Lovely Trigger

R.K. LILLEY

This one is for my husband. Thank you for caring enough to be even more stubborn than I am, when it matters the most.

BOOKS BY R.K. LILLEY

CHAPTER ONE

A FEW MONTHS AFTER THE ACCIDENT
DANIKA

Physical therapy was hell on earth. It was pain, futility, and frustration, all with a feeling of hopelessness because I knew that it could only do so much. But I gave it my all. I had too much pure stubborn grit inside of me to do anything else.

I was only twenty-one, quickly approaching twenty-two, but I'd never in my life felt young before Tristan. With him, for a while, I'd felt young and carefree, with my life ahead of me. A promising life.

As though it had all been a dream, some kind of a spell, that careless joy disappeared from my heart again as quickly as it had come. I was back to being the oh so responsible woman that I was meant to be.

I never cried a tear of self-pity. That had never been my poison. Bitter was my poison, and it took every ounce of character I possessed not to let it consume me.

I missed him. I couldn't even lie to myself about that.

I missed him dreadfully.

I convinced myself that it had all been passion, not true love. True love was a myth, a misdirection from the solid things in life. What I'd felt for Tristan had been big and all consuming, but I told myself, like a mantra in my head, that it had never been solid.

Even so, every little thing brought him to mind. We'd had too much together, been through too much, felt *too much*, and every feeling had a memory. So many songs, shows, and movies were locked away for me, never to be viewed again.

It was that kind of a breakup. The ruinous kind.

When the longing got truly unbearable, I fell back on pure survival mode, my mind going into that blank place I'd had to perfect as a sexually abused teenager. It served me well at those times. And luckily, those times always passed.

I kept so busy that I had very little time for dwelling, and no time for pining for a thing that was never meant to be. School, work, and plotting out my dream career was a very involved process.

I could throw my whole life into my ambitious future, in fact that was my only option, now that the possibility of ever having a family of my own had been ripped so violently from the table.

I did not feel whole for a long time, but I told myself, over and over, that I was strong. Strong enough to go on, with some bits of myself, or, if I was honest, some huge important hunks of myself, missing.

And I did.

TRISTAN

"Welcome to the floor," my counselor told me, the first time I walked into his office.

I thought it was a good way to start things. I wouldn't have been able to pour my heart out to him, if he didn't at least have a good sense of humor.

He was a small man in his fifties. His hair was long, gray, and unruly. His glasses always perched right on the tip of his nose as he studied me.

And he didn't even have a brown leather chaise lounge, as I'd feared. I got to sit up and talk to him like a normal person, not lie down like in the movies.

I sat in a comfortable chair on the opposite side of his desk, and, over time, told him *everything*.

"Do you ever blackout?" he asked on our first meeting, his tone idle as he looked down at his chart. I was a little fixated on that chart of his.

"Excuse me?"

"Blackouts. Periods where you were still functioning, but you have no memory of it."

I liked the way he handled things, the way he made me talk without it being a big deal, and never made the tragedies in my life seem too big for a person to handle, with his calm reactions.

"Oh yeah. I call that the weekend."

He smiled ruefully, but didn't look up. "I assume this has wreaked some havoc on your personal life."

That was the understatement of a lifetime.

It was the most bitter pill to swallow; how my own rock bottom had impacted *her*. I had always been the one to throw myself in front of a punch for my brother, my mother.

And my wife. My *wife*. I'd have done anything to take her pain, to bear her injuries myself. Instead though, I had *caused* them.

But I could not go back. I could not live on what ifs, if I had any hope of living at all.

"Well, yeah. I suppose that's why I'm here." I tried to make my tone idle, but I nearly choked on those words. "I have lost every one of the people closest to me. My brother, my mother, my wife, my unborn child. All of it was because of addiction."

"You must be a stubborn one, that it took so much to get you here." He grinned ruefully. "Stubborn is my specialty. We'll get along just fine."

And we did. Sometimes, though, I hated him, because he gave me the hard truths.

"You can't ever expect to get her back," he told me one day, when I'd been talking endlessly about Danika, once again. "This is something you need prepare yourself to accept. I can see it will be your biggest challenge, as you venture back into your life outside of rehab."

I wanted to argue, wanted to fight him. Instead, I closed my eyes and attempted to accept.

"Tell me what you're thinking," he asked, his tone kind.

"I was thinking about the first step."

"That's good. Tell me what it means to you."

"I am powerless over my addiction. My life has become unmanageable."

"That is the textbook answer, to be sure, but that's good. That one takes a while to process. Now, let's look at the twelve steps as a whole. An overview, if you will. In essence, they teach us that we cannot play God. There are some things we do not have the power to change, not just as it pertains to using or not using. This also applies to past mistakes. You must accept that you cannot change her mind, and find a way to go on with your life and stay clean. Are you ready yet to accept that?"

"I would just like to talk to her. If I could just get her to meet with me, get her to see that I'm getting better, I think it would show her that I've changed, that I'm willing to do whatever it takes to be in her life."

"Okay, I see that we still have plenty to work on here."

And so it went. Little by little, I began to accept that it really could be over between us. Not as a break, but as a permanent affliction.

It was a very rough pill to swallow.

It was months before I could open up in group therapy. Months of hearing other people's stories. Some of them didn't seem too bad, but others were worse than mine were.

One lady, a heroin addict, opened up about neglecting her

baby for so long that it died in its crib while she got high.

I processed that story for a while, haunted by the way she told it, as though it had happened to someone else.

Something in her disconnect really got to me.

Had I disconnected that much from my own life? And if so, how? How could I have been so selfish, so cruel, as to neglect the things around me for so long?

It was numbness I'd been looking for, what we'd all been looking for, and that numbness had turned us into monsters when we used.

I had to come to terms with the things the monster inside of me had done. And with the fact that I *was* that monster.

It was as I began to cope with that realization, to accept it, that I began to open up in group.

"I'm Tristan. I am an alcoholic and a drug addict. I'm here because using cost me the love of my life."

I smiled sadly as I looked down at my hands. "I think I started falling for her the first time she called me a man-whore."

It hadn't been easy to set up the meeting. She wouldn't talk to me directly, so everything went through a very slow filter via Jerry. We constantly met up with complications.

It took months just to get the ball rolling.

She wouldn't even meet with me alone, as though I was some kind of dangerous criminal.

I tried not to dwell on that.

It messed with me, my sanity, my will to stay sober, but I had to focus on the positive.

I rounded up a few friends I'd met in rehab.

Trinity was a twenty-year-old heroin addict whose parents had already put her through rehab four times. Her current clean run was the longest she'd been sober since she was fifteen years old. She was a sweet, funny girl, and I had hopes that this time she'd pull through.

She was a compact girl, and wore a uniform black T-shirt and jeans. Her short red hair was only long in the front, long enough to cover one eye, but she still managed make good eye contact.

Todd was a twenty-five-year-old tattoo artist and a pain killer addict. We wound up in the same sober house after rehab. He was a small guy, skinny, with bleach blond hair and enough tats to make me look like a blank canvas.

I'd made the fastest friends in rehab, but unfortunately, many of them weren't lasting friends. Nearly everyone I'd met had relapsed within the last eight months. The ones that stayed sober with me, though, were like a lifeline, very necessary for my own recovery process.

Trinity and Todd were both still staying clean after rehab, still fighting the good fight, like me. They were ideal company for me, going through the same things I was, and so they could understand how hard the coming meeting was for me.

They'd been in group therapy with me, so they knew all about my obsession with Danika, and all of the reasons she had to hate me.

We got there early, because I just couldn't wait around any longer. I was jittery with nerves. Wound up so tight that I couldn't sit still.

I'd been waiting, obsessed, tormented, consumed for this meeting since the last time I'd seen her. It simply couldn't end like this. There had to be something more, something I could do to make amends.

Even if I couldn't be her husband, I longed to have her in my life. In any capacity.

I'd take literally anything.

I wouldn't be happy with less than *everything*, but I'd take what I could get.

Crumbs, scraps, a taste of what she once felt for me, as a

salve for what I still felt in abundance for her.

Even that I would take.

My hands were shaking so hard that I spilled coffee on my hands as I tried to take a sip of the decaf coffee I'd ordered just to have something to do with my hands.

As we sat there and waited for her, the future so uncertain, no, so likely to turn out in a way I couldn't bear, I'd never wanted a drink more in my life.

I shared this piece of information. It was part of the process, to reach out when you felt yourself slipping. It still went against the grain for me, but I was trying my best to learn a new way.

Obviously, the old way hadn't been working for me. Not by any wild stretch of the imagination.

"Well, hell, man, let's hit the bar then. It's five o'clock somewhere." Todd said it as a joke, and that levity was what I needed.

I burst out laughing and so did Trinity.

I was facing the door of the place, on lookout, and so I saw her first.

I froze. Every part of my body just seized up as I set eyes on her. At first it, was just at the shock, the sheer joy of seeing her beautiful face, even from several feet away, through a glass door.

Some man opened it for her, and I took her in for one heart stopping moment.

She wore a long black skirt that went down to her ankles, her pale pink blouse skin tight, showed off her perfect figure. Her hair was loose and shiny, her makeup heavier than I remembered, and absolutely striking.

She was still the most beautiful woman I'd ever set eyes on. I knew she always would be.

"Holy shit," Todd muttered.

"That chick is *gorgeous*," Trinity said.

Danika began to walk through the door, and my fists

clenched.

"Oh my God," Trinity continued, in dawning horror. "Is that *her*?"

I didn't respond, couldn't, caught up in my own personal hell as I saw her struggle to make it just a few feet to sit down at a table.

Have you ever felt like someone just reached into your chest and twisted a corkscrew into your heart? No? Well, that's what I felt then.

It wasn't fucking pretty.

I reeled for an endless moment, as I saw just what I'd done, and tried to cope with it, trying to breathe for even another moment, to live in a skin that I despised down to my soul.

I didn't even realize I'd moved to her until I was at her table. My body had moved with no tangible communication to my brain.

She barely looked at my face, just one devastating, cursory glance before her eyes became glued to my chest.

Oh God. She can't even stand to look at me now. I felt gutted by that. This was going worse than my most dreadful fears.

I stared at her for the longest time, drinking her in, willing her to just look at me.

Finally, I shook myself out of it. "Can I get you anything? Coffee or tea?"

The finest tremor ran through her, but it stopped between one second and the next. I wasn't sure I hadn't imagined it or manufactured it, since I myself was shaking.

"Some hot tea, thank you," she finally answered stiffly.

I went to the counter and ordered two teas, watching her all the while.

She didn't look at me once.

I brought the tea back to the table, and she nodded her thanks, staring down into her cup. She added a sugar packet and stirred it.

"Milk?" I asked.

She shook her head, adding more sugar. She didn't drink it, just focused on it.

I shoved my own neglected tea to the side.

I put my hands on the table, fingers threaded together. I stared down at them as intently as she stared at her tea. I took a very deep breath, gathering my courage.

"I have many regrets, many bad things I must take credit for, but believe me when I say that the negative impact that all of my actions have had on your life is my biggest one." I had rehearsed this speech. I doubted I would have been able to say it without breaking down otherwise.

Finally, I felt her eyes on me, but now I didn't have the strength to meet them. I knew I'd find nothing I could bear in them.

I wished she'd say something, anything, but when it was clear that she wouldn't, I continued. "I do not deserve your forgiveness, after all that's happened, but I am asking for it."

Begging, I thought.

Groveling.

"Know that I would take it all back if I could, and know that I hold myself responsible for all of the bad things that happened. I am *so sorry* that my hitting rock bottom the way I did impacted you. Any recompense you can imagine, anything you would ask of me, I would be happy to provide." Please, I thought. Ask me for something, anything. Let me give and you take. Let me have some role in your life again. "I'm at your service. Always, Danika. And it is my most sincere wish that someday, perhaps over time, you might consider being my friend again."

Her hand went to her throat, and she shuddered, as though in revulsion.

I shuddered in pain.

She was that disgusted with me now that even the idea of a

friendship with me made her recoil?

"Tristan," she said slowly, her voice hoarse. "Consider yourself forgiven. But please don't think that I hold you responsible for everything that happened."

I was filled, for the briefest moment, with the strongest feeling of elation.

"Things didn't turn out how I could have hoped," she continued. "But no one person is to blame for any of it. So yes, I forgive you for any and all of it."

Joy, wonder, the biggest spark of hope filled my chest.

Her next words made pain, horror, denial, follow closely in their wake.

"That being said, I must decline your offer of friendship. Some things...what I mean to say is, some people, need to stay away from each other, and we are such a pair."

No, no, no, I thought. Anything but that. Don't cut me off completely. I can take anything but that.

But I saw the resolve in the set of her shoulders.

I saw the end in her downcast eyes.

The very least I could do is give her what she so clearly wanted. I did not have the right to fight her on this. Not after all I'd done.

"If that is how you feel, I must respect your decision." Those words didn't want to come out of me, but I forced them out.

"It is," she said quickly. "But thank you for the apology, and I wish you all the best." She spoke to my collarbone. "I'm glad you got yourself help."

She was done. That was all she was going to say. I couldn't quite believe it, but I made myself accept it.

Finally, I wrenched myself away.

It was an effort.

My body did not want to leave her any more than my heart did.

I did not know how I was going to move on, but it was clear

that she already had.

"I need to stay busy. I need to stay on point today," I told my friends when I'd sat back down at the table. I stared at Danika's downcast face. How had it come to this? I had the clearest picture in my head, of the way she used to look at me, like I was her whole world.

I would have given anything to have that back.

To *deserve* it.

Though of course, I'd *never* deserved it.

"I am feeling a very strong desire to use." My voice was succinct.

"We'll keep you busy," Trinity said gently.

"We'll go watch a movie, then hit up the gym," Todd suggested. "I know how you love your workouts."

I nodded, then followed them out. We passed Danika, who seemed in no hurry to go anywhere, still looking down at her drink, her face blank.

I paused as we passed her, but Trinity grabbed my arm, tugging me away.

"She hates me," I finally said, as I put my car in gear. "She said she forgives me, but she doesn't want me in her life. Not in any way. She said we can't even be friends. She could barely even look at me."

"Oh Tristan," Trinity said gently, and I could tell by her tone that she, too, had been hoping that this meeting would turn out better for me.

"I'm so sorry, man," Todd added. "It's a rough hand you've been dealt. But some things are just out of our hands."

That was a hard lesson for me to learn, but I tried my best to learn it well.

CHAPTER TWO

NEARLY TWO YEARS AFTER THE ACCIDENT
DANIKA

I'd often noted the fact that much of the humor in my life had left with Tristan. The humor, the fun, and if I was brutally honest with myself, the joy.

Everything was serious these days. Work, even my social life. When I dated, it was very serious professionals, though nothing ever got far or lasted long. My heart just wasn't in it yet.

I told myself I only needed more time.

I finished college, and James immediately promoted me. I moved to L.A. and managed the gallery there. Career wise, all of my dreams were coming true. James let me prove myself and gave me free reign over the gallery.

I missed Bev, Jerry, and the boys, but I had enough work to keep me busy literally every waking hour, and that's how I liked it.

Bev and Jerry remarried in a very small ceremony in the Bahamas. I attended, and the amount of relief I felt when I found out that Tristan, for whatever reason, hadn't come, worried me. He should not still affect me like this, I told myself, but there was no helping it.

It was a beautiful wedding. They both wrote their own vows,

and they were so sweet that I cried like a sap through the entire thing, hugging the boys, who flanked me on each side.

Later, I found out that Tristan hadn't come because he hadn't been invited. Though he and Jerry were close, Bev hadn't even considered it.

This was told to me by Bev. When I looked baffled by her revelation, she laughed and patted me on the shoulder.

"Oh, my sweet girl. If someone told you I don't hold a grudge, they were *lying*."

Her eyes and her smile were so unlike her, so bloodthirsty, that I just stared.

"You're doing great now. You look spectacular, and I have every confidence that you will get what you want out of your life. I couldn't be more proud of you, but there will always be a very clear picture in my head, my dear, and it is the stuff of my nightmares. I can close my eyes and remember how you looked, bleeding and broken in that hospital bed. Heartbroken and abused. Or of you those first few months after the accident. So sad and lost. I'm a loving woman. You know this. I love with all my heart, but a heart like mine works both ways, and there is a *wrath* in me. I will never forget the state that man put you in. You think I could enjoy a celebration if *he* was there, making you uncomfortable the entire time? That's not how I operate. It will take more than a few paltry years before I can be civil to that man."

It was hard to know what to say to *that*, but strangely, her words warmed me a little.

It would always feel good to have Bev in my corner.

I finally met my biological father face to face. It was one of the most awkward moments of my life, but I can't say I didn't feel a bit of satisfaction by the end of it.

Bronson Giles was attending a gallery showing in L.A. with his oldest son, Dermot. I'd heard somewhere that he was following in his dad's acting footsteps. He looked like a perfect younger image of his father, big, blond, and very handsome.

With my same eyes.

I think I was too completely dead to the idea of feeling anything for my father to have a reaction to him. To see him, well, it was only a sort of vague discomfort.

Dermot, on the other hand, I had not expected.

The idea of a deadbeat dad was one thing. The concept of a half-sibling, one that had no inkling that I existed, was something else. It was very strange, but I found myself staring at him whenever he wandered close as they perused the art, trying to catch some kindness in him, some redemption. I didn't want to hate him.

In fact, I quite wanted to like him.

I wasn't sure if Bronson thought it was him I was staring at, or if I just happened to catch his eye, but he watched me even more than I watched Dermot.

Finally, Bronson approached me directly. I tensed up sure he'd caught the resemblance between me and my mother, who he'd obviously known well.

That wasn't why he approached. Well, I suppose it was a twisted version of that. Marta was apparently his type, and being close to the spitting image of her, I suppose I was too.

His smile dripped with greasy charm even before he opened his disgusting mouth.

Before he even got a word out, I had the thought: Oh God, no. My own father is about to hit on me.

Please, please, please, I thought, make this not actually be happening.

Who the fuck else had this kind of luck?

I didn't even catch the first little bit that he said, more heard his tone, my mind reeling in horror.

It was just too much. Even I couldn't maintain my usual professional demeanor as I stood there and had the man that had sired me tell me how hot I was.

He didn't even have good lines. He'd been relying on his fame and money for way too long.

"So what do you say?" He reached into his pocket, pulling out what looked like a hotel room key card. "I keep a regular room at The Beverly Hills Hotel. I can meet you there in three hours. In the meantime, feel free to make yourself comfortable, order some drinks. Charge it to the room."

He said it all like it was just a forgone conclusion, even when I knew that the look on my face must have told him that I liked him about as much as something particularly smelly that had just gotten stuck to the bottom of my shoe.

He was that oblivious.

"You are just stunning. Where do you get that coloring from? A bit of Asian in there, right? I've always been a fan of the Asian girls. But the black hair with those pale eyes." He whistled long and low. "So very striking. What a beauty. Hot little body on you too."

I had to restrain myself from slapping him across the face. My voice was not quite steady when I finally found it. "What is *your* heritage?"

"I'm mainly Danish and English. Your turn, babe."

My mouth shaped into a sharp smile. "My mother is Japanese and Russian, and my father is apparently Danish and English, though I just this second found that out."

He gave me a strange look. "How so?"

"Bronson Giles, my mother's name is Marta Markova. I assume that rings a bell?"

He at least had the decency to turn green then. "My God," he whispered.

"I can see where that would be a problem, knocking up so many women that you can't keep track of your offspring. And by the way, Bronson, you are way too old for me. Even if I wasn't your daughter." I made a face. "That's just gross. If you're going to be a philandering pig, at least be more age appropriate about it. Especially with all of the random women you must have gotten pregnant over the years. Maybe stay away from women that are young enough to be your daughters, or hell, your granddaughters."

"My God," he said again. "Do you want money from me or something?"

"I don't want *anything* from you," I told him furiously, my voice low and mean. "Not one thing. I manage this gallery. You are the one that came up to me, or did you not realize that?"

He blinked a few times, turned on his heel and strode away.

Dermot, who'd been about a dozen feet away for the whole thing, sent me one probing glance and followed him.

I thought that was the end of it, but about an hour later, Dermot was back.

He sought me out, waiting while I handled a sale. He smiled and held out his hand when I was free. "I'm Dermot," he said warmly.

I smiled tentatively back, shaking his hand. "Danika."

"I just wanted to apologize for my father. He's...a throwback, and it looked like he came on a little strong back there."

I studied him. "I'm not sure why you're apologizing. You didn't do anything."

"I just didn't want you to think I was like him. He's my father, but I've known since I was a kid that he's a creep when it comes to women."

I nodded. That he was, and I didn't know what to say about it.

"Listen, this is an embarrassing way to meet, but I'd love to make it up to you sometime. How does dinner sound?"

I made an effort not to smack my own forehead.

Seriously?! What the fuck did I do to deserve this?

I realized then and there that I had to tell him, had to bite the awkward bullet and just get it out. "The fact that your father is

15

old and married isn't the only thing that offended me about his come-on," I told him, my tone matter of fact.

"Oh yeah?" he asked, smiling like I was about to tell him some funny joke.

Oh yeah, it was a real hoot.

"Bronson Giles is my biological father."

His eyes widened comically, his mouth dropping open.

"I have no proof, though if I needed it, his reaction to me telling him who my mother is would have been enough. But if you don't believe me—"

"No, no, I do. I just-I-I-I'm shocked. I am *so* sorry. I wasn't hitting on you. I meant like a platonic dinner."

He hadn't, but I grasped onto that lame ass excuse just as strongly as he did. "Of course. I didn't think you were."

In spite of that less than promising beginning, we did sort of hit it off after that.

"I like women as much as the next guy," Dermot told me over dinner, maybe the fourth time we'd met to catch up. "But if you can't keep it in your pants, the least you can do is just stay single."

"Here, here," I said, toasting him. He was preaching to the choir.

"And seriously, he's how old, and somehow never managed to grasp the concept of birth control?" He winced as he heard his own words. "No offense to you."

I laughed. "None taken. I mean, I'm glad I exist, but I could've wished for a different father, say, one that was present."

"How's Dahlia doing? And how's her boy?"

I launched into a story about darling Jack.

We always asked about the other siblings. We kept track, though no one seemed to have any urge to meet up face to face besides he and I. Dahlia had some weird resentment for our half-siblings, a bitterness for them that I couldn't fathom, considering she'd wanted to have more of a relationship with our father. *He* was the one to blame. He was the culprit. I could well understand a contempt for him and the things he'd done, but our half-siblings were no more to blame for his actions than we were. Still, there was no talking her out of it.

It was her loss. Dermot was delightful, sarcastic, and fun. We'd decided early on that we'd gotten the same twisted sense of humor.

It was several meetings before he worked up the nerve to ask about what happened to my leg.

"The relationship from hell," I answered.

This one time he didn't share the joke with me. His face shut down, and for the first time I saw that my half-brother could be a bit scary. "Some *man* did that to you?"

I shook my head vehemently. "Bad joke. Sorry. No. It's a long story, but the short version is that this happened in a car accident."

He didn't look convinced, but he did let me change the subject. It had to be easy to catch on that this wasn't my favorite topic.

"How's work going? Did you get that part you were auditioning for?" I asked him.

"I did. I start shooting next month. Also, I agreed to do a project with our dad."

My eyebrows shot straight up. He'd always been vehement about the fact that he didn't want to ride his father's coattails to success. He'd never used his connections to get ahead in Hollywood. Until now, that is.

"Hey now, don't judge me," he said with an irrepressible smile.

"What? I didn't say a thing."

"You didn't have to. You have very judgey eyes." I laughed, because he'd gotten it right. I did have expressive eyes. "The fact is, the part is a dream, and I do think I'm perfect for it. I auditioned, and I think I would have gotten the part, regardless of who my father is, just based on that audition. I'd rather he weren't part of the project, but that's not up to me."

"You don't have to be defensive with me. I'm happy for you, and I'm excited to see how it turns out."

"You still seeing that girl?" I asked, changing the subject again. He'd been really into some chick he'd just started dating the last time we'd talked.

He grimaced. "Nah, that's done. I told you she was an actress, right?"

I nodded.

"Well, I learned something. Never date an actress. She was sleeping with the director of her TV pilot. The casting couch stereotype comes from something, I guess."

"That sucks. How did her pilot do?"

He grinned. "Bombed, so there's that. I wouldn't have hard feelings, but she was lying to me for a while before I caught on. Now what about you? You seeing anybody? Did you go on a second date with that accountant?"

I made a face that got him to laugh. "I didn't. I'm very good on a first date, but I can't vouch for my second date skills. I can't recall if I've ever been on one."

We both laughed, though it wasn't far from the truth.

"Well, I know they all call. Why don't you pick up the phone?"

"This is going to sound awful, but I just don't feel like it. I'll go out to dinner once, but if I don't enjoy myself much, why try again? I like my own company just fine. I suspect that I'm just one of those people that's destined to stay single. It's fine. There are worse things than being alone."

He waved that off. "You're just young. You'll grow out of it in a few years. Or maybe you just need to find the right guy."

I didn't tell him that I had found that guy, once.

I had no desire to talk about *any* of the T words.

TRISTAN

I'd been torn apart and put back together, and though I knew the end result was better now than who I'd been before, some days it didn't feel that way. Lots of days, it just felt like like the world had lost its color, and the only things that defined my life were the things I'd lost. I spent a lot of time trying to convince myself that I was okay without her, and some days I even believed it.

It was well over a year before I could admit that she was lost to me, and that was with almost no contact at all.

James hired me on to do a show, far sooner than planned. He reasoned that it would take time to rehearse and to help get the theatre together. I had to immerse myself in the entire process, every bit of it. It was my baby after all. The theatre had to be completely renovated. He wanted me to go live within a week of his current act retiring, and it would take a year for me to prep.

It was a Godsend for me. I kept busy, productive, active. There was less time to dwell on the past.

The casino's retiring magician, Tony Biello, had no hard feelings about me being his replacement. In fact, he turned out to be something of a father figure and a mentor for me.

I'd admired his act since I was a kid, so when he started coming by the theatre to see how things were coming along, I was more star struck than I'd ever been and stressed out to boot, since I had no clue whether his retirement was voluntary.

He quickly set my mind at ease. He was a strange old coot that wore a top hat in the middle of the day and large white framed glasses that matched his wiry hair.

He was a large man, and in his seventies was heading in the direction of overweight.

I was on my semi-built stage, showing the architect I'd been working with just what I needed for the spot directly below our feet, when Tony came striding into the theatre.

He took one look at me and started laughing. "Let me guess. This is going to be some sort of act where they make you take your shirt off a lot. No doubt about it, I've been outclassed."

My mouth quirked up in a grin, and I hopped down to shake his hand.

"I made them put it in my contract that I wouldn't go shirtless more than twice a night," I joked. "Had to put my foot down somewhere."

He clutched his big belly while he laughed. "And you can take a joke. Outclassed indeed."

I scratched my head, trying to find the words to broach an awkward subject.

"Don't worry, my boy, my retirement was voluntary. I'm old, I have a bad heart, and it's time I started taking better care of myself. I've just come to welcome you to the team, and to let you know that my door is always open, if you need any advice. Hell, I'd love to help. I've been in the magic game for fifty years. I'd hate to think I was letting go of it completely.

I was inordinately pleased by this. Tony Biello offering his support was all that I, who'd been practicing tricks from the first time I'd gotten my hands on a deck of cards, could ever want. It was a surreal, dream come true kind of moment. "Thank you. I've been a fan of yours since I was a kid. That means a lot to me. I'm sure I'll be taking you up on that. Also, I wonder if you could make some guest appearances, if you're up for it."

He grinned his jolly grin. "Now that's what I'm talking about."

He came by almost every day after that, watching the work being done, giving advice, and asking a million questions about the show I was planning.

I tried to stay busy twenty-four seven, but unfortunately, there was always downtime, while I waited for contractors to show up, or found myself at loose ends. Still, I avoided downtime like the plague.

Of course, the time that I did spend dwelling was more agonizing than ever now that we worked in the same damned building.

The art gallery was made of glass, placed high above the ground of the casino floor, designed to be a piece of art itself. Watching someone inside of it and not letting them know that you were watching them, well, it couldn't have been more perfectly designed for just that.

There was a small indoor courtyard there, just some tables and chairs attached to a coffee shop. It was set below and at an angle to the glass gallery. I could sit there and stare for as long as I wanted, and she never saw, never took notice.

I did this a lot.

This was pure masochism, but I couldn't seem to stop.

Every break I had, every time I came or went I stopped at that little spot. I'd grab food from somewhere else and bring it there. I put in time at that torturous little spot.

This was all particularly unfortunate when she started seeing some motherfucker in a suit.

He must have worked in the building somewhere, because he started showing up often to take her to lunch.

It took every ounce of self-control, every minute of anger management and therapy I'd participated in, to keep from going up there and wringing his neck the first time I saw him wrap his arm around her waist, but I did it.

I walked away.

She'd smiled at him, looked genuinely happy to have him touch her.

No one deserved happy more than Danika.

Certainly not me.

My recovery had felt solid at the time, all of my twelve steps right where they should have been, but that night I very nearly had a relapse. With what felt like my last ditch effort, I called my sponsor, and he effectively talked me down. It wasn't the first time, or the last, that I knew I owed him my life.

It was a mercy when she moved to L.A., and still I hated it.

I fell back into old patterns.

I started sleeping around. At first, it felt good. Abstinence was a bitch, and I'd been damn near a monk for two years.

It took a few months to realize that this was triggering the addict in me. I began to crave alcohol more than I had since my rehab days.

I went off sex cold turkey again, then tried something in between.

I was in denial at first, for months in fact, that it was a relationship, but those things had a way of sneaking up on you. I broke up with the poor girl immediately, trying to be as gentle as I could about the whole thing.

It was difficult to sleep with only one woman and not give her the idea that it was something more than friendship, something more than comfort.

I started dating. Not just sleeping around, but dinner, the whole deal. It was a new experience for me, and spending a bit of time with a woman before fucking seemed to be a necessary component for me. The other way, with one-night stands and one clear cut agenda, hadn't worked.

I became good at it, at seeing a woman for two to three months, and then ending things in a friendly way. No real emotions were involved in it, but I didn't feel like I was using anyone, so it seemed to be the best solution for me, all things considered.

Sex with Danika had been mind-blowing for me. Incredible. Amazing. The best. It had been so good, my need to give her what *she* needed became so strong that I'd developed another level of kink from the experience. Still, it was never the same. Not even close. Domination felt like a silly game when it wasn't with Danika and the restraints were a cheap imitation.

What we'd had together; it was beautiful.   Nothing else had ever come close, and a day didn't go by that I'd forgotten that.
But I couldn't have that again.   I'd lost the privilege.
And life moved on.

CHAPTER THREE

TRISTAN

I'd barely gotten out of my car before a screaming Jack was jumping into my arms. Grinning, I lifted him high, then threw him higher, catching him. He was a fearless little guy, not a bit scared.

He giggled and clutched me around the neck. "Unca Twistan, I missed you!"

"I missed you too, buddy. It's only been a few weeks though. How did you grow so much in just a few weeks?"

"I ate my bwoccoli, just like you told me to. I'll be as tall as you soon."

I patted his head, carrying him to the single level condo where his smiling mother waited for us in the doorway.

I hugged Dahlia, and she kissed my cheek. I pulled back as soon as it was politely possible.

I was well aware of how she still felt about me, and I did my best not to encourage her.

She had cut her streaky blonde hair into a pixy cut. It made her look like a sweet kid, which was how I'd always think of her. I knew she'd celebrated her twenty-second birthday recently, but to me she looked about sixteen. She'd been my sister-in-law at one point, my kid sister by extension, and she'd never fill a different role for me. No matter how much she pressed me, that just wouldn't change.

We watched Jack play on the slide, climbing over the top like a monkey, not an ounce of fear on his grinning face even when he'd reached the top. It jarred a memory, of another perpetually smiling blond boy that feared nothing, the man who, now dead, had left behind the very image of himself as a child.

The holidays had always been tough for me. I'd been the older, bastard boy in the house, and Jared's dad had never let me forget it.

One Christmas, when I was ten, I'd run off to the neighborhood basketball court in a fit. Jared's asshole dad had been tearing into me again, calling me a punk, and worse, and I'd reached my limit. Sometimes I thought the only thing that kept me in that house at all was Jared.

I was feeling particularly sorry for myself; the boy without a dad, and I'd even worked myself up into a rare bout of silent tears when I saw the skinny form of Dean running my way like someone was chasing him.

He grinned when he saw me, sprinting straight to me. The entire left side of his face was red, one eye swollen closed. It looked like someone had taken a bat to it.

I quickly wiped away my tears. Dean was the smallest in our group of friends, but he was always the most relentless with the teasing. If he'd noticed me crying, I doubted I'd ever hear the end of it.

He had noticed, but he shocked me by just patting my shoulder as he took a seat on the bench next to me.

"Jared's dad is an asshole," I explained. Though to two ten year old boys, there was never a good excuse for crying, it was the best I could do.

"Yeah man, he's a jerk, but at least he's nice to Jared."

That was true.

He elbowed me playfully until I looked at him. He pointed to the battered side of his face. His eye was swelled nearly closed. "Don't worry about never meeting your dad, man. It could be worse. He could show up every once in a while, beat the shit out of you, and do much worse things to your mother, right in front of you. Trust me, I'd trade places with you in a *heartbeat.*"

I held up a fist. It was a big fist. I was oversized for my age. I towered over our group of friends, and was bulky enough to take any and all of them on. "Want to go kick his ass? Is he big? I bet the both of us can take him."

Dean shook his head, but he patted my shoulder again. It was a rare gesture of affection from him. "Naw. He's already gone. He ain't that big, but he carries a gun, so we should steer clear of him anyway, yanno?"

I nodded solemnly. "You know I'm here though, if you ever want to try."

"I know you are, man. That's why you're my best friend."

How had that smiling, fearless boy turned into that stranger of a man that had deceived me so easily? I'd never have the answer, but the question haunted me nonetheless. If I hadn't been so blind to what he'd become, so many horrible things could have been avoided.

I knew Dean had fathered Jack, no one could look at the boy and not see it, but we'd never talked about it directly. Considering what I knew he'd done to Danika, though, I had my suspicions.

Finally, painfully, one day I had broached that dreaded subject with Dahlia.

"Did Dean...I mean, what I mean to ask is," I stammered. I couldn't help it, the very question still horrified me, thought I'd had years to stew about it. "Was whatever happened between you consensual?"

I couldn't even look at her when I asked it. What may have happened right under my drugged out nose made me *ashamed*.

I felt responsible enough for the boy already. From the day Dahlia had called me and told me she was pregnant and that the baby had no father, I'd taken her and her child under my wing. A sense of duty drove me in that. She was, after all, my kid sister by law. Divorce hadn't changed that for me. That divorce hadn't changed any part of my heart, except to break parts of it. As the baby had grown into a little blond boy that I couldn't fail to recognize, my sense that this was my responsibility had only grown stronger.

"He drugged me. I wasn't sleeping with anyone when it happened, so you can imagine my shock when I found out I was pregnant."

I flinched. "I'm so sorry for that. I wasn't myself at the time, but I would have tried my best to prevent that, if I could have."

"I know. You did try. Every time you saw him so much as talk to me, you took him to task. I'm grateful that you tried to protect me. No one besides Danika has ever done that for me before."

"Well, I failed, and I'm sorry for that."

"But you tried, with the best of intentions, and I needed that, needed someone to be protective of me. It meant a lot. Tristan, I—"

I stopped her, because I knew what was coming, and some things were better left unsaid. "Dahlia—"

She ignored the warning in my voice, plunging ahead. "I'm in love with you. I'm sure you already knew that, but I needed to say it out loud. And what you've done for Jack, how you've been there for him, helping us financially, how you come to visit without fail, it means so much to me. To us."

"Dahlia, I'm in love with your sister," I said, my tone flat. It was best to handle this once and for all, now that it was out in the open. "I always will be. I'm very sorry. You will find someone, someone that can love you back, but it is not me."

She threw her arms around me, held on tight, and kissed me, her skinny body rubbing against mine.

I held perfectly still, letting her carry on for a solid minute. All the while, I felt nothing. Not a stirring, not even the vaguest tendril of interest. This is what it's like to have your sister kiss you, I thought.

Finally, she pulled back, panting. I could see by her hurt eyes that I'd made my point. There'd been no clearer way to show her that I could not be interested in her, of all people.

"You're a beautiful girl. Sweet and kind. You need to let go of this idea. It will never be what you want it to. It's holding you back. I'm here for you, as a brother, as a friend, and you know I'm here for Jack. I love that boy like he's my own blood. But I can't be more for you. I hope you understand now."

She nodded, her lips trembling. "How can you still love her so much? She won't even talk to you."

"Because that's how love works. It doesn't die, even when you don't feed it. That's just the way it is. I wouldn't change it, even if I could. Loving her has become a part of who I am."

"It's so unfair," she said sullenly, taking a big step away from me.

That it was.

I found myself calling Adair that night, though the thought never fully formed of what I was doing before it blurted out of my mouth. "You know Dahlia's kid, Jack?" I asked him without even a greeting. I hadn't talked to him in ages, and the band had been broken up for years.

"Dean's kid," he mused back, unfazed by the rude start. "Nice to hear from you, Tristan. I was just talking to Kenny the other day. We talked about the four of us meeting up again, seeing if we still had it."

That gave me pause, but I continued. "I've had my suspicions, but I just found out that Dahlia wasn't a willing participant in the conception. Did you know anything about this?"

"God, no!" he answered quickly and with conviction. I believed him instantly. He was a good guy, though he suffered from addiction, as well. He'd done his own stint in rehab about a year after I had. As far as I knew, he'd stayed sober, too. "That fucker. I should have known, but I honestly thought he'd suckered her into hooking up with him. I didn't know he was a rapist, man. I wouldn't have worked with him if I'd had a fucking clue, you can be sure of that. I always knew she was too fucking innocent for him. Fuuuuck, that messes me up."

"Yeah, it's hard to take, that we were there and didn't stop it."

"Yeah, it is. I can guarantee Cory and Kenny were clueless, too. None of us would have let a thing like that slide. You have to know that."

I had. I'd just needed to hear it out loud. "Ignorance is no excuse. We owe that poor girl, Adair, and that kid doesn't have a father. The least we can do—"

"I couldn't agree more. I'll call her today. I just, I don't know, I thought there was something between the two of you. I know she always had a thing for you, right from the start. Didn't want to step on your territory."

"She's like a kid sister to me. I have no claim there. Not my territory."

"So you don't mind if...?"

"You can ask her out. But treat her right. I would take it real personal if you put her through more pain that she's already been through. You understand?"

"Yes. I'm not how I used to be, man. I've grown up. I'll treat her right, if she's interested, I swear."

That suited me fine. Dahlia needed to find a new focus for her infatuation.

29

THREE YEARS AFTER THE ACCIDENT
DANIKA

The stars had aligned, and Bev threw a huge neighborhood BBQ in her backyard during one of my business trips to Vegas at the same time that Dahlia was visiting her least favorite town on the planet.

I got to spend the afternoon in the pool with Mat, Ivan, and little Jack. It was a charmed day, and so rare that I knew to savor every second of it.

The boys were nine and eleven now, and I still saw them often, but every time I set eyes on them again, I couldn't believe how much they'd grown and changed.

They hadn't seen much of Jack, but they went out of their way to be nice to him, and spend time playing games with him. They were darling boys, and they loved me almost as much as I adored them, and since Jack was my family, they treated him like their family. Bev and Jerry did it too. It was heartwarming.

Dahlia hung back a bit from it all, but I knew that it was rare for her to get a break from caring for Jack, and so she enjoyed an afternoon of sunbathing, headphones keeping her from even so much as hearing the loud pool party going on around her.

I didn't mind a bit. I was only too happy to get in all the time I could and grateful that she trusted me to care for Jack amidst the chaos.

I played pool games for hours with my three boys and several of the neighbor kids. I was still good in the water. Better than I was at walking, in fact. My knee, with all of its lost cartilage, was lighter there.

I had a blast with those boys. More fun than I'd had in ages. And all the while, I had to keep my mind from agonizing over the fact that I'd never get to have any of my own.

I'd always loved kids, always had such a knack for caring for them. I tried not to rage against the unfairness of it all.

The dark thoughts never lasted long, as the boys were always pulling me back into their games.

It was such a wonderful day, but it was ruined by the most unlikely source.

Bev and Jerry's relationship was stronger than ever, and very occasionally, they had random moments of PDA.

The boys had grown a lot, but upon seeing their parents kissing, they still howled in disgusted dismay.

I was holding Jack when it happened. He was getting big, but not too big to perch on my hip and carry around the pool.

"They kissin'?" Jack asked me.

I glanced back at Bev and Jerry. They were really going at it. "Yeah, Cap'n Jack, they are kissing. Probably giving each other cooties as we speak." I demonstrated by giving him a big smacking kiss on the cheek that made him dissolve into giggles.

"Mommy and Unca Twistan kiss, too," he gasped out when I let up.

It goes without saying, I didn't take that well.

I had to sit down, suddenly feeling weak. I'm not proud of the fact that I then had to interrogate a three year old.

My sister was just so secretive that I didn't expect to get enough answers out of her to satisfy me. I'd rather go into a conversation with her with some answers already in hand.

"You have an Uncle Tristan, Jack?" I asked, trying to keep my tone casual.

He nodded happily. "He's stwongest man in the world. He tells me to eat my bwoccoli, and takes me to the park."

I had a few insane moments where I tried to reason to myself that it could be a different Tristan, but I was an odds player, and what were the odds?

"He has magic."

Any hope I'd had disappeared in a puff of smoke. "What kind

31

of magic?"

"He teaches me card twicks and can make anything disappear. *Anything.*"

"Do you see him often?"

He nodded vigorously. "All the time. I wish he lived with us. And you. I wish you lived with us."

"I live close enough, cap'n. *I* visit all the time too. Would you say he visits you more or less often than I do?"

Jack, a three year old that was quickly growing bored with the conversation, didn't even hear that last question. He was pointing across the yard, where Ivan had begun to fill up a ridiculous amount of water balloons.

Sighing, I let him run over to help.

I had no intention of letting the subject go, though. I had to know what this meant. My very sanity depended on it.

He would not do that, I told myself. He would not go near my sister, not like that, not after everything we'd been through together. He'd have known that would kill me.

No, I told myself again. He just wouldn't. There has to be some explanation.

I tapped her bare shoulder.

She was sprawled out in a tiny yellow bikini, her pale skin gleaming in the sun. I didn't know how she wasn't burning, she'd been laying out so long.

She lowered her shades to peer at me, but didn't take out her headphones.

I tapped my own ear, feeling impatient.

She took one ear bud out, raising her brow at me. "What's up? Is Jack behaving?"

"He's fine," I told her tersely. "Bev is keeping an eye on him for a few minutes. We need to talk."

She wrinkled her nose. "Not right now. I'm relaxing."

"Right now," I shot back.

Her eyes widened at my tone. I usually treated her with kid gloves.

I didn't drag her out of her lounge chair, but it was a close thing.

I took her all the way to my old room, shutting the door behind us.

"Are you seeing Tristan?" I asked her, voice shaking. I couldn't keep my cool for even a *second* about this.

She sighed and sat on the bed. She reminded me of a sulky teenager, with the way she curled her lip at me. "Jack said something," she guessed.

I nodded, mouth tight, fists clenched. "He said he saw you kissing. Tell me the truth. Are you seeing him?"

She rolled her eyes. "I don't want to talk about this. You and Tristan! God! I refuse to talk about him with *you*."

"Are you seeing him?" I asked again through clenched teeth.

I wanted to shake her, or worse, though I knew the true source of my anger wasn't her. It was him. She was my sister, but it felt like the real betrayal was coming from *him*.

Logic had left the building.

She let out an annoyed little grunt, exactly like a teenager. "I've started seeing Adair, okay? Tristan still comes around, helps with Jack, gives him some of the male attention he needs, but anything that happened, anything between us, ugh, it's over." She grinned suddenly. "I know what you're thinking; I'm making my way through the entire band." She laughed like that was funny.

My eyes were wide on her and filled with horror. "That is not what I was thinking. Is that what you're *doing*?"

She laughed again. She was way too amused by all of this, when I wanted to tear my own hair out. Tear *her* hair out.

"No, that's not what I'm doing. It's just, you know, how it probably would look to some people."

"I'm not asking how it looks. I'm asking how it is. What

33

happened between you and Tristan? Why did Jack tell me he saw you kissing?"

She waved that off. "I don't want to talk about it, and like I said, whatever it was, it's over now." Her eyes narrowed on me suddenly. "You don't get to throw him away and then decide who he gets to see. I *never* would have thrown him away."

My heads translation for that; he'd dumped her.

I was livid. "You have no clue what he and I have been through, no clue why I had to walk away. This is none of your business, but I did not *throw him away.* I barely made it out of that relationship intact. And yes, he and I are done, but there are rules to this kind of thing. You and him…no, that's just wrong. You're my sister. He is not allowed to go near you."

"Relax, okay? We're just friends now. I'm seeing Adair now, and it's going really well. And I am done talking about this. You turn into a nutcase when it comes to Tristan. And vice versa."

She wouldn't talk about it anymore, no matter how I pried, but that didn't mean it stopped bothering me. It ate at me, because I still didn't know what had happened, and probably never would.

CHAPTER FOUR

His name was Milton Sagar. He was an NFL quarterback who'd just been drafted to play for San Diego. I met him at a gallery showing in L.A. on a Friday night. He came to visit me in the Vegas gallery on the following Monday.

He was charming, intelligent, good-looking, and very, very interested, and for the first time in a long time, I found that I was genuinely interested back.

Not good on paper interested.

Heart rate accelerating interested.

That hadn't happened to me since Tristan. I wasn't sure if I was relieved or horrified by the development.

He was very persistent. I turned him down twice.

He had huge arms, gorgeous black hair, kind blue eyes. He even had dimples. He probably flirted in his sleep.

He was just the type of guy I should avoid.

The third time he very charmingly asked me out, I said yes to having lunch with him in Vegas, on my break at work. He flew in just to see me.

I had no intention of letting it go one step further than that.

"So you live in Vegas, but you work in L.A. a lot?" he asked me over appetizers.

I shook my head. "Just the opposite. I live in L.A., but I'm in

Vegas quite a bit at the moment. I'm managing both galleries until I can train someone here."

"L.A. isn't too far from San Diego." He smiled.

I smiled back, admiring his dimples. I told myself I was utterly whacked in the head.

His smile faded just a tad. "I have the strangest question for you. I hope you don't mind my bringing this up, but a buddy of mine told me something that's been…bothering me. I guess he knows your ex-husband."

I was taking a drink of wine and nearly choked on it. "My ex-*husband*?!" I asked, trying hard to sound casual. "This friend of yours has the wrong girl."

Only a few people on the planet knew I'd been married for one hot, dysfunctional minute.

He looked surprised but not displeased. "Oh yeah? Well, that's good. Obviously I can defend myself, but he had me spooked."

I couldn't leave it at that. It was just too bizarre. "What's the name of this friend of yours?"

"Tristan Vega. I'm sure you've seen him around. He does the magic show here. It's really good."

I felt myself pale. Very carefully, I set down my glass, placing both hands carefully into my lap where I could clench them as hard as I needed to without looking crazy. "What exactly did Tristan tell you?"

"Oh, so you do know him? Not much. He just kind of… warned me off, in a vague sort of way. He said you had an ex-husband that was liable to stab me in my sleep if I laid a hand on you. He said he was huge, and insanely violent when it came to you, or rather who you date. He basically told me that your ex would go to jail for murder before he'd let you go out with a guy like me."

The sheer gall of that, the utter hypocritical nerve of it made me want to scream.

I smiled tightly. "Tristan has a twisted sense of humor. He was just messing with you. I was never married."

We did, unfortunately, run into each other occasionally, but that night was the first time I'd sought Tristan out deliberately since the accident.

Working at the hotel got me backstage before his show, and eventually, his dressing room. It was very handy to be on a first name basis with every security guard on the property.

He met me, his jaw clenched, at the door.

I barged in, fuming. I waited to speak until he closed the door, giving us privacy.

"How *dare* you?!" I hissed, shaking. It felt surreal to be alone in a room with him. The only thing that made it bearable was my unadulterated *rage*.

"I know why you're here," he said calmly. "I can explain."

"Oh please do. I would *love* to hear it."

He took a few steps toward me, but I backed just as many steps away, keeping my distance. "Don't you dare try to touch me."

He looked down, taking a deep breath. "Of course, Danika. I know how you feel about that. I take it this is about Milton?"

I nodded, biting back several sarcastic things that came to mind. "Of course it is. Why else would I be here?"

I wanted to say so much more, about how my love life wasn't his business, about how he didn't get to kiss my sister and God only knew what else and then try to interfere in *my* life, but I held my tongue. It was a herculean effort, but I did it. I would not give him the satisfaction of knowing how much that bothered me, how it had kept me up at night, the doubt, the uncertainty. Had I ever even known him at all?

"Why else indeed? Listen, I told him that because—"

"I can't believe you told him I was divorced!"

He met my eyes. His were steady, his jaw so stubborn that I didn't know if I wanted to slap it or kiss it. "You *are* divorced."

37

His tone was chastising.

"That marriage was a joke. It didn't even count."

He flinched, not even trying to hide it, one hand shooting up to rub at a twitching temple. "I told him that because he is not the guy for you."

"How cute. You think you know what's good for me?"

"He's a womanizer."

I laughed. It was so bitter that I wanted to stop, but I couldn't change it, couldn't keep it in. "Look who's talking."

"And a liar."

I began to look around, and when I realized that I was trying to find something to throw, I knew, with absolute certainty, that I needed to leave.

Every second that we stayed within each other's vicinity was bad for my peace of mind. This little scene would haunt me for months. Just seeing him up close like this and breathing him in, it would mess me up, set me back.

I met his steady stare, trying not to snarl. "That is beside the point. None of this is your business. *Nothing* in my life is your business. Are we clear?"

"Please, Danika, stay clear of him. I know you have a right to do as you please, but understand that I wouldn't have interfered if I weren't concerned. This guy is bad news. He'll break your heart, and when he does, I may well break his neck."

My mouth was trembling. With rage. With pain. The notion that he was watching over me like a big brother, that he thought of himself that way...it stung.

It cut.

It wounded.

And I was wounded enough.

I pointed at him. "You stop it. Quit acting like you give a damn, and stay the fuck out of my life. You and I...we are nothing to each other. Less than strangers."

He shook his head and that set me off. I had to restrain

myself from attacking him, but in my head, I was shoving, hitting, slapping. Grabbing his shirt in both fists.

In reality, in that pregnant, futile moment, we only stared at each other.

We were both panting. I clenched and unclenched my fists and watched his hands copying the motion.

"Please," he mouthed.

I left, and thank God he didn't stop me.

I went to a very public gala with Milton the next weekend. There was a red carpet with photographers. I smiled like I was having the best night of my life for those cameras and tried not to think about the fact that I had said yes to this mostly out of spite. Tristan would see these pictures, and he would know just how much of a say he had in my life.

I let Milton kiss me good night when he dropped me back off at my apartment, but I didn't invite him in. It was a good kiss. The man knew what he was doing. I knew I'd let him do it again.

He met me for lunch the following Monday in a posh café near the L.A. gallery.

He had a black eye and a badly swollen cheek that he claimed was from football practice. His story didn't change, even when I tried to pry further.

Still, I couldn't get the bizarre notion that Tristan had done it out of my head. I had no proof, just a strong gut feeling.

I cooked lasagna for him at my place the following weekend, and then I let him kiss me again. I even let him get to second base, and was half-tempted to let him get to third.

Though I didn't, it was nice to feel tempted. I'd half feared that part of me was permanently broken.

Perhaps I still had some shot at a love life.

He was easy to talk to, and we chatted on the phone nearly every day for three weeks. I wasn't quite letting myself think of him as my boyfriend or ready to even want something like that,

39

but it certainly seemed to be heading in that direction.

I wasn't sure how to feel about it all, but I was enjoying myself. He didn't give me butterflies exactly, but at least I felt *something,* some shadow of the fervor that I'd tasted for a brief time.

It was nothing like the inferno of passion I'd felt for Tristan, but even so, it was a relief to find that I could still be lit at all, even if it was just a tiny flame.

It was the three-week mark almost exactly when I got a call from his number, only it wasn't him on the other end this time.

We'd made plans to meet that night for dinner, and I hadn't been expecting a call from him, so my tone was a bit of a question as I answered, "Hello?"

"Is this Danika?" a woman on the other end asked. She sounded like she'd been crying.

"Yes. Who is this?"

"This is Belinda."

"Hello, Belinda. How may I help you?" Her shaky voice sent me into autopilot, which for me was a sort of detached professionalism.

"I am Milton's *girlfriend,*" she proclaimed, her shaky voice turning hard with anger.

"Excuse me?" I asked, completely caught off guard. How had I missed this?

"He and I have been together for nine years. I *live* with him. He doesn't know that I know about you, but when he gets out of the shower, I'll hand him the phone, and he can tell you all about *me.*"

I didn't have a clue what to say to that, so we shared an awkward silence for a good two minutes before I came out with, "I had no idea—"

"Well, now you do, so what are *you* going to do about it?" Her tone was animated, but there was something so off about the entire thing, like she wasn't at all surprised. How many times had Milton pulled this on her? I wondered feeling a little disconnected from the entire thing.

Finally, Milton came on the line, his tone an apology, an apology for me, which I heard quickly set Belinda off on the other end.

"Danika, I can explain."

I rolled my eyes, feeling more stupid than hurt. He'd only said four words, but all of the pieces of him clicked into place with those words, the way he shaped each syllable like he'd said it a thousand times, the perfect inflection in his cajoling tone as he launched the beginning salvo that led to the lies.

I heard the liar in him, the line he was about to tell. I had his number now. There was no undoing it. "Don't bother. Just erase me from your contact list, please."

It said a lot that my mind focused mostly on Tristan and the fact that he'd been right about Milton. If I had listened to him, I'd have saved myself that embarrassment.

That pissed me off more than any other part of the entire sordid thing.

CHAPTER FIVE

FOUR YEARS AFTER THE ACCIDENT

I'd been on only a few casual dates in the last year, when I met Andrew at a showing.

He was a photographer, an artist, but the least temperamental one I'd ever met. We hit it off from our very first conversation. We felt like very old friends, right off the bat.

He was very sweet and also very good on paper. The genuine attraction thing was obviously a pitfall for me, so I was quite satisfied with this.

Good on paper seemed to be the safest bet I could hope for.

He was gently persistent, but he always respected my boundaries.

He loved my sense of humor, and I really did love to make him laugh. It was a great foundation for a meaningful relationship. A serious one.

I let it get serious. Andrew was good at making things easier than they should be, and he even made that part easy.

We lived about forty minutes apart, and after just six months together, he wanted to move in together, citing that it would let us see each other so much more often, because driving in L.A. really was a bitch.

I put him off, explaining how important it was for me not to rush into things.

He respected that, of course. It was a talent of his, to know just how much to push, and when to back off completely.

I didn't have the heart to tell him that I didn't necessarily want to see him every single day.

I knew I should have felt bad about that. I felt bad about not feeling bad. The man adored me.

The first time we made love, I locked myself in the bathroom afterward and sobbed like a baby for three hours, the first time I'd cried in years. I tried not to dwell on the why of it.

He was even understanding about that. He let me have my space and cry it out on my own.

Tristan would have broken down the door, my traitorous mind told me. He would have made it better.

Tristan was too self-involved to ever see *your* pain, my sensible side told me.

This was the side of myself that had gotten me out of that relationship intact.

Well, intact enough. It was hard to pretend I was okay when the very idea of having sex with my boyfriend again made me hysterical.

Andrew was very understanding. I hadn't told him much, but he knew that I'd suffered through some trauma in my life and assured me that he had no problem waiting however long it took for me to be ready.

He really was the nicest man. I tried to show him how much I appreciated him.

I cooked him involved and extravagant dinners. He considered himself a foodie.

I bought him thoughtful gifts, because he was a thoughtful man.

I always had my eye out for new music he'd like. He was a bit of a hipster, always looking for something obscure.

I did everything I could with my free time to show him I cared about him, everything that didn't involve sleeping with him again and tried not to focus on the fact that my boyfriend was far more a friend to me than he'd ever be a lover.

It was in the early fall that Bev went in for a routine exam, and her doctor discovered a hard knot in the side of her left breast.

After a short series of tests, she was diagnosed with malignant breast carcinoma.

Within days, she was forced to undergo a double mastectomy.

The cancer was aggressive, and it was treated aggressively. After a short respite where she recovered from the mastectomy, she began six grueling rounds of chemotherapy, to be followed by five weeks of radiation.

I made it to every single treatment. I drove, flew, worked in the airport, and in the clinic lobby. Whatever it took, I was by her side, keeping her company, showing my support.

I thought I was strong, but Bev showed me what strength was as she fought for her very life.

She clutched my hand with her weakened one, her bald head completely smooth, her body emaciated, but her smile as bright as it'd ever been.

A fresh wave of toxic chemicals coursed through her bloodstream, making her sick, but God willing, saving her life.

All of this, and she was the one that comforted *me*.

"You think this cancer is a match for *me*?" she asked me archly. "Come on now, Danika. You know me better than that. You have to know I'm too stubborn to die before Jerry. Would *never* happen."

I laughed, and then I cried, because I was so worried about her that it made me *weak*.

"I should be the one crying," Bev told me. "I miss my fucking tits."

I wiped my eyes. "You should buy some new ones when all of this is over."

"Um yeah. That's the first thing I'm doing. Not obnoxious ones, but you can be damn sure they'll be perky."

We both laughed long and hard, and that time none of it ended in tears.

Andrew was beyond supportive through it all, sometimes taking the drive with me, or even the flight. Bev liked him; Bev approved. She was comforted by my finally moving on from Tristan.

Less than one year after the cancer was discovered, she was cancer free.

I felt like we'd all been given a new lease on life after that and impulsively, agreed to move in with Andrew.

I knew within a month that it was a mistake. I needed more space.

Good on paper was so suffocating in real life.

TRISTAN

There were only two nights a week where I didn't have a show, so the guys came to me in Vegas to work on the new album.

There would be no touring. I set that boundary up right away. I enjoyed working with them, and some occasional live shows would be fine, but I'd never go on the road again. Too many triggers for me there.

I made sure they all knew that it had to be a drug free studio, but something, perhaps having two out of five of the original members dying young due to drugs, had gotten us all sober. Kenny and Cory would have the occasional beer, but other than that, we were making a comeback as four sober grownups.

It was bizarre, but good, because if this whole band thing had turned into a trigger for me, I would have had to drop it like a bad habit.

I found, now that I wasn't getting high while Kenny did the writing that I enjoyed being involved with the entire process, and I began to write lyrics to some of the songs.

I was shit at composing music, but I was as surprised as anybody to find that I had a way with words.

Adair and Dahlia were still going strong, and she and Jack came to listen to us record more often than not.

It was good medicine. We all loved that boy, and he was spoiled with attention by every single member of the band. None of us had failed to see the uncanny resemblance to Dean, and we all felt a bit responsible and saw to it that he had everything he needed.

She and Adair were living together by then, and Jack just adored him. It was a huge relief, to say the least.

We finished recording our second album in half the time the first one had taken us and that was with me working nearly every night in my magic show. We'd all grown up, and the result was a much more finely tuned machine.

I couldn't quite believe when we got our first number one hit out of the record's first single, and when a second and a third followed, I was completely floored.

None of us could believe it. It was everything we'd talked about. Kenny, Cory, and I had been daydreaming about this since we were all fourteen, and it had actually worked out for us.

It was a bittersweet time for me. Every time we celebrated another hit, all I could think about was who was missing from the revelry.

CHAPTER SIX

FIVE YEARS AFTER THE ACCIDENT
DANIKA

It was in the summer that I met the mysterious artist.

I'd gotten a memo that the boss had himself a girlfriend and that he was insisting on giving her a gallery showing. This was told to me rather snidely by the New York gallery manager. I knew she'd had her eye on James for herself, but she'd made an advance on him ages ago, and it couldn't have been clearer that he just wasn't interested. Still, I thought, as she told me over the phone about the new development, she must have been holding onto some idea that he'd change his mind. She didn't say it aloud, but she was clearly more upset about the new girlfriend than she was about the fact that James was going to be sponsoring this mystery woman as some kind of an artist.

I was shocked myself about the girlfriend. I'd known James for years and had never thought I'd see the day he committed to any kind of romantic relationship. From what I'd observed, he was never serious about any of the legions of women he was seen with. Shocked was quickly followed by pleased, as I cared about James as a person, and I figured that if he was doing all of this, he must care for the woman.

Even so, I wasn't thrilled at the idea, at least not the one that was originally presented to me. A large, lavishly promoted showing, exclusively featuring this woman's paintings. I knew only the facts as they were presented to me. She worked with acrylics and watercolors, and had an indefinite amount of paintings, and she was without training of any kind.

It was obvious that he was in love with his new girlfriend, but that wouldn't make our jobs any easier.

And then I saw her paintings.

I was leaning casually against my tall work desk, flipping through my day's workload.

I was meticulous; so I organized my workload and made to-do lists daily and anything that came directly from the boss, which was rare, went straight to the top.

I opened the portfolio, which contained only photos of the paintings, with absolutely no expectations. One look, and I had to sit down.

Three hours later, I was obsessed.

The color, the depth, the dreamy imagination that each picture contained made my heart beat faster. This was the part of my job that I thrived on. It didn't happen often, not like this, but when it did, I just *lived* to put a show like this together.

I felt such a sense of wonder at the untutored skill behind it all. It always astounded me, the crap that came out in the art world, by artists that had impressive credentials, and years of study, and yet the results showed little in the way of skill or depth.

This was the opposite. This woman put her soul on the canvas with a skill and talent that I could scarce believe was untrained.

One phone call with James, after looking at her portfolio, and falling in love with it, and he'd put me in charge of the showing. We were kindred spirits when it came to this sort of thing, and I think my enthusiasm alone could have gotten me the job.

It all made sense to me upon meeting her. She was so composed, so reserved. I'd have thought she was cold, if I didn't have a similar approach to strangers.

Her passion, her animation came out on canvas, it was clear. It was all the expression she needed, as far as I was concerned.

I was promoted. It wasn't a little promotion. One day I was quite satisfied to be the manager of one very successful gallery, and the next I was running seven, placed all over the globe.

It was daunting, but exhilarating. I had to move back to Vegas, though I traveled a lot, so that was some consolation.

It was surreal to be working in the same building as Tristan, but after a few weeks with no sightings, I was fairly confident that we could avoid each other cleanly.

Andrew was pleased with my promotion, but not with the fact that I had to relocate for it. Still, he accepted my decision without fighting me.

He wasn't a fighter.

He came to see me every other weekend in Vegas, often surprising me with various show tickets.

Once, those tickets happened to be for Tristan's show.

At first, I tried to make excuses and to talk him into getting a refund. He seemed so baffled by that that I changed gears, bit the bullet, and just went.

If I were even a little bit honest with myself, I'd have admitted that I was dying to see the show. Morbid curiosity, I told myself.

We sat three rows back, center stage. The theatre was colossal, and they were amazing seats. Andrew had to have spent at least five hundred dollars on the tickets.

Five hundred dollars to make me a paranoid mess. We were so close that the entire time I was sure Tristan would see me, would know I'd come.

He never did, thank God, but as soon as it was over, I made sure we got out of there fast, feeling like I'd dodged a bullet.

I waited until Andrew fell asleep that night, went into the bathroom, and cried for hours. The show had been amazing, but it had hurt so much to see him again, and moreover like that, so beautiful, so compelling.

It brought to mind how much of myself I'd invested in him, knowing that this was the investment, this amazing man I'd seen tonight. He'd been a gamble, with a strong potential for loss and gain. I'd suffered the loss. Tonight I'd been reminded brutally of the promised gain.

I cried because of that. But also, because I was a fool.

I was so very proud of him.

TRISTAN

I spotted James and his new woman just as I finished my stint with the red carpet photographer nonsense.

I grinned at the way James glared at me just for glancing in her direction. The man had it bad.

I moved to them, making as if to embrace Bianca, but James was there, catching me up in a bear hug, lifting me just enough to show me that he was no pushover.

"You lay a finger on her, and I'll break those magic hands of yours," he growled into my ear.

I threw my head back and laughed. That was just what I'd needed to get over some of my tension about seeing Danika again.

I sized him up, more out of habit than anything else. I'd never lost a fight in my life, but I thought James could put up a good struggle before I took him down.

It was an arrogance born out of the simple fact that I was undefeated. He was as tall as I was, but I outweighed him, therefore I could take him. It was a simple formula that had always served me well. Also, there was no way the prep school prince had been in as many fights as I had.

He pulled away, but not before I stole his watch.

He stayed directly between me and his woman. I really couldn't get enough of this new side of him. He was just too easy to rile.

Bianca gave me a little wave and a smile.

I bowed to her, grinning. She was beautiful and really quite sweet, and I'd seen the change she'd made in James. I approved wholeheartedly. She was good for him. Even if she *had* turned him into a jealous nutcase.

I was going to have some fun with this.

"So no touching," I observed. "Can I at least see her tattoo? I heard all about it. I heard her back was lovely, just like the rest of her."

Bianca giggled, and even James grinned, shaking his head.

"Outrageous bastard," James said under his breath.

They introduced me to a guy named Stephan and his boyfriend, Javier.

I'd heard about Stephan, Bianca's best friend, and we hit it off right away. I had a feeling he was the type of guy that hit it off with everyone. He was charming and came off as very sincere. It didn't hurt that he went all fanboy on me right off the bat.

"I bet he lets *you* hug her," I told Stephan, smirking at James.

That set James off, and we insulted each other for a few thankfully distracting minutes.

It felt like I was bracing myself for a blow, and my eyes scanned the crowd constantly, searching for a shining black head of hair.

"Bianca only just found out that you're a *singing* magician," James shot at me.

"Well, it pays the bills. Some of us have to have more than one talent. We can't all get by on looks alone. Are you using a new conditioner or something? I swear your hair is even shinier than usual. I bet it smells like strawberries. And admit it, those are contact lenses."

"Please, I know what you get paid just for the magician gig. All your bills were covered before you got the band back together. And I have no idea what conditioner I used. It all just magically appears in the dispenser in my shower. And if you try to smell my hair, I'll assume you're coming onto me."

Bianca laughed, and James and I shared a smile. This was the real deal for him, and I thought it couldn't have happened to a better guy, weirdo that he was.

Bianca never seemed bored with the banter, even when she was quiet. On the contrary, she had a look on her face that made me think she was connecting new pieces of a puzzle. James had to be a strange guy to date. I was one of his closest friends, and even I didn't know much about his past.

James was complaining about how much I was planning to gouge him with my upcoming contract renewal when I glanced at his watch on my wrist. "Are you about done harassing me, pretty boy?"

James cursed, holding out his hand. "Give me my watch back," he demanded.

I waved it at him. "It's almost my birthday. Can't we just call it even?"

He grinned and shook his head. "I don't like you that much."

I shrugged and handed it back to him.

My entire body became rigid as I saw an achingly familiar figure moving through the crowd.

I thought I had braced myself.

I knew she was going to be there. No one could say I wasn't warned. Still, it was a straight up brutal punch to the gut when I saw her.

She wasn't alone.

I was taking harsh, ragged breaths, using all of my efforts just to drag much needed air into my lungs.

I'd known it was going to be hard, but nothing could have

prepared me for *this*.

I spotted her before she approached us, caught her momentary wince as she caught sight of me before she turned slightly away, her shoulders squaring, what's his name putting his arm around her for a moment before she shrugged him off. Good.

She was with him. I knew this, because I kept tabs on her. Always had. But she didn't look to be that *into* him. She didn't shoot him even one of those adoring glances that used to slay me on a regular basis.

Thank God for that one small favor.

But even so, he touched her with privilege, and I hated his guts with a deep and enduring passion. I hadn't been in a fight in what seemed like forever, but I had a sudden and persistent urge to start one with *him*. It would just be so easy to crush him. He was half my size and asking to be put in his place.

She approached our group, not avoiding me, her limp more pronounced than I'd realized.

Every jerky step made my chest ache.

She wore a dress the color of her eyes. It caressed her curves distractingly. She was as fit as she'd ever been, limp or no.

"Hello, Danika," I finally spoke, my voice coming out softer, less confident, than I meant for it to.

The punk she was with hung back, talking to the last group of people they'd been mingling with.

I was immeasurably relieved by this. I hoped to never have to deal with him directly. Nothing good could come of it.

She nodded in my direction, her gaze staying firmly fixed somewhere else, in the distance, anywhere but at me. "Hello, Tristan." Her tone was firm and impersonal.

It was hardly unexpected, but still, it stung.

Like a new cut on an old wound. One that had never scarred over, because it had never quite healed.

"It's great to see you," I told her. I couldn't seem to keep the words in. "You look exquisite, as always."

She smiled tightly. "Sure," she said.

That punk extricated himself from the couple he'd been talking to and approached her from behind. He wrapped an arm around her waist, smiling at her like he was besotted. Of course he was.

The punk didn't deserve to kiss her fucking feet.

He was several inches shorter than me and at least fifty pounds lighter. I was guessing I could have choked the life out of him with one hand. I really wanted to test out that theory.

Danika touched his shoulder familiarly. "Everyone, this is Andrew."

"Her boyfriend," the punk added.

She gave Bianca another tight smile, then introduced them.

I kept my eyes fixed on Danika's face, trying to block out that punk's hand on her. She didn't seem to be particularly happy with him, and I knew I was a bastard for being happy about that.

Danika left the group quickly and politely, only shooting me one direct glance at the very end, which only seemed to give her stare more weight when she swung it my way.

I broke out into a cold sweat, but other than that, I thought I held up rather well.

She swept by me on her way past.

Oh God, I could smell her. Just the faintest hint of her perfume mixed with the scent of her.

I made myself blink slowly, count in my head, kept from doing anything crazy, but it was pure, teeth-gritting effort.

I turned to watch them walk away, that punk's hand still on her.

I needed to get out of there before I followed them and did something supremely stupid. "If you'll excuse me, I need to go punch something now, so that I don't give in to the urge to punch some*one*." I strode away.

I took it out on a punching bag in my home gym, because that's what grown men did when they had the urge to kill someone with their bare hands, or so my therapist told me.

DANIKA

Putting together Bianca's showing was a rare treat for me. I got an absolute kick out of every little detail. She'd given me the freedom to make most of the choices without even consulting with her.

I was not a creative soul myself. I was pure right brain, analytical to my core, though I was a great admirer of artists, so a showing like this was the closest I got to a creative outlet, and I relished it.

The exhibition was broken up into rooms, as there were over a hundred paintings in her collection, which was practically unheard of. I organized them by colors, as this was her signature, trying to make each room a true complement of her brilliant eye.

She was thrilled with the results, which made me want to kiss her. The boss' girlfriend, and somehow she was the easiest artist I'd ever worked with.

I barely slept the last two days before the big event, working tirelessly to make sure that every detail was perfect. I met a jittery Bianca at the door with utter confidence that there was nothing on my end that wouldn't run like clockwork.

I'd thought of everything, and though I was anxious, as any big event made me, I wasn't a wreck. That is until Frankie and her girlfriend walked through the door, each on one of Tristan's arms.

I felt blind-sided, and for one brief crazy moment, I thought I'd lose it. What *it* was I wasn't sure.

My temper, my composure, my mind, take your pick.

Luckily, the moment passed quickly, and I got by mostly ignoring him, though he tried constantly to catch my eye.

I determined that I wouldn't let a night I'd been looking forward to be ruined by *him*.

The paintings started selling within minutes of the opening of the doors. It was thrilling.

I rushed up to Bianca after every sale, making sure she knew that the night was an unequivocal success. She seemed more than a little in shock by it all.

I had my eye on one particular piece. It was a small watercolor of desert roses. It was so crisp, the colors so vibrant it almost came across like a photo at first glance.

I coveted it, and the first few interested buyers had to make a bid. I was hoping to outbid them myself, but within a few hours, I knew it was lost to me. It was just too far out of my price range.

It was around that time that I made a hasty trip to the restroom to touch up my makeup.

I vaguely made out a set of slender ankles that I recognized under one of the stalls when the door opened behind me. My eyes widened in outraged shock when I realized that Tristan had followed me into the *women's* restroom. I'd made short work of his two attempts to talk to me throughout the evening, but this, this was out of line.

"Now you're following me?" I asked him, willing my voice not to quaver.

It didn't help matters that he looked amazing in a crisp tux that had to be custom made to fit those arms of his.

"If that's the only way you'll talk to me, then yes," he told me, just as though he had the right.

"We have nothing to talk abo—" I began.

"I still think about you *every single day,*" he ground out harshly. "Let's talk about *that.*"

That had me shaking, head to toe, in pure affront, pure *outrage*. The nerve of him, to move on from me, to move so beyond me and then torment me with this. I knew what this was, it was guilt on his part, and I was livid as I realized this. "Oh, please. Take your guilt and get the fuck away from me, Tristan. I want *nothing* to do with it."

"The guilt isn't what I was talking about," he said, his lying voice so convincing that I almost believed it. "It's you I think about. *Always* you."

I snorted. "Please! You stopped trying to call me years ago. I haven't heard a word from you since right after rehab when you went on your repentance tour."

He looked taken aback, but he recovered quickly enough, spouting more nonsense. "I didn't trust myself, Danika. I needed my sobriety. I'm nothing without it, and you were a lovely trigger for me. That look in your eyes, after all that I'd done...The way you looked at me like I was scum and knowing that I deserved all of your antipathy. I knew that if you looked at me like that again, I'd hit rock bottom, and this time I wouldn't come back from it."

"I'm with someone, Tristan," I told him, my tone hard with resolve.

"And if you weren't? Would you be willing to talk to me—to spend time with me, if you *weren't* with someone?"

I snapped. "*No*! Bad things happen when we get together, Tristan. You and I are nothing but trouble. Time hasn't changed that. Please, just stay away from me."

He moved to me, quick as a flash, his hands cupping my shoulders. "Danika, I'm so sorry. I'll never stop missing you. You were my best friend. Can you ever forgive me for what I did?"

My trembling hands reached up and pulled his from me. "I forgave you a long time ago, Tristan," I asserted, even as I took a step back, out of touching distance. "But I will *never* forget. Please keep your distance." I practically ran out the door.

I made a point of seeking out Bianca soon after, since I knew she'd overheard our confrontation in the bathroom. I cared what she thought, and I didn't want to come across like a royal bitch, so I felt I owed her an explanation.

"I'm sorry you had to hear that little exchange in the bathroom," I told her solemnly.

She looked uncomfortable but her eyes were sympathetic. "I am *so* sorry about that."

I waved that off. "It was hardly your fault. You were just using the restroom. But I saw your shoes under the stall, and I wanted to explain myself. I probably sounded like a cold bitch."

She held her hand up. "You didn't. I understand completely. Sometimes protecting your heart is the only way to keep your sanity."

She'd hit that one on the head. I nodded. "Yes, exactly. I won't get mixed up with him again, and I refuse to lead him on. When I was younger and stupid, I thought that he was the most wonderful and exciting thing in the world. I fell crazy, stupid, jump off a cliff in love with him. It was like being in love with a tornado. It took me years to pick up all of the pieces he'd left me in, but I did it, and I *won't* go back. These days I want stability in my life. I need it."

She nodded. I patted her on the shoulder, and walked away, satisfied that she understood.

I was literally forced to deal with Tristan again at the end of the evening, as he purchased two of Bianca's paintings. Unbelievably, and infuriatingly, one of them was the small still-life I'd become obsessed with.

"You have great taste," I told him as I entered his data into the system. I had other people to do this, but I always handled the really big ticket items myself. It made me nervous to let anyone else do it. My control issues were in full swing.

"I always have."

I made sure he saw me roll my eyes. He grinned at me as though I'd just given him a present, which hadn't been my intent.

"Listen, I'm sorry I came on too strong earlier, but I really think it's time we start to talk again."

"I told you, I'm with someone."

"Yes, I know. I'm not talking about him. I'm talking about *us* hanging out again. Just as friends. You live in Vegas again; we work in the same building. It would be ridiculous if we didn't go out for coffee every once in a while. Catch up a bit. That's all."

I had to work to keep from losing my temper. "You want to catch up? You want to hear how many hours I spent in physical therapy after our breakup?" He visibly winced, but I kept going. "What else would you like to catch up on, exactly? What about Milton having a girlfriend, that you had to know about, but who you didn't bother to mention when you gave me that crazy warning to stay away from him?"

"Hey now, I had no idea he had a girlfriend—"

"It doesn't matter." Though I did feel a tiny stab of relief that he hadn't known either, and I couldn't even have said why. "What matters is that the only things we have to catch up on are things I have no desire in the world to talk about. Not ever again. And certainly not with you. Your paintings will arrive at your house within the next few days, following the verification of your credit card, etcetera. Have a good night, Tristan." I strode away before I said anything else I'd regret later.

When it came to Tristan and I, there were never any winners to be had.

TRISTAN

I went to bed that night angry and upset. So agitated that, even at rest, my heart was pounding hard.

I tossed and turned for hours before I fell into a restless sleep.

I was having my morning coffee when I felt something strange move in my chest.

It felt good, but foreign, and it took me a long time to place it.

What was this feeling? I had to think for a long time to figure it out, but I grasped it after a time.

A freak streak of optimism had just entered my body.

Hope. I felt the tiniest stirring of hope. But why? She'd been as vehement as ever. She didn't want anything to do with me. Nothing had changed. But my mind had this one little thing to focus on, this smallest of contact, and so I hadn't forgotten even one detail.

On the contrary, I'd been memorizing every second of that brief confrontation.

Every last twitch.

Every time she'd blinked, or licked her lips, or swallowed with nervousness.

She'd done such a good job of showing me nothing but indifference for the last few years, I'd had no choice but to believe that was how she genuinely felt, and I'd just fucking bought it, giving her the space she needed.

She deserved that much. She deserved so much more than I could ever give her, because I'd taken so much from her, and so I'd left her in peace.

But something about last night, perhaps it was the way her hands trembled when she pushed mine away, or the fact that she'd shown me her rare temper with just the slightest bit of prodding.

And the bit where she'd said, *"Please! You stopped trying to call me years ago. I haven't heard a word from you since right after rehab when you went on your repentance tour."* That bit fascinated me. Had she *wanted* me to call her? Or was I just reading what I wanted into it?

Whatever it was, something had changed and important pieces of my life were shifting into place.

I knew what I needed to do.

CHAPTER SEVEN

DANIKA

It was a normal, chaotic day at the Vegas gallery. I was still settling in as I brought it under my own management. It was a challenge, but I enjoyed challenges, even ones that made me lose sleep, so I was exhilarated by it more than anything else.

I knew who she was the instant she set foot onto the marble floor of my gallery. Whether I liked it or not, Tristan's love life was hot news, and I was kept up to date on every little detail, thanks to the two gossip-loving ladies that worked with me.

Mona Biello was a statuesque blonde with ridiculously exaggerated curves. The blonde was out of a bottle, and at least half of those curves were added on by a doctor, but who was keeping track?

She was the daughter of the famous magician, Tony Biello. He'd recently retired his act, which had been in the Cavendish casino. Tristan had essentially taken his job. I figured there must not have been any hard feelings, since by all accounts in the media, they seemed to be close friends.

And the man didn't seem to mind that Tristan was dating his daughter and had been for *years*. She was also one of the sexy assistants in his magic act. It had even been rumored that he was planning to pop the question.

She was almost the last person on earth I wanted to see. The second to last, to be specific.

She passed right by the other two women working the busy gallery, brushing them off with a charming smile.

She headed straight to the podium, where I stood talking to a nice couple that was seriously considering purchasing one of the limited additions from this month's featured photographer. It was a $50k sale. I had courted this sale, and I would close the deal, but I figured the couple would need at least one more trip back before they made their decision. They were serious buyers. I was experienced enough to know the difference.

Mona didn't interrupt, which was considerate, instead waiting patiently while I finished talking to the potential buyers.

I sized her up with furtive glances as I chatted.

I had no notion of why she was there. My best guess was that she wanted to ask about a work of art. But whatever the reason she was there, she was dressed to kill in a tight black dress with a plunging neckline that didn't look anywhere near capable of holding her ridiculously huge breasts inside of it.

She was taller than I was to begin with, but her four-inch heels had her towering over me. I didn't like that. For some reason, I would have liked it much better if she was shorter. And certainly, I could have done without those obnoxious fake breasts of hers. I really didn't want to talk to her. Not for any reason.

I handed the couple my card, and they departed.

I turned to Mona with a professional smile plastered on my face. "Good afternoon. How may I help you?"

She smiled back, and it was friendly, engaging, even. She was certainly pretty, and striking enough, with full lips and dark, mysterious eyes. I was not particularly charmed by her beauty, but then, how could I be?

"Danika Markova," she began. It was not a promising start, though if I were to judge by her demeanor alone, she was much more pleased to meet me than I was her. "I'm Mona Biello. Has Tristan told you about me?"

I blinked at her, all sorts of confused. "Excuse me?"

Her smile widened and became amused. "Would you like to get a cup of coffee with me? We have a lot to talk about, you and I."

I sighed, seeing no way around it. She'd put me in an awkward position, coming to my workplace. "Why not? Lead on."

I nodded at Sandra on my way out. "I'll be back in fifteen minutes," I told her quietly.

"Make it thirty," Mona said loudly, that charming smile in her voice.

I didn't correct her, just glaring at her back as I followed her.

She walked fast, making no allowance for my slower gait.

That was fine. I'd get there when I got there. I knew the way, and I wasn't rushing for *her*.

She was already sitting at a table, sipping on a coffee when I reached the coffee house. I didn't bother getting one for myself, instead moving right away to sit across from her.

I crossed my legs, folded my arms, and raised a brow at her.

Her face serene, she began, "Tristan and I have been sleeping together for two years. We also happen to be the *best* of friends." Her voice was sincere and engaging.

The bitch wanted me to like her. She'd come to the wrong woman if she was hoping for some kind of a friendship.

I held up a hand, keeping my face very blank. I'd known it and though hearing it made me sick to stomach, sadly the best of friends part even more than the sleeping together, but I'd be damned if I'd let *her* know that. "I'll stop you right there. That is none of my business. If you're here to talk to me about Tristan, it's extremely unnecessary. There is nothing to talk about."

Her pleasant expression didn't waver, not for one fucking second, but I got the distinct feeling that she thought I was lying.

My spine stiffened in affront.

"I'd like to be frank with you, Danika. I've come to you because I care about Tristan, but at the moment he is shutting me out. I was hoping you and I could help each other, for Tristan's sake. I know you and he have some sort of history, and that something's been rekindled between you."

I started shaking my head, but she wasn't done, and some head shaking wasn't going to stop this one.

"You need to piss or get off the pot, Danika."

The words were inflammatory, but her tone was still pleasant, almost playful, like we were old friends.

"Excuse me?"

"I don't believe in playing games, and I've always been a fan of plain speaking. Tristan is holding some kind of a torch for you. It's very romantic, but I, for one, would like to know if it could go anywhere. Are you stringing him along, or does he have a shot here? I'm asking as his friend. Because if he has no shot, you need to let him go. You have got to stop leading him on."

I gritted my teeth and dug deep for some patience with the woman. I wasn't sure why I bothered. Nice or mean, good or bad, I wanted nothing to do with her, nothing to do with *any* of it.

It was the principal of the thing that made me answer her at all. "You're mistaken. Nothing has been rekindled. I don't know where you're getting this idea, but there is nothing between Tristan and I but some shared regrets.

I'm sure you've noticed my limp. Tristan feels that he's responsible for that. He feels guilty about it. He shouldn't feel that way, but he does, and if you've gotten the impression that what he feels for me is something other than that guilt, you couldn't be more wrong. Now, was there anything else?"

Her expression schooled itself into one of sincere sympathy. "That's very sad. I'm so sorry to hear about that. But I still can't shake the feeling that he is *obsessed* with you."

I shrugged; my face so stiff that it felt like it would crack. "Obsessed with his guilt perhaps. If that was all, I should be going."

That meeting had been agitating enough, but my day from hell wasn't done.

Not two hours later, Tristan had the sheer gall to come striding into *my* gallery.

We had clearly drawn lines of territory, ones necessary for keeping the peace, and he had a nerve coming into *mine*.

I gripped the podium and prayed for strength.

He was visibly agitated as he approached me. He wore his usual jeans and poured on T-shirt. He looked good, of course. Amazing, in fact.

"We need to talk," he began without preamble.

I looked around, feeling terribly self-conscious. I couldn't bear the thought that some hint of a rumor could be started about him and me. It was too raw of a wound to have outsiders picking at it.

"My office," I told him tersely. "You have ten minutes."

He followed me there, shutting the door behind him.

I moved to the far side of the room and then around my tall project desk, putting it between us.

"I know that Mona came to see you. I want to explain."

I shut my eyes and shook my head. I couldn't do this. I needed to stop it before it started. "Don't, please. You having some sort of a tiff with her is not something I'm willing to become involved in. I frankly could not care less what it is about. None of it concerns me. I am with someone. I am *in love* with another man."

Why did those words feel so hollow? Why did they feel like a blatant lie, and why did I feel so dirty saying them?

My eyes were still closed, but I'd have sworn, just by the very change in the air, that I could feel him recoil.

"You say you want to be friends, to catch up. That's fine. Are

66

you prepared for me to talk about *him*? It is serious between us. Are you ready to congratulate me when we become engaged? It's going to happen very soon. Are we *friendly* enough that I can tell you the details?"

He was silent for so long that I didn't think he'd answer.

"Beggars can't be choosers," he said, his voice barely more than a whisper.

"Fine. Leave your number. I'll give you a call sometime. We'll do coffee. How's that?" I would have said anything to get him out of there right then.

"It's good, if you mean it."

"Well, you'll just have to wait and see. Your ten minutes is up."

Finally, I looked at him. He gave me a tiny smile that played havoc on the stupid, traitorous organ in my chest. "You didn't let me get a word in. I want a do-over."

I shook my head, letting the tiniest hint of a rueful smile play across my mouth. "Not happening. Now make like a magician and disappear."

He laughed, and I tried not to let my heart show in my eyes.

I never made a phone call, and I never answered his.

TRISTAN

We met for lunch regularly, but it was rare for me to get a summons up to the big office. I knew the reason for it, though, the second I saw James.

One look at the pained expression on his face and I knew it.

He looked as though he was braced to step into the middle of a situation that must have put him in a bad spot.

I sat down without a word and waited for the ax to fall.

"It's about Danika," he told me with a heavy sigh.

67

I just nodded, though inside the turmoil raged on. Whatever he was about to say, I knew I wouldn't like it.

"As you know, she's recently moved back to town, and she'll be working on site regularly."

I just nodded. Again. At least this was all coming through James. Somehow, it made it easier. As far as messengers went, close friends were a better case scenario.

"She's, well, she's asked me to relay a message to you."

I flinched, but nodded at him to continue, properly braced.

"The gallery and everything west of Frankie's is to be considered her territory, everything east, including your theatre, of course, will be yours. I take it you went to see her at work?"

"Yes," I said, jaw clenched tight.

"Christ, man, what happened between you two? I missed all of the pertinent pieces. I only caught hints of the aftermath. You've both been so damned close-mouthed about it all."

I looked down at my hands. "She doesn't like for me to talk about it, but we were together. Not for long enough, but as you see, it was life-changing." I took a deep breath. "We were *married.*" It felt so good to say that part out aloud, to acknowledge that it had been real.

I could see by his expression that he hadn't had a clue.

I smiled bitterly. "No one knows. We didn't even tell Frankie. And Danika doesn't acknowledge that it ever happened. But we were *married.* It was just months after I lost Jared. I thought I was doing okay, but I did not deal with his death well."

James nodded, looking sympathetic. He'd sent his condolences at the time, but had steered clear of the funeral. He hadn't wanted to turn the whole thing into a media circus, as everything in his life tended to be.

"Obviously you know about all of the drugs and the drinking while we recorded that album with Dean. You did pay for the rehab."

"Worth every penny, to say the least."

My mouth kicked up in a grin. "We were trying to get pregnant. She was insanely young for it at the time, but there was nothing sane about us. We were crazy about each other. She miscarried our baby, and I was a complete flake about it. After that, well, the losses started piling up until I'm sure she'll say we lost more than we ever had together. That's not true. We had more than we ever lost, but either way, I screwed it up. I could blame the drinking and the drugs, but however you cut it, I'm the one that let her slip through my fingers."

He looked thoughtfully concerned, his fingers steepled in front of him. "I always got the impression that you held yourself responsible for her leg?"

I winced. "I am responsible. She came to see me after the divorce. I can't remember why she came to my apartment, I was high as a kite and wrecked over the divorce. I have huge chunks of that night missing from my brain, but I do remember yelling at her to get a ride from Dean, who I later found out had drugged her. You know what happened after that."

"My God," he uttered softly.

"I'm glad you found Bianca, James. It's not something you can describe until it hits you, but I see that you've found the one, and I'm happy for you."

He studied me, his eyes pensive, but also pitying. "I'm sorry, Tristan. I didn't realize this was what you were dealing with. I thought it was some scenario where she was wanted too much from you, and you went on your way. I knew that you loved her, but I thought that you'd let her go by choice."

"By choice? No, my friend. This was not my choice. I screwed up plenty, but if it were up to me, it would never have turned out like this."

"I don't know how you've done it. With Bianca...she turned me away for a month and I thought I was losing my mind. I can't imagine going through what you have, all the years, all the distance. I don't know where you find the strength."

I shut my eyes, the words pouring over me like some soothing torture. "I don't know either. I don't have a clue."

CHAPTER EIGHT

SIX YEARS AFTER THE ACCIDENT
DANIKA

I was beyond flattered to be asked by Bianca to be a bridesmaid. I agreed instantly. I hugged her when she told me, and embarrassingly, even teared up.

Her friendship had been very good for me. We'd particularly bonded after the shooting. I'd visited her whenever I could as she was healing.

She managed in that quiet way of hers to talk me into posing for a series of paintings for her while she recovered.

I was terribly flattered, and excited, because she'd promised me a painting for my time.

She was extremely generous with her art, offering several times to give me pieces I was taken with in the past, but I'd always put her off, insisting on paying for the two small paintings that I did end up buying from her collection. This though, the exchange of inspiration for art, didn't feel like taking advantage, and so I accepted her offer of taking my pick from her next collection after we'd finished with the sessions.

One painting turned into another, until I became her favorite subject, second only to James.

The hours turned to days, hell, to weeks, and her next show, which premiered a mere of eight months after her first, had so many paintings of me in it that I couldn't keep track. I became a bonafide part of the show. It was a strange experience, to say the least, but a good one.

We'd opened up to each other as I'd sat and she'd painted, even talking to some extent about our rough childhoods. As far as nightmares went, I thought hers took the cake, but it was good to have a friend that could relate to having and surviving a troubled past. To climbing out of a pile of rubble and leaving it behind.

It was hard, but I made a promise to myself, for the sake of two people I adored who were getting the dream wedding they deserved, to just be nice to Tristan for the whole affair.

Not just civil. Not just less hostile. But nice.

I could do this, I told myself, many times.

And when push came to shove, it was frightening just how easy it was to fall back into the old rapport.

Not just easy. *Natural.*

I had this moment every time I went to visit Bev and Jerry at their house. I'd walk in the door, and everyone in the place would just stop what they were doing and rush at me. The kids, no matter how big they got, would wrap themselves around me. The dogs, sans Mango now, but with an extra puppy in the mix, would come and crowd me until I sat down somewhere and let them all converge on me. Bev would come and kiss me on the forehead, even while Jerry did a drive by all the chaos to pat me on the head affectionately.

I was squeezed so tight that the air left my lungs, licked on every part of skin that wasn't covered, and it usually lasted for several minutes. That many kids, and people, and dogs should not have existed comfortably into one space, but it didn't just feel comfortable, it felt right. Like I was coming home.

Every single time.

That's how this felt.

Tristan and I were entering a new and unfamiliar chapter, only it didn't feel that way. It felt like no time had passed at all.

It was terrifying. And comforting, because it hadn't all just been some dream, there'd been a reason I'd gone through hell with this man, *for* this man, some true good to precede the bad. Over the years, I'd half-convinced myself that I'd imagined most of the good. It was just easier that way.

We were partnered up in the wedding party, which meant that we walked together, and at all of the parties, we sat together.

I usually took care with my appearance, but I went to great lengths that weekend, spending extra time on my hair and makeup and shopping for days to put my best foot forward.

I don't care how things stand, every girl wants to feel beautiful when they see 'that ex' again. You know the one I'm talking about. The one you never quite got over. The one that had claimed enough of you that some of it had been lost in the parting.

I wore a gold lace sleeveless mod sheath to the rehearsal dinner, going heavy with gold shadow and big hoop earrings. I wore my hair straight and parted down the middle. I kept it down, since I'd have a complicated up-do the next day.

I was in *dress to impress* mode. I'd already seen Tristan several times since the festivities began, and each time I'd decked myself out with special care.

Vanity at its most perverse.

On the up side, we'd been getting along well, both of us cautious enough to go out of our way to give no offense.

"By the way, where's that guy?" Tristan asked, sometime during the third course at dinner, his mouth making a mockery out of the words with just a hint of an unhappy smile.

His hair was longer. It looked good on him. Grippable. I gave myself a mental slap for even thinking it.

"Andrew," I clarified, something in his voice troubling me, and unwillingly, intriguing me.

We'd kept things light thus far, and it had seemed to be working. This was a new turn, or the potential for one.

"You think I don't remember his name? How likely do you think that is?"

"Where's that girl?" I asked, immediately wanting to take it back. We did not need to do this to each other.

I looked down, up, shifted uncomfortably, but his eyes stayed glued to my face, his intense regard strong enough that it felt like a physical touch.

"What girl?" he finally asked.

I made a dismissive motion with my hand. I knew her name, but I already regretted even asking. "No one. It was a very silly question."

"No, tell me. What girl?"

"That blonde one you're always with. Your girlfriend."

"That's not my girlfriend. It's weird to bring a girl that's not your girlfriend to a wedding. Your turn. Where's that guy?"

He had this perfectly even scruff on his jaw. It was distracting.

"Andrew couldn't make it." That was a lie. He'd wanted to come, but we were on a break, a very long break, due to the fact that he'd proposed several months ago, and I'd put him off again, and to say he'd been unhappy about it was a gross understatement. These days we were strictly friends, but Tristan did not need an update on my love life, or lack thereof.

"Oh, well that's too bad." His statement was so unconvincing that I had to make an effort not to laugh.

"Not an Andrew fan?"

He gave me a rueful smile, his brown eyes so endearing. I could tell he was about to say something funny. I just knew him that well. "That's like asking if I'm a fan of cancer. I fucking hate it, but do I know how to get rid of it? Not fucking likely."

That surprised one small giggle out of me. "Oh my God.

Stop it. You're impossible."

His focus shifted to something behind me, and I turned to look. In an almost comical manner, everyone seemed to be staring in our direction, all gone quiet. No one was used to seeing us interact with each other like normal human beings.

"We should really blow their minds and start making out," he whispered.

I laughed again and had to check the urge to give his arm a playful punch. "You're an ass. Shut up," I told him.

His smile grew and his eyes shone in pleasure, like I'd just given him a gift.

CHAPTER NINE

***THE WEDDING RECEPTION OF JAMES AND BIANCA
CAVENDISH***

"That motherfucker is even bigger than you," shot out of my
mouth as Tristan took his seat beside me.

He gave me one quick look and then looked at Akira, but that
look told me plenty of things that I'd rather not have known. For
starters, my statement came out sassier than I'd intended, and
Tristan still loved my sassy. In fact, he ate it up. His gaze had
been hot and...something else that I didn't want to name.

"Don't get any ideas," he said idly, taking a sip of water. "That
giant bastard is taken."

My eyes narrowed on him. "I know that. He's married to a
supermodel. I was just saying...it must be weird for you,
usually the biggest guy in the room, having to look up at
somebody. And his biceps are even a bit wider than yours..."

His breath whooshed out in a surprised laugh. "You and your
big arm fetish. Mine are still bigger than your waist. They
haven't gotten any smaller."

I didn't let myself look at them, but it was a struggle. And I'd
looked enough already to know that he was right.

Absently, I rubbed at my bad knee under the table.

I felt him staring at me.

"Does it still hurt?" he asked softly, as though he couldn't help himself.

I made my face into a very careful mask. "It's fine, just a bit stiff. Nothing to concern yourself with."

Nothing on earth could have shocked me more than when his hand touched my leg, sliding under my hand to rub at my knee, somehow knowing just where to touch to ease the ache. He'd always had a special talent for that.

"What are you doing?" I asked through my teeth. We'd been getting along for days, but this was too much, too far.

He didn't even flinch away from the look of murder I sent him, the bold bastard. "I'm just trying to help," he said, deadly earnest.

"I don't need your help." My tone was venomous.

He didn't stop rubbing, still didn't flinch away. Over the last six years, it had been way too easy to get him to back off, and I found that I had no clue what to do when my venom didn't push him away.

"I know that. Believe me, I know it. But what if I need to give it?"

"We're at the wedding of two people I adore, so I will be civil for about ten more seconds, but you had better believe that—"

"What about friendship? Can we just try that? No funny business, I swear."

I felt so stiff, and I knew hostility was radiating off me in waves.

Frankie caught my eye, her arm around her girl. This was a wedding, a joyous occasion, and her concerned look swayed me. She was worried I'd cause a scene, and it hurt me that she was right to be worried.

I'm more mature than this, I told myself. And hell, why couldn't we be friends? I didn't think he was attracted to me anymore. I knew that what he wanted really was just friendship and forgiveness, so why couldn't I just give that to him? Why

77

did I feel the need to shut him out completely?

I knew the answer. I was like a wounded animal, lashing out at his indifference, which had become the cause of my pain.

"No funny business?" I asked, then spoke again before he could answer. "I actually believe that now. I didn't figure you were into cripples."

His hand dropped limply from my knee.

I got a look at his face, right before his gaze dropped down to the table, and instantly regretted saying something so ugly.

Whatever his feelings for me had turned into, I still had the power to wound him deeply.

"I'm sorry," I told him quickly.

I opened my mouth to speak again, but was interrupted by a furious looking Frankie.

She sat on Tristan's other side, giving me a hostile look that I'd never have figured she'd direct at me.

"You okay?" she asked Tristan, her hand going to his arm.

He nodded shortly, stood up, and strode away.

"When are you going to stop hurting him? When is it going to be enough for you? You wanted him punished; he's been through hell. What more do you want?"

Part of me was livid about every word that came out of her mouth, but another part, the part that wouldn't shut up today, knew she had a point. I had been punishing him; for six years I'd been punishing him, and it had gotten out of hand.

She stood, and I knew that it was to go after him, to make sure he was okay.

I stopped her with a grip on her hand. "I've got this," I told her, standing. "You've got some best man duties to attend to."

"Please, Danika. You don't have to take him back, but please, just be kind to him. He's been through enough. You both have. You're hurting yourself with this bullshit, too, you know?"

I knew it. I let my eyes show her that as I nodded.

I found him walking aimlessly through the woods, somewhere between the wedding tents and the fortress of a building that James called a 'house.'

"Tristan," I called out loudly.

He froze. He didn't turn around, just stopped.

I caught up to him quickly, grabbing his arm.

"I'm sorry I said that. It was an ugly thing to say, and I didn't even mean it. You know how I am. I can never seem to keep things to myself, and sometimes they come out worse than I mean them."

"You've been pretty good at keeping things to yourself for a very long time."

My eyebrows shot straight up. He had a point. I had gotten better at holding my tongue, but I couldn't quite decipher what his tone meant.

"That's true. I've grown up. But what I said back there wasn't grown up, and I'm sorry for that. I don't have a grudge against you. I really have gotten over our…history together, and I think you're right. There's no reason that we can't be friends again."

"Thank you." His voice was low and hoarse, his head tilted forward. Even in the semi-darkness, I could see that his eyes stayed on the ground.

There was something so defeated in his stance, something so hopeless in his voice that I couldn't seem to help myself, I hugged him. For comfort, for support. Whether it was for him or me or both of us, I didn't dare contemplate.

I had to stand up on my tiptoes to get my arms around his neck, and that was with him slouched down.

He was stiff as a corpse for about ten seconds before he reacted, his arms squeezing me so hard that I let out a grunt as all of the air was pushed out of me.

He eased up, and I took a few breaths before relaxing into him.

My body seemed to take over, because touching him brought

back so many sensory memories. We were a train wreck, he and I, but something about touching him had always just felt right to me.

I pressed into him, my face still buried in his neck.

He pulled back slightly, and I looked up at him. I couldn't make out much in the darkness, but I knew he was looking down at me.

"Tristan," I uttered softly.

He lowered his head until his mouth was a breath away from mine, and even then, I didn't think he could possibly be going there.

"Tristan."

He moved his hands to cup my face, and at the corner of my vision, I could see that that they were trembling.

He tilted my head one way, slanted his head the other, and brought our lips together.

He kissed me.

A desperate, hungry, wild, make me forget the past and the future kind of kiss.

Most of my life was spent displaying a cool reserve to the world, my self-control assured and seemingly effortless. One brief kiss and the years dissolved; the past and the present merging into one singular thought that existed right now. And right now, all that mattered was this connection, this sensation that began at our joined lips and traveled down my body, igniting every last molecule of my being into a wildfire of sensation.

I snapped.

My hands clawed at his shoulders, my mouth ravenous on his. I'd always considered myself a good kisser, and I knew for a fact that Tristan was one, but there was no finesse in this. We simply took, and took, and gave in the form of clashing teeth and warring tongues.

His hands moved to my hips, lifting me high against his body.

I'd longed for this body, this exact shape, every bend, bulge, and curve of him all that my body needed. My legs wrapped around his waist, animalistic whimpers escaping my throat as his erection pushed hard against my belly and after I'd shifted just right, straight into my clit.

I knew he was walking, carrying me, but I didn't care, just sucking at his tongue, biting his lip until I tasted blood. The sky could have fallen around our heads and I wouldn't have cared. I wasn't letting go of this; this mindless moment where everything felt like it had shifted back into place and all of the wrongs were right again.

He tried to set me down, but I wouldn't let him, my legs a vise around his hips, my arms locked around his shoulders. He pulled his head back, and I bit his neck, rubbing my torso into his.

"Please," he whispered hoarsely.

That one small request had me pulling back just far enough to look at him. A bright lantern light shone down at us, and I took in our surroundings.

We were on the back porch of the ranch house, and Tristan was pushing my hips away from his, setting me on the thick rail that ran the length of the patio. Confused and disoriented, I let him.

I swallowed hard, opening my mouth to say God only knows what when his hands shot to the hem of my lavender bridesmaid dress, yanking it up over my hips.

That effectively squelched my urge to try to speak.

We were rushing headlong into this lunacy, and I could worry about the mess we made later.

I wanted this, needed this like I hadn't needed anything since I'd cauterized all of the joy from my life.

He pulled the dress straight up, flipping it all the way over my head until my arms were effectively restrained. I didn't know, or care, if that had been his intent.

He unsnapped the front clasp of my bra, moaning and bending down to suck one quivering globe into his mouth. His hands fumbled with his belt and fly. He groaned, and I gasped as his freed erection sprang into my stomach.

Big fingers shoved my panties to the side, and the tip of him was pushing into me as he raised his head and took my mouth again. He didn't hesitate, didn't ask if I was sure I wanted to do this.

I was relieved, because a crash this brutal could handle no brakes at all.

He reared back, then drove forward, burying his cock in me with one hard stroke.

The world stopped as we took what we needed, what I'd been starved for since the very last time I'd been in his arms.

It was a frenzied mating, a swift coming together that took me to the fever pitch of ecstasy with a few rough, heavy strokes, over too soon, the perfect testament to our torrid love affair.

We didn't move for a very long time after we finished, and more importantly, we didn't speak. Words would break the spell. Words were reality. This was a stolen moment, and I wanted to keep it as safe from reality as possible.

My forehead had fallen to his shoulder at some point, and what felt like his cheek was pressed to the top of my head. He didn't pull out, the only movement between us the aftereffects of his member still twitching deep inside of me.

We stayed like that for what could have been minutes or an hour. I had no idea what he could be thinking, and I was trying hard not to think about anything but the moment at hand, and the pleasure of being in his arms for this tiny foray of ours into utter lunacy.

It was the first impulsive thing I'd done in years, and boy was it a doozy.

"Danika," he finally spoke, his voice hoarse but soft.

I sighed heavily, pulling back. The spell was broken.

I couldn't look him in the eye and looking down was a no go, so I looked over his shoulder as I spoke. "Can you put my dress back on? We need to get back. We're both in the wedding party, so I'm sure we'll be missed."

His hands moved to start righting my gown and still he didn't pull out. I would have tried to shift away, but I was afraid it would just lead to another indiscretion.

"Danika," he said again, his voice very soft and very sad.

God, it was flooring how just listening to that deep voice of his could captivate me. For just the sound of his voice alone, I could have stayed glued to that spot indefinitely.

I shook the thought off, calling myself a fool.

"I need a minute alone, if you don't mind. I'm going to go clean up."

He tried to kiss me, but I turned my head away. "My dress, please." My voice wasn't sharp, in fact, it was gentle, but I saw him flinch out of the corner of my eye.

How did he always do that? Make me want to take back whatever I'd said that may have hurt him, even after all this time.

Reason number one thousand why I needed to stay away from him.

We both gasped in a harsh breath as he dragged himself out of me. I clenched at him involuntarily as he pulled, and that seemed to drag it out, into an act of pure torture. His girth assured that he hit every nerve ending on his way out.

I cursed.

He pulled my dress back up onto my arms, then over my head, then my shoulders. His hands were gently caressing as he eased every inch of it back in place.

I didn't look at him.

He still had his hips close, still between my thighs, even as he smoothed my dress over my back.

I felt him nudge back against my sex, seeking entrance again.

I don't know how, but I managed to shake my head. We would not be going for another round, addictive as it might be.

I had to get off the crazy train *now*, not go for another loop.

I needed just a moment, to go be by myself and think. The sooner the better.

He stepped back and helped me down. He let me go to tuck himself back into his pants, and I fled into the house.

The place had a ton of bathrooms set throughout the sprawling mansion, but I went up to my appointed guest suite and used my private bath to clean up, then combed my hair, and touched up my makeup.

I stared at my dazed expression for a solid five minutes, wondering what the hell was wrong with me.

Was this some new sickness, or had the old one persisted, in spite of everything?

Or was this the result of mishandling the situation altogether?

How were we back to square one six years later, within just a few conversations?

Had that happened because we'd never learned to cope with sharing the same space? Had never having any contact at all just made us more susceptible to a screw up of epic proportions?

Had we only made ourselves more sensitive to the other's presence, when what we'd needed was to be *desensitized*?

Was it just possible that there was some middle ground here? Some sort of closure to the romantic part of our relationship that I'd never pursued?

I had always thought of Tristan in terms of all or nothing, but clearly, that hadn't worked. That failure was currently staring me in the face, and perhaps more mortifying, dripping down my leg.

I could admit that cutting someone that had become such an undeniably significant part of me so completely out of my life had been damaging to me.

It had stunted me. Stunted my happiness. Stunted my growth.

That was a fact I'd accepted long ago, in a resigned sort of way, seeing it as a necessary evil.

But what if it wasn't necessary? What if it was *only* detrimental?

Spending some rare time in his company made me realize something new.

I'd been so focused on the bad of him, of us, the bad of all that had happened that I'd forgotten the good.

I'd lived the bad, existed with it every waking hour of every day and some nights, in my dreams, as well.

Why shouldn't I get a bit of the good?

What if, just maybe, I needed it?

What if it would help me close that chapter of my life?

Being with him was out of the question. A long-term romantic relationship was absolutely unthinkable. But a friendship? Hadn't I moved on enough to at least give myself that small bit of comfort?

Didn't I deserve it?

I was expecting it. I wasn't even a little bit surprised when Frankie made a point of cornering me.

She and I weren't the type of friends that fought. We gave each other shit on a regular basis, but that little scene earlier was as good as a full-on confrontation for us.

I'd known she was going to feel bad about it and quickly try to make it better.

The reception was still in full swing when I returned to the party. I'd have been surprised if it didn't go until morning.

I made my way quietly to my table, very acutely aware of the fact that, though I'd cleaned up as well as I could in a hurry, I hadn't showered. I was planning to slip away and do that just as soon as I thought it was politely possible.

Frankie joined within a minute of me sitting down. She was alone. Almost everyone else from the wedding party was dancing. Estella was currently going to town as the dancing meat in a Stephan and Javier sandwich.

"You remember that I set you two up, right?" I asked her as I met her very serious eyes. "You owe me. I brought that hot thing into your life."

She shot her longtime girlfriend a fond glance. "I know it." Her face crumpled slightly, not a breakdown, not tears, just screwed up a bit, as though she were in pain. She looked away. "You know I love you, right?"

It was my turn to look away. We were close friends, but not the mushy kind. Things like this were rarely said between us. "I do. I love you too. You're one of my closest friends, and I know that your heart is *always* in the right place."

"Forgive me?" Her voice had gotten very, very quiet. "I overstepped back there. I know it. It's just so hard for me to see him suffer any more, and no one can hurt him like you can. But I overreacted. I was a dick, and I'm sorry."

"Frankie, I'm well aware of the position we've put you in, and how hard it's been for you, but you've got to stop interfering, and you've got to stop thinking it's your job to protect him or even me. We are adults, and we don't need a buffer, much as I might like one, may even have depended on it in the past. He and I...we need to sort our messes out ourselves."

"Of course. And for the record, I never took his side. Or yours. You know I'm always just trying to help whichever one of you is hurting the most."

"I know. We're both lucky to have you."

I considered the matter settled, and apparently so did she as she didn't mention it again. We sat there for a long time, just watching the revelry.

There were a lot of people in the colossal reception tent, but I could still tell that there was no sign of Tristan. He hadn't returned yet, and I found that odd. I was sure he'd gone and cleaned up, but he couldn't possibly need more time than I had, even if he'd taken the time to get in an actual shower, and to change.

I was so involved with this thought process that it took me a moment to realize who else was so glaringly missing. "Did James and Bianca ditch out on the rest of their own reception, already?"

Frankie laughed. "I would bet a lot of money that they're off in the forest somewhere having a quickie. James is a kinky fuck, but they'll be back."

We continued to watch the dancing crowd. "Who is that Marnie and Judith are assaulting on the dance floor?"

Frankie squinted, then started laughing. "That's Jackie's dad. Marnie is making it clap for him. I think Jackie was right. They're going to give that poor man a heart attack. And get a load of Lana and Akira. They're making out like teenagers. God, that guy is huge."

"He's hot," I added.

"So is Lana. And this is the first time I've met her brother, Camden, but he's smokin'. This tent is chock-full of hot people."

"True. Some good dancers too."

Finally, I saw Tristan re-enter the tent. He stopped at the entrance, scanned the crowd, and zeroed in on me. The second his eyes touched on me, he started striding towards our table.

"Did you two, uh, work out whatever that was you two were having? Was it a fight?"

I couldn't quite hide my wince. "Yeah, I guess we worked it out."

"So you finally had a good talk? You both disappeared for a while."

"I guess. You know how we are. It's complicated."

"Complicated. Now there's an understatement of epic fucking

proportions."

I had to laugh. She wasn't wrong.

And that's how Tristan found us as he approached, laughing and relaxed.

The relaxed part went a bit south as he sat right next to me, and I instinctively started to tense up.

"If you'll excuse me," Frankie told us with a grin. "I have some freaking to do on that dance floor."

"Who the hell calls it freaking?" I called to her back, but she just kept walking.

It wasn't easy, but I made myself turn and look him in the eye.

I'd likely be mortified in the morning over what we'd done, but I thought the entire thing was too new for my shocked mind to react appropriately.

His face was sober. "We need to talk."

That surprised a laugh out of me. "We just tried that. Didn't exactly work out."

"I wouldn't say that. I'd say it was cut short. I'd like to try again."

I couldn't stop laughing. "I bet you would!"

Finally, his solemn face cracked into a smile. I had to clench my fists to keep from touching one of those calamitous dimples. "Well, yes, of course I would. God, Danika, I've missed you, even just to see you laughing again."

I looked down at my hands, the laughter dying a bit. "I think you're right. I think you've always been right. We should be friends. I miss that, too. I know you're worried that I'll never speak to you after this—after that little scene back in the forest, but you don't need to worry. That was insanity, and it does not need to happen again, but we can be adults here. I...won't be a stranger when we get back to town. I'll give you a call. We can sit down for coffee, or, you know, something."

There was a very long pause on his end, and I wondered which part of what I said was eating at him.

He didn't address that though, instead said, "Do you mean it this time, or are you just blowing me off like last time?"

I sent him a rueful smile. I hadn't meant it last time, and I *had* blown him off. But I found that, shockingly, I'd had a real change of heart. "I mean it this time."

I did mean it but, while I didn't avoid him for the rest of the weekend, I also made sure our contact was limited. It was necessary. I needed time to think, to have a battle plan before we started to transition into this friendship idea.

We'd been at war for way too long for me to delude myself that a battle plan wouldn't be necessary, even when we were playing nice.

I was packing to leave for home, the happy couple already having ditched the party and jetted off to God knew where, to do God knew what kind of kinky shit, when I noticed something odd.

My perfume was missing. I did a quick search of the bathroom, but there weren't that many places it could have gone, and I'd thought the small bottle was sitting right on the counter.

I was annoyed. I loved that perfume, and it wasn't cheap, but I shrugged it off. Some lost perfume was really the least of my problems.

Tristan managed to corner me one last time before I took off.

The wedding's location was remote, and so all of the guests had been flown to the nearest airstrip, and driven in limos the rest of the way. I couldn't even wrap my mind around how expensive that must have been, but there was no doubt that James could afford it.

Even so, people were sharing rides to the airstrip and planes to their various destinations. It only made sense.

Tristan and I hadn't flown or driven in together, even though we'd come from the same place.

He could not understand why we couldn't share on the way

home.

He'd actually come to my room to talk about it, charged into the space, sprawling out on the room's only chair like it was the most natural thing in the world.

I supposed it was better than the bed.

I stayed by the door, determined not to do anything stupid for the five minutes it would take me to get rid of him.

"Stop being pushy," I told him, arms crossed over my chest. It felt surreal to be talking to him as though no time had passed, but it was happening so naturally. "See, this is the problem. I give an inch, you take five more. Knock it off."

He grinned, leaning forward in his chair. "C'mon. It will be fun. We can play some road trip games. Remember all of our games?"

I sighed. Of course, I remembered. "Not this time, Tristan. I need a few days to think. Like I said, I'll call you. Now if you'll excuse me."

"No," he said casually, his smile dying. "I do not excuse you."

He stood and moved so close to me that I backed away. "I'll give you a few days, but if I don't hear from you, I am coming for you. This is fair warning."

I glared at him. "Dramatic much? I said I'd call, I'll call. I said I needed a few days, give me a few days."

CHAPTER TEN

I told myself that the reason we'd done that idiotic thing was because I'd kept myself too tightly leashed. If we could see each other more often, but casually, it wouldn't be like that. We wouldn't have to lose our minds, if we weren't scared that we'd never see each other again.

I didn't call him right away. Not because I was a coward.

Well, okay, I was putting it off because our last encounter had left me shaken. I'd lost my mind. There was no other way to put it. And that wasn't even the scary part.

What would we do for an encore? It didn't bear thinking about.

But I did think about it. Constantly, incessantly, I obsessed about what to do about him.

Even so, it was a month before I saw him again and only then because he forced the issue.

The showing was substantial in size, though not in notability. Five artists were being featured, each with two rooms in the spacious L.A. gallery devoted to their theme. It was very involved. I'd been putting it together for nearly a year.

One of the artists had recently started getting some attention in the media, due to some interviews he'd done, so what had been a promising but obscure event suddenly had some star power.

It was a bit hectic, but I was dealing with it all in stride, calming down the temperamental artists, soothing the fussy celebrities that had shown up for the press.

It was shaping up to be an invigoratingly busy but overall smooth night, when Tristan walked through the door.

He was wearing a tux, hair scraped back and showing off his strong jaw with that fascinating bit of scruff that I couldn't stop obsessing over.

He looked so handsome it made my chest ache. The effect of seeing him out of the blue, no warning, looking how he looked, was devastating.

I took a deep breath, prayed for calm, and thanked God I'd decked myself out for the event in a fitted sleeveless crimson lace dress with a high neck and a flared skirt. It showed my figure off to perfection.

He was alone, which was certainly better than the alternative in one respect, and terrible in another. He had no one else to focus on, no other reason to be there, but for me.

Well, maybe he's here for the artwork, I told myself. But even as I had the thought, he was making a beeline to me.

His expression was unsmiling and solemn as he stopped in front of me

"What are you doing here?" I asked, trying to keep my voice quiet and calm, but it was an effort.

"You never called."

I just stared at him.

"You said you'd call," he reiterated. "So we can do this easy, or we can do it hard. Personally, I prefer hard."

"Does this look like the appropriate place to have this conversation to you? I'm working."

"I gave it a month. I ran out of patience. My supply was fucking depleted to begin with."

His voice had been loud enough that I glanced around,

wanting to avoid making a scene.

"We work in the same building, if you didn't realize. Coming all the way here, on the night of a big show, is not the way to handle this."

"The gallery in the casino is your territory. You've been very clear on how you feel about me infringing on your territory. Are you saying I'm allowed to come there now?"

"Yes, that's fine," I said, to appease him. Anything to avoid what he was doing right that second, because having him there, talking to him there, was going to turn me into a basket case in the middle of an event I'd been planning for too long to flake out on. "Now please, you need to let me work."

In theory, he did back off, just not far. He didn't leave, as I'd hoped, but stayed, going through the entire building slowly, room by room, perusing the art thoroughly, always in my peripheral, hovering close enough to be distracting.

I tried my best not to be distracted.

One of the artists had done a series of paintings on large multi paneled room partitions. They each measured roughly six feet high, and the way they were set around the room turned it into a sort of maze. It was a striking series.

I'd just shown it to some potential buyers. I was taking down a few notes about some other work by the same painter that the buyers were interested in seeing before they made a decision. They had since moved on to the next room. I always encouraged this. I didn't hover, tending to let the buyer find the pieces that spoke to them on their own.

There was a small table at the back of what had turned into the maze room. It was displaying a series of small painted fans, but had enough free space for me to set my paper-thin laptop on as I typed a few details in.

I was just straightening when big hands cupped my shoulders from behind and started rubbing.

I knew who it was instantly. Of course I did. I could smell

him. The warm, spicy scent of his cologne was permanently branded into my brain.

And those hands. No one else on earth had hands like his.

I breathed in deep, taking him in, trying to get a grip.

One hand left my shoulder, and I felt a teasing finger run the length of my spine through the thin material of my dress. His touch was so light, his journey from bottom to top so slow, my nipples had tightened into hard peaks by the time he reached my nape.

I shivered involuntarily.

He moved in closer behind me, that wandering hand going to my waist, gripping. I could feel the heat of his palms, one on the skin of my shoulder, the other through my clothes. The contrast of the touches made me catch my breath.

A sensitive muscle very low in my belly began to quiver.

He moved closer by infinitesimal degrees, until I felt him leaning over me, head tipped forward. I thought he must be staring at my features, gauging my reactions.

"What are you doing?" I asked him in a shaky voice.

"You said you didn't want to have our conversation here. I'm improvising."

I shook my head slightly, then froze as, gently but firmly, the hand at my waist moved up and held my breast. His palm slid softly over the already hardened peak.

"This is not the place for *that*, either," I whispered furiously.

But I didn't move away.

His other hand moved from its scorching grip on my shoulder, covering my right hand, which was clenched into a fist on the table in front of me.

He lifted it, pried it open until he could fit his thumb against my palm, and started to rub. His touch was so soothing, so fundamentally pleasurable, that my hand fell open like he'd unlocked it with a key.

And that was when he knew he had me.

He continued to fondle me while he straightened my arm, then pulled it behind my back, palm twisted to face him. Without a word, he pulled it to the front of his pants. Slowly, leisurely, he rubbed himself into my palm, stroking himself with our connected hands. Up, down, up, down, each stroke taking its sweet time along his broad length.

My lips were trembling, my body shaking, every single muscle in my belly tight with anticipation.

I felt like all of the nerves inside of me were about to shatter. And I *wanted* it.

How was it so easy to fall into this old pattern, of all things?

Still stroking my breast and his cock with our combined efforts, he whispered into my ear. "If you say no now, I will stop. But I can't make any guarantees for after. Now is the cutoff for no."

I shuddered. After everything, the rise and the fall of us, the pain and the aftermath, why did his touch still bring such comfort? How could it unearth such a sense of security?

I made my mind into a temporary ally with my want, my desire, yet again, and took the plunge.

I felt so out of control that I didn't even care what happened after.

It was madness.

And yet, completely necessary.

"Yes or no. I want to hear it."

My eyes fell closed and I gripped him harder. "Yes."

His breath shuddered out harshly, and he fumbled at his pants, working them open.

I gripped and started stroking as soon as he spilled, bare and hard, into my open palm.

I felt him working my skirt up, his other fingers plucking firmly at my nipple through two layers of fabric that I would have liked to make disappear just then. But there was no time for undressing, not here.

This was a direct access; get at it as fast as you can kind of fuck. And yes, it had a name. Thanks to the devastating power of our history together, nearly every damn thing did.

The hand in my skirt lifted it high, and he fit himself behind me, his swollen flesh pressing hard into my thigh.

He pushed the heel of his hand against the throbbing nub of my clit. It pulsed against him like a heartbeat.

"Oh," I cried out before I could stop myself.

The hand on my breast moved up to cover my mouth. I mewled softly into it while he rubbed at my needy flesh.

"Shh, sweetheart," he rasped in a hushed voice. "I don't know if you've forgotten where we are, but this is not the place to make a lot of noise."

I shook my head, my body shaking, throbbing with unfulfilled need as he shoved my panties to the side and rubbed the thick head of his cock slowly along my wet entrance.

His mouth moved to the sensitive tendon between my neck and shoulder, biting down gently, he plunged in hard.

I bit his hand (not gently) as he started to fuck me in earnest.

I had to brace both hands on the table in front of me. It wasn't all that sturdy; it began to shake, clanging into the wall with each movement.

I didn't give a damn.

A few delicate fans fell off, and still I couldn't make myself stop, even knowing I'd be sorry later.

That was the all-encompassing, undeniable control he had over my body, the absolute power.

The power to make me forget, and to make me let go.

He stretched me, my flesh clenched around him. He surged in and out of me, filling me, taking all of the emptiness away for that brief respite.

I throbbed in time to his steady rhythm. As ever, he played my body to his beat. Who else? It had been tuned for his hands alone. The years apart had only illustrated that fact even further.

In huge glowing neon letters.

His mouth stayed on my neck, licking, sucking, his free hand digging into my hip, anchoring me for his relentless thrusts.

The pressure inside of me built with each sure thrust, until I was biting so hard at his hand that he pulled it away.

I tensed as I felt the wave coming, muscles drawn tight as he continued to pound into me. I bit back a cry as my entire body began to convulse.

I broke, shuddering, clenching, wave upon wave of pleasure washing over me, crashing relentlessly, again and again.

Like it was rinsing me clean.

I couldn't quite stifle one tiny sob as I came down from that impossible high.

He was folded against my back, himself shaking and emptying inside of me, as I came back into my trembling skin. I'd missed the beginning of his release, as I'd been so involved in my own.

"My God," he gasped. "Are you okay?"

I nodded weakly.

"Well, I'm not sure I am."

He started to pull out, and I let out a little involuntary noise of protest. He hugged me tight from behind. "Sweetheart, you are going to be even angrier with me if we get caught like this, or I'd stay inside all night."

His words jarred me into remembering where we were. I couldn't quite believe it. I'd been transported, for a few addictive minutes, into another place, another world.

His pants were fastened, my skirt straightened, when he spoke again, "Can we agree that we need to talk? Not in a week, not in a month, but tonight."

"I'm work—"

"When you're done. I can wait. Obviously."

I nodded, not looking at him, focused on the pile of fans we'd knocked over onto the floor.

I got to work picking them up and straightening them. None were damaged, thank God, but not for lack of trying. We'd knocked every single one of them off the table.

Tristan tried to help me, but I waved him off.

"Go away. Go look around, or mingle, or something. I can't get anything done with you around."

Instead of offending him, that made him smile. The man was still perverse.

I got back to work, but I was so distracted that I felt like a basket case for the rest of the night.

Every time I turned around, there he was, looking my way, smiling at my annoyed looks.

What was wrong with him, behaving like no time had passed since we'd been close? Acting as though we still *were* close.

It was disarming me, and I *needed* my arms.

After a time, as I did my usual hurry back and forth through the different exhibits, answering questions, handling sales, placating artists, I noticed that he'd stopped following me around.

Somehow, that was even more distracting.

The event was winding down before I saw him again.

I happened upon him in one of the smaller rooms, alone with some woman. They were laughing together, and as I very nonchalantly moved in for a closer look, pretending to straighten a picture on the wall, I realized that I recognized her.

She had deep red hair and a pale but luminous complexion. She was beautiful and very young.

She was a famous singer. I knew the name of at least three of her songs, so she was *very* famous. She was one of those young starlets that were always being linked romantically to other celebrities.

And at the moment, she seemed to be very interested in my ex-husband.

I couldn't recall them ever being linked in the gossip rags. Though I liked to pretend I didn't keep track, I was up to date enough that I thought I would have remembered this connection.

The girl was just so young. Nineteen, if I was recalling it right.

She wasn't too young to make him laugh, or to appreciate whatever he was saying enough to laugh herself, and to touch his arm several times, and just in general seem ecstatic to have his attention on her.

I turned around and left. I didn't need to see that, or hear it, or ever think about it again.

I couldn't, however, manage to keep my mouth shut for even a second when he approached me again, several minutes later.

"God, it was bad before you were famous. You must have to beat them off with a stick now. Or not, I guess. There's plenty of *you* to go around."

His expression, which had been smiling, wiped clean, becoming very blank. "I don't think we want to go there. Either of us."

I rolled my eyes, because it was no competition. His revolving bedroom door and my locked one were not even in the same category.

"Am I allowed to ask if this is jealousy?"

I bristled. "No, you're not. You do whatever you like. It's no business of mine."

I started to move past him, but he caught my arm, turning me slowly back to him.

"That's quite an invitation. Anything I like, huh? Let's go back to your hotel room. Right this second."

I rolled my eyes, jerked my arm out of his hold, and stormed away.

CHAPTER ELEVEN

TRISTAN

It took her hours to finish up, but I waited patiently. Better to wait hours here, then days, weeks, months, somewhere else. And in spite of all that had happened, I had no doubts that it was a very real possibility she would just cut me out again, if I didn't press the issue now, tonight.

"This can't be convenient for you," she told me sassily as I held the door open for her. Even her walk, limp and all, was sassy.

I felt myself getting hard.

"This isn't really about convenience, now is it?" I asked her pointedly.

She didn't answer, just folded her arms across her chest and stared at me.

The gallery shared a parking lot with a Cavendish resort, so I assumed she had a room there for the night, since it was clearly too late for her to make it back to Vegas.

"Let's go talk in your room," I said with a smile, watching her face for a reaction that I was way too excited about, considering that I knew it wouldn't be a positive one.

She gave me a dirty look, and I shoved my hands in my pockets, my cock twitching restlessly.

"I'm so not taking you there. No way in hell."

I tried not to let my grin grow too big. "I saw an all-night diner on my way here, maybe five minutes away."

She gave her narrow eyed agreement to let me take her there.

We stared at each other across a tiny table and ordered cheeseburgers. The table was so narrow that our legs would have touched if I hadn't spread mine wide, letting hers rest between.

It was surreal, just to get to stare at each other under bright, unforgiving lights.

Of course, Danika didn't need forgiving lights. She was perfection, even under the harshest of conditions. So beautiful that my chest was aching enough that my hand had been rubbing at it for a solid minute before I caught myself and lowered it. And the entire time, I just kept drinking in the sight of her.

There were so many shocking, drastic changes and painful, wrenching similarities between the girl and the woman. The girl had been playful, fresh-faced, and beautiful as a freshly bloomed flower. The woman was quiet and elegant, and so heart-wrenchingly exquisite I would have given up another piece of my soul just to keep looking at her.

I couldn't believe she'd let me have her again. Even as I clearly recalled the encounter, how she'd let me inside of her, bare; let me come in her, skin on skin; let me empty myself deep inside of her, I almost felt as though I'd dreamed the whole thing.

That was all we did for the longest time, just stared at each other. I was hesitant to be the first to start talking. The faster we talked, the sooner this was over, and I was content to drag this out until dawn.

"Does this place even have good burgers?" she finally asked. "Because I'm warning you right now, I'm not wasting calories on a bad one."

I smiled fondly at her. "What, you think I'll get upset with you if you don't eat the food you order? Who do I look like, Ike Turner?"

She stifled a laugh, and then refused to look at me for a while, not talking either, just staring down at her hands in her lap while I marveled at how even the curve of her brow was just lovely.

Very slowly, I closed my legs until my knees touched each of hers. I reached under the table, cupping her clenched hands in my grasping ones.

Her chest shuddered as she took in a very deep breath. "So what are we doing here? Tell me how you see this playing out."

I wasn't sure which version to give her, but I didn't think I should start with the brutal truth. I sugarcoated the hell out of it, going into pure survival mode. "I think we should become friendly again. I come say hi to you at work, we grab a bite to eat, and make each other laugh, etcetera, and so on."

"And the rest. What happened at the ranch, back at the gallery. What's your solution for that?"

To do it every chance we get, day or night, until we pass out, or hell, fucking keel over and die.

I had a very vivid but too short vision of her sprawled out naked on this very table, taking every inch of my cock, no, not just taking, begging for it. I figured my chances of fucking her again this very night were slim to none, but a guy could dream.

I smiled pleasantly. "Ball's in your court. You want platonic, I can do that."

"I think that would be for the best."

I tried to keep my expression neutral. "Okay. I think it's pretty obvious; I'll take what I can get."

"Want to hear my theory on that insanity back there?"

I sighed. I knew I wouldn't like whatever she had come up with, but I humored her, "Yeah, shoot."

"I think it's some survival instinct kicking in, some biological, physical drive that kicks in when we're near each other, because we never got real closure, so our bodies want to cling to each other, because we're worried we'll never get the chance again. You can't cut someone out of your life like that and not have closure. We need closure."

I wanted to quote my therapist to her. He always said closure was a myth, or at least what people had turned it into was, but I stayed silent, because I wanted her to cling to this theory of hers.

This theory was my ally. It clearly had her changing her tune after all these years.

I mean, I hated the theory, and I thought it was complete bullshit, but I was in no position to dispute it. If I could have said what I wanted and not scare her off, I would have pointed out that it'd always been like that between us, there had always been the drive to touch, to feel each other in every way one human could touch another, inside, outside, body, soul.

But I couldn't say what I wanted to say. Not yet.

Step one: Get back into her life again.

Everything else was secondary. The rest would come with time, God willing.

"Maybe we should set up some ground rules, like only go out with a third wheel, some type of chaperone."

My smile felt like it wanted to crack my face. I really, really didn't like that idea. "Whatever you think is best."

She sighed, as though conflicted about it. "We're two mature adults. We shouldn't have to resort to a babysitter."

Here, here.

"We'll keep our hands to ourselves. It's just that simple."

The fuck it is, I thought, giving her my blandest smile. I wasn't optimistic enough to think I'd get to fuck her again anytime soon, but I spent a lot of time plotting out how I could get her to let me eat her pussy. She became very receptive after I went down on her for a few minutes, I recalled.

I had a brief and intense fantasy where I buried my face between her legs and made her lose it. I wanted to taste her, even if it was only for a moment. I needed to know if I remembered even that last detail as well as I thought I did. How long did a tongue's memory last? I badly wanted to find out.

My mind wandered to our encounter from earlier. It had been so incredible. The feel of her hot walls closing on me; God, I needed to get a grip.

I couldn't believe that, even as I sat there, my dick was still covered in the evidence of what we'd done. That got me thinking about how it couldn't be that hopeless of a cause.

I started plotting ways to get up to her hotel room with her.

She was still talking, and I tried to pretend that I hadn't been daydreaming about the things she was talking about never doing again.

"I don't need conflict, I need peace. I don't need chaos, I need order. I'm dealing with needs here, not wants, not wishes. And you need to understand that. You need to respect it."

I made her look at me, straight in the eye, when I spoke. "Whatever you need me to be, I'll be that. Whatever you want me to do, however we need to make this work, we will do it." And it was as I spoke that I realized that I couldn't seduce her again so soon, certainly not tonight.

I needed to bind her to me again with more than the most incredible sex of my life.

We needed to become best friends again. Yes, that was how I would do it. I needed to become so essential in her life that she couldn't conceive walking away.

I meant to break her.

Needed to break her.

Whether it be with deceit, subterfuge, cold calculation, or sheer willpower alone, I was set in my course.

She'd built a wall up against me. A wall that seemed to me to be interwoven into her very soul.

For years, I'd thought that wall was impregnable. But a few words, a few brief encounters had shown me that the wall wasn't stone, but glass.

I meant to break it, and her, and anything that stood in my way. I was going to shatter all of the things she used to keep us apart.

It had become my sole purpose. And if she failed to give, to yield, I'd break myself in the process.

I was prepared for that. At this point in my life, with what I'd learned from our separation, I was willing to risk it.

"So it's pretty obvious you're never going to call me. Let's start with baby steps. How about you just start to actually answer when I call you?"

She chewed on her lip for a minute and then nodded.

"And we work in the same building, so how about I come by sometimes, and say hi, and you don't call security, or hell, our boss, to get me to stay away?"

That got me a rueful smile and another nod.

"And you let me walk you up to your hotel room. We can cuddle for a few hours, no funny business." I smiled. She'd say no, but it would be sassy and cute, so I tried anyway.

She rolled her eyes, a corner of her pretty mouth kicking up. "Not happening."

"Well, I had to try."

Our cheeseburgers arrived, and we ate. The burger must have been good, because she ate the whole thing, wasting lots of her allotted calories on it.

I finished mine too, but I couldn't have said if it tasted good. I was too distracted, too focused on her, to notice I was even eating until the food was gone. I'd inhaled the thing, the fries too.

She shook her head at me, still working on hers. "Must be

nice to get to eat however much of whatever you want and still have a perfect body."

I grinned at her, the word body making me think of nothing but what mine could do to hers. "I do spend two to three hours in the gym every day. Weights and calories go hand in hand." I flexed my arms a bit, loving the way it drew her eyes and made them glaze over. Only with Danika could workout talk become foreplay.

I ordered a milkshake after she finished her burger. She declined dessert, though she eyed mine up hungrily when it arrived.

It was banana, not the real banana flavor, but the fake banana flavor.

I knew that was her favorite kind of shake. I'd only ordered it to stall and draw the night out longer but when I saw the chance to torment her, I took it happily.

I took a long drink, moaning appreciatively, like it was the best shake I'd ever had, though I barely tasted it.

"Want a drink?"

She shook her head stubbornly.

"One drink won't affect your diet."

I slid it her way, and she tried it. Apparently, it did taste good, because she just kept drinking, and as she always said, she didn't waste calories on sub-par food.

She finished the whole thing, then blamed me for letting her have it. "Now I have to hit the gym extra hard tomorrow."

"*I* could always give you another workout tonight." Even if we were in friend mode for the moment, what could it hurt to flirt?

Of course, if she'd taken me up on it, nothing on earth could have kept me from following through.

Unfortunately she didn't. Instead, she glared.

I ordered cherry pie a la mode, just to keep dragging the night out, then proceeded to go on and on about how much I loved to eat pie.

Just to make her laugh.

And it did. And her laugh made me happy, as it always had.

Next I ordered coffee, and she had a cup as well.

I was stuffed, but I ordered an omelet next.

She'd caught on by then, folding her arms across her chest. "I'm tired. I need to get to bed, sometime *tonight*."

"You want me to go to bed undernourished? Let me finish this last thing, and then I'll take you back."

I finished the entire omelet, and all of the sides that came with it, dragging it out to the last.

"You flying or driving back to Vegas?" I asked her, as I finally took her back to her hotel.

"I have a flight in the morning. Early."

I nodded. I'd driven, as this trip had been a last minute impulse; I'd learned about the show the morning prior. Also, I liked to drive. If I thought I had a chance in hell, I'd have put some real effort into getting her to drive with me.

"Well, I drive in the morning. Let me know if you miss your flight, or just want to sleep in, you can come with."

She didn't respond. I hadn't thought she would.

I walked her in and got a room there myself.

I tossed and turned all night, obsessed with the fact that she was under the same roof, somewhere.

CHAPTER TWELVE

DANIKA

I'd bought a house the year prior, less than two months after I'd moved back to Las Vegas.

It was an odd move, because I'd never even considered buying a place before. I'd been a pretty happy renter.

But I made good money, and I'd just started looking at houses, with a mind to planting some roots. Very quickly, I'd found a cute little place in Seven Hills. The commute wasn't bad into work. The traffic was a dream, compared to what I'd gotten used to in Los Angeles, and my location gave me a few route options, if I hit it at the wrong times.

It was a quiet area, and for the most part, my neighbors kept to themselves.

The lady next door had what seemed like thirty cats, but that didn't bother me. I didn't have pets, but I *loved* pets, so I found myself buying cat food, and putting it on my back porch, shamelessly feeding the felines so they'd like me.

I traveled too much to have my own pets, so I just borrowed a few sometimes.

There was an orange tabby and a blue point Himalayan I was particularly fond of, and those ones even got to come into my house.

I had a promising future as a lonely cat lady.

I'd been back in town for two days and still hadn't had any contact with Tristan. I'd gotten right back into work, and I knew Tristan'd had his show the last two nights.

Some days I enjoyed the peaceful solitude of my little house in Seven Hills. Some days there was nothing I loved more than coming home from work, putting on a pair of sweats, collecting my furry friends, and curling up with a good book, shutting out the world, getting lost in fantasyland. Nothing beat an absorbing book in terms of distraction.

I wasn't feeling that need for solitude so much that night. I wasn't in the mood for reading or borrowing cats.

In fact, I felt so lonely that I found myself doing something I almost never did.

Logging onto Facebook.

It was my personal account, so there wasn't much going on. I had two friend requests, but only one of them had my heart racing. I clicked confirm on both before I could talk myself out of it.

Less than two minutes later, a little red number one appeared above my message box, and breathless, I clicked on it.

Tristan had left me a short message.

Tristan Vega: Thanks for accepting my friend request. I promise to try my hardest to refrain from sending you too many dick pics.

That surprised a laugh out of me, and then a smile that just wouldn't go away.

Danika Markova: How sweet. What a gentleman you are.

Tristan Vega: By too many, I mean more than a dozen,

just so you can't say I didn't give you fair warning.

Danika Markova: Don't make me find the unfriend button.

I sent it as a joke, but his response back was effusive and apologetic.

Tristan Vega: I'm very sorry. I was totally joking.

Danika Markova: I was only joking, too.

Tristan Vega: You have any exciting plans this weekend?

I sighed, not knowing what to tell him, not knowing what to do. What I wanted to do and how I needed to handle things were two polar opposites at the moment, actively working against each other.

Danika Markova: I do have plans. How was the show tonight?

Tristan Vega: Good. Want to have lunch tomorrow, at the casino? I'll be in early, and I know you're working.

I shut my eyes, knowing that I should find an excuse to say no. I needed to slow this thing down, and if we started seeing each other on a daily basis, that wasn't going to happen.

He was easing his way into being a big part of my life again, and I knew that it was nothing that I should encourage. He took a mile for every inch I gave. He always had.

Still, I told myself it was only lunch. And if he was already going to be there, it seemed over the top rude to turn him down.

Danika Markova: Sounds good. Just let me know when you want to go. My lunch hour is flexible.

Tristan Vega: Perfect. I'll text you around noon, when I get close.

I logged off quickly after that, making a note not to go on Facebook again.   That had backfired on me in a hurry.   But even as I had the thought, I was smiling.

I dressed with care the next day, wanting to look my best for the most obvious reasons.

I loved clothes, loved fashion.   I always had, and my fashion sense had been constantly evolving through the years.   I had a great job, and little in the way of expenses, so I indulged myself in this.

I'd been very into pleats and collars last season, bringing a bit of prep into my business attire.   I liked this look because it was cute and feminine, but still classy.   My hemline was usually at my knee or lower, my neckline high, and though everything was usually fitted to complement my figure, it was all very modest. My color palette was usually neutral, with lots of creams, beiges, grays.   Colors, when I'd worn them, had been muted.

I found myself shopping more than usual the last few weeks, though (specifically since the wedding), and it seemed that my style preferences had changed seemingly overnight.

Now what caught my eye were plunging necklines and raised hems.   A bit more skin.   A flash of vibrant color.   Still classy, still professional, but I'd definitely found my sexy side again.

I didn't have to think hard to know why this had changed for me.

Needless to say, I'd been shopping a lot, updating my wardrobe, turning it up a notch.   Lucky for me, I worked in a building with some of the best shopping in town.   And Vegas was a town with some killer shopping.

Today I wore a fitted black tuxedo jacket, and a white pleated skirt that hit me mid-thigh. I kept the jacket buttoned, because underneath I wore nothing but a violet bralette. It was modest enough, as long as I kept the jacket buttoned, just a glaring flash of lace showing at the neckline.

I wore bright white patent leather loafers with it. They were flats. That couldn't be helped.

I parted my hair down the middle and curled it into thick ringlets, then tousled it a bit. My makeup got as much care, with a dark eye and glossy pale lips.

My extra time paid off when I walked into work feeling sexy. Pride was a perverse thing.

The morning dragged and right before noon, I went to the bathroom, refreshing all of my makeup. It was foolish, but even if we were just being friends, I wanted to look my best in front of Tristan. And by my best, I mean sexy as hell.

It was Frankie who came strolling into the gallery at about eleven forty-five.

"I hate to be the one to break it to you," I called out to her, smiling, "but I'm ninety-five percent sure that some wild animal ate the bottom half of your tank top."

She smiled ruefully. "You're just jealous because your job has a dress code that doesn't include belly shirts. I can recall you rockin' your own under boob a time or two, or have you forgotten?"

I hadn't forgotten. I still had a few of the trashy shirts, for the random rainy day indoors.

"Tristan is going to meet us at the restaurant," she continued. "I invited myself to lunch with you guys. Hope you don't mind."

I shook my head, eyes wide. "Not at all. Sounds like a great idea."

She laughed. "Well, your reaction was better than Tristan's, at least. He actually threatened to start getting his tats elsewhere. Can you imagine?"

I blushed, pleased at the notion that he'd wanted to have lunch alone with me. But again, I knew I was being foolish. Stupid, even.

To say I was conflicted where Tristan was concerned was the understatement of a lifetime.

"Where we headed for lunch?" I asked her, going to grab my bag.

I waved at Sandra before we started to walk. Frankie naturally slowed down for me. She was used to my slow walking.

"The Mexican place. What else? I love to get the enchiladas when I'm with Tristan so he can rant about how much better he makes them, and then I rope him into cooking for me. Works one hundred percent of the time. Try it. See if I'm wrong."

I just shook my head at her and smiled.

Sounded like Trouble to me. It didn't help that just thinking about his cooking had me salivating.

We were seated and chatting when Tristan showed up promptly at noon. We were in a booth, so he had to sit next to one of us.

He squeezed in next to me, throwing an arm over the back of my seat.

I flushed when he said quietly into my ear, "Jesus. You look beautiful."

I tried to order a salad, but that about gave Tristan a conniption.

"Don't tell me about your fucking diet again," Frankie chimed in, taking his side.

I made a face and shrugged. "Must be nice not to have to diet and keep a great figure, you two, but that isn't how it works for me."

Tristan ignored that completely, and then ordered tamale combos for all of us. "It's their best dish. Trust me on this."

"I was craving some enchiladas," Frankie complained.

"Well then come have dinner at my house tonight, before my show. I'll cook."

"Done," she stated before he'd even finished talking.

"Both of you," he added.

I was looking down at the menu, but I felt his eyes on me.

"Oh, well, thanks for the offer, but I have plans tonight." It was lame, but it was the best I could do on short notice.

"Oh yeah? What are your plans?" Tristan asked, and if he was trying to disguise the tense new note in his voice, he was doing it poorly.

I looked at him, and his attitude seemed to rein itself in before my eyes.

"A rain check then," he told me.

I shrugged, refusing to commit to anything.

It was a strange meal, though I couldn't deny that it was enjoyable.

He was big and the bench wasn't, so we sat hip to hip and ate and joked with Frankie for a good hour.

It was like being transported back in time. I didn't begin to know what to feel about that.

Frankie headed straight to her shop after we finished, but Tristan walked me back to work, strolling slowly beside me, hands in the pockets of his slacks. He was well turned out, in an all-black suit with no tie. The effects were devastating, though I tried not to dwell on them.

"You're all dressed up today. What's the occasion?" I asked him, my tone idle, my eyes hungry.

"Don't you like it? I know you aren't a fan of my T-shirt and jeans uniform."

My mouth twisted as I shot him a look out of the corner of my eye. "I do like it, but why on earth would you say that? I have never in my life complained about the way you dress."

He shrugged, fidgeting with his collar. "I haven't failed to notice that you only date professionals. The kind that wear suits, not jeans."

I stopped to give him my full attention. "Don't tell me you dressed like this for me."

He looked distinctly uncomfortable. He shrugged again. "I wear suits sometimes. Not a big deal."

We started walking again. My eyes were glued to the carpet on the casino floor. It was elaborately patterned in blue and gold, very nice, but somehow managed to look like the floor of every other casino I'd ever been in. What was with that? Why did they all look the same? Was it all of the slot machines, the sounds, the sights?

I realized I was trying to distract myself and snapped out of it.

"I *am* a fan of T-shirts and jeans, Tristan."

Especially when they were wrapped around *his* spectacular body, but I sure as hell wasn't telling him that.

He stopped abruptly, looking at me like I was supposed to be reacting to something.

I didn't care for the look. Something in it scared me. Threatened me, or at least, my well-being.

I glanced around. We were near some slot machines and to our left was a women's restroom.

My eyes widened, then narrowed.

I started walking again.

In my mind, I'd systematically gotten used to moving past that spot, just as I had the sports book that we would pass next.

There were memories in this place, memories that I'd had to push far back in my mind, to keep sane.

"Do you remember—"

"Don't. We're not doing that. We're not taking a walk down memory lane. We just aren't. Is that clear?"

He sighed, but agreed.

But I did remember. Oh Lord, did I remember.

I remembered so well that it had me seeing into the very near future, that very night in fact, when I would go home by myself, go to bed by myself, and fantasize, obsessively, about getting fucked in the stall of that bathroom over six years ago.

We walked the rest of the way in silence, but he didn't leave me at the entrance, following me all the way to my office.

I went and stood at my tall project desk, looking down at it, knowing I had things to do, but unable to focus on anything to do with work.

Forgetting, for a moment, what my work even was.

"What are you doing?" I asked Tristan, who was in my office, leaning against the wall, just looking at me.

"I want to cook for you. When can you come to my house for dinner?"

I should have turned him down flat, but something he'd said and something I'd heard made me too curious to pass up the chance to ask about it.

"Your house?" I questioned. "I heard the strangest rumor that you live in the casino."

His mouth quirked up just enough to flash a dimple. "It's required in my contract that they keep a room available for my own personal use for the duration of the show. It's a suite, my own personal suite, for nights that run late, but it is not where I live. I do have a house, out near Seven Hills."

My eyes widened, but I didn't tell him that I lived in that direction, as well. Then he'd ask questions, and possibly find out exactly where, and I did not need that on top of everything else.

"How about tomorrow?" he asked, tucking his hands into his pockets.

I shook my head, admiring the lines of his suit. It was amazing how well it fit him, sexy, giant biceps and all. "No. No. That sounds like a date. We are not dating. Friends don't date."

"Frankie is coming to my house tonight, by herself, and I'm cooking her dinner. Same damn thing that I'm proposing for tomorrow. You going to tell me I'm dating Frankie now?"

As far as arguments went, he got the award for best angle on a shitty one.

I had a thought. "I bet Estella is coming too, so that makes it completely different."

"She's not. Estella is busy. Tonight is just me and Frankie, since you refuse to come."

"I said I have plans."

"Okay, fine. So come tomorrow. A friendly dinner. You can see my house. Aren't you curious about my house?"

I sure was. He knew me so well. I was utterly fascinated to see what kind of place he'd ended up in, where he called home now.

"Tomorrow isn't a good night for me, anyway," I hedged.

"The next night then. That's better, actually. I'm off that night. Friends have dinner with each other. This is how friends work. Now work with *me*."

I shut my eyes, caving. "Okay, fine. Day after tomorrow, we will have a platonic dinner, and I get to check out your house."

"Thank you," he said, closer now.

I opened my eyes to look up at him.

His hands went to the lapels of my blazer, smoothing them absently.

"You going to see that guy tonight?"

"I'm not talking about him with you. That's out of line."

"Does he know about me? Did you tell him that you and I—"

"Stop. Stop this instant or I'm done."

He closed his eyes and took a deep breath. "I'm sorry. You're right. I can't do that." He opened them again and focused on my jacket, or specifically, the buttons of my jacket.

Quick as a flash, and nervy as all hell, he unbuttoned it, sucking in a gasp at the tiny scrap of cloth I had on under it.

I took two quick steps back, buttoning it up again in a hurry.

He ran a hand through his hair, eyes wide. "Fuck. You wear

117

shit like that to work often?"

I shrugged in a noncommittal way.

"Fuck. Well, *that* messes with my head. What can I do to convince you to let me see that again?" He smiled. "I barely got a glance. If I'm going to be fantasizing about that tonight, it would be nice to have a very clear picture."

I pointed my finger at the door, trying to hide my smile. "You need to go, before you talk yourself out of cooking me dinner in a few days."

He cursed, sent me a comically longing glance that had me trying not to laugh, and left.

CHAPTER THIRTEEN

I dressed with care the morning of my non-date with Tristan. Of course I did. I always put time and care into looking well put together for work, but that day I woke up an hour earlier than usual, taking extra care, and picking out my clothes with a giddy fire in my belly.

I went with a cream-colored pencil skirt that hit a few inches above the knees, and a fitted lavender silk high-necked halter top with a cutout design at the collarbone that revealed a bit of skin, and a hint of cleavage. It also left my arms, the top of my back, and the upper section of my sides bare.

When paired with a matching cream blazer, it was quite professional. When taken off, very sexy.

I was pleased.

I parted my hair down the middle and pulled it back in a severe chignon. The severe style brought out the paleness of my eyes. A heavy, smoky eye shadow gave them extra pop. A pale pink lip finished the look.

Work moved at a snail's pace, but that was to be expected. I overcompensated by staying as busy as humanly possible, putting details for various showings together that didn't need to be done for another month.

Kate and Sandra, the two women that worked the gallery with

me, both part time, seemed to know something was up with me.

Sandra, who'd known me for years, cornered me in my office and shamelessly fished for information. "So Kate tells me that Tristan Vega came by yesterday; that he went into your office."

I looked up from what I was doing to give her a very bland look. "Yes, he stopped by briefly."

Her head tilted curiously, and she just kept studying me. "So he's shopping for some art? Is that what you're helping him with?"

I sighed. To say I wanted to avoid this conversation like the plague was putting it mildly. "I'm in the middle of something. Is this urgent, and is there a reason you're asking?"

"Oh, sorry, no," she said, looking like I'd just burst her bubble. We were friends, and her natural curiosity had been about anything other than Tristan, I likely would have indulged it.

I felt like a jerk, but it was necessary. The last thing I wanted was for rumors to start up about Tristan and me.

I normally stayed at work until six, and today was no different. I stayed until five o'clock sharp, not indulging even a small break in pattern.

It was pretty much torture to wait, and when it was time to go, I had to rein in the urge to rush to my car.

The entire drive there, I kept asking myself: What on earth are you doing? Why did you agree to this, no matter the justification?

No matter the temptation.

This didn't fit in with any of my plans, small scale or large.

Going over to have him cook me dinner. Just he and I, alone.

No pretenses, or none that I could convince myself weren't bogus.

How could we call this anything but a date? How could we act like *this*, of all things, was purely platonic?

This tarnished facade that we were calling a friendship was quickly coming clean, before it had really even begun.

I was disappointed in myself, because that pretense, if nothing else, would have let me have more time with him.

My self-control, in the face of this blissful infatuation, had no chance at all.

His house was intimidating, but I should have anticipated that. It was common knowledge that he had one of the best contracts in town and was paid handsomely for his talent.

It had its own gate and a long drive up to the actual house. Dayum, the man must be loaded. It was a hard concept to reconcile in my mind. We'd been so young and poor together, back in the day.

He met me at the door before I even knocked. He beamed at me.

I took him in. He was wearing a white dress shirt open at the neck, with the sleeves rolled up, but still a dress shirt. And slacks. It was so strange that I just gaped at him for a moment. Where was my T-shirt and jeans rocker?

"You look amazing," he told me, bending to kiss my cheek before I saw it coming. He was in and out in a flash, too fast for me to take exception.

"You too," I said through numb lips and a suddenly dry throat. "Did you just come from a meeting or something?"

"Nope. Been cooking for hours." He pulled me inside.

I was instantly assaulted by the divine smell of his too die for enchiladas. I'm not kidding; I almost started drooling, mouth filling with saliva, jaw going slack in anticipation.

"Oh God," I said, giving him wide eyes. "I'd convinced myself that I had invented that smell in my mind, but it really exists."

His smile was playful. "You've been missing out, boo. Feel free to use me for my cooking any time the mood strikes you."

"Do I get the tour of the house before or after we eat?"

"After. Food's ready now. And get this, homemade tortillas."

I shut my eyes, like he was talking dirty to me.

He continued, "Pico and guacamole from scratch. And

dessert is a surprise."

The man was diabolical.

We ate in his formal dining room. It was a beautiful room, huge, with twenty-foot ceilings, and ultra-modern decor. One of Bianca's spectacular paintings hung on the wall.

I could tell he'd gone to some trouble, with a centerpiece of fresh flowers and lit candles set throughout the room. He'd set his long black table with intricately folded white napkins and very nice dinnerware.

He sat me at the head of the table, taking the spot at my right, and didn't let me lift one finger to get the food, serving me like I was royalty.

I wouldn't have been surprised if he'd tried to feed me each bite by hand, but thank God, he did not.

We had an awkward moment when I took my jacket off and he got a load of my shirt. Yes, I was sporting side boob, and yes, I knew that would drive him crazy.

We got past it though, after a few minutes where all of the oxygen left the room, and he just stared at me like a man starving.

I looked down at my food and started eating.

He could still cook his ass off. I found myself closing my eyes to savor each bite and eating way more than I needed to, when I rarely ate for enjoyment. I liked to think of food as fuel for my body and ate accordingly, but Tristan's cooking had always knocked that theory right out the window for me.

I didn't look at him as I ate. It was bad enough that I'd given in enough to even be here, but finding out if he still watched me like he used to would do nothing for my peace of mind.

And if he was indifferent now, well, there was no doubt that would be even worse.

"Is the food okay?" he finally asked me, his tone a little hoarse.

I just nodded, though okay was the biggest understatement in the world.

After stuffing myself to the brim, I finally made myself set my fork down. I wiped my mouth with one of his fancy white cloth napkins, still not looking at him. "Thank you, Tristan. It was very nice of you to cook dinner, but I really should be going."

"Wait, you can't," he burst out, sounding more than a touch panicked.

Some thread of desperation in his tone had my heart twisting in my chest, and I finally looked at him.

He was watching me, his face deceptively blank, except for his eyes, which were pleading with me in a way that I'd never been able to resist.

"Why can't I?" I finally asked, after we'd stared at each other for an uncomfortably long time.

"You can't skip dessert."

"I don't think I could take one more bite of food. You know I can never stop eating your enchiladas until I'm stuffed."

"So stick around for a while, and I'll make us some dessert when you're up for it."

"Tristan—" I began.

"Please. Just hang out for a while. What's the harm? We can watch the new episodes of Arrested Development and just chill. No funny business. I'll sit on a different couch, if you want. I just want to hang out with you, like old times. Like friends."

The pleading tone he used got to me. I never could tell this man no.

"I heard about those new episodes. I haven't had a chance to watch them yet. Are they good?" We'd watched the old seasons at least half a dozen times each and had quoted the funny parts to each other more times than I could count. It wasn't a show I'd been able to watch without thinking of him, so I'd avoided it very deliberately over the last six years.

"I haven't watched them, either. It wouldn't have been any

123

fun without *you*."

I bit my lip and gave him a rueful smile.

We'd ruined each other for *so many* things.

"Jerry tells me they're good," I remarked. "Can't compare to the original, but good, is what he said."

"Well I'd take a bad episode of that show over a good episode of anything else."

We shared a smile.

As though it had been inevitable, I found myself relaxing on the sofa in a cozy media room just off his kitchen and watching the show with him.

He did behave himself at first, even sitting on a different couch, as promised.

But that didn't last long.

Had I thought it would? Best not to think about.

"Relax, put your feet up," he ordered, when we were two episodes in, and I was still sitting with my feet flat on the floor, my hands in my lap.

His plush sofa was huge, and it had been a struggle to sit up straight on it. I put my feet up, because it was just more comfortable, and I was starting to feel ridiculous.

We were another episode in, both of us laughing, when he moved to sit at my feet.

I shot him a warning look.

"Oh, relax. I'm not going to attack you."

I felt silly and turned my attention back to the TV. I was clutching my belly and laughing when he started to rub one of my feet. His touch was firm, hitting just the right spot, so when I looked at him to tell him to stop, my mouth was already a little slackened with pleasure.

"Tristan," I tried to warn, but it could as easily have been construed as a plea.

He kept his eyes on the screen, ignoring me completely either way, and kept rubbing.

I was basically a relaxed puddle on his couch by the time he moved to the second foot, and when he moved his hand up to rub my bad knee, I was done for.

It was three more episodes in, all the while with his pleasurable hands rubbing my knee, my calves, my feet, when he moved to lay behind me, his arm going over my ribs, hugging.

"Tristan," I whispered. I didn't even know what I was trying to tell him, let alone how it was actually perceived.

"Please," he whispered. "Just for a moment, let me hold you. Nothing else."

Nothing else, except for *everything,* I thought, my mind going fuzzy.

He was pressed hard into my back, and so I could feel that he wanted to do more, but he didn't. He just held me and it wasn't for a moment, but many moments, and for every second of it, I *trembled*.

"Thank you," he said into my hair after a time, kissing me softly on the side of the head.

He got up and went into the kitchen, but quickly returned to sit at my feet. He resumed with the rubbing.

The house quickly filled with the smell of baking cookies.

"Oh God," I said, somehow hungry again. "Chocolate chip?"

"You know it."

I looked at him and smiled, and his hands froze.

I started to shake my head when I saw the look on his face, but he ignored that, moving to lay behind me again. He pressed hard against me, one arm thrown over me, and his big hand moved to my stomach and started to rub. To stroke.

He lifted up my shirt and kneaded at the skin over my ribs, then snaked his hand down into my skirt to massage the flesh around my naval. I lay there, stiff but trembling. Eventually, his hand moved low enough to dig into a rope of scar tissue, and that little tinge of discomfort was enough to give me some willpower.

His fingers had begun to feel at the hard ridge of the scar, as though to determine what it was, when I grabbed his hand and pulled it away.

His voice was rough and worried. "Danika, what was—"-"

"I don't want to talk about it."

The oven timer began to chime, and I stood, going to sit at the round table in his breakfast nook.

I listened to him as he went into the kitchen, mapped out every move as he took the cookies out, and switched them onto a plate.

I looked down at my hands the entire time.

He joined me at the table, setting the large platter of cookies directly in front of me. He sat down beside me, and the second he did, on the side of my bad leg, he began to rub my knee.

That got me to look at him, which I was sure had been the point.

"What—" he started to ask again.

"No." I shook my head, and tried to still the hand on my knee. It was persistent, though, and just kept rubbing. "I'm not doing this. We have a relationship with boundaries now, Tristan. I'm not going to give you what you want, every time you want it, just because I'm incapable of telling you no. I've changed and you've changed, and we need to have some rules, if we are going to be able to spend time together like this."

"Yes, I know that, but I just wanted to know what that was—"

"No," I said again, firmly. I would not waver in this. "I refuse to talk about it, and your hands should not be going there in the first place."

His jaw clenched, and I saw a glimmer of his now rare temper flash in his eyes, but he shut them quickly, hiding it, shutting it down. "Okay," he said finally. "I'll drop it."

Things were stiff after that. I ate two of the delectable cookies, then told him that I had to go. He didn't protest, just packing me up a container of cookies to take.

"Oh, you don't need to—"

"Take them," he grumbled. "I made them for you. The least you can do is pretend that you want them."

I nodded and took them. He walked me to the door and then to my car. He opened the driver's side door for me, but then blocked me from entering.

He took the cookies carefully from my hand, setting them on top of the car. He turned to me, then slowly, softly, embraced me. He hugged me under the arms and lifted me against him. He pulled me right into his neck, and my arms went up to hook at his nape, holding on, since my feet had been lifted cleanly off the ground. He put his lips to my temple and just held on.

Neither of us said a word, but we didn't let go. Not for a very long time.

I didn't think of it until I was nearly home, but he'd never given me a tour of his house. Dammit, now I'd have to go back.

CHAPTER FOURTEEN

He came by my gallery again the next morning, dressed in a suit. Again.

I was in the office, standing at my tall worktable as I got organized for the day.

I glanced at the clock. "Isn't this way early for you?"

He shrugged, staring at me.

It was too intense of a regard, and I looked down at my hands while I moved some papers around.

"Come to my house for dinner tonight. I have a new recipe I want you to try." There was no question in his voice.

I shook my head. "You know this is a mistake."

His laugh was low and a touch bitter. "*I* don't know that. Come home with me tonight. I'll drive us straight from here."

"And leave my car? How will I get home? And how will I get to work tomorrow?"

"I'll drive you when I come back for the show, or whenever, wherever. I just want to share a meal. What's the harm?"

I tried to give him a chastising look. Neither of us were naive enough to think that leaving my car here would end up in us just sharing a meal.

"I'll come for dinner, but I'm driving myself."

He smiled, flashing big, happy dimples, and I saw his move.

He'd asked for too much, so I would concede more than I'd planned.

He moved to stand directly behind me. I shut my eyes as he pressed against me slowly.

"What are you doing?" I asked him, my voice catching.

"Shh, sweetheart, just let me. I need this." He spoke against my temple, then kissed me there.

I let him.

He covered my hands with his own, and still, I didn't pull away.

I wasn't sure what he was up to, what he intended, and I wasn't sure how long I would have let it continue, how far I would have let it go. It was taken out of both of our hands when Sandra popped her head in the office, effectively breaking the spell.

Which was embarrassing, but for the best.

"Um, sorry, but you've got a call on line one." She disappeared.

"I need to work," I told him.

He took a step back. "I'll see you tonight."

He left.

I tried to make myself call him and cancel, but my workday ended, and I found myself driving to his house, instead of home.

I still wore my clothes from work. It was business attire, a sexy twist on a simple navy sleeveless shirtdress, with a shorter hem, and the neckline open to reveal my cleavage down to the lace of my bralette. I'd taken the time to retouch my makeup before I'd left my office.

The pretense of this being platonic was flimsy indeed. Less believable by the minute.

He met me at the door in another dress shirt and slacks. I really wanted to know why he was dressing like this now, but he wouldn't give me a straight answer, stubborn man.

We shared another spectacular meal, a homemade linguine

with creamy pesto sauce.

I assumed he had a show that night, but as we lingered over dinner, he started talking about watching more episodes with me.

"Don't you have to get back to the casino soon?"

"Nah, no show tonight."

That baffled me, as I was quite familiar with his schedule. This wasn't one of the shows normal blackout nights.

"How is that possible?"

He just shrugged it off. "I have a good contract, and sometimes, if I just need an extra night off, I get a night off."

I didn't want it to, but that warmed me from head to toe.

I kept him company in the kitchen while he made us a totally unnecessary dessert.

He started making chocolate cake from scratch, and I perched my butt on the counter and watched him, as fascinated as I'd ever been to watch him working in the kitchen.

He shot me a sideways smile. "Sweetheart, you've got to stop giving me that look if you don't want me to ruin dessert."

"Don't call me that," I said weakly.

His smile grew as he turned back to his task. "That's right. You prefer pudding. I remember now. Be careful with those looks, pudding."

That made my fists clench, because it brought back memories, and that made me realize that every time he used his endearments on me, *my* endearments, it brought back memories. Those memories were going to break down all of my defenses in no time. That couldn't happen.

"Boo, sweetheart, pudding. You have got to stop it with all of those damn nicknames," I told him, making my voice firm.

"Endearments."

"Well, call them what you want to, but knock it off." I wasn't even sure why I bothered. He clearly wasn't getting the message.

He stopped what he was doing and turned to me. "Is this wager material? Do you want me to stop that bad?"

"Oh, no. You are not going to turn this into a bet."

"You win, I'll stop calling you boo. I win, you stop complaining when I do."

"Nuh-uh. I already told you, not falling for it."

"I'll bet you one spoonful of cinnamon."

"Excuse me? Is that a metaphor or some kind of a dare?"

"A dare. You eat one teaspoonful of cinnamon and you win."

"I'm not you, Tristan. I can turn down a dare."

"Prove it."

"Now you're daring me not to take the dare? Either way, I'll be taking a dare. You're setting me up."

"Well, take the cinnamon dare and I'll drop it.

It did sound easy. My eyes narrowed on him. "Just a teaspoon full? Not even a tablespoon?"

He grinned, showing every white tooth. "You don't watch YouTube much, do you?"

"No, but what does that have to do with anything?"

He bit his lip and shook his head.

"Okay, you know what? I'll do it."

His response to my acquiescence was pure glee.

That should have clued me in, but hell, I'm as stubborn as he is, the crazy bastard.

First, he made sure a glass of water was on standby.

He spoke while he got out the cinnamon. "Here are the rules: No water for one minute, and the entire spoonful has to be swallowed in that amount of time. You spit it out, or go for the water, you lose. You swallow it, you win. Any questions?"

I was studying him, getting more paranoid by the second, but how hard could it be, really? One teaspoon, a teeny, tiny spoonful of something I loved the taste of?

"Nope. Let's do this."

I didn't draw it out, grabbing the spoon and the cinnamon out of his hand, and getting it ready.

"Do you mind if I record this?" he asked. He already sounded like he was trying not to laugh.

"That was not part of the deal."

"I have to warn you, this is going to burn your throat and you might throw up."

I ignored him, pushing the spoon into my mouth, planning to swallow fast.

I hadn't even pulled it out before cinnamon was shooting out of my mouth and nose as I went into a painful fit of coughing. I grabbed for the water, took a long swig, and spit that out too.

My throat felt on fire, eyes tearing up and running in mere seconds.

"Oh my God, it burns!" I gasped, going for another drink. I did this three times, then started to look around for paper towels. Not seeing them right away, I moved to Tristan and started rubbing my tongue on his very nice shirt.

The bastard deserved that and worse.

He was laughing so hard he was doubled over.

"I hate you," I told him.

"Hey now!"

"This is disgusting. It's stuck to the roof of my mouth! Ick!"

I went to the sink and started rinsing again, then back to his shirt to scrape my tongue again.

"My nose is running! My mouth is burning!"

It took a while, but when I felt recovered enough, I whirled on him. "That was awful. I can't believe you made me do that."

His eyes were twinkling; he couldn't stop smiling. "You know I adore you, but there are times when I just like to torture you. It makes me happy."

I didn't know what to say to that. I focused on the obnoxious part and ignored the part that made my stupid heart pound faster. "Well you don't have to look so satisfied about it!"

There it was, that most Troublesome smile. "Oh, boo, you of

all people should know that this isn't how I look when I'm satisfied."

I supposed I'd walked right into that one. Infuriatingly, I blushed. "Don't you use that tone on me," I warned, but it was so feeble that I knew it didn't faze him.

We watched our show while the cake baked. He behaved himself, staying on his couch. I didn't even have to insist. He just did it. I eyed him suspiciously all the while, not trusting it.

We were eating his chocolate cake when I caught him staring at me.

Not just staring. Eating me up. He was gazing at me with an unabashed longing in his eyes that I couldn't let stand. I could only take so much.

"Don't look at me like that," I told him, setting down my fork, my voice turned as cold as I could manage.

He kept doing it, until his faced transformed into a too warm smile, a soft, affectionate stare.

"Like what?" he asked, and I knew that he was toying with me.

Torturing us both just to get a taste of the old feelings.

"You know. I will leave. I mean it."

"I'm not doing anything. I've just…missed you. I'm glad to spend time with you again."

I knew he was full of it. "We can't go back, Tristan. We can't take any of it back. We can't pretend that you are just you, and I am just me. There is too much bad history between us to pretend."

Something passed over his face. It was hard to name all of the things I saw there with just one brief glimpse. Pain, regret, hope?

I discounted it all, even while I felt it myself.

"This is nostalgia that you're feeling. It is transient. It will go away."

He swallowed hard, looking anguished for one brief moment

before he washed his features back into that soft smile. "For you, maybe. But not for me. Want to know how I know?"

I started shaking my head, but the question had been rhetorical. He was going to tell me, regardless. "Because it never went away. Nostalgia suggests that the feelings are coming back, and they can't do that, when they *never went away*."

I couldn't breathe.

I stood up, then started to look around, trying to remember where I'd left my bag, and what I needed, before I got out of there.

He stood, his hands going out in front of him, as though in appeal. "I'm sorry. That was out of line. I'll behave myself, just don't leave yet, not when you're upset like this, okay?"

"We should make another don't list, cause this is already getting out of hand."

He laughed, long and hard.

I didn't mean it to come out as a punch line, but hell, it *was* a punch line. I shook my head, and I couldn't hold back a baffled smile. "I'm doing my level best here, but you need to promise me you'll get a grip. No more of those impossible looks, okay?"

He didn't hesitate. "Yeah, yes, of course. I can do that. Just don't shut me out again."

We finished the cake, and he walked me out to my car. He behaved himself, mostly, not kissing me, instead folding me into his chest for a long hug. He inhaled deeply once, as though he were about to say something, but he held it back.

"I still taste cinnamon," I said into his chest.

He laughed and I smiled.

I was curling up in my own bed when I realized that I'd still never gotten that tour of his house.

CHAPTER FIFTEEN

He came by the gallery the next day, wanting to cook me dinner again.

I put him off. It wasn't easy. Not to make myself do it or to get him to accept it.

I agreed to share a quick bite to eat with him after my shift and before his show, but not for three more days, and not at his house, but somewhere public.

It wasn't what he wanted. He was used to bigger concessions from me, but he took it, believing I was resolute.

I was relieved when he did, because my resolution had been wearing more thinly than he'd realized.

I was a little shocked, and not altogether pleased, when I didn't hear from him for those three days. That messed with my head, and I had to wonder if that had been his intent, because it had me *obsessing* about him more than ever.

It made me wish I hadn't said three days. He didn't have to do a thing but stay away, and I saw the error of my ways.

Why had I thought I didn't want to see him for three days? That small amount of time with silence on his end had me realizing that I hadn't expected not to see him for those three days, and that's why it'd been so easy. He may have been playing some game by staying away, but I'd clearly been playing a game, when I'd told him to. The 'Who wants it more?' game is what I would have called it if I had to give it a name.

How quickly we fell back into the old, addictive patterns. The scary part of that? Even looking at it that way, I didn't so much as consider not seeing him again.

Of course, I went to great pains to look my best those long three days later. Hair—loose, smoothed and then tousled. Makeup—heavy on the dark eye and soft on the pink lip.

I wore an airy, lightweight, sunset orange knife-pleat maxi dress with a slim gold belt. The hem was so long it nearly brushed the floor. It was comfortable, but the thin, gauzy material, and the belted waist made it cling in a way that upped the fit from relaxed to straight up seductive.

It was a very trendy look at the moment, but managed to make me feel sexy and feminine.

I was happy I'd gone to the trouble when Tristan set eyes on me, and his face went a touch slack. He was in my personal space in a flash, restaurant forgotten, outside world forgotten, even though it was just the briefest hug. Still, the embrace lasted long enough for him to get a few hits in.

"Still the most beautiful thing I've ever set eyes on," he said into my ear. He turned his head, kissed my cheek, then took a step back, his face set back into neutral lines.

We were seated instantly at the casino's upscale steakhouse instantly. This restaurant fell on Tristan's side of the casino, and the hostess knew him on sight.

I ordered a small cut of prime rib, and he ordered a large one. And then we just looked at each other.

I studied his tailored suit, wondering what the hell was up with his wardrobe. I'd seen plenty of pictures of him over the years, and he was never dressed the way he'd been dressing every single time I'd seen him lately.

Hell, even his billboard out front had him in his signature poured on T-shirt and edible jeans.

"Are you dressed like that for your show?" I asked.

He shrugged. "Sure. I can dress however I like for that. I'm in charge."

I gave him a level stare. "Okay, what is up with your clothes? You've been dressed up every time I've seen you."

"So have you."

"I dress like this for work. I don't have a choice."

He shrugged again. "I can dress professional, too."

Something he'd said before came to mind. "You said something, a few days ago, about me going out with professionals. Is that what this is all about? Are you dressing like this just for me? Tell me I'm imagining that."

"You're imagining it."

I glared. "Tell me if you are or not. Don't just parrot what I said."

He tugged at his collar, looking distinctly uncomfortable. "It's not a big deal. I'd just like for you to see that I can be accommodating and understand that I'm not the guy I was six years ago."

I sucked in a few deep breaths, my face getting so stiff that it felt like it might crack. "Tristan…"

Our food arrived, and I began to cut into my steak.

"Like I said, it's not a big deal. Let's drop it." He paused. "You should come see my show tonight."

I chewed on my lips. "No, thank you." I couldn't even come up with an excuse.

He took a few bites, looking up to watch me while he chewed.

Finally, he wiped his mouth and asked, "Aren't you the least bit curious about it?"

I debated for a minute. "I've seen it. It's very good, amazing in fact, but you know that."

He just blinked at me, and then stared for the longest time. "You really came to see it? That's unexpected, I have to say. When was it, and where did you sit?"

137

I stared back. "You ask the oddest questions. What does it matter where I sat?"

"It will tell me what kind of a show you got, and it can be a very different show, depending on where you sit. And the when, well, of course I want to know how long it took for your curiosity to get the best of you."

"Center stage, three rows back. It was nearly a year ago, just a few months after I moved back into town."

He studied me for a minute, then went back to eating.

"Those are great seats. I'll have to put you in the balcony next time, though. That's a different experience altogether."

We were nearly finished before either of us spoke again.

"Were you alone?" asked Tristan, a tense thread in his voice.

I took a long drink of water and finished chewing my food. "Excuse me?"

"When you came and saw my act." He spoke very slowly, tasting the words, as though he wasn't sure he really wanted to know. "Were you alone, when you watched me, three rows back, center stage?"

"No." I watched him when I said it, felt his flinch with him.

I was familiar with what he was thinking and feeling right then. I'd thought and felt the same, when I'd watched his show, performing parts of it with a woman he'd been sleeping with for *years*.

"I don't suppose I should assume that you went with Bev or Frankie, huh?"

Why did it feel like a betrayal, when I looked at it through his eyes? Why did I feel like I needed to explain myself?

Because I'd known, even then, that he'd want me to see him perform, but also, I'd known very well, that he wouldn't want me to be with another man when I did it.

I suddenly felt just awful about it. Which was so stupid.

The feeling was not rational, but it was powerful. Enough so I felt the need to offer him an excuse.

"He surprised me with tickets. That's the only reason I went to see you with him."

His jaw clenched, and he tossed down his napkin, nostrils flared. "And by him, you mean…"

"Yes, Andrew."

"Don't. Please, don't say his name to me."

That had me bristling. "Tone it down, will you? Don't ask the question if you don't want the answer. You haven't been an angel yourself. In fact, if we're keeping score, you have a *lot* more names in your column that I don't ever want to hear you utter."

He didn't say a word, but his eyes screamed at me. This was a hurtful subject, for both of us, and we needed to get way better at avoiding it.

When he finally spoke again, his face was composed, his voice calm. "Well, you need to come see the show again, alone. That's all there is to it. I'll snag you a balcony for tonight."

"How about this? I'll come see you, but not on a night when you're performing with anyone that you have fucked or are fucking."

It came out harsh, but that was how I meant it. This was harsh stuff, for both of us. And I was not going to sit through another one of his shows, with fucking Mona assisting him.

He took a deep breath. "Jesus. I'm not fucking any of the assistants, if that's what you mean."

I set my jaw hard before I could say her name. "Not even Mona?"

He winced, and I had to restrain from shouting out an immature, 'Ah hah'.

"Not even her."

Well that was something, but certainly not everything. There was so much wiggle room in 'not fucking.' It could mean he'd only stopped yesterday, for all I knew. "I said, *have* fucked, too."

He looked unhappy. "Okay, I'll get you set up in the balcony on another day, when she's not working, but I want to come by your house when I'm done tonight."

"No." I didn't elaborate or offer any excuses.

"We'll play a round of 'tell me something.'"

That was tempting, but not quite tempting enough. "God, I almost forgot about that stupid game." I fought not to smile. "But no."

"I want to see your house. I want the tour."

I snorted. "Not likely. I've been to your house twice, and I haven't even seen the second floor. You aren't getting a tour of mine until I get one of yours."

"Okay. Come by my house tonight. I'll give you a key, and you can let yourself in and wait for me."

"No."

"Okay. Back to the original plan. I'll be by your place later tonight."

"I work in the morning. If you want to come by after a performance, at least do it when I'm off the next day."

He smiled big. "Tomorrow night then. That's perfect."

I glared at him. He'd done it again. That tactic seemed to work on me every time. "You can only get away with that trick so many times before I stop falling for it."

"I can live with that. I'll just move onto another one. You're forgetting just how many tricks I have up my sleeve."

I rolled my eyes, though I couldn't seem to stop smiling.

CHAPTER SIXTEEN

DANIKA

I found myself challenged with the issue of non-dressing up for his visit to my house. Obviously, by the time he showed up after his show, it would be late at night, and I'd look like I was trying too hard if I was still dressed up for work.

I changed my clothes four times in the hours I waited for him.

Also, I typed out three texts to him, canceling our plans, because what were we thinking? This wasn't even dinner, which was bad enough.

This was straight-up booty call hours.

In the end, no texts were sent.

I was only human, and I wanted to see him.

Why did he have to be so much fun on top of everything else? It was just so unfair. And so addictive.

I put on a pair of gray sweatpants and a slouchy, off the shoulder gray sweatshirt. This was outfit number one, my 'It's past my bedtime, and I'm not even trying to be sexy for you' getup. I put my hair up in a messy ponytail, put on makeup that made it look like I wasn't wearing makeup, and then stared at myself in the full-length mirror in my bedroom for a solid five minutes.

I went into my home office and caught up on work for less than ten minutes before I headed back into my closet and changed.

I switched into some white cheer shorts, but left the sweatshirt on. This was outfit number two, my 'I'm dressing down, but that doesn't mean I can't be a little bit sexy' getup.

That one lasted less than five minutes.

I changed into a half shirt that barely covered my breasts (I had to dig deep in my closet to find this one) and rolled the waistband of my white shorts up, making them miniscule. I took my bra off and my hair down. This was outfit number three, my 'Let's see how long you can last until we're fucking tonight' getup.

That outfit lasted nearly an hour, and my vibrator got some serious attention just because of where my mind went when I thought of how he'd react to seeing me dressed in it.

I buried that outfit back into my closet after I took it off.

Next I changed into a loose, pale pink, lace edged camisole with a built in bra, and found (after much digging) my favorite old pair of shorts. The ones that read 'sassy pants' on the butt. I'd had them forever. Tristan loved them, I knew. This was outfit number four, my 'Yes, it's sexy, but at least I didn't have to masturbate for a half hour after I put it on' getup. This one ended up being the winner. I left my hair down, and glossed my lips up three times in the five-minute window when I was expecting Tristan, before he actually showed up.

I opened my door to him with trembling hands and a racing heart.

We smiled at each other, him looking too devastating, still dressed in his suit, me in my thoughtful loungewear that I could tell he appreciated at a glance.

He stepped inside without a word, heading straight into my living room, which was directly accessed from my small entry hall.

He shrugged off his jacket, his back to me, and tossed it on the back of one of a set of armchairs. He rolled up his sleeves as he turned back around, then, looking up at me, unbuttoned the top two buttons of his dress shirt. It was baby blue today.

"How was your show?" I breathlessly asked.

He strode to me, hands going to my hips. It was so unexpected that it made me jump.

He smiled that heart-stopping smile. "Relax. I'm just saying hi." With that, he pulled me closer, putting his arms over my shoulders, and kissed the top of my head.

Since my face was already there, I let it rest against his chest, rubbing my cheek against the swollen flesh of his pectoral. I kept my hands at my sides, attempting some form of restraint, no matter how feeble.

He pulled back, then stepped back, shoving his hands in his pocket. He watched me, keeping his expression neutral.

I wasn't sure what to do. "You hungry?" I asked him.

"If you're cooking, yes."

I led him into my kitchen, and started pulling various items out of my fridge. I knew how much he ate, so I'd planned for feeding him, though I'd only prepped, not cooked, just in case.

He made an appreciative noise when he realized what I was planning. He went and preheated my oven without having to be asked.

He'd been the one, after all, that had taught me the recipe.

He helped me stuff several jalapeños and then wrap them in bacon. We didn't talk much, I don't know why, but I was just enjoying the company, even in silence.

After I'd put the appetizers in the oven and set the timer, we went into the living room.

He sprawled out on the couch, and I took an armchair.

We smiled at each other.

'Tell me something' was a game we'd played back in the day. It had started out as a game we'd played over the phone when we were doing the long distance thing, and evolved into a bullshit test, where we lied half the time, only admitting it was a lie when we thought we had the other convinced. The best get, though, was when you said something legit and got called bullshit on the truth. I'm not even sure why, but we'd both decided that was the win of all wins. It was the most fun, I supposed.

We were twisted, but it was so much more fun to be twisted when you had a partner.

"Tell me something," he said fondly.

I propped my feet up on the coffee table, chewing on my lip. We hadn't played in so long; I didn't even know where to begin. I beamed as I thought of a good one. "I'm a huge Josh Groban fan now."

He barked out a laugh. I'd known he'd get a kick out of that. That kind of music was so not his cup of tea. "You are shitting me. This one is easy. Lie."

"I'm not joking. Bev got me hooked on him last year. I'm not a rock snob, like you. I like all kinds of music."

He shook his head. "I call bullshit."

"Is that your final verdict?" I asked cheerfully.

He squinted his eyes at me. I'd stumped him now. "Well, hell, now I can't tell if you're lying."

"The man can sing his heart out. There's so much power in his voice. Gives me chills."

"Fuuuuck. Okay, you stumped me. Let me think, let me think." He started stretching his shoulders like he was prepping for a challenge.

I giggled.

He pointed at me. "Name one Josh Groban song."

I pretended to have to think about it. "Um, hmm. Oh, I know. *Remember When it Rained.*"

"Well, shit."

I grinned. "You don't know any of his songs, I presume."

"No, of course not. But that song has to be a fake. It's just the sort of thing that you'd come up with. It sounds made up. You are lying. That is my final answer."

I clapped my hands. "*Wrong!*"

"Well, hell. Pick your prize."

"I'll pick after your turn, in case I lose, we can cancel each other out."

He shook his head, both dimples out in full force. "Hell no. I'm picking a prize if you lose, regardless. You know I never mind paying up."

"Well, I'll have to think up something extra special for you, then."

He winked at me. "I'm counting on it. Okay, hmm, oh yeah, I've got one. I bought a painting of you, one of Bianca's. It's hanging in my bedroom."

That one did stump me. "I call bullshit." It seemed too easy, because there was simply no way he had one of those paintings. I'd put the show together, had handled the sale of each one. There was no way I'd have missed it if *he* were a buyer.

"You're wearing a vintage dress. I know it's called that, because a card with a long description came with the piece. The dress has lots of beading. It's silver, the color of your eyes. It covers you up to your neck, but it shows off your shoulders, and if I weren't a pervert, I wouldn't have to point out that it shows off a bit of side boob too. The most spectacular side boob in the world, but your eyes in it were what slayed me. You know which painting I'm talking about."

I glared at him. There was no way he should even be able to describe that picture, let alone claim to have it in his home. "There's just no way."

"Is that your answer?"

I shook my head, back to glaring at him. "I believe you; I just don't know how you did it."

"Dammit, you always were better at this. You win that round. It was the truth."

"How?"

"Second party buyer. Cost me a fortune."

"That's insane. You weren't even at the show."

"He texted me all of the pictures, and I picked it out the second I saw it. I picked out three, actually, but that was the only one he got before it sold to someone else. The asshole was slow as hell, considering how much I was paying him to do it."

"You do realize that's insane, right?"

"Yes. Now ask me if I'd do it again." His tone had gone from playful to so tender that I couldn't look him in the eye for a long moment.

I looked down at my hands instead, wringing them restlessly.

I should have chewed him out, just on principle, but I didn't seem to have it in me.

My heart *ached*. What was I going to do about him? About *this*?

"Your turn, boo."

It took me a while, but I composed myself, reined in my reckless emotions.

"I think I'll stick to my music theme tonight. Fun fact about me. I have three songs about eating pussy in my music library." I said it deadpan, and surprised a throw your head back, let loose kind of laugh out of him.

It was official, I still loved to make him laugh.

"I bet you can't even name three songs about eating pussy. In fact, that's it: name three."

"Hmm?" I played dumb.

"Name three songs about eating pussy off the top of your head."

"Birthday Cake."

"That's one."

"It's a good one. You love it, too. Admit it."

"Eating your pussy? Absolutely. I fucking love it."

That got a giggle and an embarrassed blush out of me.

"Two more, boo."

"I Love the Pussy."

"That's not a real song."

"It is. I Love the Pussy by Alpa Chino."

"Fake songs from movies don't count."

"They do. It's a song. I know the words. I could sing it to you."

"I'd pay to see that."

"I'd have to lose a round for that."

"Noted. Fine, I'll give you that one. One more pussy song."

"Pussy by Iggy Azalea."

"Never heard of it."

"Well look it up. Real song. Definitely about eating pussy. So now we've established that I can name the songs. The question you have to ask yourself is. Do I have them on my iPod?"

He pursed his lips, but couldn't hide his irrepressible grin, his irresistible dimples. "Okay, I believe you. I win this round."

I tried to look innocent. "I can't remember, does that mean that you get to pick a prize, too?"

"Ha! You're full of it. You know the rules. There's always a loser, which means I owe you two, you owe me one."

I threw my arms up. "Oh fine. How about we cancel out each other for one? Win, win for both of us."

"Hell no. We already covered that. Quit backpedaling, and let's negotiate. I'll go first. Mine is easy. You sing that Alpa Chino song for me. Here and now. Let's hear it."

I covered my face with my hands. "I'm not doing that," I told him.

He was closer when he spoke. "And I get to record it. I want to use it as my ringtone."

"Oh Lord. That's messed up."

I started giggling when he scooped me clean out of my chair, carrying me back to the couch with him. He perched me on his lap sideways, tilting my chin up with his finger, his eyes so warm they left their permanent brand on me.

"I won't hold back on you, if you make me do this," I warned him, reaching up to touch a beloved dimple.

"Promises, promises. Start singing, sweetheart. And sing it sexy."

I did sing it for him, but it was the opposite of sexy. I couldn't stop giggling for the entire stupid song.

And he hadn't been joking, he really did record it, though I doubted he'd be able to hear me singing on the playback, we were both laughing so hard.

"Okay, okay, your turn. Hit me with your best shot."

"Only one appropriate prize comes to mind. You're going to owe me a dick pic."

He hooted with laughter, spilling me out of his lap and onto the couch, and standing up. "You don't have to ask me twice." His hands went to his fly.

I slapped his arm. "I'm not finished. Not just any dick pic. I'm going to text you, it could happen at any time, and no matter when it does happen, you have to run somewhere private, take a dick pic, and send it to me."

"That's evil. What if I'm in the middle of a show?" He sat down again, pulling me back onto his lap.

"This will count for both of my wins, both of my prizes, so even if you're in the middle of a show, you have to do it. You'll get a ten-minute window. And your face has to be in the photo. And there has to be something in the picture to timestamp it."

"You are one diabolical woman, but I suppose I have to do it. You were a good sport about that song."

His finger was tilting my chin up again, his warm smiling eyes making their mark on me. Again. I wished he would stop doing both. One was distracting, the other riveting.

More weapons in his endless arsenal.

"What am I going to do with you?" I asked him, voice breathless, lungs breathless.

He took the air right out of me. And the fight.

"It boggles the mind," he said with a smile, though his hoarse voice contradicted the playful line.

He ran his nose along my jaw, breathing on me. "We're friends, right? This is going well, don't you think?"

The man was demented. "By what criteria are we judging it? If going well means we've both lost our ever-loving minds, then yes, I guess it's going well?! If we're basing it on us being just friends, we're failing epically."

He pulled back from me and grinned, just looking tickled by my answer, the stubborn man. "Don't be so salty. We're getting along great, and we're having so much fun. Tell me you didn't miss this. I dare you."

That I couldn't do, unless I became a much better liar in the next five seconds, and as for the dare, psh, I wasn't falling for it.

CHAPTER SEVENTEEN

We ate bacon wrapped jalapeño poppers, and then, because he harassed me into doing it, I gave him a tour of my house.

I'd forgotten that I'd let the neighbor's orange tabby in earlier, but I remembered as I was showing him my small home office, and we found him, passed out on his back, sleeping under my desk.

Tristan, who loved all cuddly creatures, went for him with a smile, picking up the cat, and stroking it without even seeming to disturb the animals limp sleep. Magic hands and all that.

He looked up at me, cat cradled in his arms like a baby. "What's its name?"

My mind went blank. It was over all the time, but I just called it kitty, and thought of it as the orange tabby.

I improvised. "I call him Ginger, on account of the orange hair."

He laughed, and sent me an odd look. "Um, Danika, this cat is a girl. How on earth do you not know that you have a girl cat?"

I chewed my lip, not wanting to tell him. It was embarrassing, but oh well. "It's the neighbor's cat. I just let it hang out here when I'm around."

He set Ginger down, laughing so hard that he stayed doubled

over. "Oh my God! You stole your neighbor's cat?"

I was defensive. "Borrowed. And she has, like, thirty cats. I doubt she even misses her. I travel too much to get any of my own pets."

He just kept laughing.

After a while, I was laughing with him. Even I could see that it was funny as hell, and that was with the joke at my expense.

"See, this is why it's handy to have a man," he finally said, moving to sprawl out in the chair behind my desk. He looked ridiculous in it, it was so small, and he was the opposite. In fact, the whole room suddenly looked as small as a closet, with his larger than life presence dominating it.

"I'm not following," I said wryly.

"Well, I'll just throw this out there. Crazy cat lady next door is single, right?"

I nodded. "What, you think the cats scared all the men off?

"She's not single because she has thirty cats. The one happened after the other, I guarantee it. And if she had a man, he would have stopped the crazy cat train after, like, four, five tops. So you see, men can be handy to have around." He wiggled his eyebrows suggestively, sending me into peals of helpless laughter.

"That's an interesting way to look at it," I gasped. "Are you getting at something in particular?"

"Yes. You should let me live with you. I know you love pets, and I'll stifle the crazy cat urges before they even start. And I cook."

I shook my head at him, still smiling, as I backed out of the room. "You're impossible," I called out to him, as I moved down the hall, towards the next stop in the tour.

I didn't even have to look, I could *feel* his presence behind me.

My mouth twisted as I showed him my room. I hadn't cleaned it, hadn't made my bed. I wasn't messy, but it was messy tonight, due to all of the wardrobe changes and the masturbation session.

His eyes were glued to the bed from the second he stepped in the room. I looked with him and knew instantly what had him transfixed.

They were cheap cotton sheets, but the wonderful thing about cotton was that, if you abused it with enough washing it got really, really soft.

And I loved those sheets. I'd been using them for years. Just how many years, I refused to think about.

I had other sheets, nice sheets, much nicer sets, in fact, than these, but those were only used when I laundered the good stuff.

Unfortunately, the cheap ones were also distinctive sheets, white and patterned with bleached out yellow rosebuds.

I'd known when he said he was coming over that we'd end up here at some point. Why hadn't I changed the sheets?

And of course, he'd noticed right away, the overly observant bastard.

"I remember these," he said, reverence in his tone. He moved right to the bed, running his hands over the fabric, bending down to bury his face in it. "We were on these the first time we..." he trailed off.

"I know." I sighed. I should have put the sheets away. Now he was going to want to talk about things that I wasn't ready to talk about.

"Come here," he said huskily.

I shook my head, but he wasn't looking at me, his cheek pressed to one of the yellow rose pillowcases.

"Come here," he said again.

Biting my lip, I went to him.

Slowly but firmly, he pulled me down to lie beside him, both of us on our backs, the sides of our arms touching. "Remember these sheets?"

I swallowed. "Of course I do. They're *my* sheets."

"Remember the first time we made love?"

I shouldn't have indulged him in this, I knew it, but my mouth refused to listen to my brain. "I remember being on top, and it pissed you off."

He smiled, rolling on his side to look at me. His eyes were so soft that my whole body went soft with them. "I remember that. God, you were riding me so good, and I knew that you were just trying to drive me wild, but even knowing it, it fucking worked. Best fucking ride of my life."

I blushed and started smiling. I couldn't help it. And I also couldn't help asking, "Yeah?"

"Up to that point. You weren't done blowing my mind, though, and you know it, because the next time was even better."

"We put these things through their paces."

He tensed suddenly. "Have you been using these the whole time we've been apart?"

I knew what he was asking. "Only when I was by myself."

I'd kept the sheets faithful to Tristan. Bully for me.

We were so freaking screwed up.

So freaking *screwed*.

His hand moved to my stomach, stroking with a light touch through my thin shirt. "I love these sheets. I'm going to steal them from you when you're not looking, or, you know, when you are."

I laughed. "They wouldn't even fit your bed. They only fit a queen."

"I don't care. I'll use them like a blanket."

I laughed harder, then stopped abruptly as he moved to loom over me.

I stared up at him, wondering when I had lost this fight. It was likely before it had even begun. No wonder Andrew had never stood a chance. No wonder no one had. Who could compete with this beautiful, larger than life specimen of a man?

He didn't make a move on me, or at least, not in the way I was expecting. Instead of bending down to me, he lifted the hem of my shirt, exposing my belly, and then pulling my shorts down enough to unearth my skin, from my navel down to my pelvis.

Several long, jagged scars marred the skin there. They'd faded more than I had ever hoped for, but still, they were impossible to miss.

He ran his fingers over each one, his expression going very blank, but not as blank as mine was. "Will you tell me what these are?"

I wasn't happy to talk about this, but I was anxious to get it over with.

"They're nothing. Completely superficial," I lied.

Not remotely superficial.

Just the opposite.

Profoundly detrimental, that's what those scars were.

"From the accident?" he asked, face still blank.

"Yes. I just got scratched up a bit. Like I said, totally superficial. Didn't hurt a thing but my vanity." Slowly but firmly, I pulled my shorts up, and my shirt down to cover the marks.

He sat up, rubbing his palms into his eyes. "I know it's not your favorite thing, but there is some stuff we need to talk about."

That pissed me off. Couldn't we go even a few weeks before we delved into that? Couldn't I just enjoy myself, for once? But even as I had the thought, I recalled several things that I'd just been dying to have him clear up for *me*.

I stood up and began to pace.

"Okay you want to talk? Let's talk." My tone was tense, my arms folded in front of me like I was ready to do battle.

Because I was.

I kept pacing as I asked, "Did you beat up Milton back when I was dating him?" I snapped my neck around to look at him.

He tried to give me a very innocent look, but I was not buying it. "Excuse me?"

"Don't play dumb. Answer me."

"When are we talking about, exactly?"

"Oh, did you beat him up more than once?" I shot back, voice dripping with sarcasm. "I went out with him on a Friday. Some charity event. There were photographers there. The next time I saw him, on a Monday, he looked like he'd lost a fight. Was that fight with you?" I spoke slowly, sharply, determined to get a square answer.

"Oh, that..." He gave me an engaging sort of grimace that turned into an audacious smile. "Yes. That was me. In my defense, I was provoked beyond all sanity. And the next time, well, he was asking for it. Don't get all pissy about it. He's a big boy, he can handle it. I was literally picking on someone my own size."

I shook my head, beyond exasperated, because he clearly wasn't sorry, and moreover, perversely, I found his shameless confession sort of endearing.

And worse still, I couldn't keep myself from asking, "You weren't hurt, were you?"

I was a stupid, stupid girl. Hopeless really.

He stood and approached me, and I got the tightest hug for that one, his face buried in my neck. "You're such a sweetheart, you know that? He didn't hurt me. Not at all. It was kind of a letdown, really. He looked like he'd be more of a challenge. Do you know that second time was the last time I've been in a fight?"

"You beat him up a *second* time?"

"I knew he kept calling you, after you'd said to leave you alone. Before you ask how I knew, I made a point of finding him and asking him. That was the second time. He stopped calling, right?"

I didn't have a clue what to say to that, so I just stared.

"Okay, my turn," said Tristan.

He pulled back and all of the happy bled out of his face as he pondered his question. A twitch started pulsing in his temple, but he plunged ahead. "Did you sleep with Milton?" The words churned over in his mouth, like he didn't have the stomach for them.

I rubbed my temples. "Tristan," I warned him.

How quickly we'd wandered out of safe territory.

"I'm not going to interrogate you about the last six years. I just want to know about *him*. Consider it my one free question."

I stood and started to pace, getting more agitated by the second. "He bothers you more than, say, someone more faceless? Someone you don't know?"

"Yes," he said simply.

"Fine. No. I never slept with him. It never got that far. Now, my turn."

"Your turn," he agreed warily.

"Tell me about you and my *sister*."

His brows shot together. "Dahlia?"

"Yes. That sister. Tell me what happened between you two."

"Nothing. Nothing happened. I tried to help her and Jack out whenever I could, tried to be a phone call away if she ever needed help, but that's all."

"Bullshit. When Jack was three, he told me he'd seen you two kissing. I confronted Dahlia, and she as good as confirmed that it was true, though she stubbornly refused to give me any more information. I want to know *exactly* what happened. Did you date her?"

His breath puffed out in an agitated sigh. "No, of course not. You really thought I'd do that?" His voice was full of chastising affront.

I set my jaw stubbornly. No guilt trip was going to keep me from hearing what had happened. Not even a very good one.

"Tell me what happened. Did you kiss her? And if you didn't, tell me why Jack thought you did."

"I started checking in on her, as soon as I found out that she was pregnant and alone. Like a big brother would do. Because that's what I was. I'd married into her family. You know I take family seriously.

And she, well, she always had that silly crush on me. Frankly, it was annoying. She never even knew a thing about me when she started with that nonsense. But I always tried to be nice to her, because she was your baby sister, and I tried to look after her, because she was *your baby sister.* I guess she was reading more into it. One day she kissed me, planted one on me right in front of Jack. I let her get it out of her system; let her see that there was nothing on my end to feed whatever delusions were happening on her end. That was it. She got the picture. The end."

"Why wouldn't she just tell me that?"

"Who can say? She always resented the way I felt about you, the power you had over me. Maybe she saw it as a small way of getting back. The point is, there was nothing between us. Of course there wasn't. I'd never do that to you. Your baby sister? Come on. *Never.*"

I felt such a wave of relief I nearly staggered with it.

I believed him. I just did. Moreover, I wondered how I'd ever been so certain he could do such a thing.

Perhaps I'd wanted to believe it. Perhaps I'd been looking for more reasons to bring him down in my esteem.

I had been in survival mode for a very long time. And whatever was happening to me now, well, that could only be the opposite.

It had only taken a few questions to get Tristan out of his fishing for information mood. I'd known that would work, had counted on it.

He wasn't the only one with an arsenal in this war of ours.

157

What I didn't plan on, though, was him behaving himself. He left not much later without even kissing me, or even trying to, and I told myself that was good. Maybe we were getting better. Maybe my theory (Familiarity breeding self-control) had been correct.

CHAPTER EIGHTEEN

I didn't hear from him for a few days after that, and then when he did call, wanting me to come over, I was in an airport, heading to New York for five days.

Within a five-minute conversation though, he convinced me to come over to his house the day I got back.

In fact, jet lagged, travel weary, I found myself driving directly from the airport to his place. What could I do? He was bored and waiting for me, he'd told me over the phone. Who could turn that down?

Apparently not me.

I grabbed us takeout from this old, Italian place, Sophia's, that was conveniently located just five minutes from the airport. We used to have it delivered to Bev's, back in the day. It was killer, and I hadn't had it in six years.

I wanted that takeout.

We shared a long hug when he opened the door for me, looking delectable in a white T-shirt and jeans.

We pigged out on stuffed shells and the greasiest garlic bread I'd ever consider worth the calories.

I had almost stopped to grab a bottle of wine at a liquor store on the way to his house. I'd parked the car before I'd remembered why that was a bad idea.

That calculatedly absent alcohol was the only thing that made our dinner together that night any different from the old days. No, not the old days. The *good* old days. The great ones.

After dinner, I found myself on the couch again with him, watching our favorite show together and letting him slowly take liberties that I knew from the start were going to lead farther.

Eventually, he eased into lying behind me on the couch, an arm thrown over me, the other under my head, being used like a hard pillow.

I laughed at the show we were watching, and my body moved just enough to brush him. With that brief contact, my back arched instinctively, pushing my butt hard into him in an artless invitation.

My head said no to that, but it was, unfortunately, several seconds slower than my traitorous body.

He sucked in a harsh breath.

We were on the thinnest of ice, so when it cracked, and we both went crashing through, I couldn't even pretend to be surprised.

Any vague remnant of caution I'd felt walking through his door was quickly overrun by the promise of sheer carnal oblivion.

Physical need could be a terrible thing, and I didn't even need to get into how messy the rest of our baggage was.

His hand covered my breast over my clothes, fondling, fingering my hard nipple, kneading at my pliant flesh.

My top had a built in bra, so when his hand delved into the side of my blouse, it made direct contact with skin. I pushed myself into his hand, gasping.

His mouth was on my neck, my eyes closed with pleasure, when my hands went to the front of my slacks. I felt him working at the fastening of his jeans behind me.

I didn't get my pants all the way off, just pushing them past my hips to bunch around my knees.

I didn't even manage to turn around. The second I felt his

bare skin against me, his hardness digging into me, we shared but one goal. To get him inside of me, by the fastest means possible.

One of his hands gripped my hip, anchoring me as he pushed hard against me.

My back bowed; my body contorting until I was angled to allow him entry.

He started to surge into me with a rough curse. He had to work in slowly, the fullness of it overwhelming, the voluptuous sensation of every raw tender nerve being worked making me so frantic that I bit my fist in some desperate attempt at restraint.

His hand snaked down, rubbing my clit with a light, fast touch, meanwhile the progress of his cock into my cunt was at an all-time slow.

"Please," I called out.

"I can't rush it. I don't know when you'll let this happen again, and the last time few times were so fast, so fucking rushed, that I've regretted that I didn't savor them more."

I wiggled my hips impatiently. He kept moving deeper, stopping completely when he was fully submerged. Instead of pulling out, or thrusting, he began to circle his hips, shifting inside, dragging his shaft around and around, hitting nerves, setting off sparks.

The sensations that caused had my eyes rolling up into my head, and I was shaking like I had a fever.

"It's too much," I gasped, one hand flying up to grip at his hair, the other reaching for the coffee table. I could just reach the edge of it. I scored my nails across it, and the soft dark wood finish gave under my fingers.

He'd have a bitch of a time hiding the damage.

He brought me over like that, with that torturous circling and his relentless fingers. I was still clenching on his cock as he shifted, rolling me until I was pinned flat on my belly below him, his hand pushing down hard on my shoulder. He began to move with purpose then, deep thrusts that pounded me into his couch.

"Fuck, Danika. Do you have any clue how often I think about this? It's a wonder I get any fucking thing done, when my mind is always right here, buried in this divine cunt. Do you have any idea how much I've missed this? Missed you?"

I whimpered, but he wasn't done bombarding me—with his thrusts or his words. He kept at it, cursing, praising, rutting, caressing.

Meanwhile, I could barely get a breath in, my face was being pounded so deep into the sofa.

He shouted, his voice rough and low, as he came, grinding into me at that perfect angle.

I was close to coming again too, so close that I started cursing him as he pulled out.

"Shh, sweetheart. I got you. Let's go to bed. I'm not even close to being done."

He got off me and helped me up from the couch.

I pulled my pants up awkwardly, feeling disoriented. "I stood up too fast," I told him. You couldn't go from facedown, ass up, to upright and not have to pause to get your bearings.

He pulled me close, propping me against him, his arm thrown around me. He nuzzled into my hair, into the sensitive spot just behind my ear. "Come to bed with me," he said very, very quietly.

I didn't respond, didn't think I needed to, since he'd already begun to tug me with him to the stairs.

I paused in the door of his bedroom, needing a moment to take it all in.

The huge painting on the wall, of me, was of course the first thing I focused on. I still couldn't believe he'd done that. Who the hell bought a ninety thousand dollar painting of their ex and put it in their bedroom?

It was so twisted. And dammit, some part of me thought it was the sweetest thing he'd ever done.

After a time, my attention shifted to the rest of the spacious room.

I sized up his bed. I wasn't pleased with what I saw. It was intimidating. It was huge and red and built more like a miniature house than a bed.

I shot him a look. "That your torture chamber?"

"It's a modified reproduction of a Chinese wedding bed."

"That didn't exactly answer my question."

He began to undress me, starting with my slacks. When his hands went to my panties, I moved away.

"Let's get in bed," he urged softly.

I shook my head, still staring at that bed, getting more agitated by the second. "Why do you have a bed like that, Tristan?"

"Come on." He grabbed my hand, trying to tug me toward it.

I shook him off. "Is there anything you want to tell me?" I licked my suddenly bone dry lips. "Any *surprises* you have for me?"

He sighed deep, ran a hand through his hair, and just stood there, looking very uncertain for a man with a bed that looked like it belonged in a BDSM playground.

I set my jaw and moved to it. When he tried to follow me, I held up a warning hand. "Stay there." My voice was cold.

It was beautiful in a way, painted red and carved intricately. Determinedly, I climbed inside. The mattress was soft. It didn't even hurt my knee as I crawled across it.

When I spotted the row of drawers at the head of it, my suspicions were confirmed. I didn't even have to open them, though I did.

Handcuffs. Ropes. And a shitload of other things that I couldn't have named, but knew the purpose of.

I moved back to the opening of the bed, swinging my legs

out, and just perching there for a long time, my mind racing.

My eyes snagged again on the picture of me. He must've had it for months. How could that possibly go over well, a sexy painting of your ex looking down on all of your sordid kinky bed activities.

I pointed at the painting. "What the fuck is with this kinky shit? I think that's actually worse than the restraints. You like my painting to *watch you* when you fuck other women?"

"Such a pretty girl, such a dirty mouth." He sounded resigned, but still fond.

I glared at him. "Don't get cute with me. Explain this messed up shit to me. *Now.*"

"I haven't had anyone in this bed in ages, okay? There's nothing for the you in that painting to watch." He paused. "Well, except for copious amounts of jacking off. But other than that, Painting Danika should have nothing to complain about. And frankly, in my mind, Painting Danika loves to watch me jacking off."

Eyes wide, I just kept shaking my head at him.

He shrugged, trying and failing to look sheepish, then looking down while he outright smiled. "Too far?"

I ignored him, still fixated on those restraints and the comment about no one in the bed for ages.

The comment was easy to reconcile, when I recalled that he had that hotel suite at his disposal.

And the restraints, well, it'd be a lie to say I hadn't had a clue he was kinky. I just hadn't thought it was this essential to him.

The bed reminded me of a lifestyle.

It reminded me of Frankie.

"It was Frankie and James, wasn't it? Did those kinky fucks bring you over to the dark side?"

He started laughing. Hearing my own words, I started laughing, and neither of us could seem to stop for the longest time.

"It was you, actually."

That confused the hell out of me. "How do you figure?"

"It started with you. The submission, the restraints. I don't have a fetish, but I definitely found a preference. With you. When I started dating again, my, um, sexual triggers were just desensitized. Not being able to get high didn't help, not back then. I just needed a little extra something, to make things exciting, because it was hard for me to get excited about anything at all, for a very long time."

I looked down at my feet. "You know what? Let's not talk about this anymore. I get the picture. But just to be clear, if you ever try to spank me, I'll probably knee you in the balls."

He laughed. "I don't spank. You know what I do. You *like* what I do."

"God, the things that can happen in six years and still it feels like no time's passed."

"I don't know how I even did it," said Tristan softly. "Looking back from here, I have no idea where I found the strength to let you stay out of my life for so long."

I looked down at my fidgeting hands. "You're a strong guy. It looks, from where I'm standing, like you handled it just fine."

"You were always the strong one."

My brows drew together. "Bullshit."

"Let me finish. You were. Just because you're a girl, and you don't get into fistfights, doesn't mean you aren't tougher than me. You faced your pain head-on. You always have. I can't tell you how much I admire that. I wish I were like you. I have from the beginning. There is no one I admire more. You don't run away from *anything*."

I was sitting on his bed, we'd just had sex on his couch, and we were pretending this was *friends*, and so this made me crane my neck to look at him, my smile wry. "What do you call all of this? Being together like this, pretending it's only friendship? Don't you think *denial* is a form of running away?"

165

He came and sat beside me on the bed. Without a word, or seemingly any effort, he plucked me into his lap. He pulled me hard against him, wrapping his arms tight around me so I was facing forward. I couldn't see his face in this position.

"You aren't in denial, so this isn't running away for you. For me, perhaps, but not for you."

I barked out a short laugh. "So what would you call it, in my case?"

"Pity." His voice was a quiet, reverent utterance. "You've taken pity on me. And I'm in denial, telling myself that it's more for you, like it is for me."

I couldn't breathe in his arms. He wasn't playing fair. He knew it and I knew it and still, I didn't walk away. "We can't keep doing this, Tristan. You can't keep saying these things to me if we're going to have any hope of staying friends." There was more desperation than conviction in my words.

"I can't stop, Danika. Please don't ask me to. Even if this is the set up for the fall of a lifetime, I still can't walk away, and I can't back off. Don't you see? I feel alive now, and I can't go from feeling this and back to *nothing*, back to getting by a day at a time, *surviving*, instead of gripping onto every second that passes, wishing that each day would never end. Knowing every day that you're in the same building as me, that you'll talk to me when I come to see you, that you'll laugh for me, and make me laugh, and even, if you're feeling very charitable, you'll let me hold you sometimes, let me touch you, and even be inside of you. Don't you see that I'm living on hope right now, and that hope is sustaining me like nothing else could? So I'm sorry, but I have to keep doing this. I'm not strong enough to stop. I never was. Like I said, *you* were always the strong one."

My eyes were shut by the end, my lips trembling. "Oh Tristan, what are we going to *do*?"

"Whatever you want, sweetheart. Whatever you allow."

I knew I needed to leave, to get out of that house before it went too far, but I didn't have the strength to try to break free of his arms just then. They weakened me, not with their strength but with their tenderness.

I let him hold me for a very long time, but sometime in the night, I did find the strength to get up and leave.

CHAPTER NINETEEN

DANIKA

Tristan was either suddenly very interested in one of the Vegas gallery's featured photographers, or he'd found a new approach to getting me to spend more time with him, because he set up a private showing after hours in the gallery the following Thursday.

I'd been putting him off, so I tended to think it was the latter. The alarming thing about that was my reaction to it. I felt giddy with anticipation even after all of the things he'd said that should have had me running in the opposite direction.

It was the evening of my day off, and since I was the only one that handled showings like this, I found myself getting dressed up and coming in to work at nine p.m.

I dressed seductively and not subtly so. This was not an outfit I could have gotten away with on a normal day at work.

From ribs to knees, the dress was a fitted black sheath. The only immodest thing from the chest down was the slit that run high up one thigh.

The top, though, was completely out of hand. It was made up of cream silk, with a neckline that plunged so deep, I never could have worn even a strapless bra with it. The sleeves were gathered, and hooked onto my shoulders lightly, nothing but a prayer holding them there. And the material was very fine, so the slightest breeze would have my nipples popping to attention.

And there was something much bigger than a slight breeze heading my way that very second.

I came into the gallery and began to set things up, knowing Tristan was just minutes behind me.

I tried to move about like everything was normal inside of me, but that was a lie.

The deepest throbbing had taken root in the pit of my stomach. It was persistent, staying with me, day and night.

Awake or asleep, I couldn't escape the fact that my body had straight up turned on me.

It was the most delicious sort of agony, to be constantly *throbbing* from within. Every single one of my senses had been brought to life.

He arrived, got one look at me, and became very formal, almost stiff.

I was taken aback, because without even so much as a kiss on the cheek, he asked to be shown some specific photographs in the current featured collection, as though he'd done research on it. His interest in the art seemed genuine, like that really had been his reason for arranging this torturous meeting.

And that's when I knew that I hadn't thought this meeting was anything more than a charade, not for one second had I even considered it.

I was not a good sport about being so mistaken. And the state my body was in, which was unequivocally his fault, only antagonized the matter.

The throbbing inside of me, which had been bad enough when it was contained within, slowly, insidiously, was spreading. One look at him, one slight feel of his presence sharing my same air, and that flimsy container *broke*.

I tried to work with him as I would have worked with anyone who had scheduled a private showing like this, setting up the photos that caught his interest in what we called the black room, where we could adjust the lighting to best show off the range of colors in this particular photographers crystal imbedded paper.

I set up one particular red canyon piece, doing a quick mockup of what the actual framing would look like. He sat on the long couch at the back of the room, and I backed in his direction as I played with the lights, illustrating how even the fading color tones could be brilliant.

But that feeling, that *throbbing*, had made its way to my thighs, my breasts, my lips, my belly, until I could barely move without grimacing, and sometimes, even moaning out loud. Within a few minutes of being in his presence, I was willing to fold, once again, just for another brief taste of relief. It became not an issue of resisting him completely, but a matter of folding gracefully, and hopefully, to save my pride, to make it seem like his idea.

But he hadn't even coerced me. No seduction whatsoever this time. And that was so much worse.

I acknowledged that some perverse part of me just had to know that he felt it too. I'd worn a dress open practically to my waist for him tonight, and he'd barely looked at me. Somehow, that was the fastest seduction of all.

His indifference feigned or otherwise, undid me completely.

"What do you think of this one?" I asked, moving to sit beside him as I adjusted the light in the room to play across the photograph. I started it on bright, then faded it to near dark, then repeated the process, showing how vibrant it could still look without full lighting.

I sat too close to him. It felt like a desperate move, but I could acknowledge that I was desperate just then.

He grunted. *Grunted*, like a caveman. It was bizarre, and I had no idea how to respond.

"I'll try another. I know you liked the red in this series. I have another with a beam of light in it that really plays with the color."

I stood, moving past him toward the door. He stopped me with a hand on my hip, then slowly turned me to face him, gripping my waist in both hands. I stared at him, breathing hard, but struggling not to show it. I was panting like I'd run a mile.

It was insanity.

He didn't look up at me. It was still dark enough that I could just make out the top of his head. I tried to be quiet enough to hear if he was breathing like I was, but my heart was beating so loudly that I couldn't make out anything beyond it.

"Turn the light back on," he told me, voice low and hoarse.

I had to move away to grab the remote, my hands fumbling, trembling as I slid the lights back to bright.

"Come here," he ordered roughly.

Some sarcastic remark tried to make its way out of my mouth, but the look in his eyes stopped any sound from leaving my lungs. I moved to him, my hands not so much clenching as folding in on themselves with the effort to keep from touching him.

He had no such qualms, dragging me close to straddle him the moment I was back in his reach. He slid my tight skirt up to my hips, hauling me on top to straddle him. His hands were all over me, hungry touches that took a bit of everything, his ravenous eyes taking so much more.

"How do you do that?" he whispered roughly. "How do you keep talking, keep moving around like you don't feel it, too?"

I shook my head, finally unfolding my fingers and digging them into his scalp, gripping at his silky hair.

He moved my hips with his hands until my sex was flush against his erection. Through my panties, and his pants, he moved us together, grinding against me until I moaned and shook.

"Tell me you feel it and I'll give you relief. Admit I'm not alone here."

I shrugged out of the sleeves of my top, leaving me bare from the ribs up. I arched my back, my breasts pushed up high for him, like an offering. They were slightly fuller than they'd been all those years ago, and I wondered if he'd noticed. I was still in good shape, but I'd filled out a bit. I wasn't dancer skinny anymore, and my breasts now overflowed a C cup. The curve of my waist was just as small as it had been, my stomach just as toned, but my hips had a slight curve to them now that wasn't all hipbone.

The way he took in the sight of me let me know that, whether he remembered enough to notice the difference, he appreciated what he was seeing.

In fact, he was panting for me, desperate for me.

I'd worn the dress specifically to do this to him. How could I have fooled myself for even a second that I was doing anything else?

I watched his downturned face watch my upturned body. He was biting his lower lip, which made his dimples stand out starkly.

His thick eyelashes cast deep shadows on his passion-slackened face, just the tiniest hint of his eyes visible to mine.

But it was enough.

I loved to see that look in his eyes, even if it did drag me back in time six years, to when I'd believed that love could conquer *everything*.

He tongued a nipple, and I bore down on him, tilting my hips until his zipper was digging directly into my clit. It heightened the ache to the point of pain, but I couldn't stop doing it.

"Say it," he mouthed against my skin, no actual sound coming out.

"Yes," I panted. I would have said almost anything just then to get the relief he promised. "I feel it. I need it. Now, Tristan."

He exhaled heavily against my skin, which made my entire body shudder in anticipation. It knew what was coming.

Rapture, ecstasy, a few brief moments of forgetting everything in the world but what this beautiful man could do to my body, to my very soul.

He reached between us, still sucking at my skin. His fingers brushed against me as he went for his zipper, and I rubbed against his knuckles, moaning as I hit just the right spot.

He cursed, fumbling to free himself. He had to peel his mouth away from my skin and look at his hands before he finally pulled his stiff length out and up, shoving my panties aside so he could push straight into my entrance.

I shifted my hips until he was sliding into me slowly. I was wet, but he was substantial, and it took some work to get him inside of me at this angle.

Even when he'd worked himself all the way into me, he didn't rush it, taking his time, pausing while I moaned and throbbed on top of him.

He gripped my hips and began to move, lifting me high, until just the tip of him stayed inside, then jack knifed his hips up, thrusting deep again.

So many sexy things still came out of his mouth as he had me. He wasn't a ranter, not like me, except for during the act. As he took me, he never could keep a word in. Praises, curses, endearments, more cussing, more compliments. I soaked it up. Basked in it.

I was too undone or too outclassed to do much but hold on. This was not a good position for me, with my bad knee, but you wouldn't know it just then. Just then, he was taking the brunt of the weight, and I couldn't have cared less about the discomfort that left in the mix.

My body was there, oh God yes, it was, but *I* was not in it. I floated weightless somewhere, just a few feet above, as my helpless body got *rocked.*

He propelled himself in and out of me, his hands and hips working in sync to fuck me, not fast, not slow, but *hard* and *deep*.

His hands on my hips guided me until, at some point, they weren't so much leading the rhythm as they were simply holding me together, bringing floating me back into my heavy, throbbing body right as it detonated, and rapturous waves of absolute pleasure lapped over me, into me, soaking every pore of my body.

I lay limp against him and let my body and mind come back together.

It wasn't a peaceful union.

Tristan and I were having some kind of a fling. With all of my determined denial, even I couldn't call it anything else. I was letting it play out, barely resisting anymore. What else could I do? I would let him play with my heart, handle it like a toy, and when we were done, I'd hope that all we left this time were bruises. I didn't let myself hope for even one moment that it could ever be more. This was more than friendship, sure, but it was *temporary*.

Even if he was too blind to see it, *I* couldn't see anything else.

My limp was more pronounced when we finally rose from the couch and I began to move about, straightening up, keeping busy.

Tristan noticed right away. "Fuck, Danika, did I hurt your knee?"

I waved him off. "It's just stiff. Stop fussing. Seriously."

He was impossible, as ever. He literally picked me up and carried me back to the leather sofa, rubbing at my knee like it was the cure.

"I think I'm going to have another surgery on it," I said quietly while he worked at it. Saying the thought aloud was the first time I'd acknowledged that I was even considering it.

He paused, then continued the rubbing. "Well, that sounds

encouraging. They can still do something? To improve it?"

"Bev has been bugging me to try some new thing they're doing. It's going to suck. Physical therapy will take over my life again. But yeah, it sounds like they can do something. I'm sure it won't be a huge difference, but better than this."

He couldn't seem to look directly at me. "I'm glad you're considering it. I promise to help with the physical therapy. I'll go with you, make it less boring."

That made me so uncomfortable that I had to stand up and move away from him. "That's a nice offer, but it's really not something I want company for."

"I'll change your mind about that, sweetheart. You'll see."

It was a struggle not to snap at him. I had to compose myself before I could say very calmly, "Stop it, Tristan. I give an inch, and you just keep taking. This isn't what you're pretending it is. You're not my boyfriend, and it's not your job to—"

"You're right, I'm your *husband.*"

He'd done it. He'd gone and flipped the psycho switch in my brain again. Just a few words, and I was reeling, my reason leaving me. Enter hair-pulling rage. "What did you say? Are you *deranged*? We got divorced, *years* ago!"

"That wasn't my choice then, and it isn't now. You're absolutely right that I'm not your boyfriend. This is not some trial period in a relationship, where I'm not abso-fucking-lutely clear on how I feel. I know what I want."

That did it.

I was done. I walked into the bathroom, bolting myself in. I didn't trust myself to continue with that conversation.

I straightened my clothing and my hair, wiping the bits of mascara from under my eyes. I waited a very long time, calming myself, before I came back out.

"I'm sorry," Tristan burst out the moment I stepped out. "I was too pushy."

"You were out of line."

"Yes, that too. I'll drop it, okay? Just don't shut me out again. Not for this."

I nodded, too weary to put up a fight, when that fight would involve delving back into a subject that had the power to undo me.

"Show me the rest of those pictures?" he asked, his voice all cajoling charm.

Too late for that, my glaring eyes told him, but I nodded. I waved him back into the viewing room while I grabbed a stack of samples.

My hands were shaking. What he'd said terrified me, but it wasn't his fault. What had me shaking was the little thrill of joy, of hope that it'd sent through my system. I needed to get a grip.

Tristan was far from done with his private showing, going through dozens of pictures, and finally settling on a particularly stunning photo of a field of sunflowers, some fully bloomed and reaching for the sun, but with a small circle of flowers still stubbornly facing down. What was stunning about the picture, though, was the way the sun was washing over the more closed off blooms, as though giving them special attention, giving them another chance.

I was handling the transaction, him standing silent behind me, when I spoke. "This picture is up to forty grand now, since it's limited to one hundred editions. You really filthy rich enough to just drop that kind of cash like that?"

"Not drop it, no. I just like it that much. I love the name of it. Makes me feel hopeful. I want it over my mantle."

I paused in what I was doing, my eyes scanning over the photos title, *Second Chances*.

He was smiling, I could hear it in his voice, when he added, "And I could tell it was your favorite when you showed it to me. I figure I have a better chance of getting you to come back to my house, if I fill it with the things you love."

He'd hit his target with the opening salvo. That second part

was just overkill.
I finished up and got out of there, fast.

CHAPTER TWENTY

I was working, minding my own business the next day, when he texted me.

Tristan: I'm at Frankie's parlor. Come see me. Getting my yearly sobriety tat.

I tried to resist that one. I worked for another hour and tried to pretend I wasn't curious to see what was going on inside this very building.

I went to the restroom, freshened up my makeup, tousled up my hair, fidgeted with my pale rose dress. It was lightweight and silky, with a clingy, belted shape, and one big ruffle at the hem that hit a few inches above my knee. I had a scoop neck, which was sexy, that hugged low along my sides, and shaped into a racer-back, which was sexier.

It was hot and flirty, and I was happy I'd worn it, as I was about to cave and go see the man I'd worn it for.

An hour was as long as I lasted. I told Sandra that I was taking lunch and hurried to the parlor as quick as my faltering step would take me there.

One of Frankie's artists led me to the back room where Tristan was being worked on. I knew the room well. I'd gotten my own tattoo there. I didn't let myself think about the other things that had gone on in that room.

I almost turned away when I realized where it was, but I was too late.

Frankie had spotted me.

She lifted the needle from that gorgeous back, grinning at me. "Danika!" She completely ignored the camera crew. She was used to them.

I wasn't. So when they turned to me, my face was stiff. I moved past them, getting closer to the shirtless man on the table that, in spite of everything, still consumed my every waking thought.

Tristan lifted himself up enough to smile at me. I tried not to linger on the way that made the muscles of his shoulder and back shift, but it was too delicious of a sight to ignore.

"How's it going?" I asked him, moving close to his side.

"It hurts," he said, lying back on the table. He reached a hand out to grab my hip, pulling me closer. "Hold my hand?" I could hear the smile in his voice.

The man was working me, but I found myself taking his hand, gripping it tight.

"Mmm, thank you. Much better."

Frankie went back to work, and I studied the back of Tristan's head, letting my other hand stroke over the silky strands of his hair. I loved the new length. It was just perfect for gripping.

"Do you like the tattoo?" Frankie asked.

I didn't look at it. "I'll look when it's done. I can never get a clear picture, until I see the final result. It's what makes me a good appreciator, rather than an artist myself."

"But this is a work in progress tat. It will never be done. He'll be getting one of these blossoms, every single sober year, for the rest of his life."

That had me looking. The word blossom raised some red flags, and I thought, *oh no, he wouldn't have.*

But he had. On his back, scrolling over most of one shoulder was a cherry branch. It wasn't on the same spot on his back as it was on mine, but there was no mistaking that it was a mirror of my tattoo.

On the branch were five small blossoms, each a slightly different shade, each with a number, bold and in red. One, two, three, four, five, and soon, already more than half finished, a six.

I clenched my jaw, closed my eyes, and bowed my head. I couldn't stop the tears, but I could keep them quiet and hidden, bowing my head far enough to let my hair fall over my face.

I still held Tristan's hand, and gripped his hair, but now I was doing it just to stay upright.

"Cut," Frankie called. "I need a break, guys. Let's take it outside for a minute, grab a coke."

I didn't acknowledge her thoughtful maneuver, didn't so much as look up.

"Do you like it?" Tristan asked, his voice telling me that he knew I was reacting, and not reacting well.

"Am I supposed to like it?"

He didn't answer me.

"Am I supposed to *like it*?!" I asked again, voice raised, filled with rage. With pain. "Or be *ruined* by it?"

He moved so fast that it startled a yelp out of me. He raised his body, and flipped up into a sitting position so fast that it was like a trick. Part of his act.

He grabbed me, not timidly, no, aggressively, yanking me against him, between his legs, pushing my face into his chest. "No, sweetheart, no. Not ruined. It was a tribute. It was not supposed to hurt you. It was as much for me as for you. However we ended, however you hated me, I didn't ever want to forget what we had, or to forget what I'd done to deserve losing it."

"That's not a good recovery tattoo, Tristan. It sounds more like an albatross around your neck to me. Aren't you supposed to celebrate your successes, not wallow in your mistakes?"

His lips were on my jaw, his breath hot. "I'm not wallowing in the mistakes, Danika. I acknowledge them, give them their proper due, but those mistakes aren't my obsession. *You* know what is."

His lips were open, moving down my neck, then up again, until he was breathing at my mouth, his minty breath mingling with my own. "Do you remember this room?" he breathed.

I closed my eyes and trembled.

It was too much. I was done for. Defeated.

I hadn't had any of my defenses left coming in here, and he'd pulled no punches at all.

He gripped my hair in both hands, anchoring me while he tilted his head, and brushed his lips across mine. Softly, too softly, his mouth teasing back down to my neck, rubbing that irresistible scruff of his into that most sensitive area.

I moaned, loudly, and he covered my mouth with a short bark of a laugh. "I don't suppose we can take our time right now, huh?"

I just shook my head, my trembling hands going to his chest, tracing over his glorious ink.

He moved in a flash, grabbing me, turning, and perching me on the table, until our places were reversed. He started inching my loose skirt up my hips, and once it was up around my waist, he parted my legs wide and stepped in, two fingers pushing into the side of my panties, feeling at my sex.

He cursed and praised me as he found me wet and ready for him.

It was a rush job after that. There wasn't even time to take my bra or panties off. He just opened the front of his jeans, pulled his jutting erection out, and guided it with his hand against my pussy.

His other hand pushed my small panties to the side. We both watched, rapt, as he thrust forward hard and his cock disappeared inside of me.

I braced my hands behind me, still watching as he slid out, then in again, a few test drives before it turned into a full-on hell bent fuck.

I didn't last long, my head dropping back as I started clenching on his plundering cock.

He grabbed my ass in both hands, lifted my hips off the table, and started drilling into me, keeping it up until he was emptying himself.

I stroked his hair, his shoulders, his face as we leaned against each other and panted, taking forever to recover from that madness.

"We weren't quiet," he murmured against my cheek. "I was trying to be quiet, because this clearly isn't private enough, but I failed."

I giggled. "Yes, you did. What's your problem?"

He pulled back to give me a playful glare. "I'm not sure if you realize this, but you were *much* louder. There is no way Frankie isn't going to know exactly what just happened. I hope you were ready for her to know."

I flushed. I didn't think I was ready, but it was too late now. My complete lack of self-control where Tristan was concerned had just shoved all discretion out the window.

"She's going to ask me," he said quietly, back to kissing my jaw. "What would you like me to tell her? The truth, or some other version to buy you time to come to terms?"

I wanted to take exception to what his words implied, but that was sort of difficult as I was still squirming on his cock, and little shivers of aftershock were still running through my body from an incredible orgasm. "I guess, just tell her that you and I have become close again, friends again, and the rest is none of her damn business."

"Tell that to her favorite tattoo table."

In the end, I'm not sure what he told her, because I ducked out right after the tattoo was finished, and left it for him to handle.

Frankie shot me a few inquisitive glances, but I ignored them, and that was that, for the moment, at least.

I was still trying to figure out how I felt about the whole thing; I certainly didn't need anyone else to weigh in.

CHAPTER TWENTY-ONE

DANIKA

I avoided him for a few days after that, but he was persistent, and even I knew that it wouldn't last long.

It was the evening before a day I knew we both had off when I broke.

I found myself stalking him on Facebook. It was embarrassing, but I didn't stop doing it, in fact spent hours going through his photos, wondering about every damn chick that he'd taken a picture with in the last two years, even knowing that most of them were likely just fans.

Finally, I found myself messaging him. I told myself it was just boredom. The quiet time I'd once enjoyed alone in my house had suddenly turned into tedium for me, and it didn't take a rocket scientist to figure out why.

Danika Markova: Want to hang out tomorrow?

He didn't respond, and that messed with me. It wasn't what I'd come to expect from him. Was he getting bored with this whole messed up thing? I hated to think it, but that was where my mind immediately went.

When I realized I was acting desperate, I walked away from

my computer.

I'd brought two portfolios home from work. I went through them, taking notes, feeling aimless, despite the fact I was doing a task that almost always drew me in.

When even work couldn't distract me, I went to the market. I shopped for an hour for nothing, going up and down the aisle. I spent two hundred dollars on food, then wondered the entire way home what I would do with it all. I just didn't eat this much. Some of it was canned, which would keep, but a lot of it was produce and meat.

I was still berating myself as I pulled up to my house. My heart started pounding when I saw a familiar black Challenger parked at the curb.

I was smiling as I got out of my car and met him in the driveway. "Hey, what's up?"

He didn't answer at first, instead helped me unload my groceries.

I thought his silence was strange. "Did you get my message earlier? About tomorrow?"

He looked distinctly uncomfortable. "Yeah. I've got plans."

I blinked. This was different. I wasn't accustomed to hearing no, not from him. I shrugged. "Okay. That's fine. No worries."

"I'd cancel, but it's a sponsored charity run. Nothing big, just a 5k, but all the press attached is going to take forever. And there's an after party. We do stuff like this all the time." I really tried not to dwell on who the *we* was in that sentence. "It's usually an all-day thing. I could come by after."

I nodded. "Yeah, whatever. I mean, call after, and we'll figure it out."

I wasn't sure what to say. I didn't know if he didn't want to invite me to participate or if he felt awkward asking me. Maybe he thought I couldn't do something like that? He had to know that I could walk three miles. I had a limp, but I was still in good shape. I made sure to work my knee out every single day.

"Is it a serious 5k? I mean, strict runners only, or are there some slower participants?"

He sat on one of the barstools at my counter, his eyes steady on mine. "Anything goes. It's all to raise money for some local charities. I'm just going to bring some attention to it." He swallowed. "You're invited, if that's something you could do, that you'd want to do. I didn't want to pressure you or to come across like an insensitive prick. I know you do your stationary bike every day, and that you swim, but I wasn't sure..."

I shrugged. "I can do it, but only if you want me to go. I don't want to impose, and I don't want to slow you down. You can, you know, feel free to run ahead of me."

"You're not imposing. I want you to go. And you won't be slowing me down. It's not that kind of a race. I won't raise more money for charity if I finish faster." There was a very long pause. "Mona will be there. All of the girls from the show will be."

I rolled my eyes, none too pleased about seeing Mona, but it was certainly the lesser evil. At least he wouldn't be spending the day with her without me now, with me at home alone on my day off.

"Do I need to sign up somewhere or do anything special?"

He shook his head. "I'll get you signed up, and I'll drive. I know where it is. The only rule is that you have to wear white."

I thought that was odd, but I went into my room and started going through my closet. "Tops *and* bottoms?" I called to him.

"If you can," he answered from close behind me. "Just make sure it's not any clothing you're real attached to. It may not survive the day."

"What, you going to rip it off me?" I shot him a sassy look, and he laughed how I loved, from deep in his chest.

"It's quite possible. I certainly wouldn't rule it out."

I pulled up a pair of white track shorts and a white modified muscle shirt. "These work?"

"Perfect."

He didn't stay long that night, which was disappointing, but I supposed it was good that at least one of us was showing some restraint.

"I'll be by at eight to pick you up in the morning," he told me as I walked him to his car.

He kissed me goodbye, pulling back quickly. "I need to go get some stuff done, and I know that if we get into this we'll never stop."

I nodded, stepping back. "Goodnight," I murmured, then went back into the house without looking back. If he could pull away, I told myself, then so could I.

I was ready, dressed in white down to my shoes, my hair tied up in a messy ponytail, knee brace on, when he pulled up the next morning. I didn't make him come to the door, going out to him before he could walk up to the house.

We met halfway, in my driveway. He looked so different, dressed all in white, in a V-neck T-shirt and athletic shorts. Each piece had a small Cavendish Resort logo embroidered on it.

Even his shoes were white, and he was wearing a white sweatband.

"You'd look so preppy, if I couldn't still see all of that ink."

He grinned. "There's a perfectly good explanation for why I'm dressed like this. You'll see what it is when we get there."

Before I could respond, he was bending down, lifting me into a tight hug that took my feet clear off the ground. My arms wrapped around his neck.

I lifted my face and closed my eyes as his lips made their way to mine, wishing he'd shown up earlier, or stayed the night before, or something, anything to give us a few more stolen moments we could have had to feed this hunger enough to keep it at bay.

We were not in any way assuaging this need of ours. With

every encounter, we only seemed to be making it more acute.

His lips became insistent, his hands grabbing my ass so he could keep me anchored while he ground hard against me.

It was a few drugging minutes before he tore himself away.

"Christ. Do you want me to fuck you on your lawn, or was I misreading that?"

I giggled as he set me down.

"You're right. We can always just apologize to your neighbors later."

I backed up a few steps, warding him off with my hands. "One question. Is the race going to start without you, if you're late?"

His breath whooshed out of him in a noisy, annoyed breath. "Not likely."

"Is there any way we have time to run into my house and have a quickie, and still make it on time?"

"Not fucking likely," he growled, his mood darkening by the second.

"Okay then. Get in the car. We've got to go. You are not going to make everyone wait on you."

He cursed his entire walk to the car, kept it up as he held my door open for me, and even for part of the drive there.

"You should have come early," I told him.

"Well, thank you for the invitation, but it's a little fucking late."

I laughed. I don't know why, but I'd always gotten a kick out of grumpy Tristan.

I saw when we got there that everyone participating wore white. There was a huge banner at the starting line that read *Color 5k for Charity*, and I began to get an inkling of what I was in for.

"White, huh?" I shot him a look.

He grinned. "It's fun. You're going to love it. Trust me."

Those were the strangest words.

Trust me, coming from him of all people. My head and my

heart went to war when he said those words, even in a lighthearted way.

Because I wanted to trust him. A part of me needed to. I wanted to trust him with the best of me, the worst of me, and everything in between.

So much of me instinctively reached for that trust. Sometimes it felt like my very soul had cast its lot with him, and even in the years apart, it had clung to him, leaving the rest of me to *wither*.

But I *had* trusted him. Trusted my whole heart with him, and he'd crushed it into little tiny pieces, seemingly uncaring of the carnage he'd left in his wake.

But he'd changed.

It was hard to deny that the things about him that had destroyed me once had been transformed, or disappeared, or been left behind.

And so, the battle inside of me raged on, and that charming devil of a man just went about his life, smiling while he slowly broke down all of my defenses against him.

Defenses I'd worked hard for.

Defenses I'd earned.

It wasn't fair, just as it wasn't fair when he gave me a mischievous grin that made me melt, and I quickly lost my train of thought.

That was what I was dealing with.

I was outclassed and outgunned, and I was only realizing it when it was too late to do a damn thing about it.

A heart could only break so many times before the cause was lost.

We were separated once we got near the starting line. He was hosting the thing and had to wade into the center of the chaos, so I waved him on, hanging back.

I could do a 5k, I knew it. But I hated that I'd be the slowest one, and everyone knew why just by glancing at me. Even after years of dealing with it, it was a difficult pill to swallow.

Still, I swallowed it every day and did my best. Today was no different, just a bit more public.

There might have been people I knew there, I wasn't sure. I didn't look for anyone. I didn't want to slow anyone down.

I suddenly wished I hadn't come. It wasn't like I'd really be spending time with Tristan. But it was also too late to back out.

Still, I briefly considered hailing a taxi and just cutting out.

For some reason I didn't. For some reason I stayed.

I caught some glimpses of the spectacle that was Tristan and all of the girls from his show towards the front of the line.

The assistant/showgirls were all wearing white belly shirts and white hot pants, as they posed with him for photographers. Briefly, I got close enough to see him putting his arms around some of them for the pictures, and by them, I mean that one of them was Mona.

I got far away after that, wondering why he needed to have ten showgirl/assistants in his act, and why they all had to sport double Ds. It was depressing.

CHAPTER TWENTY-TWO

I was at the very back when the race started. It only made sense.

I started moving briskly as soon as the starting shot was fired. I didn't look up or to the side, just down at me feet as I trudged along

I'd been doing this for about five minutes when I saw his shoes come into view, walking beside mine. "You don't have to slow down for me," I told him without looking up.

He grabbed my hand. "Stop it," he said quietly.

I kept going, kept watching the ground, and moving.

"Is your knee hurting?" he asked.

"It's fine," I said. It was sore. It was always sore, but I was very used to that. "I'm not what I used to be, huh?" That had slipped out, and I wasn't happy about it.

I tried not to look at my bum knee or my barren belly.

"Stop it," he said again, halting me in the middle of everything. "You're everything you were. You're still you. The rest are details."

I wanted to take strong exception to that statement, but I couldn't think of a single thing to say that wouldn't come out sounding like self-pity, so I kept my peace, and started walking again.

"Is there a reason that every single one of your assistants is sporting a huge rack?" I asked him. I was more than slightly perturbed by this.

I glanced at him, and was gratified at how uncomfortable he suddenly looked.

"This is Vegas."

"That's the reason? This is Vegas is the reason? Did you pick these girls out yourself?"

"I did. I had to make sure myself that every single one of them was competent. They don't just roll props out. Some of them are really talented."

"And they all just so happened to have double Ds?"

"This is Vegas," he repeated.

"That's disgusting. My opinion of you in general just took a nosedive." I'd meant it sassy, but it came out a touch angry, and I realized that's because it was. I was bothered by this preference of his.

He stopped me again, giving me a stern look. "Listen to what I'm saying. They have huge racks, because girls that audition to be magician's assistants in a Vegas show already bought themselves huge racks before they ever showed up to try for the job. Do you get it? Hell, most of them now have butt implants too. I chose the most competent girls that auditioned. Bust size never even entered into it."

I was somewhat appeased, and curious about something he'd said. "Butt implants? You're making that up. No one would actually do that."

"I don't get it either, but they do."

"How is that even possible? How could someone get an implant in a spot that they sit on? Doesn't that seem like a bad idea? What if you sat down too hard and popped the implants? What if you fall and land on your ass?"

He laughed. "I have no clue; I just know it's a thing."

We walked on for a bit, when he said suddenly, "Close your

eyes. This is the fun part."

I squealed as he grabbed me by the waist, setting me up on his shoulders like it took no effort at all.

I clutched at his head and closed my eyes, but I'd already seen what was coming.

"Keep your mouth closed," he said, a smile in his voice. "And your eyes."

That was easier said than done. When someone threw colored powder at you, it was hard not to gasp.

When I opened my eyes again, all I saw was pink.

I was pink.

I looked down to find Tristan's head and the rest of him, pink.

"How many paint throwing stations are on this thing?" I asked him, laughing.

"At least five on the way, and I think it's a free for all at the end."

"You know I saw this coming, right? If you thought you were pranking me, you failed. It's called a *Color 5k for Charity*. Wasn't hard to figure out."

He squeezed my leg, and I could hear the smile in his voice. "It wasn't a prank, it was a pleasant surprise. You're having fun though, right?"

I glanced down at us, at me, getting a ride on the broad set of shoulders that I dreamed about, my hands free to roam all over that beloved head, and covered in pink powder.

Yes, I was having fun. It was a perfect day, and even me, the Queen of Denial, could not deny that Tristan had waltzed back into my life, and brought my joy back with him.

I shifted on his shoulders, stroking his hair. "Yes, Tristan, I'm having fun."

He turned his head, kissing my bad knee, one hand moving up to start rubbing at it. And just as though our thoughts were as interwoven as our souls, he said quietly, "You make me happy. You know that, right?"

I teared up and cursed about it, because tears would leave obvious tracks down my powder-covered face.

"Don't," I said weakly.

"Don't what? Be happy? I can't help it when you're in my life.

I took a few deep, steadying breaths, hand to my racing heart. He was relentless.

When I'd been silent for a long time, he took pity on me and changed the subject.

We were pelted with yellow at the next paint station. I rubbed it into his hair, saying, "Dammit, I really wanted some pictures of you covered in just the pink. For blackmail purposes."

"Boo, you can take pictures of me buried in your pink anytime you like."

I pulled his hair for that one.

"I need to give you fair warning. I ran into Natalie earlier, before the race, so she's here somewhere."

I stiffened. "Twatalie Natalie? She's still hanging around?"

I felt his shoulders shift under my thighs. He was getting uncomfortable, which made *me* stiffen even more.

"She works at the casino. Has for years. She bartends at Decadence on the weekends, and I think she's a cocktail waitress in the casino a few days a week. She's mellowed out some, but she can still be a handful, thus the warning."

"So you and her are still close, huh?"

I felt him sigh under me. "No, we're not. We're friendly enough, when we run into each other, but that's about it. She gave up on getting me back a long time ago."

"I always wondered if you two would get back together if you and I broke up."

"Well, there's your answer. No chance in hell."

"Not even one hookup?"

"Fuck no. Not a chance. You happy or sad that you were so wrong?"

I made a noise of noncommittal, but I was pretty damned

ecstatic about it.

"She did come up in therapy a few times, mostly because my relationship with her pointed to the fact that back when we were teenagers, I wanted to save her more than I wanted to be happy. Savior complex, my therapist called it."

My chest was tight. "Is that how you felt about you and me? Were you trying to save me?"

He turned his head and kissed my knee again. "God no. You've got that so twisted. You were the one saving me. Always."

I closed my eyes and let that wash over me. The only thing that brought me out of it was some bright blue colored powder to the face.

"So Mona and Natalie are both going to be at the after party for this thing?" I finally asked him.

"Yes. If it makes you feel better, I think Natalie hates Mona even more than she hated you."

That did not make me feel better. In terms of things in the world that didn't make me feel better, that one got a top spot.

I made him put me down and walked briskly for the next few paint stations.

He ignored my protests, throwing me back on his shoulders to cross the colorful finish line, dragging me to one of the pack of color throwers, holding still until every inch of us was drenched.

I was giggling and dusting off the top of his head when a smiling, colorful Mona approached us.

She greeted us both warmly. She didn't act at all threatened by me, and I didn't know what to make of that. I hadn't gotten the impression, for even a second, that she was over Tristan.

But perhaps that was my baggage, since six long years later, I was still completely infatuated with the man.

"They're setting up a photo op with the other girls," she told Tristan. "They want to do it while all of the paint is still fresh."

She pointed towards a stage that was being set up. "They want us all there in five minutes."

"Let me down," I told him, tugging on his hair. He did so without a word.

"You can come too, of course, if you want," Mona told me.

"No, thanks," I said instantly.

Tristan was looking at me, and Mona was looking at him. I wanted to be literally anywhere else on the planet right then.

"Go on," I told him. "I'll be around." I tapped the armband on my bicep that held my phone.

He moved close, as though Mona wasn't even there, and cupped my face in his palms. "Come with me. I don't want to get separated in this crowd. It could take me hours to find you again."

I shook my head, but it didn't dislodge his gentle hands. "I have my phone. Go on. I'll be fine."

He bent and started kissing me, powdered faces and all. He didn't pull back until I was clutching the front of his shirt in both hands, and Mona had long since moved on without him.

I still refused to go with him, but when he left, I trailed slowly, intending to watch the shoot from a distance.

All around me people were dancing and in general just having a blast, everyone so covered in paint powder that it was peppering the air with every movement. A few people had even brought their children, and they seemed to be getting as big of a kick out of it all as the adults.

Only with Tristan would I find myself in a place like this and the second he was away from my side, I wanted to leave.

I stuck with it, though, watching the drawn-out photo op that involved him putting his arm around a lot of busty, paint colored women in half shirts.

I was about one second from saying to hell with it and catching a cab when a female voice spoke just to my right.

"I guess the bitch is back."

It took me a minute, while I turned and studied the paint-colored, hostile woman that had taken up residence beside me.

Finally, I recognized the collagen injected, puffed up features under the powder. Even under a pound of color, I could tell she wasn't aging well. She was going overboard with the surgery.

"Natalie," I said, then turned away again.

I ignored her as much as I could. I figured that was the nicest thing I could do. And the mature thing to do.

Even she didn't deserve the things I wanted to say to her. The last six years of our mess wasn't her fault.

"I saw you and Tristan during the race. It's so sweet that he was helping you out back there. He's such a nice guy, helping the disabled."

"Disabled?" I said softly, giving her my full attention now. *Now* she deserved it.

A part of me kind of lived for that moment when my claws could come out, and I didn't have to feel bad about the consequences, because I felt I'd been properly provoked. This was definitely one of those moments.

"If you ask me, those giant silicone filled balloons on your chest that have you nearly tipping over every time you try to stand upright, and those clown lips of yours have to make it hard to eat without drooling. Now those are a disability."

She made a disgusted noise, but had no comeback.

I smiled. She moved away and that was that. It was sad, but I actually preferred dealing with her to dealing with Mona.

I found a place to sit, on a picnic table that was set near what was turning out to be quite the dance floor.

Almost the second I sat down, I felt my phone vibrating on my arm.

It was Tristan. I didn't think I had a chance in hell of hearing him over all the noise, so I dropped the call and texted him my location.

CHAPTER TWENTY-THREE

He was there in less than a minute. Sitting down next to me, then pulling me unceremoniously onto his lap.

I turned until I was sideways, staring up at him. "You can go dance if you want to. I don't mind."

"Not without you," he said, kissing my nose.

"I still have a few moves," I told him, watching his face.

I loved to make him laugh.

I was flattered by the admiring look he gave me for that. "Yes, you do."

I laughed. "I wasn't talking about that. I'm talking about dance moves."

He looked intrigued. "Yeah?"

"Yeah. There's the lasso." I showed him that classic, and he laughed. "And the 'make it rain,'" I put my fingers to my palm and imitated flinging cash. "And the slap that.'" I put one palm down, and the other moved in a rapid spanking motion. "And of course the 'going down.'" I pointed my palm down, cupped it to imitate it holding the back of a head, and pushed it down, to mimic him going down on me.

I'd just made that last one up.

He was laughing hard by the time I was done. My whole chest went warm when he laughed like that.

And then we were kissing, making out like teenagers in public again. I knew I should pull back, but I couldn't seem to stop. I gripped his shirt while he gripped my hair, and let our mouths just go at it. It was a special kind of bliss to just let go like that, for a time.

He was laying me on the bench, his hands getting a touch indecent, when I found the will to pull back.

"We can't. Not here. There are kids around, Tristan. Not to mention *other people*."

He pulled back and sat up. "I'm going to go grab us something to eat."

He disappeared into the crowd.

He was back maybe ten minutes later, his arms full of sodas and hotdogs.

I didn't even complain, just ate the hotdog and drank the coke. I was so hungry that even that was worth the calories.

We shared a smile as we finished eating, my mind on that ridiculous make out session earlier.

He had a bit of ketchup on the corner of his mouth, and I took a napkin, dabbing at it, smiling into his dear face.

He tilted my face up with his chin. His expression was raw with things I couldn't name or didn't want to. "Oh, no, you've done it now," he whispered softly.

"Done what?"

"You're giving me that look. You know we can't go back, if you're looking at me like that again. You get that, right?"

"I don't know what you're talking about," I told him, which was a lie. I could feel it spilling out of my eyes, covering him like some pain-relieving salve. This was something I gave, and he took, and we were both more lost for it, or at least, that's how it had worked out the last time.

"Yes, you do. You can't give me that look without *feeling* that look." He took a deep breath, and then another.

"It's probably all this powder. You're seeing things."

That didn't even faze him. "I swear, it feels like there's been a bullet lodged in my gut, buried there for ages, and it just got pried out. Thank you."

I looked away. "Don't thank me. Just do what you need to not to hurt me."

His breathing grew ragged. "Do I get to ask the same of you?"

We shared a raw look, but I didn't answer him.

"I didn't realize how hard it would be, to be around Mona," I said, changing the subject. "I think it's best for me to avoid that in the future."

He was the picture of yellow, purple, and pink faced remorse. In spite of myself, I found that so incredibly endearing. "I'm so sorry for that. It's turned into a bad situation."

I shook my head at him. "What were you thinking, sleeping with someone you worked with? When does that *ever* turn out well?"

He looked wildly uncomfortable.

I shook my head at him some more. "Oh you naive bastard. Still thought fuck buddies could work, huh?"

He flinched. "I did. I was an idiot. But let's not do this to ourselves, okay?"

He had a good point, and I dropped it, since I was done making mine.

We went to his house, and I finally got that tour.

"It's huge," I told him before we'd even finished with the first floor. "What single man needs this much space?"

He gave me an enigmatic look for that bit of sass.

We fucked our colorful way all over his kinky bed. Afterward, we took a shower together that bled into a rainbow down the drain and he took me again against the shower wall.

It was as I was drying off that I noticed a half used bottle of women's perfume on the counter, near his own assortment of colognes.

I grabbed it, holding it up. "Care to explain this?"

He smirked. "Sure. Don't get mad, but I stole that from you back at James and Bianca's wedding."

I just blinked at him. "You went into my room at the ranch and took something? And what on earth could you possibly use my perfume for?"

"You probably don't want to know."

I blushed, head to toe, and I couldn't look at him for a solid five minutes. It didn't help that he was naked and I was close to it.

He took me into his closet to try to find me a T-shirt. I froze in the doorway, staring inside.

With just a towel clutched to my chest, I stared at his closet for the longest time. It was huge, and much stranger, it was full. Long lines of suits, a wall of ties, racks upon racks of dress shirts. There was only one small space allotted for T-shirts, and the wall of shelves that held his folded jeans wasn't much bigger than the section allotted for ties.

"Holy shit. What happened here? This is not you."

He looked sheepish as he ran a restless hand through his hair. "I have a dresser."

"Huh?" I made a face. "Explain that to us poor people. A dresser?"

"For the show, there's a lady that does my shopping, puts clothes together for the act. A stylist, I guess. She put this closet together, as well, for all of the events associated with the casino. An extensive wardrobe is part of the job, I guess. So you got that part right, this is not me."

He snagged a T-shirt down from where several were folded, and I dropped my towel, going for it.

He held it out of reach with a smile. "I just rethought the whole giving you clothes idea." He tossed the shirt over his shoulder and reached for me. He kissed my forehead softly while he cupped the back of my head, gripping my hair; he turned my body so he was behind me, then prodded me forward.

"Grab my wrist," he told me, and I reached my arms up and behind, gripping the hand that held my hair. This exaggerated the arch in my back, and he stroked his other palm up my torso, gripping a breast as he led me into the bedroom.

He walked me up to a strange, dual arched leather bench. It was about six feet long, with one arch that reached three feet high before it sloped down low then rose into another arch that was maybe a foot shorter than the other one. It was a narrow bench, as well, and I didn't imagine for a second that this wasn't for a reason.

I gave it a squinty-eyed look. "Okay, I give up. What is that thing?"

He walked me directly to the rounded edge of the higher side. He pushed me forward until I lay with my ass was pointed straight up, and my feet dangled off the ground.

His hand still held my hair, and I still had a tight grip on his wrists.

"It's called a Tantra Chair. In case that doesn't describe it well enough, let me put it this way: We are going to clock in some hours on this chair. *Days.*"

I wriggled, the position alone a turn on, with my hips flush to the soft surface of the chair. Of course, having Tristan naked behind me was more than a little responsible for getting me wet and ready for another round.

I couldn't share with him that I'd forgotten what it was even like to have a sex *marathon.* I'd only been with Andrew in the years between, but I doubted many men could put in so many rounds, like Tristan. The man was superhuman. I'd always known it, but having this, and losing it, made it even sweeter the second time around.

He kept my hair gripped tight as he played against my entrance with his tip.

"Sweetheart, here's how it's going to go. You aren't going to come until I tell you to. No matter how unbearable, you will *hold back* until I give the word. Also, don't move your hands until I say to."

I bit my lip, shutting my eyes tight as he sank in deep. He started moving right away, but so slowly, so leisurely that it was torturous right off the bat.

I was already primed. What I needed was another hard fuck. I told him so.

He chuckled, kissing my back, his lips playing over my tattoo. "Let's be clear; you are far from in charge here."

As though to illustrate his point, he gave me a few rough, jarring rams before he went right back to that infuriating pace.

He palmed my left breast and kissed my back as he maintained that smooth as hell and torturously unhurried rhythm.

This went on for so long that I was mewling, then cursing him loud and vehemently.

His reaction to that was to laugh against my back. "I already got you off twice. I must be spoiling you, if you're this greedy for a *third* round."

"I know you're good for more than three, you sadistic bastard," I told him.

I got a few rough jolts for that one, and as soon as I realized that taunting him would get me what I wanted, I began to insult him in earnest.

It backfired. Badly. He pulled out of me completely, letting go of my hair. I tried to take back every insult, but it was too late.

"Relax your hands," he told me, and when I did, he lined them up straight at my sides, twisting my arms just enough to face my palms up, then pulling my arms high and far enough behind my back to hold them taut.

I felt him kneel behind me, still holding my hands captive, and start to eat me out from behind with the most teasing little strokes of his tongue.

My feet arched up, and I hooked them until they were crossed behind his head, resting on his nape. He began to plunge his tongue deep, using my captive hands to move my pussy on and off his busy tongue.

I was close, and I told him so. He pulled back, and I felt him stand. He tugged at my arms, pulling me back onto his cock, and started up the slow pace from before.

I bounced my hips and started to beg.

He took pity on me, working into the pace I wanted, needed. "All right, sweetheart, you can let go."

I came hard, convulsing, shaking, clenching on his cock as I felt him grinding hard as he followed me.

I was so limp after that round that he had to carry me to bed.

I passed out, sated and content in a way that had been lost to me for as long as Tristan had. Even with the touches of drama, it was the best day I'd had in as long as I could remember.

CHAPTER TWENTY-FOUR

I met him offsite, at a restaurant near Tropicana and Pecos, right next to a huge gun store with the biggest shooting range in town.

It was a great little Italian joint that I'd have bet money was run by the mob. The place was open twenty-four seven, and it was always completely dead except for a few overweight Italian guys that chatted quietly in the corner. One of them, the owner, would almost always stop by our table to make sure that we'd enjoyed our meal, giving a long speech about taking care of his customers.

Super mob vibe. And come on, this was Vegas.

The food was so good that I kept coming back, regardless. Bev and I had a bi-weekly lunch date there, rain or shine.

Usually, Andrew and I met up at one of the restaurants inside the casino, but I didn't think that was a good idea at the moment, for obvious reasons.

Not because I was hiding it, but more because I didn't want to deal with any potential drama because of it.

Okay, maybe I was hiding it a little. Though I wasn't doing anything wrong.

I told myself that firmly and repeatedly. Somehow, it didn't help.

We met for lunch a few times a month, even post breakup. That's just how we were. I thought we'd always be good friends. Andrew was just that type of guy. Even if he'd rather not have been broken up, he respected my decision.

He never resorted to dirty tricks or Troublesome smiles to get what he wanted from me.

Of course, he didn't have those in his arsenal.

In fact, Andrew didn't have an arsenal.

That had always been my favorite thing about him. Too bad it hadn't been enough.

It was hard to sit across a small table from him and not make comparisons to a certain tattooed bad boy. Impossible, actually.

And it was hard not to feel guilty at just how unflattering those comparisons were for poor Andrew.

I ordered a salad, Andrew ordered lasagna, and we picked at our food while we waded through some stilted conversation. It wasn't usually like this.

I felt like shit for even being there. I should have canceled, but I'd been too stubborn to admit to myself that my life couldn't just keep going on as usual.

"So are you seeing anyone special?" I asked, feeling way too hopeful about it. The day he moved on would be a big weight off my conscience. I knew I'd broken his heart, and though it'd been several months since all of that had gone down, I still felt bad about it.

He winced slightly. "I'm still carrying a bit of a torch for you, if you hadn't noticed." There was no censure in his tone, just honesty.

That was so much harder to face. I looked down at my plate.

I thought I'd been clear for a while now, but apparently not. Had I inadvertently been stringing him along? It had never occurred to me before, but, of course, I hadn't been sleeping with someone else before.

That thought threw me, the part about someone else.

Tristan being the someone else was just off. It felt wrong to even think it.

I knew why, too.

He was the someone, so he could never be the else.

This was the else, my morbid mind told me.

The last six years have been the else, and poor Andrew was just another casualty in the Great War of T&D.

Dear Andrew had been on a no percent survival suicide mission, and he hadn't had a clue.

"I wish you wouldn't," I told him as gently as I could. "Carry a torch for me, I mean. You're a great guy."

"Uh oh," he said with a sad smile. "That sounds ominous."

"You are. You've been wonderful to me, patient and kind, but I was broken long before I met you, and I'm afraid that neither you nor I ever did have the tools to fix me. I'm just beginning to see that. I'm sorry I wasted your time; sorry I hurt you. Truly I am. We are good as friends though. I'll always have the utmost respect and fondness for you."

He looked much more broken up by my words than I was ready to deal with. "It wasn't a waste of my time. Falling in love never is." He covered his face with his hands. "I didn't know you felt this way. I thought you just needed more time. More space. Is this coming up for a particular reason?" His hands dropped, and his solemn eyes met mine. "If I may be blunt, is there someone else?"

Still there was no censure in his tone, only a gently wounded concern.

I flushed, feeling ashamed at my insensitivity. I should have told him sooner. "I have been seeing someone. I can't say if it's serious, or even has the potential to be. It's a very complicated situation. But—"

"It's Tristan Vega, isn't it?"

That took the steam right out of me. "How did you know?"

"It was always him, wasn't it? I knew," he said emotionally. "I knew there was someone that had your heart, something that always made you hold back from me. I should have realized we were doomed, after that first time, when you locked yourself in the bathroom and wouldn't stop crying. Obviously I knew there was something wrong, but I didn't know it was *hopeless*."

He paused for a long moment, regaining his composure. "You shouldn't be sorry, and you shouldn't feel as though you've done something wrong. I know you tried your best to love me. We just never had a shot, huh?"

I shook my head, wishing I knew better how to comfort him. I could tell he was in pain, and I hated that I was the cause of it.

"That time we saw him at the red carpet last year. Christ, I should have seen it coming then. I could tell you weren't over each other."

"Was I so obvious?" The thought was alarming, to say the least. At times, it'd seemed that my pride was all I'd had. Had even that small comfort, that I'd kept my feelings hidden, been denial on my part?

"You weren't, no. You have always been remarkably good at hiding your feelings. It was him. He wasn't hiding a thing. He looked at you like, I don't know, like he couldn't even *breathe* at the sight of you. I could tell he'd been your lover, and I admit to being jealous, but still, I had to feel for the guy.

And the way he looked at me, well, he barely glanced at me, but when he did...I've never had that much animosity aimed in my direction in my entire life. I know it sounds crazy, but I think he wanted to attack me. Like, bodily attack me."

That didn't sound crazy. That sounded like Tristan.

I wondered briefly if I should warn him that it was a very real possibility, if they had a run-in in the future. Tristan wasn't half the hot head he used to be, but the way he felt about Andrew might just cancel out all of his newfound self-control.

"About that," I began. "I'd tread carefully, if I were you and I happened to see him. He can be, well, volatile."

His eyes widened. "Is he dangerous? Wait, are *you* safe with him?"

I waved that off. "I'm safe with him. He'd never hurt a woman, and he'd cut off his own arms before he'd hurt *me*. If there's one thing I'm sure of about him, it is that. And no, he's not dangerous, not ordinarily, but his animosity towards you is not ordinary for him. I'm not saying he's going to come to your house and strangle you, I'm just saying that if you happen to see him somewhere, you should turn around and walk the other way."

His eyes were no less wide, no less horrified. "I don't fight. I've never been in a fight in my life, but you're saying this guy could just walk up and attack me?"

I shrugged, grimacing. "I don't think he will, but though I can't say for sure, I'm also not positive. He can't even say your name. If I talk about you, this little twitch starts up under his eye. It's not good. I'm just warning you to be extra cautious, because he *has* been in a fight before. Many fights. It used to be almost a hobby for him. I'm not trying to scare you, I just don't want you to get hurt. Bodily hurt, on top of everything else."

"At least you talk about me to him. That's got to mean something."

"It does. I'll always care about you. I'm sorry it worked out like this."

"So you and him? You're making it sound like a done deal."

I shrugged helplessly. "I have no idea. Who can say? We have a powerful history together, one that goes back years, and that ended in some of the worst tragedies of my life. Nothing is a done deal, not at all, but I've just begun to realize that I might have it in me to give us another shot."

"Well, you seem different. You seem happy. That's got to be a good sign that things are going well."

I smiled tremulously, so happy that he seemed to be

accepting it all. Hopefully this would give him a few steps in the right direction, towards moving on. "They seem to be. I'm taking things one day at a time."

"It does worry me that you're talking about it more like a cancer treatment than a relationship, but then I know you well enough to appreciate your little quirks."

I laughed. A weight had been lifted. He was a good man, and he would not be trying to hold me back with guilt.

I finished our meal with a lighter heart, feeling that things with Andrew were settled, once and for all.

Before I started the drive back to work, I checked my phone and saw that I'd missed a few texts from Tristan.

Tristan: How's work?

And then, not twenty minutes after.

Tristan: I'm coming to take you to lunch. I just got some good news, and we need to celebrate.

That had been about forty minutes ago.

My mouth set in a grim line, cursing silently, I texted back.

Danika: I'm on my way back to work now. Coming back from lunch.

I didn't elaborate, but I did wonder the entire drive what was wrong with my luck. Some people could get away with all sorts of deceptions.

Not that this was a deception, I told myself. I just hadn't bothered to tell him, because who I had a friendly lunch with was not his business.

But still, I had a long rant in my head about the fact that I did indeed have the worst luck in the world.

I also spent a good chunk of that drive wondering what I would tell Tristan if he asked who I'd gone to lunch with. I could easily say Bev, or simply say it'd been business. It was unlikely he'd catch me in either lie.

I didn't entertain the thought for long. I wasn't a liar, and I hadn't done anything wrong. If he asked me, I was just going to tell him. Easy peasy.

CHAPTER TWENTY-FIVE

Tristan was at the gallery waiting when I got there. He was chatting with Kate. He had a deck of cards out, no doubt wowing her with one of his mind-boggling tricks.

I smiled fondly. He was charming her into a moon-eyed mess. I could certainly relate.

I'd seen many of his tricks, and I'd even gotten that sneaky viewing of his stage act.

Even so, he still had the ability to shock me with his talent.

He pointed to a magazine that had been strewn carelessly onto the podium. Some sort of Vegas events brochure, I noticed, as Kate picked it up.

"Page sixty-two," he told her with a grin.

She flipped it open to the page and started freaking the fuck out. "Oh my God. Oh my God. Oh my God! How did you do that? How could you possibly, I mean, I picked that card myself. It was *my* choice, which means, oh my God, I don't know what it means. Holy mother of God."

I shook my head, disbelieving, approached them. On page sixty-two of the magazine was a picture of a deck of cards, with one card flipped up on top. It was a king of spades.

"You picked a king of spades?" I asked her, studying her face.

She nodded vehemently. "That is some freaky shit, right?"

I swung a narrow gaze Tristan's way. "How on earth?"

Those Troublesome dimples came out to play. "You know. Magic."

I pulled him into my office, not even giving a gape-mouthed Kate any explanation. "Seriously, tell me how you did that, because unless you really have sold your soul to Satan for some magical powers—"

"Hey now!"

"Unless that has happened, there is an explanation for that trick back there, and you really need to tell me, because that one freaked me out."

He shook his head, smiling. "I can't just give out trade secrets. I need some guarantee, boo, some sort of contract between the two of us that assures your loyalty."

"I swear I won't give away the trick," I told him.

He tilted my chin up with a light touch, his eyes so affectionate that I had to blink rapidly and look away, to stay unaffected.

"Okay, I'll take that, and now I just have to keep you close, as insurance, you understand." He smiled. It was overkill. "It was actually a two-bit trick. The cheapest kind of all. The really difficult involved stuff is never fully appreciated, which, as a professional, is vexing. But this one was simple."

"You somehow have an extra page that you carry around and slip into the magazine, after she picks a card?"

He laughed and shook his head. "No. That would be a feat, there. I've seen the magazine before, and I knew about the page, about the card. I'm actually responsible for that page being in all of the copies of that publication, and it's a popular one around town."

"Well, that seems pretty damned involved to me. But that makes no sense. She picked the card."

"It's not involved, since I do the damn trick all the time, and I get many uses out of it. I make James provide copies of those magazines all over the property, which is easy for him, since he owns the publication."

"But that doesn't explain why she picked that card. She said so."

"She thinks she picked that card. But she didn't. I suggested it, not in a way she realized, and that is all there is to it. Like I said, cheapest trick in the biz."

"Wow. They all work like that?"

He shrugged. "It depends. To say I have a lot of tricks up my sleeve is like saying James has a lot of money. Not even touching on the surface of it."

"You think a trick like that would work on me? Could you have suggested which card to pick to me like that?"

His mouth twisted, and he stroked a hand over my hair. "Well, no, certainly not now. It's all out in the open, for you and me." Something dangerous was bleeding out of his eyes.

I backed away. "I need to get to work. Tell me your good news fast, because I'm heading out on the floor."

He shook his head, his eyes on my body.

I was wearing a fitted navy polka dot halter dress with a big bow at the neck, and a sweeping hem that hit just above the knees. I hadn't been dressing to impress when I'd put it on, but suddenly it felt like the dress was too sexy to wear to work.

That's what his eyes did to me. They had the power to transform. The way I felt. The things I wanted.

"You aren't going to tell me your good news?" I asked, breathless now.

"I can't even remember what it is."

"Must not have been that good of news."

A ghost of a smile played around his mouth. "It had some stiff competition, in terms of my attention. Never had a shot."

He took a step in my direction, and I inched a careful step back. There had to be boundaries, somehow, someway, and it seemed like not having sex in my office in the middle of business hours was a good place to start.

"I really do need to get back to work," I told him, when he'd backed me to the wall.

He picked me up by the waist, carrying me straight to my desk. He set me on the edge there, and it was high enough that he could squeeze his hips between my thighs, and hit just the perfect spot.

"This won't take long."

I snorted. "Well, that's hardly selling it."

He smiled, and sank down to kneel in front of me.

I'd never realized before just how multi-functional a stand-up desk could be.

He buried his face between my legs without even pulling up my skirt. He just inhaled, making me squirm.

His hands began to inch my hem up. I helped him, officially gone to the dark side for the immediate future.

Sanity rushing out of me between one ragged breath and the next.

And in that same breath coming back, I let sensation in. Blissful oblivion in.

It seemed like a good trade. Impossible to turn down, really.

He bunched my skirt up around my hips, nuzzling into my sex. I sucked in harsh breaths as he pulled my panties off.

With this teeth.

I struggled to watch, when my eyes wanted to drift closed in pleasure.

It was a sight worth seeing.

I dragged a fistful of my skirt up, stuffing it in my mouth in an attempt to muffle my own cries.

How could I have forgotten the magical things his lips could do? And his tongue.

And his hands. Once those magic hands set to work on me, there was no setting up boundaries, no stifling cries.

He licked, lapped, tortured and teased, while my hands in

turn stroked his hair or tried to pull it out. That delicious scruff on his jaw added to the torment, tickling at the skin of my inner thighs.

It wasn't long before I was tensing, my thighs gripping his head hard, the torrid sensations reaching their fever pitch.

I came, crying out his name, no thought, no care to where I was or what the hell was happening to my self-control.

He was smiling when he straightened. Very smugly, I thought. "Well, what do you think? Did I sell it?"

I just shook my head with no concept of what he was talking about.

Rational thought would return.

Eventually. But not yet.

"You said I wasn't selling it. I was asking if I changed your mind."

I just shook my head, gone mute. It wasn't a no, it was a 'I have no idea what the fuck is going on.'

He kissed me, one long drugging taste; before he pulled back. "Come by my place after work. Don't find any panties between now and then."

He left.

It took me a few minutes to recover, and it was only as I was straightening my clothes that I caught the full implication of what he'd said.

The bastard had made my underwear disappear.

He hadn't given a time, but I ducked out of work early.

I'd been basically worthless for the two hours I'd stayed. Who could concentrate on anything after that? Not me. I could barely focus on the road while driving there, nearly ran myself onto the shoulder as my mind ran rampant with visions of the encounter in my office and then continued to wander to the night ahead.

I had to ring the doorbell several times before a shirtless Tristan opened the door.

He was gleaming with sweat. It would have taken inhuman willpower not to drink in every inch of his muscled, tatted up body.

And I was human. Oh Lord, was I human.

He'd clearly been working out by the no shirt, athletic shorts, and running shoes he was wearing.

He'd always been in incredible shape, but this new, disciplined version of him had taken it to a whole new level. He'd taken all of that antsy energy that he'd once used alcohol to mellow out, and applied it to a workout routine of epic, addictive proportions.

And I was addicted to the results.

His shorts hung low and his sweaty, cut to within an inch of its life, pelvic V muscle, was giving a silent but clear invitation to my tongue.

I knew what I wanted first. It was all I could do to keep from getting on my knees and going down on him on his doorstep.

I moistened my lips, then reached out a finger, running it down his slick chest. He didn't so much as twitch.

That should have been my first clue that something was wrong.

But I was blinded by all of that gloriously bared flesh, oblivious to all but the physical.

"You're early," he panted.

"You changed my mind. You sold it." I took a step closer, watching my hand trail south. I could see his erection moving, growing through his fluid shorts.

I wasn't even going to let him shower before I wrapped my lips around his spectacular cock.

He turned abruptly, striding back into his house, leaving me to follow.

And I followed, shutting the door behind me and locking it. I toed off my shoes in the entryway, and unbuttoned my dress. I pulled it over my head and threw it behind my shoulder before

I'd made it through two rooms. I unsnapped my bra, tossing it behind me somewhere between the living room and dining room.

I was completely nude by the time he stopped, his back to me, in the kitchen.

"Let's go upstairs," I told him huskily.

He rounded on me, took in my state, and set his jaw.

"Who were you out with this afternoon, Danika?" he asked me in a terrible voice.

I stiffened, wishing I'd kept my dress on.

I didn't know how to answer, and the first thing out of my mouth was perhaps the most incriminating thing I could have said. "Who told you?"

His eyes clenched tightly shut.

He reached up a hand and raked it through his hair. It was trembling. Badly.

"You answer first. I want to hear it from you. Who were you with this afternoon?"

I swallowed hard, feeling sick to my stomach. Why the reaction? I asked myself. It was illogical, but even so, undeniable.

I felt bad about this.

Guilty.

Because he wasn't angry. I'd seen Tristan angry more times than I could count, and though he was difficult when he was angry, I could manage it. Could manage him.

But this wasn't anger; it was pain. My actions hadn't enraged them; they had hurt him. It was so much harder to navigate than simple rage.

"I went to lunch with Andrew. He was in town, and we're still friends. It's not something you should be getting this worked up over." There, it was out of my mouth and nowhere near the deal he was making it into in his head. "Now tell me how you found out, and what you heard that's upsetting you like this. It's clearly been blown out of proportion." I began to inch back, intending to locate my dress and have this conversation with a bit more dignity.

He followed me, out of the kitchen, through the formal dining room. He followed until I reached my dress, menace in his every step.

The second I had the dress in my hands, it was wrenched away.

He didn't use his hands but his body to force me back and down onto the sitting room's sofa. He followed me, covering my body, his eyes liquid gold as they bore into mine, lit with accusations that I couldn't bear to face.

He crawled between my legs, pushing my arms above my head, clutching my wrists. "When I was leaving your office I heard Kate and Sandra talking. They were wondering if you were going to tell Andrew about *me*. They weren't sure which one of us was your boyfriend, and which one of us was the other man."

I winced. The girls were being harsh on me behind my back. That was never fun, but especially when the bite of that gossip could leave some lasting marks.

One of his hands snaked down, and he fingered my sex. He rubbed until I was nice and wet, then plunged two fingers in deep.

He was thrusting them in and out when he asked, his voice so pained that it made me ache, "Did you...?" he couldn't finish. He had no stomach for this, but I knew what he was trying to ask, knew what his mind had fixated on.

"No, of course not," I said unsteadily.

His eyes closed, fingers coming out of me. I looked down between our bodies as he pulled his stiff, quivering cock out of his shorts, and guided himself to my entrance.

With agonizing slowness, he rubbed the head of his shaft against my tender flesh.

"Did you kiss him?" he asked, as he began to push inside.

"No, no, I told you. He and I are just friends now. That's it. Friends."

He kissed me, shoving home.

I sucked at his driving tongue as his shaking body took my shaking body in hurried, desperate thrusts, my hands still pinned above my head by one of his.

I arched my back, rubbing my aching breasts into his hard, sweaty chest. I couldn't get enough of him, couldn't *feel* enough.

He groaned into my mouth and moved faster, thrusting harder, deeper, until I felt each heavy drive, an invasive, numbing pleasure filling my lower body, then bleeding in great gushing hemorrhages into the rest of me.

He pulled back, still moving in and out. Eyes raw, nostrils flared, he rasped, "How could you fall in love with him? How could you *do that*?"

He always knew when to strike, and I was at my weakest here.

I shook my head and closed my eyes, feeling lost, feeling found, my body, heart, and mind at *war*.

But even war was forgotten as, gasping, mewling, trembling, and holding on for dear life, I fell over the edge. Broad pulses of sensation moved in beating waves from my cunt, from deep in my womb, and reverberated unrelentingly through my entire, defeated body.

Tristan fared no better as shouting, grunting, gasping on top of me, shaking head to toe he came, emptying himself inside of me in long heavy spurts that were perceptible as my clenching sex milked him dry.

I didn't speak after. He didn't either, not at first.

He lay still on top of me, though raised enough not to cut off my breath. The only sign of life in the room for endless minutes was the harsh drum of our heartbeats racing against each other as they met through the pressed flesh of our chests, and the pulsing of our sexes still joined together.

Finally, he pulled back to look at me. Something wild flared in his eyes. The pain, as it always does, was turning into something akin to rage.

"Last year you told me you were *in love* with him. Those words came out of your mouth, directed at me. You cared about him enough to *destroy me* with that. You were planning to marry him, you said. You felt confident enough about that marriage to tell *me*, of all people, that it was a foregone conclusion. What do you imagine that did to me, to hear you say that? What would the reverse do to you? *Tell me.*"

I just shook my head. I remembered so clearly where I'd been when I'd heard a rumor, just over a year ago, that he and Mona were engaged. It had messed me up.

Being apart was one thing, but the idea that some other woman could be his *wife*? That was out of fucking line.

And I'd planted the same poisonous idea in Tristan's head about Andrew and me. I was fully culpable here. I'd given him that idea, knowing that it was utter nonsense, knowing quite well that it would mess him up like it had me.

I felt guilty enough about it to offer some small recompense.

"First of all, let's be clear. You have no claim on our years apart. You don't own *any* of them."

His golden eyes were filled with a supplication so raw that I couldn't take it at close range. One small rant had reduced him from the rage back to the pain.

I pushed him away, wrenching him off me, out of me, scrambled back, then stood, and backed up until my shoulder blades hit a wall.

"No claim," I repeated. I was naked, but I didn't even try to cover myself from his eyes. My body wasn't the most exposed part of me just then. I wanted to cover my heart.

"No claim," I repeated again, voice quavering. "But of course

I didn't love him. I wanted to love him, but love is not about *want.*"

His eyes had gone pure liquid.

I shuddered, then started to shiver, and not from the cold.

"He was good for me, but love is not about *good.*"

My hand jabbed at him, then at me, then back again, the motion wild, chaotic. "This is what love gets you, okay? I cared about Andrew, do care about him, but I walked away *clean.*"

Lips trembling, voice trembling, I continued, "*Love* doesn't let you walk away clean. Love is *messy.* I don't have to tell you, of all people; Love takes a fucking piece of you before it's done."

If it is ever even possible to be done.

I couldn't say that part aloud. Fear still held too strong a hold on me, and I respected that fear enough to give it the time it needed.

He rose and moved to me. His shorts rode low on his hips, the waistband in front still pulled under his scrotum. He hadn't bothered to raise them enough to cover his heavy, spent cock. I didn't think he even noticed.

It was distracting, but not as distracting as the unrelenting glint in his eyes. His mood had altered with the flip of a switch.

My rant had appeased him, to put it lightly.

I wasn't sure that had been its desired result. I'd wanted to solve a problem, not create a new one.

He cupped my face in his hands, his eyes tender enough to *break* me.

"Come here," he urged softly, taking his hands away from my face, and opening his arms wide.

With a shuddering sigh, I fell into them.

CHAPTER TWENTY-SIX

TRISTAN

I wrapped my arms around her and clutched her to my chest, letting her words wash over me, allowing them to soothe me. She hadn't been happy to say them, but they still worked as balm to my wounded heart.

We stayed like that for a long time, but it couldn't last forever, especially since we were skin on skin.

Eventually, we started shifting and soothing rubs turned into lingering touches.

Her hand moved to my stiff erection. Her teeth bit at her lush lower lip while her palm pumped at me, her grip firm as she ran it up and down my length. I loved the feel of her hand on me, the way her delicate fingers curved so perfectly around my throbbing length.

I watched her face while she touched me. That dear, beautiful face. Her hair was parted down the middle and pulled back tight today. Even our efforts on the couch hadn't loosened it. It was a severe style, but somehow it only enhanced the raw beauty of her features, her clear gray eyes standing out like pale crystals, her trembling lips so lush I couldn't stop picturing them wrapped around my cock.

Not yet, I thought. Maybe next time.

This time I needed to feel her against me again, to press my whole body to her whole body and *feel*.

My lips latched onto hers, plundering hers, bruising in their conquest.

Mine, my lips told her.

I backed her flush into the wall, dislodging her hand from me.

Lifting her high, I held her propped up with a hip braced between her legs, gripping her ass in both hands.

I buried my face against the soft mounds of her breasts, rubbing my stubbled cheek against the hard nub of her nipple.

She squirmed and gasped at the abrading contact, clutching my head to her.

I worked my way over to her other quivering breast, nuzzling into the tight crest, turning my head to lick and suck it into my mouth.

I drew hard on her nipple until she whimpered. Until she begged.

Mine, my body told her, as I pinned her to the wall.

She was panting in short, heavy gasps, her breaths puffing against the top of my head. I swear just the sound of those labored breaths could have gotten me off.

I twisted my hips, rubbing my jutting cock hard into the soft flesh of her inner thigh. I shoved against her until I felt a spurt of pre-come coat the skin just below her pussy.

She moaned and reached a grasping hand down, gripping me, pumping.

It was too much, too soon, and I pulled it away. It seemed a waste to come all over her thigh, when I was more than welcome inside of her tight cunt.

I flicked my tongue against her throat as I shifted, positioning us both so I was snug between her thighs, her feet lifted clean off the ground.

I took her mouth with ferocity as I impaled her slowly onto my aching cock.

She was suspended only by one hard hand on her hip, and my hard member working her on the inside.

She gasped and trembled as I nailed her against that wall.

I gripped my free hand into her hair, holding it at the nape, keeping her mouth anchored to mine.

I pulled back to watch her face as I began to move.

My eyes drank in the sight of her face, tight with longing, her eyes wide and moist, her lower lip trembling uncontrollably.

I glanced down, watching as I slid in and out, watching my cock pull out until just the thick head remained lodged inside.

My eyes flicked to her heaving chest, slick with sweat, her breasts so high and lovely.

I met her stunned gaze as I crammed back into her brutally.

She screamed, and I lost my mind, fucking her hard, harder, jamming into her, dragging out roughly, again and again, mindless with lust.

She was so tight that I felt like I was stretching her with every mad drive, and I couldn't get enough of it.

I gripped her hips in both of my hands and bounced her forcefully on my cock.

She screamed louder, and I kept fucking her in earnest.

She was so close that she was starting to clench on me in anticipation. I didn't let up.

I bit softly on her lower lip as she came apart in my arms.

That, I thought, that right there is what I need. The ability to fulfill her needs, the power to make her weak, weak enough to lean on me.

Mine, my heart cried out to her.

I didn't stop, riding out her clenching walls and her digging nails.

I shouted and cursed as legs shaking, back bowed I hit the end of her one last time, and erupted deep inside of her with explosive force, clenched so tight that I could feel each rough pull of semen being milked out of my pulsating cock by our combined efforts.

I came and came, so far gone that I felt shaky with it. Even my vision went fuzzy for a few long, intense moments.

I slid us both to the ground, pulling out of her on the way.

Laying her gently on her back, I propped myself above her. I spread her limp thighs with a light touch, fingering her sex.

I'd spilled in her twice already, and trails of liquid were running down her thighs. Watching her face, I shoved some of that errant fluid back inside of her, my thoughts on our lack of protection.

It wasn't that it'd slipped my mind. On the contrary, I'd noticed that even on that first time at the ranch, when I'd lost every ounce of sane thought. How not? Being bare inside of her was my own little kind of heaven, and the fact that she hadn't protested at the time, well, that I'd chalked up to the fact that the lust had made her lose all control, like it had me.

But she hadn't said so much as a word about it the next time, either.

Or the next.

And neither had I.

For my part, I had no motivation to so much as mention it. I was clean, and knew she would be. As for getting pregnant, I figured she was on the pill, but the fact was, even if she wasn't, I didn't care.

That wasn't true. I cared. I wanted her off the pill. I *wanted* her to get pregnant.

Right or wrong, I'd never stopped wanting that. I doubted I ever would.

Things were still unsettled between us, but I couldn't even pretend not to wish for some small chance I could have gotten her pregnant. I wanted that. I was more than ready to try my hand at being a father.

And there was only one woman I'd ever have considered for the role of mother to my children.

She gasped and turned her face away. "Oh God, Tristan. What are we doing?"

"I don't know, but neither of us work tomorrow, so we're about to do it for two days straight, whatever we want to call it."

She didn't even look like she'd heard me. In fact, she looked like she was drifting off.

I sprawled onto my back beside her. "I have to say, I'm tempted to sleep right here on the floor. Seems easier than trying to move at the moment."

She snorted.

"What? You can't move either. Admit it."

"I could move, if I wanted to," she said, a hint of a smile in her voice.

I turned my face to look at her. "Prove it. I bet you can't even get up right now."

"You and your bets," she said, but she'd started moving, rolling onto her side.

She'd never admit it, but the woman couldn't turn her back on a dare to save her life.

It took her a minute, but she made it onto her stomach, and then pushed up with her hands, dragging her legs underneath her.

Slowly, giving me a hell of a view, she rose onto her elbows and knees.

She braced herself there, facing away from me

And the view she gave me right then. *Jesus.*

I bit my own fist I was so turned on by the sight.

I wasn't tired anymore. Every part of me woke right up, and in fact, one particular part went to great lengths to rise to the occasion.

I'm not proud of this, but that was the precise moment when my errant cock decided that it had to be buried in her tight little ass in a hurry.

Everything was just lined up so perfectly. She was relaxed to the point of limp, natural lube was dripping down her thigh with every shift of her body. Who could resist? Not me. Not fucking likely.

She hadn't quite worked herself into a crawl when I covered her, my chest pushing into her back.

She reared up. "You've got to be kidding me!" she said, not quite stifling a laugh.

I was already parting her thighs from behind, dragging me cock against her, using the moisture between her legs to make my member slick. I grabbed a bit of extra moisture, dragging it up to her back entrance.

That's when she got the picture. "Oh," she uttered softly, then held perfectly still.

I didn't ask for permission, just moved into position and started to enter her. "Tell me if it gets to be too much," I gasped, working to get my tip in. That first shocking inch would be the challenge.

It wasn't easy. She was not accustomed to this, and her body was firmly closed against me.

I reached between us, burying two fingers in her pussy. I started to move them, and as she accepted my fingers, her back gave just enough to let me push my throbbing tip into her.

After that, I was able to sink into her, going as slow as I could stand. I was big, and I knew it wouldn't be easy for her to take me like this, but with patience I was able to sink in a few aching, precious inches.

"Am I hurting you, sweetheart?" I groaned, finger fucking her hard, because that seemed to soften the rest of her.

She couldn't even speak, just writhing and moaning below me.

I could live with that. What I couldn't live with was the superhuman control it took not to start fucking her ass harder.

With a rough grunt, I thrust in another intense inch, and then another. I stopped when I had a thought.

"Am I hurting your knee?"

"Don't stop!" she gasped, because my fingers had stopped moving. I started working them again, jerking hard, and pushed my cock in farther.

I pulled out a bit, head tilted down to watch my progress. I wasn't sure I'd be able to bury myself to the hilt. I wanted to, bad, but I couldn't stand the thought of hurting her, and I really was too big to do this particular act comfortably.

"Just fuck me," she moaned.

My eyes shut on a groan of pleasure and I sank back in, farther than I'd been before I started pulling out. "Say that again," I urged her, my voice rough with effort.

"Fuck me. Fuck my ass. Don't hold back."

"I'll hurt you if I don't hold back."

"I don't give a fuck. So I'll be sore tomorrow. Shit happens. Bury that gorgeous cock inside of me. I can take it."

That was a full on tirade for her during a sexual act, as she usually wasn't coherent enough for words at this stage.

I started pumping my fingers fast, swinging my hips hard against her, driving in until just two inches at my base weren't buried. She seemed okay underneath me, in fact she was writhing in pleasure, so I let myself drive in those last few inches.

I stayed like that for a full minute, hoping it would help her adjust.

Finally, snapping, I shut my eyes tight and let go, pulling out halfway, then shoving back in.

I dragged out again, farther this time, then plunged back in deep with one jerky swing.

I heaved nearly entirely out, biting my lip hard as I rammed back in hard.

I told her how beautiful she was, how perfect, how good her toned little ass felt to bury myself in. I barely registered what I was saying as it came out of my mouth, but it was all the blunt truth. Her flesh, any of it, wrapping around me, sucking me in, had always acted as a truth serum for me. I could not be inside of Danika and keep to myself just how damned glorious I thought she was. Never had been.

It was ironic, because I wasn't a talker during the act with anyone else.

Only her. Always her.

I dragged out and jammed in, still going slow, being careful, well, careful as could be considering.

She started coming around my fingers, I felt it, and when she let go, so did I.

With a harsh cry, I pushed her shoulder down, grabbed her hip, and started fucking in earnest, rocking in and out with great, heavy drives.

I was rough, but the rough part was quick, as I was already far gone before I'd started up the rhythm that finished me. My eyes rolled up into my head as I felt my sac filling, the great rush of my orgasm building into an eruption that shot out of me in heavy waves.

I was just starting to ejaculate when I pulled out, coming on her back, her ass, even crawling as far up as her sexy shoulder blades, watching each heaving spurt landing on her. I even painted her tattoo.

Her voice came muffled but amused. "You giving yourself a money shot back there?"

I grunted an affirmative like the caveman she liked to call me.

It took a while, but I managed to get us both upstairs, showered, and into bed.

I lay on my back, tangled with her, profoundly and irrevocably entwined. She nestled into me, and I pulled her cheek over my heart, arranging her, trapping her against me for the night.

I watched her face for a long time, until I was sure she was deeply asleep. "I love you," I told her, voice hushed, reverent.

CHAPTER TWENTY-SEVEN

DANIKA

I tried to make my expression less unpleasant than I felt when a decked out Mona came striding into my gallery just a few minutes before closing time the next day.

There goes my day, I thought, my face so stiff it would have cracked if I'd tried to fake a smile, which I didn't.

Her gown was short, gold, and heavily sequined. I'd have bet good money it was one of the many dresses she wore in Tristan's show.

She gave me a warm smile as she approached me directly.

Like we were old friends.

We were not. I nodded at her, setting my jaw, bracing myself, as she drew close.

My eyes were drawn to her enormous chest. I'd forgotten it was quite so huge. It looked extra ridiculous in her tight dress. It had a round neckline that she practically spilled out of. She had the kind of rack that should have lost at least one plastic surgeon his license, because seriously, who would agree to do that to a person? She was more than a little in danger of tipping over on the spot.

I felt sick to my stomach, and she hadn't even opened her mouth. I really didn't like dealing with this woman, or looking at her, or remembering that she existed.

"Danika! How are you?" Her voice was filled to brimming with what honestly sounded like genuine affection. I just couldn't credit it.

I didn't buy it, not for a second, but I had strong doubts that that had anything to do with her. More likely, I just didn't like her, and I was looking for things to back up that dislike.

Things other than the fact that she'd been intimate with my own personal lifetime obsession.

"Hello, Mona," I kept my voice civil, if nothing else. "What can I do for you?"

She beamed. "I just came to see if you wanted to go and grab a bite to eat, since your shift is ending, and mine doesn't start for a few more hours." Her tone was engaging and personable, as though this was the most reasonable of requests.

I didn't hesitate. "Sorry, I have plans."

"We can be quick. I actually wanted to talk to you about a few things, sensitive things that I'm sure you don't want to discuss in front of your co-workers." She glanced around, her eyes finding Kate, who was likely not even out of earshot.

It was a threat, though nothing but her words were communicating that, her tone as warm as ever.

I took a few deep breaths. It was immature, but I wanted to call Tristan and chew him out for having to deal with this. "I'll meet you in ten minutes," I told her, voice deceptively calm.

"Perfect! Bistro near the theatre?"

"That's fine."

She left, and I glared at her back.

It took me longer than ten minutes to get there, more like thirty, while I closed up I took my sweet time, because really, what was my motivation for rushing into this mess?

I honestly thought about ditching out completely, but I didn't want her to feel she'd gotten the better of me, so I went, my mood black.

She was eating when I approached, but I didn't order anything. I was leaving as soon as my pride would allow.

She set down the fork she'd been using to eat her salad, opened her mouth to speak, but we were interrupted by a couple that had seen her in the show the night before and wanted her autograph.

She smiled sheepishly after they'd left. "That almost never happens. Bizarre timing."

I just nodded. "What did you want to talk about?"

She looked vaguely uncomfortable for a moment.

Finally, some understandable reaction to something. Everything else about her was just so off to me.

"It's about Tristan."

Of course it is, I thought.

"I'm sure you know he and I are very close. I assume he's told you about our longstanding friendship."

I smiled thinly. "Strangely enough, no. You haven't come up. Though I do recall *you* telling me that you two were the best of friends, last time we met."

She blinked. "Yes, I remember that. That same meeting where you told me there was nothing rekindled between you and him. Let me ask you something, is that still the case?"

I gave her a level stare. "I really don't like to talk about my personal life with people I barely know. If you have a question about this, perhaps you should ask your very close friend, Tristan."

She was unfazed, as friendly as ever, not even a hint of temper evident in response to my words. "He's been very close-lipped lately. He's been different, edgy, less happy, for the last few weeks. This worries me very much, you see, because I've been there for him for so many years, and I know he counts on our friendship to help him through rough spots. Tell me, did you and he have a similar relationship? Did you help him through rough spots, Danika?"

I was shaking, but my voice was firm. "If that's all, I'll be going." My composure was hanging on by a very thin thread.

"Wait! I'm sorry, I didn't mean to come across so pushy, but something happened yesterday that worried me. You see, Tristan is trying to get me hired on for a different act, for a different magician, when my contract is up in two months. I don't understand this. Do you have any clue where this might be coming from? Did you tell him that you didn't want me working with him?"

The scarred, raw, burned organ in my chest got just a tiny bit less sore. He was getting Mona out of his life. I wanted to celebrate, then smash my own head into the wall for being so happy about it.

"I've come to you, woman to woman, because I think that us women handle things like this better than men do." She smiled.

I prayed for the strength not to throw something at her. "Well, that's an interesting way to look at it, but I don't share the view. Here's what I think: You should be taking this issue to the person who it involves, the man you say is your very close friend, instead of a woman you barely know who has nothing to do with your friendship with this man."

She was still unfazed. "That's fair. I don't blame you there. So are you two back together, or is this a casual type of situation?

I stood. "We're talking in circles. Take this to Tristan, please."

I left, feeling like an uncivil bitch, because even as I'd left rudely, I hadn't rattled her pleasant air.

I called Tristan when I got to my car. It was the first time I'd actually called him since this crazy train had started up again. We'd been communicating mostly through messages, but if we did talk on the phone, it had always been him calling me.

He answered on the first ring, his low voice sounding

delighted and surprised. "Danika, sweetheart. I was just thinking of you."

I paused. I hadn't been prepared to start like that. I had to get my bearings for a long moment. "I just spoke to Mona," I began.

Long pause. "Was she bothering you? What happened?"

"I think she wants to be buddies. I think she'd like us to hang out and talk about you, because we're all such *very good friends*."

Another long pause. "I'll talk to her. I'm very sorry about that."

I tried to leave it at that, but... "How would you like it if Andrew went out of his way to corner you, to talk to you *about me*?"

He cursed, long and low. "I'm very sorry. I'll handle her. Are you okay?"

I shut my eyes, letting his concerned voice wash over me. "I have a weird question for you. Last time I met her, she told me something...was she...is she your best friend?"

This thought, more than anything, was getting the best of me.

Longest pause of all. "In my whole life, there are only two people that I've *ever* called my best friend."

My eyes filled from his raw tone as much as his words.

"You and Jared."

I sucked in air. "I'd like to see you tonight," I managed to get out.

"Yes," he said quietly, vehemently. "I'll be at your house, right after my show, okay?"

I opened the door for him the second he got to it. I'd been waiting, watching out my front window like a lovesick puppy. I wore nothing but the T-shirt I'd pilfered from his house a few days prior.

He took one hot look at me and took me to bed.

There I was, topless, and him, the most gorgeous creature to ever lay his hands on me, nuzzling between my breasts, cupping them, kneading them, paying each one very special attention.

And all I could picture was Mona, nearly tipping over with those giant boobs of hers.

I had the sudden and overwhelming urge to bolt. That would have been the wise choice.

Instead, I opened my big mouth. "They're pretty tiny, huh? Compared to what you're used to, I mean."

He froze, then pushed up on his elbows, giving me a puzzled look. Puzzled and a bit glazed over. He'd definitely been into what he was doing.

I held my hands out a good foot in front of my chest, to illustrate just what I meant.

His expression stiffened, and he started shaking his head, still looming over me, one of his legs wedged high between mine.

I needed to get away and take a breather. I was embarrassed that I'd even brought it up, no matter that it'd been bothering me.

"We don't need to go there, Danika. Who I've been with, who *you've* been with, in the lost years. I don't have the stomach for it."

"I was just surprised...I mean, how did I never know that you preferred huge, fake boobs. I'm surprised you never tried to talk me into getting some."

He pushed back from me until he was sitting up, feet over the side of the bed, his hip still wedged high between my legs.

I started to push myself away, but he stilled me with one hard hand on my hip.

"You want to do this? Fine, but you're starting." His voice

was resigned and more than a touch resentful. "How long had it been since you'd fucked Andrew before we were together at the ranch?"

I flinched at the crude language, feeling somehow ashamed when I shouldn't have. Logically, I knew that. But being here, with *him* and talking about how I'd shared my body with some other man made me look at it in a way I never had before. Made me compare it to the awful way I felt when I thought about who *he'd* been with.

"How long, Danika? How many weeks, or was it *days* before you moved from his dick to mine?"

That was too much, and I pushed away, wrenching out of his hand, turning until I was on my knees on the bed, intending to leave.

His chest covered my back, pinning me in place before I got far. "I'm sorry. That was an asshole thing to say. As you can see, this is a touchy subject for me. I don't prefer huge, fake tits, if that's what you were asking. I've only had what I *preferred* with one person, and that was you, Danika. I wasn't with her because I liked her boobs. I was lonely, and she was a friend, okay? There's not much more to it than that, and I'm sorry I asked about Andrew. Truth be told, I don't want to know about you and him. Just saying his name makes me feel sick to my stomach."

I shut my eyes when I told him, "I broke up with Andrew long before the ranch. Several months, actually. We were just friends at the time. There was no overlap. Not even close."

He didn't answer with words, but his breath grew ragged as he moved tight against me. I felt him working at his fly between us.

"At the wedding, you made me think you were still together," he accused, but there was no heat in it. Even without seeing his face, I knew he felt nothing but relief at the revelation.

"I know. I'm sorry. I was using that to keep you at a

distance."

He barked out a laugh as his hands pushed my skirt up, yanking my panties down. "How did that work out for you?"

I didn't answer right away, because he was pushing his cock into me from behind. I braced myself on my hands and knees as he worked himself in hard, my eyes trying to roll up into my head with the pure sinking pleasure of it.

"Not well," I finally admitted on a gasp, when he'd buried himself to the hilt.

His only response was to slowly glide out of me, then thrust back in hard.

I whimpered, arching my back.

"This right here," he growled, pulling slowly back out. "This is what I love." One of his hands palmed my breasts and he started to move in earnest, jerking in an out in a rough rhythm. "This is what I crave, what I need. This, sweetheart, is what I prefer."

He gripped my hips, lifting them so all of the weight was off my knee, and began to work me hard.

I lowered myself to my elbows, reached a hand down and felt for him. His scrotum was slapping into me with every hard thrust, and I palmed him, cupping, scoring my nails on him lightly. I felt them tighten up when he started to come, and lowered the arm still bearing weight, going facedown into the bed so I could cup him with one hand, and rub my clit with the other.

He was still thrusting, deep in the throes, when I caught up to him, eyes rolling back in my head.

In more ways than one, I was done for.

CHAPTER TWENTY-EIGHT

Lana and I had hit it off during James and Bianca's wedding weekend, but as she lived in Maui, I didn't get to see too much of her, though we'd met for lunch twice when she'd been to town on business. The last time, she'd revealed that she was over four months pregnant, though she was barely showing. I chalked that up to supermodel genes.

I was so happy for her and excited to hear that Bianca was throwing her an impromptu baby shower the next time she came to Vegas for business.

I was surprised to learn from Bianca it was happening that very weekend, as Lana had decided to stop traveling from her island home for the rest of the pregnancy, since it was wearing on her.

Another surprise was that it was co-ed. Of all of the men in the world I'd ever met, Akira seemed the least likely to me to enjoy a baby shower. But what did I know?

Tristan was invited as well and wanted to carpool to it, but I shut that down right away. I didn't know what exactly was going on with us, and it would be awkward enough if it all fell apart to our circle of friends. There was no reason to go out of our way to advertise it now, I reasoned. We were still taking things one day at a time.

That didn't mean I didn't go out of my way to look good for the party.

I wore a smooth and fluid lavender matte jersey wrap dress. Not only did it hug every inch of my torso just so, it had a plunging neckline, and with a few swift tugs of the tie at my hip, the entire front would open.

Spectacular access, is how Tristan would describe this dress. It was just the sort of dress that would drive him out of his mind. I couldn't wait for him to see it.

I knew it was dysfunctional, but I needed constant proof that he couldn't control his need either.

Somehow, a runaway train was less Troublesome to me than a charging one.

In some respects, I'd rather if *neither* of us were driving this thing.

I didn't see him right when I got to Bianca's house, instead did a round of hellos to what was quickly evolving into my favorite crowd of people.

Bianca and Lana met and embraced me at the door, crowding me until I felt like I was being cornered by a team of Swedish bikini models. They were both so tall, and that was before their heels. I'd have loved to be able to sport some ridiculous platforms so I didn't feel quite so short, but flats were my fate, so I worked them as best I could, but I did stand up straighter around these two.

I rubbed Lana's tiny baby bump, congratulating her, feeling only the slightest twinge of pain. I'd had a lot of time to deal with the fact that this could never be me.

"Do you know if it's a boy or a girl?"

She was positively glowing. "A boy. Get a load of Akira. You could guess it was a boy just by the way he's strutting around and pounding at his chest."

I glanced around, saw him across the room, chatting with James. He did look particularly smug.

Bianca pinned a pink diaper pin to the neckline of my dress. "Now, you aren't allowed to say B-A-B-Y, but if you do, whoever calls you on it gets to have your pin. At the end, whoever has the most pins gets a prize.

I fingered the pin and nodded, thinking *Oh Lord, baby showers.* We'd all likely be forced to eat baby food by the end.

I greeted Estella with a big hug and Frankie with a long one, then moved to shake Akira's hand, and nod with a smile at James. He gave me a very warm smile in return. I still found myself amazed at the change in him over the last year. He'd always been a great guy, as far as I was concerned, but he was just so much *happier* now. It was heartwarming.

As I had the thought, Bianca returned to his side, and he snatched her to him, like he'd just been lying in wait for the chance.

I went to mingle with the partygoers that I didn't know quite so well, but was friendly with.

Camden, Lana's brother, was in a corner chatting with Bianca's stylist, Jackie. It struck me what an odd pair they made as I greeted them with handshakes and hugs.

I smiled extra wide as I ran into Stephan, coming out of a hallway that led somewhere at the back of the house. He was Bianca's best friend and just one of the nicest human beings I'd ever met. He had literally taken a bullet for Bianca. That right there told you all you needed to know about Stephan. He was nearly as obsessed with her as James was.

We shared a long hug. "How are you?" I asked him. I hadn't seen him for nearly three weeks, which was unusual for us.

"Great. But you need to come visit more."

He and his husband, Javier owned and operated a swanky bar in the casino. I usually made a point of coming and hanging out at least a few times a week.

"I'll come have a drink tomorrow or the next day. It's just been a crazy couple of weeks."

Javier approached us, dragging me into a deep hug without a word. He kissed my cheek, murmuring, "Miss you, girlie," and pulled back to smile at me.

I smiled back.

I adored Stephan, and I got along great with him. Everyone did. But Javier and I were something of kindred spirits. He was quiet and very sweet, but he had a wicked sense of humor that he didn't reveal to many. Our personalities just complemented each other, I thought.

Our quiet conversation was interrupted by two loud squeals that erupted behind me.

I turned and grinned as Marnie and Judith rushed me. They were a funny pair, but two women less likely to be close friends with the reserved Bianca I'd never met. Still, every party she threw, these two were invited and showed up.

"Is Lana happy you're here, tempting her brother?" I asked them.

Marnie rolled her eyes. "We've been warned off, and pregnant Lana scares me."

I made a face. "You poor things. What are you going to do for three whole hours with no one to hit on?"

"I've been wanting a piece of that magician," Judith said, sounding forlorn.

My expression tried to stiffen, but I smoothed it out with great willpower.

"He is *not* interested," Marnie added, making me feel instantly better. "Not at the wedding and not now. He's fucking hot though."

"He must have a girlfriend or something," Judith continued. "But I'm telling you, if he was up for it, whew, we would have some fun."

Stephan patted my shoulder. I wasn't sure what he knew about Tristan and me, but I figured it was as much as Bianca did, which was that we had a painful past together.

I'd made a full circle around the room, introducing myself to those I hadn't met before. It wasn't a huge gathering, but it was substantial.

Bianca approached me. "We've turned the living room into a onesie painting studio."

That made me smile. "If *you* paint one, it will be worth at least five figures."

She laughed. "Well, that's only because of you."

I shook my head. She would always underestimate her own talent. It was such a gift that she just did it, was compelled to do it, but I'd never overpriced her work. I'd given it exactly the value I would any work of that quality.

She glanced behind me suddenly, chewing her lip. "Um, Tristan is in there already. Just giving you fair warning. I know it can be...touchy between you two."

I nodded, feeling guilty. We were close. I should clue her in at least a little bit about the strange changes that had been taking place between Tristan and I, and I was determined to do so at a more appropriate time. I knew for a fact that Bianca didn't care for the role of hostess, so I didn't want to take up any of her time today.

"Can I help you with anything?"

She rolled her eyes, glancing back, looking for James, I presumed. I was sure he'd be along shortly. "No. There's nothing to do. James, who always has a team of people on hand, hired an *extra* team today to make sure I wasn't stressed out."

I laughed. "And that probably stresses you out," I guessed.

"Exactly. He even turned the backyard into a full on daycare for anyone that brought kids, with five lifeguards on deck. Who else does that? But what can you do? I knew he was a lunatic when I married him." There was a fond twinkle in her eye as she said it.

We shared a good chuckle, and then I moved into the living

room turned onesie painting studio.

Tristan was the only one in room. His back was to me, and he was painting away on a onesie. As I approached, I saw that he was painting a deck of cards, and it was actually good. "That's impressive," I told him quietly. "I didn't know you could paint."

He set down his brush, then held up his hands and wiggled his fingers as he turned to me. "Magic hands, remember?"

He zeroed in on the dress right when he saw me, his eyes glazing over a bit.

That just tickled me.

He shoved his hands in his pockets, just staring for a long time.

"Hey," I said with a smile.

He cocked his head to the side, running his tongue over his teeth, eyes glued to the careless knot tied at my hip. "Um, is that, hmm?"

Wow, he was speechless. My entire body flushed in pleasure. "Is that what?" I prompted.

He waved at the fastening of the dress. "Is that little tie there all that is holding that thing closed?"

I watched his face and nodded slowly. He cursed, turned on his heel, and walked away.

I couldn't stop smiling as I set to work on painting one of the many stretched out white onesies mounted on an easel.

I felt it when he came back, felt his eyes on me. He spoke very quietly behind me. "I know where a guestroom with a lock is."

I shook my head, and started moving towards the door. "Nu-uh. Not here."

He stalked me into the next room, but I evaded him, going to stand near Lana, who was busy making out with her powerhouse of a husband.

Tristan had no choice but to retreat.

Over the next thirty minutes, I proceeded to collect four diaper pins around the room by walking Javier, Jackie, Akira, and Bianca into saying the word baby.

In my peripheral, I could see that Tristan was doing the same thing. From the loud commotion that occurred, I figured that he collected pins from James, Stephan, Marnie, and Lana.

Tristan and I wound up sitting next to each other for the diaper/candy bar smelling game. This was the game where they smashed different melted candy bars up into diapers, and we had to guess which candy bars they were.

It was disgusting, and funny, and I'd never been to a baby shower where they didn't play it.

I was just sniffing something that I thought smelled and looked like a Snickers bar when Tristan's phone started ringing.

Loudly.

It was the most bizarre timing, because I'd never even heard his phone ring before, but suddenly his ringtone started playing *loud*, and it was my giggling, out of tune voice rapping, *"Pussy, pussy, pussy, that is all on my mind..."*

I blushed but couldn't help giggling as the room erupted in laughter.

"I'd swear that sounds just like Danika's voice," Bianca said, her gaze swinging to me.

"Oh that's definitely her," Frankie assured her. "I've heard that out of tune singing before. No mistaking it. It's great to learn you love pussy that much, Danika. How did I never know this?"

I shut my eyes, and shook my head, blushing down to my toes. Even so, I couldn't stop laughing. "I lost a bet," I explained.

I shot Tristan the stink eye, plotting revenge.

The bastard winked at me.

CHAPTER TWENTY-NINE

It was ten minutes later, and I was sniffing a diaper that smelled like an Almond Joy when I passed it on to Javier, then reached down into my bag, grabbing my phone.

Danika: I'm ready for my dick pic. Your ten minutes start now.

I sent it and watched Tristan as he felt his now silenced phone vibrate and reached into his pocket. He pulled it out and checked the screen.

I was already biting my lips to keep from laughing when he looked up, his eyes wide, and said loudly, "Really!? Are you fucking kidding me? You're doing this now?!"

I was doubled over laughing, but I still managed to nod.

He stormed from the room. I finally straightened to find everyone looking at me in wide-eyed shock.

Frankie was the only exception to this. She looked frankly gleeful. "Wow. So the crazy train is going full speed ahead, huh? 'Bout fuckin' time."

I waited about five minutes before I felt my phone vibrate in my hand. I had one new text. I checked it, and sure enough, I'd gotten nothing but a picture from Tristan. It was taken using the mirror in the bathroom, not thirty feet away.

He'd taken his shirt off, and unbuttoned his jeans. He was giving a very toothy grin to the mirror, one big hand fisting his big cock. He'd gotten himself hard.

I blinked. I'd done the whole thing because it was funny. I'd never imagined a dick pic could actually be hot. It looked like he was inviting me to join him in the bathroom, which he probably was.

I ignored the possible invitation, putting my phone away, my face so red I could feel it.

My eyes went nowhere but the crotch of his pants when he came strutting back into the room. At least he'd gotten a handle on his hard-on, though I wasn't going to ask how he'd done it.

He raised his brows at me expectantly as he sat down beside me again. "You get it?"

"It's not time-stamped. Do it again."

I couldn't keep a straight face when I said it and neither could he.

"You can see that it is in their fucking bathroom," he said between heaving laughs. It was a straight belly laugh for him. My absolute favorite. I would have gone through hell and .back to hear that laugh come out of him.

Had gone through it.

Would again.

"The conditions were very clear. Time. Stamp."

He looked around the room, shaking his head in laughing disbelief. He pointed at me. "This woman is evil. Never lose a bet to this woman. What, do you think I anticipated that you'd make me do the picture in this very house, and just happened to have one already taken, in that same bathroom?"

I tapped my imaginary watch. "Time's a wastin'."

"James, do you have a newspaper somewhere? I need to timestamp a picture."

James, who was across the room, chatting with Akira, gave

Tristan a thoroughly disgusted look. "Seriously? You think you need a newspaper to timestamp a photo? Get out of the stone ages, Tristan. Just hand me your phone and I'll do it."

"Trust me, you don't want to see this. Newspaper?"

James stood up and went, I assumed, to get a newspaper.

Tristan turned his laughing attention back to me. "You need to erase the other one. I did not agree to two, and you are being a snot, so I'm not giving you a freebie."

I looked around, hoping we hadn't brought too much attention to ourselves, but of course we had.

Still, I looked back at Tristan, smiling at him with my eyes. "Make me," I mouthed.

He got up and walked out of the room, headed down the hallway that led to the bathroom.

He looked agitated. The good kind of agitated.

James came back into the room carrying a newspaper.

I intercepted him, holding out my hand.

"I'll take it to him," I told him with a smile.

He looked taken aback, but he handed it over with no hesitation.

"Thank you," I said cheerily, heading down the hallway, where Tristan had disappeared.

The bathroom door was slightly ajar, light on. I stepped close to the door, as though to knock, when it swung completely open, and a smiling Tristan snatched me inside.

He'd surprised me, and just going on instinct, I smacked him in the chest with the paper I was holding.

I did it again, holding it out for him. "You better hurry. I think you have like thirty seconds left."

He shut and locked the door behind me, swung me to sit on the long bathroom counter, then started shrugging out of his shirt.

"If you don't hurry, you're still going to owe me on this bet."

With a curse, he pulled his dick out, grabbed his phone and

the paper, and took a hurried shot in the mirror.

I was still laughing when he hit send.

I stopped laughing when he moved close, his hands going to my thighs and parting them so he could step between. His eyes and his hands were all over the one knot that was keeping me dressed, but not for long, since he untied it faster than I could say, "We shouldn't. Someone will hear."

He was parting the two sides of my dress, folding it back over my shoulders. "You didn't wear this dress so I wouldn't fuck you the first chance I got." He unsnapped the front of my bra, pushing both cups to the side. "And look at this. I got a chance."

It was by all definitions a quickie. A panties shoved to the side, cock shoved in, yanking out, rocking, rutting, quickie.

A fast, swift, brief, hasty, fleeting, hurried, rushed, quickie.

A hard, rough, vigorous, brutal, crude fuck of a quickie.

That's not to say it wasn't awesome. I got off, he got off, and I could have spent the rest of the day sleeping on his chest and dreaming about how sweet life could be.

And that was the problem with quickies. They were always quick for a reason, and then you were thrust back into real life, when all you wanted to do was loll about, sated.

I washed up as well as I could, then started straightening my clothes while Tristan cleaned up. I was just tying my dress when Tristan moved close and kissed my forehead, then my cheek, then the corner of my mouth.

"Love you, sweetheart," he said quietly but vehemently, then walked out the door.

I stood there, frozen, staring into space like a lunatic, for the longest time.

The words just stayed there, right at the edge of my thought, distracting enough, but somehow hard to focus on, in the light of day.

And then, as though I'd just snapped out of it, I went back to the party and had a mostly good time.

Not all the way good, but mostly.

Mostly because there was one very bad moment when I walked out back to find Tristan performing one of his tricks for the handful of tiny kids that were having a pool party while the grownups had a baby shower. He was so good with kids. Amazing. I watched the entire thing with what could only be an infatuated smile on my face.

That wasn't the bad part, not yet.

The part that turned the day just a touch sour was when he walked up to me after moving close, and with no hesitation, he stroked his hand over my lower belly, stroked it right *there*, and he didn't have to say a word. I could read his mind.

I got away as fast as I could, going inside, trying to stay far away from him until I could breathe again.

And I did bounce back, even tricking Tristan into letting me win the diaper pin game. It was easy. I had some dirty tricks up my sleeve, too.

I grabbed a marker, a Sharpie to be exact, from one of the tubs of supplies in the living room turned painting studio, and went into the bathroom. I pulled my dress down all the way to my bra, and wrote BABY on the skin right above.

I tugged my dress back into place, dropped the sharpie back in the bin, and went in search of Tristan.

When I found him talking to Akira who was on his way to feeling up a giggling Lana, I quietly pulled him aside.

He raised his brows, looking very happy. "You ready for another round?"

I shook my head and pulled my dress down far enough to show him what I'd written.

He cocked his head to see the words, and read slowly, "Baby."

His eyes widened, neck straightened, and he pointed at me. "Wow. You *are* evil."

I held out my hand, and slowly, grudgingly, he unfastened all of his pins and gave them to me. "I hear it's a deluxe spa package," I taunted him. "I'm pretty stoked."

"I know. I was going to use it to bribe you into doing me sexual favors." He said it in a pout.

As though he needed a bribe.

It was only later, at night, as I lay in the dark that his words began to move in my head. To circle. In a crazy loop.

Here's all you need to know about crazy: Crazy's favorite shape is a circle.

Broken records, crazy urges on a loop. Any of this ring a bell? That's how crazy works, and why it keeps repeating itself.

And boy was it repeating itself now.

It was all happening again. Every insane fucking bit of it was back.

The all-consuming infatuation. Back.

The tight pull in my chest every time I looked at him. Back.

Falling asleep in his arms and still dreaming about him. Back.

Insane psychotic jealousy. Back. Doubly, because we were both afflicted with it.

Public make-out sessions, as though we were teenagers. Back.

Vibrating tongue and magic hands that made me lose all brain function. Back.

The heaven and hell of being with a man I couldn't stand to be parted from for even an hour. Back.

His smile ruining me for every other smile in the world.

The joy and the pain of being undeniably, unquestionably in love.

How could one person, who'd proven to be so inherently bad for me, so *wrong*, still be so utterly necessary for my happiness?

It wasn't fair.

I wasn't lying there thinking about Trouble. And I wasn't even thinking of how to avoid it. I simply wanted to co-exist with it.

The question was, as well-adjusted, okay, somewhat well-adjusted adults, could we turn this crazy thing healthy a second time around?

I was trying to plot it out, trying to find a game plan that could work, because I *wanted* this.

I needed goals, and rules, and a clear picture of what the future could hold.

But I *didn't* have a clear picture of where this could be going, not long-term. And that terrified me.

CHAPTER THIRTY

The first three times he brought it up, I changed the subject. I really didn't think it was a good idea.

Just the thought of going to one of his performances had me thinking of old times, bringing up long forgotten memories of the days when I'd lived to see him on stage.

The fourth time, he had a ticket for me, and he didn't seem to be taking no for an answer.

"We don't do these very often," he cajoled. "I want you to be there. It could be a year before we perform live again. It's a toned down venue. It won't be some wild audience. Everyone will be sitting down, I swear."

"Oh Tristan."

I was hopeless. Truly.

"Please. As a favor to me. It would mean a lot to me for you to be there. For support."

Just hopeless.

Why had I ever pretended that I was capable of telling him no? Utter denial, that.

I thanked the usher that showed me to my seat.

I glanced around nervously. I was in the first row, right by the stage. I knew that Frankie was attending. James and Bianca, too. But I sat alone, per my request. I knew that this was going to be an emotional undertaking for me, and I preferred to experience it without company. And besides, I knew I'd see them at the after party.

It was an intimate venue, set up for an acoustic performance that I'd been told would be aired live.

Even being in the audience made me nervous. What happened if I sneezed? Would they have to reshoot a song or just kick me out? Just thinking about it made my nose start to tickle.

It was a powerful set they played.

It was rock, there was no denying that, but still they had a soulful, gritty feel that gave the music such an emotional core. It was beautiful. Moving.

They were better than they'd ever been. *He* was better.

He could still suck the very breath out of the crowd, in fact he was more compelling as a front man than he'd been even before. His voice was better trained and age and discipline had only helped to refine it.

I couldn't take my eyes off him. I ate up the sight like a flower soaking up the sun.

The song had me tensing from the first note. It was slower than their usual style, with dark, haunting notes that made my breath catch.

He closed his eyes and began to sing. Even his voice, as he sang it, was different, too. So raw, so emotional.

I listened, entranced, and suddenly, in spite of the crowd, it felt like we were the only two people in the world.

Remember when you told me that I was yours and you were mine
Every heartbeat, every breath,
Our love was perfect, our vows were sacred
And, oh sweetheart, you know I tried so hard to tow that line,
* * *

But there was a poison in my heart,
And a darkness in my mind
I wasn't there when you were drowning
Though I'd give my soul to take it back
You had to leave me behind

Looking back, over the years of empty space,
Through the harshest rearview mirror,
Remembering the things I put you through
Now left to wonder, who's come to take my place

When I looked at you the world dissolved
My poison cured, my darkness light
I never did deserve you, sweetheart
But in your arms my wrongs were solved

My head was lowered, hands clenched, face wet with tears.
And somehow, in spite of the agony of it, my body swayed
gently to the music, as though it was casting some spell on me,
or curing some ill. Therapy via concert. That was a new one.

Though it echoes loudest in my tortured heart
That night was not my only crime
Despite all the ways I failed
I still longed to make things right
Somehow we ran out of time

But there was a poison in my heart,
And a darkness in my mind
I wasn't there when you were drowning
Though I'd give my soul to take it back
You had to leave me behind

Somewhere, in the great expanse of space,

There is a home where souls reside,
Yours and mine were joined together
I have not moved from that place,

God help me, I'll never move from that place

But there was a poison in my heart,
And a darkness in my mind
I wasn't there when you were drowning
Though I'd give my soul to take it back
You had to leave me behind

You had to leave me behind
How did you leave me behind?

The music faded down to just one soft guitar rift and Tristan's passionate croon.

Everything you promised, everything I need
What I'm willing to give to you is what I want from you.
Can't you do that for me, sweetheart? Isn't there enough of you left?

I'd told him that exact thing once. I'd had no clue he'd remembered it; he'd been so high when I'd said it to him.

"What did you think?" he asked gently, after the concert was done, the theatre emptied.

I'd just been sitting there, still and silent, while everyone else had filed out.

"That last part didn't even rhyme," I told him through my tears.

He laughed, tugging me out of my chair and into his chest. "Are you mad at me?" he asked, face buried in my hair.

I didn't know what I was.

All out of escape routes, my twisted brain told me.

Conquered, my traitorous, white flag waving heart told me, but it didn't get a vote, since it had always, *always* been on *his* side.

"I take it you have a hand in the lyrics now?" I asked, trying to brazen through my shaky voice. "Unless Kenny wrote that and if he did, that's really awkward."

"Oh, you thought that song was about me and you?"

I punched him in the arm, and he laughed harder, and held me tighter.

"Yeah, I've taken up songwriting, though Kenny still writes the bulk of them."

We stood there for a long time in silence before I looked up at him and spoke, "I'm so proud of you. You were always so talented. It is a daunting thing to stare into potential like that and try to do it justice. You have."

His expression tightened, and he buried his face in my neck.

That had gotten to him.

I patted his back soothingly.

"My only criticism is that you didn't take off your shirt," I told him to lighten his mood. "That used to be my favorite part of every show."

It startled a laugh out of him. "Did I really used to take my shirt off at every show?" he asked, like he couldn't remember.

That made my chest tight, thinking about all of the memories he'd lost. "Close enough," I said lightly.

Looking up at him, seeing the way he looked back, I started to just *freak*.

I took two steps back away from him.

I'd tried to lock my feelings away in some corner of my heart and mind.

I hadn't forgotten about them, had never failed to realize they were there, but I'd convinced myself that if I could just keep myself from looking directly at them, they would hold no sway over me.

But now, now they were creeping up on my peripheral, becoming brighter, more clear, with each passing breath, until the urge to look, the pull of it, consumed more of my thoughts than just looking would, I was sure.

Even when I'd known better, I'd just decided that those feelings could be put off. But how long could a thing like this be put off?

I was shaking, head to toe.

Slowly but inexorably, I was coming undone.

I couldn't hold it together. Not for another day. Not for another minute.

It was happening. In spite of how I fought it, some steady unraveling was happening inside of me, had been happening. It was nearing its finish, and I *was not prepared*.

Tristan moved to put his hands on my shoulders, but I warded him off with both of mine.

"Oh Danika," he said softly.

I started shaking my head vehemently.

"Tell me, sweetheart. Whatever it is, I'll fix it."

I closed my eyes, my face crumbling.

"Oh sweetheart," he said, softer now, closer now.

"I feel so lost."

He took my hands in his. "Not anymore. I'm right here. I've got you."

"There is this hollow place inside of me, where my faith in you used to be. I am so full of fear, and I *do not know* how to let myself trust you again. I don't have the strength to do this. Not again."

"I've got enough for both of us." He moved closer, wrapping me in his arms. "It's about time I got a turn letting *you* lean on *me*."

He'd set me adrift, so very long ago, and I had wandered into deepest waters, with depths far too vast for me to navigate alone.

And here he was, swimming out to save me. Had he been following me all the while? Had I been so blind?

Still, even knowing he was rescuing me, some part of me had to fight him. "What are you doing to me? Don't you know I can't take this, Tristan?"

He groaned and pulled me even closer. "You can. You don't think you can trust me again, and I understand that, but you need to learn. However long it takes, you need to learn that being with me won't turn out the way it did before. I won't let it."

I shook my head, but he was kissing my jaw, my neck, behind my ear, and I didn't stop him. "You don't seem to understand, Tristan. I don't think it will turn out how it did before, because all of the damage has already been done. There's not enough left of me to break this time."

"No, you're wrong."

Of course he couldn't know what I was referring to, because I hadn't told him, hadn't built up the stomach for it yet.

Even now, when every single defense of mine was disarmed, I couldn't find the courage to tell him.

"And I won't be doing any breaking," he continued vehemently, "I swear it."

My arms had gone limp at my sides but I raised them now, wrapping them around his neck.

"It's not only about breaking *me*." I took a very deep breath. "I saw it with my own eyes, Tristan," I told him quietly, wretchedly. "That day at the café, that last time we met up, after the accident. After you'd moved on from me, and you were happy, laughing, healthy. That was when *I* moved on."

"Oh, Danika," he breathed.

"I saw how you were without me, how you'd gotten so much *better* with me out of your life, and that was when I really let you go."

"Oh, Danika," he said emotionally.

"How can we be so good for each other in so many ways, and so bad in just as many others?"

"We were never bad for each other. *Never.* That's not what happened with us."

"What did then? Explain your reasoning to me here."

"*I* was bad for us. I was bleeding out. I'm sure you caught on, but I was fucking wrecked by what happened to Jared and everything after, well, I went into free fall, but don't put that on us. That was on *me.* All of it. Every fucking ounce of it."

"Oh Tristan. That's just not true. I changed too, with you. I enabled you. I made you worse, not better."

"Oh, Danika." His voice was still gentle but chiding.

"Don't 'Oh, Danika' me. I obviously couldn't help you. I tried and tried—"

"And you thought this was your job? To *help* me? You thought this was *your* responsibility?"

"Well, yes. But everything I tried only seemed to make you worse."

"Oh, sweetheart—"

"Don't call me that."

"Sweetheart," he emphasized. "No one can help a person in that condition. Sometimes, if we're really lucky, we come out of it, and we help ourselves, and we do this *because* of the people we love. You were not responsible for making me *worse.* But I'll tell you one thing, it's a fact that you were responsible for making me better. I'd resigned myself to dying. That I could have handled. But when I saw what I'd done to you—"

"That wasn't on you."

"That may be your reality. You're entitled to see it how you need to, but I can only see it one way. What happened to you was on me, *is* on me, and when I realized that I wasn't only hurting myself, was in fact hurting you even more than I was my own numb mind, I found the motivation I needed to stop using, to stop trying to check out of my life. *That's* on you."

CHAPTER THIRTY-ONE

I was just finishing up at work the next day when he called.

"Let's go out tonight. I want to take you someplace special," Tristan's deep voice started purring into my ear before I'd even managed to get a 'hello' out.

I took a deep breath. "I can't tonight." After the fit he'd thrown about a lunch with Andrew, I knew to brace myself for the worst.

There was a long pause on the other end. "Why not?"

He'd never been a shy one.

"I'm going out to dinner with a friend of mine."

"Is this a private dinner, or can I come along?"

I thought about that dynamic. I didn't think Dermot would like him. I couldn't see the two men getting along well enough for a quiet meal. They were both too overprotective of me in completely different ways. "It's just kind of a monthly thing. It's complicated, but I don't think you'd get along with my friend. I'll tell him about you. Maybe next time, after I've given him fair warning."

Of course, he only heard one part of my statement.

"*Him*?"

"Yes. We've been over this. I have male friends."

"Are you going on *a date* tonight?"

I sighed. Caveman post therapy was still caveman. "No. I am going out to dinner with a friend." I debated telling him that Dermot was my brother, but decided to ask Dermot about that. His father was still married to his poor mother, and I didn't want to cause any problems in his family, so I kept it under wraps. Tristan could keep a secret, so I knew I'd be telling him about it, but I wanted Dermot's go ahead first. It didn't feel like my secret to tell.

"A *male* friend. That's a date. What's his name? Where does he live? I bet I can take him."

I giggled, though he was only half joking. "It would only be a date if we were romantically involved, which we're not. Listen, it's complicated, but I promise to explain it to you, after I talk to my friend about it."

He was so distraught after that I almost canceled.

He wasn't yelling, or screaming, or even trying to talk me out of it.

He just became so quiet and withdrawn on the other end that I could barely stand it.

"Okay, you know what? You need to knock it the hell off. Do you see me telling you that you can't be friends with Mona anymore? No. And you've slept with her. I have never slept with Dermot."

"His name is Dermot," he interrupted dully.

"Yes, Dermot, who I would never sleep with, not in a *million* years. Not even if we were characters in *Game of Thrones*."

That drew him out of it, or confused him out of it. "What the hell does that damn show have to do with anything?"

I'd recently started making him watch it, and he went from grudgingly liking it to hating it from one episode to the next. He was only on the first season though. If I just got him through the one, I knew he'd be as hooked as I was.

I smirked. "You'll figure it out, eventually."

I tried to tell him goodbye.

"I want to come with you," he growled into my ear.

I took a deep breath. Why on earth did I still have such a hard time telling him no?

"Boundaries, Tristan."

He let me off the line, but I knew he wasn't happy.

Dermot and I never told anyone that we were related. We never had to. Neither of us were answerable to anyone, so the world just thought we were close friends, or so I'd assumed.

It hadn't occurred to me that my meet-ups with Dermot looked like dates. I'd never had to worry about it before.

Andrew had been the kind of boyfriend that was understanding to a fault. He'd never even questioned that I often liked to go out to dinner with another man.

"I'm seeing someone," I told Dermot, after we'd ordered our food.

He looked surprised but not displeased. "Well, that's great. Is it serious?"

My mouth twisted. "Like a heart attack. Whether we have a shot at anything lasting is another matter entirely. I'll keep you posted."

"Have you known him long?"

It was the strangest thing. I'd been raised with Dahlia, but Dermot was so much easier for me to open up to. It'd been like that with us from the start.

And somehow, I found myself telling him our story, the long version—The Saga of Tristan and Danika.

The battles and the victories.

The defeats and the triumphs.

The tragedies and the trials.

Somewhere in the middle, I had him tearing up, which I'd never seen him do, and I tried to tell it all with less dramatic flair, but it was what it was.

"Wait, so you haven't told him that you can't...?" he asked, somewhere near the end.

I looked down at my lap. "I don't know how."

"I'm so sorry, Danika."

I shrugged it off. "Anyway, do you mind if I tell him that you're my half-brother? I thought I should ask first, because of, well, you know. And as I'm sure you've gathered, he's the insanely jealous type. He was none too pleased when he heard I was going to dinner with a man."

"I don't mind at all. I don't keep our relationship under wraps, Danika. I'm sorry you thought that I did."

"Well, I just thought, because of your mother, you'd want to keep it secret."

"You're not a secret, you're a person. My parents' mess of a marriage is their business, and it will never affect the fact that you are my sister."

That warmed my heart. He was a good brother.

I went straight to Tristan's after dinner.

He was still tense and upset, but nothing like he'd been when I'd gone to lunch with Andrew.

"Okay, let me have it," he started in on me right away. "What's the big mystery about this buddy of yours?"

"He's my brother."

That deflated all the sass right out of him. It was kind of nice. I had a brief moment of wishing I could bottle that ability up. It would make a good superpower.

I found myself storytelling for the second time that night, giving Tristan the full rundown on my deadbeat dad.

"Your dad *hit* on you?" he asked, shocked.

"You saw my mother. I look just like her. I guess he has a type."

"Don't try to pretend that is even remotely normal! I ever see that guy, I'm kicking his ass. Period. That is happening. Fuck, I think I've met that dude. Un-fucking-believable."

I thought that about summed it up.

He started tugging me through his house, up the stairs,

straight to his bedroom. He cornered me against his unorthodox bed and started stripping me. "You just tortured me for hours," he said, voice low and gravelly. "Now it's my turn."

TRISTAN

She loved to make cracks about what she called my 'kinky' bed. I thought it was time I showed her what it could do.

I stripped her down to her little tiny thong and blindfolded her. I looked my fill of that intoxicating sight before I took her into the bed and made her stand.

I fastened her arms above her with padded leather cuffs that attached to the ceiling of the sturdy bed.

And then I went to work on her with my mouth, starting at her jaw, working my slow way down her neck, her collarbone, spending extra time sucking at her puckered nipples. Gripping her breasts into two perfect handfuls, I rolled them against my tongue, kneading.

I loved her body. In fact, it was a little alarming how obsessed I was with it, the vast amount of hours I'd spent fantasizing about this right *here*.

I fisted my cock as I nuzzled into her navel. I was loud with it, and when she heard me working at my own fist, she moaned and squirmed.

I knelt in front of her and buried my face between her thighs, throwing her legs over my shoulders. I shoved her panties to the side and went to town, using every tongue trick I had to bring her, again and again.

And then I went to work on her with my hands.

When I finally stood up and started fucking her vigorously, she was pliant under my hands.

After I came, I just kept pumping into her, letting her milk at me for a long time.

This right here. Heaven.

"I love you," I told her, not in the throes of passion, but in the clear moment after. I would keep telling her, conditioning her to it. I'd keep trying forever, if I had to, to make her trust me again.

I knew she still loved me. I could see it now, even if she was still in the throes of denial. She didn't have to say it in words. She spoke to me in so many other ways. Her love spoke to me in every surrendering line of her body.

It spilled out of her pure silver eyes every time she looked at me.

She was mine again.

And, even when she hadn't wanted me, when I'd lost all faith, I'd always, *always* been hers.

I took her down and arranged her on her back. I peeled off her panties and parted her legs. She was so satiated that she was as good as limp, so deliciously pliant that it made my brain go a little fuzzy with the heady pleasure of it.

My fingers slid along the soft skin of her thigh as I straightened, catching one of her sexy little feet and digging into it, rubbing until, even in her complete relaxed limpness, she began to make little writhing motions on the bed.

I kissed the arch of her foot, then her slender ankle. She was so delicate and soft under my hands that every touch I gave her held a shaky restraint.

I loved this body, this slender waist, these lean hips, her slim thighs. I adored that what appeared so dainty had a core of steel so strong, so relentlessly solid, that it was the only thing I'd found on this earth fit to cast my lot with, to make my home.

She humbled me to this day.

My hands were reverent, my lips worshipful as I made my trembling way up her trembling body, so thankful for every touch she allowed me that I was giddy with it, *shaking* with it.

Because, whether she would admit it or not, every time we gave in to this hunger, this unforgiving passion, we showed our true feelings to each other. She couldn't give herself to me without showing me her vulnerability, and I couldn't take her without revealing my utter devotion, my forever love.

I never could keep the filthy diatribe in when I got my hands on her perfect little body, but more and more, the words were as desperately emotional as they were dirty.

"How did we do without this, sweetheart?" I asked against her satiny smooth belly. "How could we think that was an option?" I nuzzled along her ribs into the underside of one plump breast. "How could I ever stop this? You know we can't go back now, don't you? We can't go back to that."

She didn't answer me. I hadn't expected her too. I knew she was far past the point of a coherent sentence. I'd always loved her smart mouth, but at times like these, I liked it even better when it was incapable of forming whole words.

I took off her blindfold and covered her. I took her again, hungrily, desperately, like a man starved. Even as I was twitching inside her, still shaking from my release, I felt that hunger.

Just on the edge of sleep, I caught it. "Fucking Game of Thrones," I muttered.

She laughed beside me.

We fell asleep entwined, and I woke up still wrapped around her from behind. In fact, my hard cock was right in the middle of trying to find an entrance before I'd even blinked awake.

I sat up, rolling her to her back. It was like eyeing up a feast. I didn't know where to start.

Her jaw was slack in sleep, her lips parted. My hard-on told me very clearly to start there.

I climbed up her body, and managed to dig one knee into the bed next to her head, the other stretched clear of her body. I pushed my tip between those inviting lips, trying to go slow, but once I got to her throat, a knee-jerk reaction had me shoving in a little too forcefully.

I gagged her twice before she pushed me away, laughing.

"You're too big for that angle," she told me.

She made a good point.

"I wasn't quite awake yet when I thought of that."

She pushed at me, and I sprawled out on my back for her. "Next time, just wake me up."

Her head started bobbing, and I gripped her hair. "Anything you say."

CHAPTER THIRTY-TWO

TRISTAN

I always felt the date approaching like a magnet, my mind constantly pulled to it.

This year was a little better. I got out the black wristband and put it on with a lighter heart than I'd had, well, since his death.

Having Danika back in my life helped me with this, there was no question.

Even so, I'd tried to talk to her about it, tried to tell her what was coming up, and hadn't found the voice to do it.

It was the morning of and I'd slept over at her place. I was in her kitchen, sipping coffee and staring off into space, when she finally realized something was off.

She studied me for a while, checked her phone for the date, I think, and then approached me looking contrite.

"Oh, Tristan," she said softly, wrapping her little body around my big one. "I am so sorry."

I kissed the top of her head.

"I'll call in sick to work. Tell me how you handle this day."

"Frankie usually comes over, and Cory and Kenny, if they're around. We tell stories about him. Good stories. We watch all the videos I have of him. We never focus on the bad."

We got dressed and went to my house. Frankie and Kenny

showed up at noon. Cory was out of town.

I baked a ridiculous amount of cookies, keeping Danika hostage in my kitchen the entire time.

We all sat down in my living room and talked about Jared. I started.

I held up a chocolate chip cookie. "Jared's favorite. He's actually the reason I learned to bake. As a kid, he had us all wrapped around his little finger, me, my mom, his dad." I looked down at my hands. "This one time he got hurt. I'm not even sure how it all went down, but he was horsing around with Dean in his room, and wound up falling out of the second story window. I was twelve, and I was supposed to be watching him. It was terrifying, but he hadn't broken anything. I think he was just scared, but he wouldn't stop crying. He was inconsolable, and the only thing that got him out of it was the promise of cookies. We didn't have any cookies, but we always had baking supplies, so I learned to bake cookies that day. He loved them so much that he started to fake getting hurt, just so I'd bake. I never minded. It was never a secret; I'd have done anything for that kid."

How do you recover from a loss like that? One day at a time was the only way I knew how. We'd been so close that he was still a part of me, always would be.

Danika, who'd been sitting directly to my right, hugged me hard. I threw my arm around her. Having her here, right now, meant *everything*, and I savored it, even amidst the bittersweet reminiscing.

Kenny went next. "It was Jared and I that originally started the band. We both picked up the guitar, but he was always so much better than I was. I was so impressed with that kid. He was five years younger than the rest of us, and he put me to shame, talent wise. He never had an ego about it, though, he just enjoyed it. He had the purest love for his craft."

Frankie was bawling by the time we got to her. She didn't

hide her grief and that had always made it easier for me to express mine.

"He was just the nicest," she began. "I've thought about this a lot. I spent so much time with him. We had a lot of fun together. And in all of that time, I can't ever remember him saying one negative thing about anybody. How is that even possible? He was just so *good*. I miss being around him. I miss his smiling face, and how he'd come to me when he needed help solving a problem, no matter how silly the problem. To Jared, the sweetest angel in heaven." She took a big bite of her cookie, like it was a toast. You had to get creative around alcoholics like me.

I held up my cookie like a toast, then took a big bite.

I hadn't expected Danika to say anything, I don't know why, but of course, she did. She'd always had a way with words, a way to shape them into something that could bring me comfort.

Her mouth quirked up in a half smile before she began. "He used to call me sis. I loved that so much. And I loved talking to him on the phone. For hours. He was the best talker. And listener." She bent down and reached into her bag, pulling out a flip phone. The thing was a relic.

Her smile died, turning into the face she made when she was trying hard not to cry. "This thing can't keep a charge for ten minutes, but I'll never get rid of it. I didn't find this until after he passed."

She pushed some buttons, and then the sound of Jared's voice came out of the phone. "Hey sis. I know you're upset with him, but trust me when I tell you he regrets everything he said. Just give me a call. We'll talk it out, okay? The Vega brothers love you, sis. Never doubt it."

That one gutted the room, and no one talked for a long while. Even with the way it'd hurt, it'd still felt so damn good to hear his voice.

"Remember that night he and I got completely blitzed at the

sportsbook in the Cavendish casino?" Danika finally spoke to say. "We had so much fun. He was always so much fun."

Frankie smiled, mascara trails all over he pretty face. "I remember that night. You were off with Jared, while Tristan and I complained, for hours, about how crazy women are. Your name might have come up a time or two, in the crazy column."

She rolled her eyes. "I'm sure I took up most of the crazy column. Hell, I probably had my own page."

I'd pieced together every video ever taken of Jared years ago. There were only a few of us as kids, but thank God there had been several years worth of camera phones before he'd passed. That made up the bulk of it. We watched them all, then told some more stories.

It was a good day of remembering. It hurt, sure, it would never stop hurting, but it was better with her there. Everything was.

I'd missed a few calls over the hours we'd been reminiscing and had a few messages. I grimaced when I saw that one was from Mona, and I almost just erased it. I'd gotten her contracted to another act in two months, and she was not happy about it. But she'd been acting strange since Danika and I had gotten back together, and it made me realize not to trust her, to in fact keep my distance, and that's what I was doing.

Still, I listened to it, because it was unusual for her to leave a message. I was a little stunned at what I heard. And sad. What were the odds, on today of all days?

I went to sit back with the group. "Tony Biello just died," I said numbly. I knew the numbness wouldn't last. He'd been a mentor to me, a father figure. He'd been scheduled to make a guest appearance in a few weeks. "I guess I shouldn't be this shocked. He retired his act because his health was bad."

Danika hugged me hard. I'd never talked to her about Tony, but I had a feeling she knew everything. She'd been more secretive about it than I had, but we'd both been keeping tabs on each other over the years.

CHAPTER THIRTY-THREE

DANIKA

I showed up at his house already dressed in a conservative black sheath dress, my hair pulled back in a chignon, my makeup neutral and soft. I was in full funeral mode.

I didn't want to go.

I felt bad about it, but I still didn't feel right about going. Mona always tried to be pleasant, but her father had just died, she had to be hurting, and I just didn't think she'd want me to be there.

I searched for the words to explain this to Tristan without sounding like an insensitive jerk about the whole thing. He knew I didn't like Mona.

As though to pre-empt my attack of the flake-outs, he came to the door just shrugging into his dress shirt. It was still unbuttoned, and I ran my hand over his bare skin. The crisp white against his tanned, tatted skin was just too delicious not to touch.

He caught my hand and pulled me inside his house, and then tight against him, kissing my forehead. "Thank you for coming to this. It means a lot to me to have you with me right now, and I know you don't like Mona, so I'm doubly grateful that you're willing to do this."

I hugged him hard, feeling like a royal bitch for even considering backing out. And for being so obvious about disliking Mona. She'd really done nothing to earn it, aside from sleeping with a man I wasn't speaking to at the time. (Logic meet feelings. The two of you will never see eye to eye. Let the lifelong catfight commence.)

"Of course. Want me to pick out your tie?" Of the two of us, I was the only one that cared enough to try at fashion.

"Yes. Thank you."

No matter how I tried to look at it, I didn't like the woman. The fact that she seemed to like me just fine didn't sit right. I was torn between thinking she was completely, convincingly fake, or worse, that she was just that bigger of a person, because I couldn't act like I convincingly liked her for even a minute. It was all I could do to be civil. Though, with her dad recently passed, I knew that even I would have no problem offering her sympathy today.

But, fake or not, bigger person or not, I just couldn't convince myself that she'd want to deal with me today.

The point was moot, since Tristan had expressed his need for me to be there. I never was any good at telling him no.

I went straight to his closet and picked out a soft gray tie for him. He stood very still for me while I knotted it, his eyes closed, head tilted slightly back.

"I like this, you knotting my tie," he said quietly. "But I'm afraid to ask where you learned to do it."

My hands paused for a moment, then continued to tie the knot.

His breath shuddered out. "Andrew," he guessed correctly. His mouth twisted down on the name, like he couldn't say it without scowling.

I finished, started straightening his collar, smoothing it, and then running my hands along it, just touching for the sake of feeling. "Don't. You wound up with kinky cage beds, and learned to tie knots; meanwhile I learned to knot a tie. Rehashing this stuff, over and over, isn't healthy. And if this is going to work, it has to be healthy."

He nodded, mouth still shaped into a deep frown. "You're right, but it's not easy. I'm still...processing. I need a grace period for adjustments."

"Me too. Trust me, going to your girlfriend's dad's funeral is not something I ever thought I'd be doing."

"She's not my girlfriend. She never was my girlfriend."

I really didn't want to get into it, but I couldn't let that one go. "Well, she isn't now, but you can hardly say that she *never* was."

"You know what? You're right, let's not talk about this right now. I'm in a shitty mood, and we don't need to actively work at making it shittier."

I winced. I'd forgotten for a minute what was going on today. He was putting a good friend in the ground today. I needed to remember to be more soothing of a presence.

I put my arms around his waist, laying my cheek on his chest. "I'm sorry. How you holding up?"

"I'm doing okay, just in a foul mood."

"That's understandable. Would it help if I promised not to antagonize you for the rest of the day?"

He squeezed me, kissing the top of my head. "Frankly, your antagonism has never been the problem. In fact, I kind of like it, for the most part. You leaving is my problem, so it would help if you promised to stick around for the next few days. I could use the company."

I thought this was a result of all of his therapy. Back in the day, he'd needed me plenty, but he'd never been able to communicate in such a specific way before. "You got it. I have to work tomorrow, but I could bring a few things over, stay at your place, if you want."

"I want. Thank you."

"Of course. Anytime you need me."

"I always need you," he said solemnly.

I shut my eyes and swayed against him, feeling like I was floating. Whether it was floating on a cloud, or floating unmoored, in the middle of the ocean, I could not have said.

The verdict was still out.

He pulled back after a time to study my face.

I just blinked at him.

I tried to get my bearings, but I had no time to recover, not from being back on solid ground, hell, not even from being off it.

The funeral was an ordeal, though I didn't breathe a word of complaint. Funerals weren't supposed to be pleasant, and who could be picky about the method of unpleasantness, really?

It was a huge event, and the itinerary was daunting. There was a private eulogy with close friends and family, followed by an open casket to the public, where anyone could pay their respects for about five hours. I wasn't judging, but I would have found that to be a difficult way to handle things, if I'd been his family. For their part, they were being generous with what remained of him.

Mona seemed remarkably composed. She was holding court at the entrance to the casket room. Her hair was pulled back tight from her face, her makeup heavy. She was conservatively turned out, from the neck up. The neck down, now, that was a different story. She was dressed in a sexy black dress that had a slit up the thigh, and showed off enough cleavage that I was surprised she'd worn it to a funeral.

Maybe they didn't make dresses that could carry that much boob without some of it spilling out, I thought snidely. Yes, I knew it was bitchy.

The only telltale sign of her grief at first sight were her slightly red eyes, and the fact that she threw herself into Tristan's big arms the second she saw him.

I determined not to say a word. They'd been close friends for years, and I didn't blame her for needing a hug. There was endless comfort to be found in Tristan's arms. I never imagined I'd been the only one to notice.

"I'm very sorry for your loss," I told her.

She didn't look at or acknowledge me, throwing her arms around Tristan's neck, and burying her face against his throat.

Tristan patted her back, sending me a helpless sort of look.

I gave a little shrug. It was awkward. I didn't know what to do either, so I gave them space.

I offered my condolences to the rest of Tony's family, who all stood in a line. I didn't go to the casket. I didn't think it was necessary.

I was infinitely relieved when I saw a familiar face in the form of Bianca. I rushed to her, giving her a quick hug.

She looked good in black, her light skin luminous. She barely wore a scrap of makeup, just a touch of mascara and some light pink gloss on her lips, but she didn't need any more than that. She was stunning, with those incredible icy blue eyes of hers. They were hauntingly pale and expressive. Her all black attire only seemed to enhance the effect.

"Hey," she said in a hushed voice, a world of affection in that one neutral word.

"Did you know Tony?"

She shook her head. "No, I'm just here for James."

I glanced around. "Where is James?"

"Talking to the family."

I spotted him even as she spoke. He was patting Tony's wife's hand while she spoke to him earnestly, tears running down her cheeks.

"You're here with Tristan?" she asked in that soft-spoken way of hers, studying my face. I knew we confused the hell out of everyone. No one could ever keep track of if we were even speaking to each other.

"Yes. I didn't know Tony either."

"Let's sit down. I don't think anyone cares if we make our rounds and mingle here or not."

I smiled at the way she said it, as though mingling were the bane of her existence. "Does James make you mingle often?" I asked.

Her nose wrinkled. "He tries. Now ask me if he succeeds."

I bit my lip, trying not to smile. "I don't think I need to."

"I guess you could say I mingle if by that you mean, does he stay glued to my side wherever we go. He has to talk to people. They come up to him everywhere. I don't see why that means that I should have to talk to them all or listen to them, for that matter."

"You make a good point."

"Where *is* Tristan?" she asked, looking around.

"In the foyer with Mona."

"Oh."

The way she said it made a corner of my mouth turn up. I shot her an amused look.

"You're surprised that I left him out there with her," I guessed, my voice a low whisper.

"Yeah, that's what the 'oh' meant," she whispered back.

"It's her dad's funeral. I'd feel like a bitch if I got jealous about her grabby hands today."

"Just how grabby are they?" She sounded intrigued.

"I have a feeling you'll get to see for yourself.

As I spoke, Mona and Tristan passed by our seats, going to the front row.

Mona was walking with both arms wrapped around his waist, her head on his shoulder.

I had the uncharitable thought that she was milking this for all it was worth.

Tristan sat down with her, his head bent down to hers. He was speaking quietly, his voice too soft for me to hear from this distance.

It seemed to take a lot of time and effort, but he disentangled himself from her, and stood, striding to where Bianca and I sat, and taking a seat close at my right.

"Hey," he said to Bianca with a small smile.

She smiled back. "Hey."

"I'd hug you, or shake your hand, but James threatened to put a hit out on me if I so much as touched you with my pinkie."

She bit her lip to hide a smile. "I think you made that up."

"Keep living in that dream world of yours, where James isn't a nutcase, but if you ever get over the Stockholm syndrome, just signal to one of us, and we'll get you out. Wink three times if you want us to help you escape."

She covered her mouth, her eyes twinkling. "I'm going to tell him you said that."

"I know you are. I look forward to it."

He turned to me, his face turning serious. "Tony's family has asked me to sit up front. Would you like to come with me, or are you more comfortable sitting with James and Bianca?"

I didn't hesitate. The idea of sitting in the family row at a funeral of a man I'd never met made me highly uncomfortable. "I'll stay with Bianca."

He just nodded and gave me a quick kiss on the cheek before getting up and going back to Mona.

I didn't realize Frankie was there until she was stroking a hand over my hair as she moved past me down our aisle.

She and Bianca were friends, but Bianca's hair didn't get the same treatment. James had very strange rules about who could touch Bianca, even if it was just casually.

For instance, I could hug her, or kiss her cheek, or stroke her hair right now, and he wouldn't be bothered. At least, I didn't think he would.

If Frankie or Tristan did any of those things, though, it was a fact he wouldn't take it so well.

James was crazy about Bianca. Literally crazy.

Whatever strange rules they had for each other, though (and there were a lot) it seemed to make perfect sense to them, and no one could say it wasn't working.

I knew more about the inner workings of their relationship than most. Bianca had opened up about it over the many hours I'd posed for her.

For instance, she had a gorgeous choker around her neck that I'd just thought was an obscenely expensive piece of jewelry. I'd learned that not only did James refer to it as her collar, but he never let her take it off, in fact it was locked on, and he had the key.

Apparently, it was a very big deal.

But who could really knock their methods?

I couldn't, not when I'd seen firsthand the way they looked at each other.

Estella arrived at our row next, and she hugged me *and* the untouchable Bianca.

I knew what that was about. Frankie had me well versed in BDSM etiquette. Estella and Bianca were both subs, which made all the difference when it came to friendly, casual touching.

Estella sat next to Frankie who sat beside James, who took up possessive residence on Bianca's other side, his arm thrown over her shoulders. You couldn't have slid a credit card between the two of them, he was plastered so close to her.

And then there was me, on the end of the chain, watching as Tristan got felt up at a funeral.

CHAPTER THIRTY-FOUR

James leaned forward, aiming his electric gaze in my direction. Of course, he looked good in black. James looked amazing in everything. "He holding up okay?" he asked me.

I nodded, eyes wide.

"Are *you* holding up okay?" he questioned, looking concerned.

I nodded. "I didn't even know Tony."

"That's not what I meant. In general, are you okay?"

My mouth twisted ruefully, but I just nodded. I had to bite my tongue to keep from making any comments about what was going on in the front row.

But seriously, it was ridiculous. Mona was as plastered to Tristan as James was to Bianca. And there was so much ownership in it, as though it was the most natural thing in the world, as though she did it every day, as though he was hers.

Tristan had his arm around her, and seemed to just be taking it in stride as she nuzzled into his chest. I didn't even think she was crying, so it looked more like canoodling than it did mourning.

I told myself I'd never lost a father, hell, never even had one to lose, so I could hardly decide what form Mona's grief should take.

Even so, I was upset, and that upset was growing into something stronger by the second.

I must have been showing some outward sign of what I was feeling, because Bianca, who was not normally demonstrative, reached over and grabbed my hand, squeezing it comfortingly.

Tristan kept turning his head, trying to catch my eye, but every time he did it, I looked away, pretending to pay attention to the ongoing eulogy speech by Tony's tearful wife.

Finally, I stopped glancing their way altogether, which is how I should have handled things from the beginning.

Finally, Tristan got up to say a few words, going largely over Tony's mentorship and career and how it had affected his own life and work.

It was a touching speech, and I marveled at how polished he was at public speaking. When I'd first met him, he'd been a good performer, but I thought this new articulate speaker part of him must have come from performing in front of a large audience five nights a week.

All of Tony's grown children, of which there were four, got up and spoke briefly about what they had most enjoyed doing with their father. It was all very moving.

Even Mona's story about how she'd grown up to become a magician's assistant because of her father's influence was quite touching.

His children seemed to genuinely adore him, and a man couldn't ask for a better sending off.

I stayed with Bianca and James after the ceremony was done. Tristan made it over to us eventually, still with a clinging Mona glued to his side.

Tristan opened his mouth, to say something to me, I presumed, when Mona opened hers, speaking before he could. "Tristan, will you ride with the family to the reception? My mother wanted me to ask you. It would mean a lot to us, in our time of need."

She looked at me while she said it, and I had a hard time thinking nice thoughts about her as she stared at me and made a guilt-play for the love of my life.

Tristan sighed, expression neutral. "Do you mind riding with the family, Danika?" he asked.

Oh, Lord, I didn't want to do that.

"She can come with us," Bianca butted in quietly. There was something about her that made it so hard to tell her no, possibly because she never spoke up unless she meant to follow through. I'd seen her do it with James several times, and once she made up her mind about something, she was un-budgable. "We'll see you there."

Tristan's jaw clenched briefly, and he stared at me for one pregnant pause before he nodded.

As I made my way slowly, arm in arm with Bianca, out of the building, I had to wonder if he'd really be riding with the 'family' or if Mona would use this as an excuse to get him to herself. I wouldn't put it past her.

The intimidating Cavendish security detail ushered us from the building to the car.

Bianca patted my hand after we'd become comfortably ensconced in their limo. "Mona can only use this for one day. One day to make this play of hers. It'll pass."

"They work together several nights a week," I shot back quietly, acutely aware of the fact that I did not want to be having this personal discussion in front of James. But I just couldn't seem to keep it in. If I didn't talk about, I felt like I'd burst.

"Whether she's around or not, she'll only be able to milk the guilt-trip for so long."

"You saw that too, right? That's totally what she's doing."

"Yes," she said simply. "Want my advice?"

I nodded, fascinated. James was silent for our exchange, doing something on his phone, one proprietary arm thrown around Bianca's shoulders.

"She wants him, you have him. Don't give him away. Fight for him. Stake your claim."

"You think he'd just go for her if I don't fight? I don't want a man that's that easy to lose."

"That's not what I'm saying. In fact, I know he wouldn't. What I mean is, you need to show him that he's worth fighting for; that you'd never give him up. Don't you think it's about time for that?"

I didn't have the answer for that, but I certainly burned some calories stressing about it.

The reception was held at the Biello mansion. The property was huge, but it was still a crush inside.

The interior decor was pretty much exactly what you would picture when thinking of an old Vegas magic act's house in Viva Las Vegas. Lots of white and gold, and hell, even pictures of white tigers.

I found almost right away that it was best just to stick close to James and Bianca. The crowds parted for them, which was good, because there was no telling what an obsessed James would do if, God forbid, someone accidentally bumped into Bianca.

We hadn't exactly rushed there, but it was a full hour before I spotted Tristan, and it was as he came through the front door, Mona on his arm. They had only just arrived.

An entire hour later.

I told myself they must have just been held up at the funeral home. I had to tell myself that, or I would have started screaming and throwing things, and I wouldn't have stopped.

He hadn't even spotted me yet, but I turned my back on him.

Bianca's eyes were sympathetic as they met mine.

"Tell me, am I overreacting? Am I being selfish and insensitive right now?"

"It's a bad situation. I think you're doing your best. James is almost done making rounds. You want to catch a ride with us?

I could abscond with you to my painting studio, again. I've been wanting to start on that painting with you that I was telling you about, with the yellow scarf, and you could vent at me to your heart's content."

That was tempting. There was nothing I'd have liked better than to slip away before Tristan even saw me, and spend the afternoon with Bianca in her peaceful studio. I loved that studio. And I could undoubtedly use a good venting session.

"I would love that, but I did promise Tristan I'd stay close for the next few days, for moral support. Still, it's not like he needs me right this second, and he could be here all day. Let me talk to him and see."

I bit the bullet and approached him.

Mona was just holding his arm now, one big fake tit pressed into his bicep. It was still a vast improvement over what she'd been doing before, which had been just shy of dry humping him in public.

They were talking to another couple, people I didn't recognize, but I approached anyway.

"Tristan," I said quietly.

He started and looked at me. He seemed off, some stiffness in his expression cluing me in that something was wrong.

"Hey, I'm taking off with Bianca, but maybe I'll catch you later tonight, okay?" My words came out stilted, almost cold, which hadn't been my intent at all. I just wanted to get the *hell* out of there.

He started trying to pry his arm out of Mona's death grip. "Excuse me," he told her. "I need to talk to my girl."

She let him go, giving me very solid eye contact. I never could read her. I'd considered briefly that she might be high, with the way she'd been acting, and everything else that was going on, but looking at her up close, I didn't think it was that. Still, she seemed just as off as Tristan did. Something had definitely happened between the funeral and the reception.

R.K. Lilley

I dreaded figuring out what.

"Hurry back," she told him in a breathless voice.

I had to bite back a response to that.

Tristan tugged me down the nearest hallway and into a small sitting room that somehow didn't have any occupants. He shut the doors behind us, but there was no way to lock them.

"You're upset," he began quietly.

I shook my head, though he wasn't wrong. "I don't think you need me here, in fact, I think it would be better if I left and leaving with Bianca seemed like the best solution."

"I do need you here, and I know it's tedious, but it would be really nice if you would just stay by my side."

"Your side's been occupied."

He rubbed his temple while I began to pace around the room. "Yet another reason I'd like you to stay close. She's...not herself today, and I would like to discourage her without making her day any worse than it already is."

"You want me to, what, stake my claim?"

"That would be nice, yes. What would be really nice is for you to mean it."

Ha. That really wouldn't be a problem. "Oh, I can do that."

He started moving to me, and I had to stifle the urge to start backing away. I didn't want him to touch me until I knew what he'd been up to between the funeral service and here.

"So you rode over here with the entire family?" I asked him, watching his face very carefully.

He grimaced, and I tensed up. "No. Mona set it up so it was just she and I in a limo."

Well, at least he hadn't tried to cover that up.

"Did you fuck her?"

He didn't take that well, which was understandable, because I hadn't meant it well.

I didn't really think it was a possibility, but I couldn't seem to keep it in. I had to vent somehow, or I'd go nuclear. Even so, I regretted saying it instantly. This was not the time or the place.

His nostrils flared, his eyes gone wild. "Is that a serious question?"

I chewed on my lip, reluctantly admitting, "No."

"Good. And no, I stayed far away from her."

He finally had me backed into a corner when he cupped my face in his hands.

"This is why you don't sleep with the daughter of a close friend," I told him. I was angry about that, how his naiveté could potentially harm what we had, what we were still trying to build into *something*. "Especially one that you work with. What were you thinking?"

"I was a fool, clearly, but she didn't present herself as she is now. She was, I don't know, the opposite of you. She's not a relationship girl, or so I thought. She always tried so hard to prove that she was just the cool chick and just as disinterested in having anything serious as I was. She was all too happy to volunteer for fuck buddy status. It made sense at the time. None of it is an excuse. I was an idiot."

Yep, I was done with that line of conversation. I tried to pull my face out of his hands, but he wasn't having it.

He bent down to me. "Stay by my side. Stake your claim."

"That's just what Bianca told me to do."

"Well, aside from her taste in too pretty men, she's a smart girl."

That got a small smile out of me, as though he took that as permission, he brushed his lips against mine.

I gripped his wrists, whether to keep them where they were, or push them away, I wasn't sure.

He took my mouth softly, in slow, drugging pulls, running his velvety tongue very slowly along my lips, begging for entrance.

With a small moan, I opened for him.

"Do it, Danika. Claim your man," he pulled back to murmur against my mouth.

I wasn't proud of it, but I let him have me, quick and fierce against the wall.

We were straightening our clothes when Mona opened the door. She didn't say a word. She didn't need to. She just wanted us to know that she knew what we'd been up to.

I felt bad. I'd just participated in making her bad day worse.

A few days later, I couldn't believe I'd ever had a kind thought about the woman.

Always trust your gut, even when it makes you feel like a total bitch.

That's what I learned from Mona.

CHAPTER THIRTY-FIVE

I was at work, minding my own business a few days later when a smiling Mona came waltzing into my gallery.

Every time I saw that smile, I became more certain that there was just something wrong with it.

"Is it about time for your shift to end?" she asked, her tone pleasant enough but lacking any inflection. Her eyes were sort of glazed over and vacant.

Curiouser and curiouser.

Even so, I didn't really want to know where this was headed.

I sighed. I still felt bad about what she'd been through with her dad, so I'd be humoring her. "I run the place. I can leave any time I want. I take it you wanted to talk again?"

She nodded. She was just off. I wondered if she'd taken something, but I didn't know her enough to be able to tell for sure.

"I'll meet you at that bar, Twist, when I'm done."

She left.

I finished up with a few things, and then tasked Sandra with closing up in thirty minutes. I headed to Stephan and Javier's bar with the hope that I could get rid of Mona quickly and then just hang out with the guys.

Stephan saw me coming and came to greet me with a big

hug, kissing both of my cheeks. "Finally, you come to see us."

Javier followed closely behind him, and we had a quick love sesh.

"Come sit at the bar, chat with us. Tell us what's going on with you." Javier wiggled his eyebrows suggestively. "Because we've been hearing some things."

"Hell, we've been seeing some things," Stephan added, referring, I knew, to the baby shower.

I scanned the plush lounge area for Mona and sighted her easily enough. "I've got to talk to someone real quick, and then I'll be right there."

I excused myself, knowing they'd have a million questions for me to answer about this in about five minutes.

I sat down next to Mona on a plush white leather couch. Next to, as in three feet away.

"We need to talk," she began.

I had to make a concerted effort not to roll my eyes. "Shoot."

"I just want you to answer one question for me."

I studied her, finding nothing in her face or her demeanor that I understood. I never had. "Just ask it. Enough with the drama."

"Are you in love with him? Just tell me that."

I shook my head. "I'm not doing this. Nope, not doing it. I don't know where on this earth you got the idea that I owe you answers about Tristan and I, but that is *not* the case."

"I am. In love with him. No hesitation here. Your turn."

I wanted to slap her. I felt my upper lip trying to shape into a snarl, and I had to take a few careful moments to smooth it out. "There was a six year window. I'm not sure when you came into the picture for him, but that was the window. That's how much time you had to make your I love you matter for him, for it to be enough. That window is closed, and I am sorry for you, but if he didn't love you before, I can promise you that he will *never* love you now. Is that a good enough *answer* for you?"

There it was. The thing I'd been looking for, and if I was honest, hoping for, since I'd first met her.

Perhaps I'd driven her to it; perhaps she'd been hiding it all along. Needless to say, I preferred the latter.

But did it matter? No.

The point was, the ugly from inside of her spilled out, contorting her face, her kind smile shaping into a hateful sneer, eyes gone bright with edgy fury.

She pointed a shaking finger at me. "You think you own him? You think you've had some invisible hand on him, through it all, but he was doing just fine until you came back into his life. *Just fine*, until you sabotaged his life again, with that pathetic limp, and those fucking manipulative guilt trips of yours."

"I'm going to stop you right there. You're going to keep going on with this rant and it is not going to matter. Whatever you had with him, it doesn't have the power to affect what he and I have. So go on. Go. Get on with your life, because you don't have the power to influence mine."

She gave me the most bitter smile. No, not bitter.

Triumphant.

That worried me, and I felt my heart rate accelerating with more than my temper. Dread swirled deep in my belly. I watched her mouth, fearing what she would say before she even fucking said it.

And then she proved me so very wrong, because she could affect Tristan and me. In fact, she could destroy us with two short sentences. Just five little words.

"I'm pregnant. It's his baby."

My mind reeled. I don't know how long I just stood there in stunned, unadulterated horror, but she was still sitting there when I came out of it.

"So now you'll try to trap him with a baby." Disgust dripped from my voice. For her, for him, for all of us.

"Who are you to judge me? I'm better for him. I don't have to wonder if I'm in love with him, I know. I never would have left him, pining and alone, to suffer for years, to look for comfort in other women, for years. You did all of that. Who are *you* to judge me?"

"How far along are you?" I asked her. I couldn't believe how calm my tone sounded.

Inside, I was a mess.

A bloodbath.

"Does it matter? I know he's the father. I haven't told him yet, but you know Tristan. He could never turn his back on something like this."

I stood up. I wasn't sure how. I made my way slowly, unsteadily, to the bar. I didn't look back at Mona again. I would have done a great deal to never have to set eyes on her again for the rest of my life.

Stephan met me halfway, and just swooped in and picked me up. I studied the chiseled line of his jaw.

"You look like a blond superman," I told him.

He smiled. "You don't look well, Danika. I'm driving you home, unless you have an objection."

I shut my eyes. "Will you take me to your place? I need to keep away from my life for a bit."

"Of course. We have lots of room. You can stay for as long as you need to. I'll take you, and Javier will bring your car, later, so you aren't stranded."

"Thank you. Absolutely everyone on the planet should have their own Stephan."

"I think you might be a little bit in shock, Danika."

I only wished. Shock smacked of numbness, and I wasn't that.

To say I didn't handle the news well was a gross understatement.

I lost it. Just *lost my mind.*

The first stage was avoidance. It was pure cowardice. And utterly necessary.

I avoided him with skill. With talent. I not only anticipated where he would be, I anticipated where he'd think *I* would be, and steered clear of it all.

At one point, he camped out in his car on the curb in front of my house.

That night, I got a hotel room.

The next stage was worse. It was anger.

Rage, fury, outrage, utter devastation. I stopped avoiding him because I *wanted* him to feel my wrath, needed it.

I went to his house and strode up to his door. He opened it before I could knock. I had no clue how he'd known I was coming. What, had he just been watching for me out the window?

No matter.

I walked in, not even looking directly at him.

I took a deep breath and turned to face him, raising my trembling chin to meet him in the eye.

"Sweetheart," he said, his voice so, so soft, his golden eyes softer.

My arm jerked back and swung forward. There was no tangible communication between my brain and my arm as I slapped him as hard as I could, hard enough to leave my arm sore and my palm numb.

I staggered back, eyes wide on his face. I suppose I expected some sort of an angry reaction from him, something volatile, or perhaps mean. Some normal response to being struck in the face.

His eyes were wild, but not with anger, not with rage. Something else moved there, something more worrisome, though I could not put my finger on what, precisely. At least, not right at first.

He followed me as I took jerky steps backwards, still with that light in his eyes that was trying to *break* me. It was unholy.

"I'm sorry," I gasped out. I wasn't even sure if I meant it. It just seemed like the appropriate thing to say.

"Don't be. Not for that. In fact, you do that again, if you want to."

That sent a jolt of a shock through my body. "What is wrong with you? You *want* me to slap you again?"

"I'll take it. I'll take any reaction you need to give me, as long as you're not walking away."

"What were you thinking? How could you get her pregnant? *How could you?*"

"I didn't."

It happened again. One minute my arm was at my side, and the next it was whipping across his face hard enough to sting my palm and send a shock through my arm. "Don't you lie to me. *Don't you dare.* You might not know if it's yours, but you were sleeping with her, so you cannot tell me that you're sure it's not!"

"Yes, I can. I am not lying. She knows it's not mine. It is a matter of days before this lie of hers comes clean. But go on, do what you need to, say what you need to, to vent your feelings about this. As long as you don't leave."

I felt all semblance of control slipping away from me. I felt myself getting hysterical. I backed away from him, step by step, sobbing uncontrollably.

He followed me, step by step, a world of sympathy in his unholy eyes, and I did not want it. All I wanted on earth in that moment was to go back in time, and get the picture out of my head of some other woman *pregnant with his child.*

"If you're lying to me," I warned him, voice shaking, knees shaking, hands shaking, "I don't ever want to see you again. Not ever. If you're lying about this, I want you out of my life *forever.*"

That made his mouth twist down, and my mind instantly

latched onto that as a sign of his guilt. "Oh my God! You liar! It *is* yours. You-you got-got her pregnant?"

He shook his head, but I was past the point of all reason. He was standing so close now that I slapped him again, and again, and *again*, then clutched at his shirt with both hands. I gripped it so furiously that it ripped, and I raked my nails into his chest, scoring deeply into his flesh.

Lashing out like a wounded animal.

I glared up at him, barely seeing past the tears, but seeing enough.

Enough to make me shake. Enough to break me.

It was as though every blow I landed only softened him, tenderized him, and with each abuse I inflicted, more love would pour out of his eyes.

"Shh, Danika, shh. Listen to me. Calm down and *listen*. I did not get her pregnant. The only woman I have ever gotten pregnant is you. The only woman I *would* ever get pregnant is you."

I sobbed harder at that, though he couldn't have known why.

"Look at me. Look me in the eye and see the truth. I have not touched that woman in well over a year. I have not been with *anyone* but you since I saw you with Andrew on that red carpet. I was celibate for a full year before the ranch."

Slowly, gradually, the sobbing stopped and his words sank in. I began to study him, looking for the truth, or God forbid, the lie.

If he was lying to me now, if he could make his eyes do what they were doing *right now* with artifice, then I was done for. There was no limit to what he could get away with, if he could fake a thing like that.

Because I was incapable of cutting him off when he looked at me *like that*.

My entire body froze.

"Excuse me?" I finally asked him, not processing all of it right away. He'd given me too much information all at once.

"I did not want to do this now, but I will if you need it. But first, I need to know that you understand that that woman is not pregnant with *my* child. Do you understand that?"

My head started nodding before my brain gave the order.

He still had way too many weapons in his arsenal against me. And he still used them mercilessly.

"Good. I was celibate for a year before the ranch."

The impact was just as severe the second time he said it.

"After I saw you with that punk on the red carpet."

I took in one deep trembling breath. "Andrew."

He flinched. "Yes. *That* punk. I saw you with him, and I knew you were together. I saw it up close, not from any distance at all, with no filter, and I realized that I couldn't live like that anymore. It was *wrong*."

"Stop." My voice was a whisper.

"You never should have been with him."

"Stop." My voice got louder.

"And I never should have touched another woman, no matter that you wouldn't speak to me, wouldn't look at me. I was celibate for two years after the night of the accident and for one year before the ranch. Everything else was *wrong*. It should have never happened like that. My only excuse was that I'd lost all hope." His voice went from unsteady to breaking on each word. "If I'd had even an ounce of hope left that you would let me so much as kiss your fucking feet again, I would have *waited for you*." He made a visible effort to calm himself.

He took a very deep breath. "And then I saw you with that piece of shit—"

"Stop it! He's not a piece of shit. He's actually a very nice man."

"Well, I fucking hate him, so please don't talk him up to me." His voice was shaking, and getting louder by the word. "When I saw you that night, the way he was with you, touching you with privilege, I knew that I couldn't go on like that anymore, couldn't go on pretending that I was okay with the way things turned out.

I tried it your way, Danika. No one can say, *that six fucking years later,* I didn't try to respect your wishes, but I am *done.* This was *wrong. You* were *wrong.* And I'm here to tell you that, if it takes me the rest of my fucking life, I am going to make this right again."

I had no words, for once. And I couldn't move, couldn't begin to imagine how to react to his statement. Something was happening inside of me, some hardened part of me had thawed out and the repercussions of that thawing were not something I was ready yet to contemplate.

"So that is how I know for a fact that it is not my baby," he continued relentlessly, "and she knows it too. She's turned malicious. She's not who I thought she was, and that's unfortunate; it has cost her job, but she does not have the power she thinks she does to hurt what you and I have. *No one* has that power, with the exception of you and me. So, sweetheart, please, I just need you to have a little bit more faith."

"Why didn't you tell me before now that you hadn't been with anyone in so long?"

"You hadn't even admitted to me that things were over with Andrew. Did you expect me to admit to a thing like that, when I didn't even know if you were jumping from his bed to mine? I do have some pride left, even when it comes to you."

"I told you about Andrew—"

"Yes, well, that was later, and by then we were avoiding this subject, not finding new reasons to talk about it."

I'd been so full of anger, so fueled by wrath, that when it left me, I was completely deflated.

I would have fallen to the ground if he hadn't caught me.

But caught me he did and swung me up into his immeasurably comforting arms. I laid my head on his chest as he kissed the top of my head. I could have stayed there

forever.
It felt like coming home.

CHAPTER THIRTY-SIX

We were in the kitchen of his house, cleaning up after one of his amazing dinners.

"What did you come to the apartment for that night?"

I didn't have to ask what night he meant, no matter how we'd been tiptoeing around it. We talked about the before and the after like reasonably well adjusted adults. But the other, the incident, *that night*, and the sequence of events that led directly to it, that we'd been avoiding. Well, okay, *I* had been. He'd been quietly but persistently asking and then waiting me out for answers.

I would have loved to keep avoiding it. It had already caused us so much pain. What was the point of dragging it all out in the open and letting it hurt us again? Because it could. I knew it was only a question of when.

There was no doubt in my mind that we weren't done bleeding for that night. Weren't done *suffering*.

"What could it matter, Tristan? Why do you keep *digging* at this? What's the point? Just let it go."

"I *can't*. It's always bothered me. I find myself thinking about it all the time. On the edge of sleep, at the oddest quiet moments, that's where my mind goes. To this day. I need to know. What were you doing at the apartment that night? Did you come to reconcile? Is that what happened?"

"Yes," I said quietly. "That is what happened. I came there to try to work things out."

Out of the corner of my eye, I saw him jerk. As I'd suspected, he hadn't taken that well.

"My God. You came to make up and I—I—"

"Yes. You were too far gone to talk just then. You couldn't be reasoned with."

"There are so many holes in my memory that night. In rehab, they call it a blackout. You function, sometimes almost like normal, and have no memory of it. It's a sign of alcoholism."

I, unfortunately, had had no such mercies. I remembered the details of that night so clearly that they haunted me. I had been so *stupid*. I remembered *that*. So completely naive, thinking I was tough, meanwhile a predator had been lurking in our midst, taking advantage of our every emotional misstep.

I had a thought. "I have a question for you. Something you said that night never made sense to me. Do you remember when I sent Jerry to you with the divorce papers?"

I'd even gone so far as to ask Jerry about this, but he'd assured me that he handed the papers and the note directly into Tristan's care, so I'd gotten no answers there.

Tristan had seemed so ready to take on the subject when *he* was asking the questions, but something about my question seemed to have weakened him.

He moved to the table in his breakfast nook, felt for a chair, and sat down, looking at his hands. "Yes, I remember."

I moved to sit as well, but not facing him. No, I turned my chair away, staring out the window. This subject was hard enough to face, without having to face each other, as well. "Do you remember the letter I sent with the papers?"

There was a very long pause, then some agitated movements behind me, as though he'd taken exception to his chair or the ground it was sitting on.

My stomach churned when he answered behind me, his tone just awful with pain and confusion, "What letter?"

My eyes squeezed shut. I didn't want to dig into the old wounds, but ignoring them had obviously never made all of the questions go away. "When I sent Jerry to you with the divorce papers, there was a letter with them. A very important letter. For you. Jerry swears to me that he handed both directly into your care."

A longer silence passed with more agitated movements.

"What did it say?" he finally asked in the most wretched voice.

I wished instantly I'd never brought it up, but I trudged on. There was no going back now. He'd been like a dog with a bone before I'd opened my big mouth about the letter. There was no question he'd be even more relentless with still more questions in the mix. "I'll tell you. First, though, I want to know what happened to it. Were you alone when he came to see you? He told me he didn't see anyone else at the apartment."

More silence, then the sound of something breaking in the kitchen. Near the sink, likely a plate, I thought, but I didn't look.

This was rough enough, just hearing what it was doing to him.

"Dean was at the apartment with me. He came out of his room after Jerry left. He'd heard Jerry's voice, wanted to know what was going on."

"The letter was tucked into the papers," I explained, keeping my voice gentle. I'd come to terms with this years ago. No new fresh wounds for me here, just sore old ones. Not so for Tristan. Some of this was very new to him. "Impossible to miss once you started going through them. Is there any chance you set them down before...before you read them?"

More silence, more things breaking in the kitchen. I could hear his heavy, ragged breaths catching as he moved. He was not taking this well.

"I did. I set them on the coffee table and went to pour some shots. I didn't want to read the papers without a drink. I didn't think I could handle them."

There it was. All of the puzzle pieces fit right into place.

"And Dean, I take it he was near the coffee table when you turned your back?"

More things broke in the kitchen. And then his ragged breaths were directly behind me. "What did that letter say, Danika?"

I took a few deep, steadying breaths. "It was short. An ultimatum. Essentially, it said that if you went to rehab, I wouldn't divorce you."

I sat there for a long time, even after he'd left the room, my mind in dark places.

Regrets were such useless things, and even so, it seemed impossible to dislodge some of them.

So many mistakes on both our parts, and here we were, six years later, still dealing with the aftermath.

I loved him every bit as much as I ever had, and that love was more useless than it had ever been, even now, when I could get through to him.

I found him out back sitting on a lawn chair, staring into his pool. He was bent forward, fists clenched. He looked wound up so tight that he might just curl into a ball at any second.

I stroked his shoulder and he jerked like he'd been shocked.

I touched him again, and this time he seemed prepared for it. "Come on. Let's go to bed."

I led him by the hand up to his bedroom, and he let me. I certainly couldn't have moved him otherwise.

Slowly, tenderly, I stripped him and then he me. I tugged him under the covers with me. I hugged him tight, trying to ease the frigid remorse that was gripping him. It had me in its grip as well, so I knew better than anyone how the touching helped.

We held each other for a very long time before he spoke, his voice rasping out, breaking on some of the words. "I would have gone to rehab, even as fucked up as I was back then, if I had seen that, I would have gone. I thought you were dead set on staying away. I thought you were *so* done with me. If I had read that letter, *everything* would be different."

"It's no use," I told him gently. "We have enough to contend with. We don't need to harbor these regrets, as well. We've got to let it go. The past is the past, and we cannot go back."

Those words weren't only for him. I was still convincing myself, as well.

I pulled his face closer, and laid my lips very softly on the corner of his mouth.

He shut his eyes, and I turned his head just so, pressing my lips gently to the pulse in his neck. I held them there for a prolonged moment, then pulled back, tilted his head down, and rubbed my lips against his forehead, then down, brushing against his stubbly cheek, his jaw.

He held still and let me, compliant, even passive, under my soothing hands, my forgiving lips.

He was shivering relentlessly, and I warmed him with my touch. I warmed us both.

CHAPTER THIRTY-SEVEN

I was in his large foyer, about to leave for work the next morning, when he stopped me with a question.

He said it from behind me. I'd left him soundly asleep and had hoped he'd stay that way for a few more hours. It had been a rough night. He needed it.

Also, I'd wanted to avoid *this*.

"Wh-what—" his voice trembled, and I thought that perhaps he'd guessed the next part. "What changed to make you want to work things out?"

The closest chair just seemed so far away. Like a limp doll, I leaned against the closest wall, then sank down to the floor.

What could it hurt at this point to just tell him? What more damage could it possibly do? All of the damage had already been done. Of course, it had. Years ago. No one knew that better than I did.

So why had I run so hard from telling him?

We'd been on borrowed time, and I'd wanted to borrow more. Another minute. Another day. I wasn't picky.

No. Just greedy.

I looked up at him as I answered. I could give him at least that much. "I was pregnant."

The words barely carried, and the journey seemed to take

forever, but when they hit their mark, it was a solid blow.

He just sort of folded in on himself, his shoulder hitting the wall next to him.

I shuddered, looking away.

A gross miscalculation.   There was so very much left to damage here.

Our ragged breaths were the only sounds to be heard for long, painful minutes.

He came at me then in a way that I had not expected or prepared for.

"How could you keep that from me? How could you *hide* that from me?"

Was that anger in his voice?

Outrage?

I was outraged just to hear it, so my answer, when it came, was inflammatory. "I wasn't hiding it. I didn't need to hide it. It was *no one's* business but *mine.*"

He came at me then in a way that I had not expected or prepared for.

"How dare you!" he shouted, his voice booming as he pointed at me. He didn't come even one step closer to me, as though he couldn't trust himself. "You had no right! *No right* to keep that from me!"

I was shocked. I was appalled.

Furious.

"No right? I had *every* right!"

"That was my child too! I had a right to know about its existence and of its loss. You kept it from me. That was wrong. You know it was wrong."   There was a fine tremor in his low, pain roughened voice and madness in his eyes.

I shook my head, over and over, eyes wide on his face, studying it in hopes that I'd find something I could understand there, because his words were not something I could stomach. "You have the nerve to talk to me about *rights*? Maybe once, for a brief moment, you had a *right,*" I bit out scathingly. "And I did tell you. I came to your apartment and told you to your face, and that is when you sent me home in a car with a rapist. You lost *all* of your rights in that car, along with our child."

I was shaking in rage, in remorse. I hated myself for saying those things, even if they were true.

I made my trembling way to a trembling stand, turning to leave, but his words stopped me.

"Liar! You're a liar!" he shouted, voice shaking with fury.

I turned back, wondering what awful thing I was about to say or do, because I felt provoked beyond all reason. "What did you just say?"

He crumpled where he stood, his knees hitting the floor hard, his hands pushing out in front of him to keep him upright.

It was incongruous, a man so huge, so powerful, brought so low with a few awful words.

He knelt, prostrate in front of me. His pose was a direct contradiction to his tone.

"I called you a liar." The shaking in his voice turned to a quaver. "You said you forgave me. You told me that six years ago, and you've told me since, and that was a *lie.* There is no forgiveness in the things you're holding onto. You don't even have a concept of what that word means. Tell me I'm wrong."

I took a few steps closer, fists clenched hard. Even in my fury, I could not help but want to comfort him in his pain.

It was a sickness, I thought.

"Forgiving is not forgetting."

"You are doing more than remembering, and you know it. I don't remember that night. To this day, the vital parts still escape me, but I want to know. I *hate* myself for it. Don't you see that? No matter how horrible, no matter how much it will damage me, I can't move on, no more than you can, until I hear it all."

I sat down on the ground, slowly lowered myself until I

mirrored his defeated pose just a few feet away from him. "I will tell you," I conceded.

We stayed how we were, on the floor, heads bowed for a very long time, and I told him almost everything.

Almost.

We huddled on the floor and cried together, though we did not move close enough to touch. I couldn't stand any contact while I gasped out the sordid details, the painful losses, and he, I thought, didn't have the courage to seek to comfort me just then.

The sun was starting to rise, streaming into the window beside his front door, when we picked ourselves up, and made it to the kitchen table. We sat, not close, not touching, not looking.

"Please," he finally spoke, after I'd fallen silent, and been silent, for a very long time. "Everything we had, everything we planned for. All the things we talked about before I messed everything up. I want marriage, babies, forever. With you."

I looked at my hands. I couldn't look at him. Not for this. No part of me wanted to tell him, but I'd gone long enough keeping it from him, and it wasn't fair to go a step further, when we could never have what he was talking about.

I took the deepest breath. "I can't have children. I'm barren."

One furtive glance showed me the slightest shift in his expression as his head tilted up and his brows drew together. "How can you say that? You got pregnant *twice.*"

I swallowed, not knowing how to broach this part. I knew I'd make a mess of it either way, so I just told him all of it. "I told you that I lost the second baby in the accident. I haven't explained just how.

Right before impact, Dean was trying to...touch me. I had a framed picture in my hands—"

"The one I gave you back that night?" His voice was choked, as though he couldn't quite believe it.

"Yes. That one. I had the picture in my lap, and I used it to block his hands from going up my skirt. I was focused only on that. On stopping him. I didn't see the accident coming. I had no time to brace myself."

He made a soft grunt of a noise, and one stolen glance showed me that his shoulders were shaking with silent sobs.

I hadn't been even close to crying. I'd been feeling pretty numb, actually. I was only cataloging facts for him, after all, but watching one big tear fall from his thick lashes and hit the table had me tearing up.

I took a few long moments to compose myself before I spoke again, castigating myself the entire time. This wasn't about making him feel bad. I had only meant to tell him what he needed to know. This was my curse: to always say too much, and say it all wrong.

"The collision smashed in my side of the car. This crushed my leg, my knee, but that was actually just one of the injuries. The impact also broke the picture into sharp pieces of wood and glass, and several of the pieces stabbed deep into my abdomen."

He gasped in a harsh breath so violently that I found myself breathing with him, as though I couldn't suck air into my lungs fast enough, as though we were *both* suffocating with my confession.

"It did enough damage that the doctors knew right away that I could never get pregnant again. It is not just unlikely for me to get pregnant, it is impossible. I was hemorrhaging badly. They were forced to perform a hysterectomy."

This little reunion had been a hopeless fantasy from the start.

He was sobbing now. Brokenly. I'd never seen a grown man cry like that, great heaving sobs, as though the world were ending, and there was no earthly reason to hold back the despair. He hadn't even been like this for Jared, and we had both done our share of crying for his dear brother.

"It was a long time ago, Tristan, and it was *nobody's* fault. It was a tragic string of events that no one could have seen coming, let alone stopped, and we've both suffered enough for that night. Please stop blaming yourself. I did a long time ago." I was sobbing by the end, right along with him.

He was inconsolable. I tried to talk at first, making good, valid points to him between my own sobs, but he seemed to hear none of it, just cried as though he'd never cried before, the dam had broken, and he would never stop.

Finally, back bent, body slumped, I went to him. It was a hard thing for me to do, because I knew that at the end of this, I'd be saying goodbye to him and letting myself comfort and take comfort from his touch would only make it harder. I wasn't going to try to hold onto him forever through his guilt.

I knew more than anyone how much he wanted children.

As much as I did.

I would let him go. I was capable of that much, at least.

I touched his head softly as I finally reached him. Two arms had never been so grateful as the ones he wrapped around me. His face burrowed into my neck. He said the same thing, over and over, between those raw, awful, gasping, wrenching, sobs. "I'm so sorry. I'm so sorry. I'm so sorry."

I stroked his hair, tears flowing freely down my face and into the soft strands. I tried words again. "Things worked out how they were supposed to work out."

He shook his head, his face in my belly. "No. No. No. This is *not* how things were supposed to work out. I wanted that baby. Our baby. Our *babies*." He sobbed brokenly for torturous minutes, before he continued. "I wanted *our family*. I've never wanted anything so much in my life."

I took a few deep, steadying breaths, wondering how I would do this, how I would be able to collect myself enough to walk away.

I had to try.

"It's not in the cards," I began, haltingly, gasping with the effort, as though my body were so at war that my lungs would not cooperate, and my vocal cords would no longer take direction from my brain. "I'm sorry, but I can't do this anymore. It's not an option. I know you think I'm good for you. I get that now. But can't you see that you aren't good for me? I'm trading my peace of mind for split seconds of bliss here. I look at you, and I *remember*. I remember what I've lost, what I should have been, what I could have had. Some of it feels good, but just as much of it is near unbearable for me. I could find someone, someone else, who didn't only remind me of the things I'm *not*. Of the things I've lost. In fact, I intend to. And you, you can find someone else that doesn't make you remember, either, doesn't tear you up with guilt. Some relationship without a lifetime's worth of baggage, weighing it down. I'm sorry, but I can't see you anymore. I wish you the best in your life, and so I'm setting you free."

Somehow, I peeled myself away from him and left.

He let me.

I couldn't even look at him after that last bit, so I had no clue what it cost him to keep his silence while I sliced us both open and walked away.

CHAPTER THIRTY-EIGHT

I did what I always did when I was too weak to stand. I went home.

Bev welcomed me with her warm heart and her open arms, as she always had.

I poured my heart out to her and told her everything I'd avoided telling since Tristan and I had started seeing each other again.

She took it well, didn't judge, only soothed and listened and soothed some more.

I hadn't even been there for five hours when Frankie showed up, and I wasn't at all surprised. It seemed to be her MO.

She was like our combat nurse, always showing up after a battle to help each side nurse its wounds. I must have been the one she'd decided was more badly injured, if she'd found me this fast.

Bev let her in and poured her a glass of red wine.

"Why do I always take life so seriously?" I asked them both.

Neither had an answer except to give me sympathetic looks.

"You know, I've never smoked crack," I told mostly Frankie, but of course, Bev had the stronger reaction.

"What the *hell* are you talking about?" She sounded appalled.

"We used to have this homeless guy that would creep into the gallery, like a couple of times a week."

"Dirty Jim," Frankie guessed.

I nodded.

"He sounds charming," Bev said, sounding appalled.

"Not so much."

"He had Hep C," Frankie added her two cents. "Liked to talk about it. In fact, he had a rap about it. Shit, I can't remember what it was, but he actually found a word that rhymed with hepatitis."

"We'd always have him escorted out," I continued, ignoring her. "Since he tended to shout obscenities at the other patrons. But whenever security would start to drag him out, his last line was always, 'You haven't lived until you've smoked crack.' Hell, for all I know, he had a point."

They both stared at me like I was crazy, and that's when I realized that I was drunk. I started laughing.

"Now I remember! It was meningitis. That's the word he used to rhyme with hepatitis in his rap. Not as clever of a rhyme as it seemed like at the time, but oh well. God, he was a crazy motherfucker. I shit you not, he asked me to tattoo some balls on his chin, like, a dozen times."

I shook my head at her, laughing harder.

"He offered to pay for it by donating his sperm to the parlor. He was a dick, always trying to get on the TV show, but he never said anything that could get past the censors, the weirdo. The producers even tried to coach him, because they thought he'd be a funny touch for the show, but he couldn't go two words with dropping the F-bomb."

I lost it.

"I thought you both worked in a nice casino," Bev gasped as if in outrage, but I could tell she was trying not to laugh.

"You've been cooped up in your office too much," Frankie told her. "This is *Vegas*. It's like the weirdo capital of the universe.

Just drive down Boulder Highway sometime, if you don't believe me. There will be at least one crazy motherfucker wandering around in his boxers, looking like he just walked off the set of *The Hangover.* Guaranteed."

"Well, what does it say about all of us that we live here?" Bev asked.

"We like spontaneity?" Frankie tried.

"I hate spontaneity," I pointed out. "God, I hate surprises. How did I get so screwed up?"

I started bawling. Neither of them could seem to get to me fast enough, but it was Bev that got there first, pulling me into her, patting my back, and making soothing noises while I cried it out.

I'd calmed considerably when she spoke.

"I've never smoked crack, but I swear snorting coke helped me get through law school," Bev revealed.

We couldn't stop laughing after that, and I hadn't a clue if she was joking or not. I knew she'd been through some serious partying days, once upon a time, so it was anybody's guess.

"But I digress," she continued, voice gone from wry to soft. "You don't need to follow every impulse in life; you don't need to take on every gamble. But some, even ones that have burned you before, well, some of them you do. Some of the sweetest moments in life come from second chances." I knew this was Bev giving me her blessing, and I gave her a teary smile for that.

Who knew better than Bev that second chances could work?

He was dressed nicely in a plain navy suit. It was simple and severe, and he looked just gorgeous in it. His face was pretty neutral as I opened my front door. It was a surprise visit, and I was certainly surprised. Without even thinking, I opened the door to let him in. I'd missed him and had half expected never to see him again.

"What's going on?" I asked him, instantly suspicious by his smile. It was a sweet, bland smile, which made me think he was up to something.

"I wasn't expecting to see you again," I told him.

"Oh Danika." His soft voice was full of reproach. It was almost...comforting, as though nothing had changed since our last meeting.

He was carrying a briefcase, something I'd never seen him do before. I was instantly suspicious.

"What's in the case?" I asked him. I automatically thought it must be for some kind of magic trick. That was, after all, what he did. "Don't tell me. Magic, right?"

The sweet smile got bigger, lost the bland, and became mischievous. "You could say that, I suppose."

What the hell did that mean?

He moved immediately into my living room, making himself at home on my sofa. He set the briefcase on my coffee table, popping it open. He took out a small laptop that looked ridiculous as he opened it and started typing with those huge hands of his.

I moved in front of him, one hand on my hip, the other pointing to the small black velvet bag in his case. *It* reeked of a magic trick.

He just smiled, shaking his head. "It's a surprise. Let me pull something up on here, and then I'll show you."

I moved around him to look over his shoulder, trying to make out what he was looking at on his screen.

"Step one: Pick an adoption agency. I already found one. I hope you don't mind me just deciding. I've been doing nothing but researching it for the past week, so trust me when I say I'm making an informed decision."

My heart was trying to pound its way out of my chest, but I managed to keep my voice calm. "What on earth are you talking about?"

"Step two: Choose the country of adoption. I've thought this over a lot, and I was thinking, and tell me if I'm wrong, that it doesn't really matter. But I heard that the process goes faster if you choose a country yourself, so I went to the liberty of putting them all in a hat."

He bent forward, plucking the black velvet pouch out of the briefcase and pulling it open until there was just enough room for my hand to fit in. "I think you should do the honors."

I put my hand in, mostly because it was so surreal that I couldn't quite believe what was going on. I pulled out a small piece of paper that only said *China*.

"China. Perfect. Now that that's out of the way, Step three: Do a shit-ton of paperwork. I've heard that part is a headache, but it'll be well worth it."

"Tristan—"

"Oh, wait, I forgot something important. Reach into the bag again."

I don't know why, but I just did it, though I knew we needed to talk more than he needed to continue with this.

Whereas before my hands had skimmed over several small pieces of paper, now it held only one thing, at the very bottom. He hadn't so much as twitched, that I could tell, since the last time I'd reached in.

I yanked my hand back like it had been burned the second I felt what was inside. I knew what it was instantly.

I started shaking my head as Tristan started nodding that yes, it was just what I thought it was.

He got down on one knee in front of me.

I covered my face with my hands.

He started laughing. "I learned my lesson the first time. Notice my clever location is very much private."

"What are you doing?" I asked, my voice muffled by my own hands.

"You know," his deep voice was affectionately amused.

He moved my arm a bit, but not to take my hands from my face, as I originally thought.

Instead, he covered the spot on my chest just over my heart. He kept it there for a few beats, and then he was shifting, standing, then pulling me against him, pushing my face down on his chest with one hand, the other moving to cover my chest again.

"Do you hear that?" he uttered quietly.

"Hear what?" I whispered back.

"It never stopped, did it?" he asked softly. "All this time. Years. And my heart is still beating in time with yours, still working, above all else, to keep that even pace. Fight it all you want, but even our bodies betray our feelings."

As though in direct contradiction, my heart tried to pound its way out of my chest at his words.

I clenched my eyes shut tight, clenched everything as I spoke. "I can't have children."

"Oh, sweetheart. You haven't been paying attention. Did you think the way I felt about you would change because of that? I am not that guy. I am the guy who has been in love with you for over six fucking years. I am the guy that has thought about you every day. I *miss you* every day. What happened—what we lost together—breaks my heart, but it doesn't change anything. I still want to marry you, and I still want you to be the mother of my children."

"Tristan, I can't—"

"It is a technicality. We can't conceive, so we will adopt."

I started sobbing.

"You know, if you get hysterical every time I propose to you, it's going to start to hurt my feelings."

I laughed, then sobbed harder.

"Give me my family back. Marry me. Be my wife again."

He didn't wait for an answer, taking the ring out of the bag and putting it on my finger.

"Yes," I finally told him, holding on for dear life.

He stroked my hair, his eyes closing, a look of utter peace overtaking his face.

"I missed you *so much*," I sobbed, then burrowed into his chest.

"Never again."

I waited until I was calm. "I love you," I said quietly and vehemently.

I heard the smile in his voice. "Love you more."

CHAPTER THIRTY-NINE

DANIKA

To say that our wedding got the royal treatment was a huge compliment to all things royal. The moment James got wind that we were even considering using his resort to say our vows, the diamond encrusted red carpet was rolled out, and the rest was sort of history.

The ceremony itself was held in the Cavendish Hotel & Casino's world-renowned atrium. The atrium was a huge draw for the casino, so the fact that they roped the entire thing off for three hours just for our vows, was huge. In fact, I'd never heard of such a thing. And what was even more extravagant, James had an entirely new all white garden arrangement put together just for us.

I confronted James directly when I heard a rumor about how much the new arrangement had cost.

He'd just smiled charmingly, and diffused the situation with ease. "We do these floral arrangements all the time, and they're often expensive. We won't take it all down right after the wedding. We'll make full use of it."

I was appeased, because, grand gesture though it was, at least I could be sure it wasn't wasteful.

I told all of the bridesmaids that I wasn't wearing a strapless gown when we went shopping for my dress, but by the end of the day I'd found my dream dress, and lo and behold, it was strapless, and it was just perfect.

It was ivory but the fitted, elongated bodice was so heavily beaded and exquisitely embroidered that the top looked silver. It had a curved neckline that made my curves apparent, but didn't give too much of a show. It was undecided what was more of a showstopper, that beaded bodice or the tiered ruffle silk organza skirt with a chapel train.

It was the most elegant of princess gowns, and I adored it.

I'd tried on twenty dresses, and the instant I walked out in that one, everyone agreed that it was the one.

The bridesmaids wore white floor-length lace gowns with pale yellow sashes.

Tristan wore a classic crisp black tux, with a white shirt and tie. The groomsmen wore the same, but with yellow ties.

Frankie and Estella, arm in arm, were the first of the bridal party to walk down the aisle.

As the maid of honor, Frankie had tried hard to get me a female stripper for the bachelorette party. She'd only given up on the idea when I'd pointed out that it was clearly a Homer gift.

It hadn't been a real bachelorette party, anyway. We'd combined with the guys and James had wound up throwing us a party at his house. I thought the guys had gotten the better deal, as there were two hot lesbians making out for half of it.

Bianca and James were next. They didn't walk arm in arm, but with one of his hands at her hip, the other in the loop in her choker.

Next followed Lana and Akira. Lana had given birth just six weeks before, but you wouldn't know it by looking at her. She was one of those lucky bitches that bounced back right away.

Even as they walked, I saw them both steal a peek at the row where Tutu sat, holding their new son, Kaiko. I'd gotten to hold him earlier. He was calm and already clearly took after his father in looks, except for his blue eyes, though it was too soon to tell if those would change.

Dahlia and Adair were next. They'd eloped about a year prior, and seemed to be doing well. Stephan and Javier walked down together. Todd and Trinity, two of Tristan's very close support group from rehab, walked next. Cory walked down alone, since the numbers were uneven, and Kenny paired up with Bev, since Jerry was walking me.

Bev gave Tristan her blessing after one tense lunch at her favorite Italian restaurant. The mob place. And while Jerry and me watched as Bev interrogated Tristan for a solid hour, a few tables away from the godfather, I'd of sworn she was the scariest person in the room.

But it had all turned out well, and she hadn't hesitated to join the wedding party.

It was a very long aisle to walk and a beautiful one. Big heaping bouquets of every white flower imaginable lined the pathway, dwarfed by colossal white vases filled to brimming with even more painstakingly arranged bouquets.

I clutched Jerry's arm hard, but that was for emotional support. I didn't need to use him as a crutch. After having partial knee replacement surgery over five months ago, my gait was smoother than it had been since the accident. I'd never be taking up ballroom again, but I could take a turn or two around the dance floor now, which would surely come in handy later.

It would never be perfect, but it was better and close enough for me.

The minute we began to walk, a soft guitar began to play, followed by Tristan's voice, singing our song. Incidentally, it'd been the biggest hit off their latest album.

I met him and his devastating smile at the altar, and we said our vows again.

I didn't hope, but *knew,* that this time would be different from the first.

ONE YEAR LATER

It was the longest flight I'd ever taken. Well, at least it felt that way. I'd actually taken the exact same route twice before, but this time was different.

This time that flight felt like the longest thirteen hours of my life.

It didn't help that it felt like Tristan wasn't even sitting next to me. When booking the flights, the idea of first class was all well and good. A rip off money wise, but I'd been excited to experience it again, as we had on the first two trips.

At the moment, I'd rather have been in coach sitting next to him, instead of in an isolated pod, feet away. We couldn't even touch. The best we could manage was to talk through a lowered partition.

Our pods were at least next to each other, and we were face to face. Still, I felt restless and antsy, and I knew that if we'd been sitting together, if I could have just held his hand, it would have helped.

He was reclining, his eyes closed. I didn't understand how he could be sleeping at a time like this.

I wanted to shake him awake. I needed company right now.

"Psst," I called to him.

He smiled, eyes still closed. He hadn't been sleeping.

I looked around, grabbed a grape off my fruit plate, and threw it at him.

He laughed, opening his eyes. He looked so relaxed and

happy. I had no idea how he could be so calm.

I reached for an almond, and beaned him in the forehead with it. He just kept laughing.

"What if we can't...? What if they won't...?" I was speaking in a furious, agitated whisper, so stressed I couldn't even get the full questions out.

He moved his chair until he was sitting up, giving me the Troublesome smile. The one that had changed my life.

"Come over here," he said softly.

I looked around. "I can't. We have to stay in our assigned seats. And besides, there's no room over there."

"Come over here," he repeated softly, his smile even softer.

I glanced around, saw that the two flight attendants in our cabin were working in the galley, then moved quickly around until I was standing in the entrance to his pod.

He didn't hesitate, pulling me down to sit on his lap.

"We can't do that!"

He shifted until I was squeezed in next to him, his arm thrown over me. It was a very tight fit, but I felt instantly better.

His free hand reached for mine, and he threaded our fingers together while I burrowed my cheek into his strong chest, breathing deep as I listened to the steady thud of his heart.

"Stephan told me the trick to having sex in an airplane bathroom. I think the flight attendants are too busy to notice us. Whataya say?"

I elbowed him hard in the ribs.

He grunted then started laughing. "Not the time, huh?"

He stroked my hair for a while before he spoke again, voice serious now. "Everything is going to work out just how we want it to." He said it softly against the top of my head. "In just a few days, we'll be flying home as different people. Everything is about to change. It's going to be everything we've talked about, all we've dreamed of."

I squeezed his fingers until mine turned white. "I'm just so afraid we won't get to—"

"We will. I promise you this: We're not going home without her, not this time."

"She won't understand us. What if she doesn't like us?"

"Love has its own language, sweetheart, and of course she'll like us. We're her parents. It might take some time, but we'll teach her what that means. It's going to be just perfect. You'll see."

Her name was Ming, and I loved her before I ever met her.

I fell in love with a picture, and it was true love. The unconditional kind. I didn't get to take her home with me until she was nine months old, but that didn't make me any less her mother.

It wasn't blood that created a mother. It was love. Ming taught me that.

Tristan and I clutched hands as we entered the orphanage. I recognized her instantly. They had her in an outfit I'd sent her, a little dress with strawberries all over it. They'd even put her in the matching ruffled shorts and bonnet.

I started crying, but Tristan kept pulling me along.

"I'm a mess," I told him, patting my cheeks.

"You'll be fine. And don't cry. I'm not even proposing to you today."

It helped. I laughed.

Ming looked right at me, blinking her big dark eyes.

Tristan got to her first.

I hung back, watching.

He crouched down in front of her. She was being held by one of the ladies that worked there. Ming seemed attached to the woman, clinging to her.

Tristan held out his arms to our daughter, his smile so tender it made my breath catch.

Ming touched his hand, studying him. He had to be the biggest person she'd ever set eyes on, but she wasn't scared.

She looked fascinated by him.

"Hi Ming," he told her very softly, his voice rough with emotion. "I'm your daddy. You have no idea how long your mommy and I have been waiting for you."

She was too young to understand, and even if she'd been older, she had very little exposure to English. Still, some communication seemed to make it through to her, and she launched herself at him. He hugged her tight, straightening. Her little head looked so perfect, so trusting, laying on his strong shoulder.

Like they'd done it a thousand times. Like it was fate.

His tender eyes swung to me, and they were bright with tears. He smiled at me, biting his lip. "Come here, Mommy."

I moved as if in a dream, touching her little back, stroking her short black hair.

She pulled away from his chest to look at me, her little face so solemn.

"Hello Ming," I choked out. "I'm your mommy, and I've been waiting my *whole life* to meet you."

She touched my face, running her tiny fingers over my brow, my nose, over my tear-streaked cheeks.

I held my arms out to her, holding my breath, and after one endless minute, she launched herself into my arms.

I held her tight and never let go.

We sat in economy class on the way home, as babies weren't allowed in first class. We sat side by side, and Ming was our lap child. I couldn't have been happier.

We took turns holding her. I couldn't stop staring at her, even when she slept.

"Pinch me, Tristan," I told him quietly, as we just stared at her in wonder. "I must be dreaming. This little angel can't be ours."

He actually pinched me.

"Ow!" I said, giving him a dirty look. I didn't dare punch his arm with the baby.

His smiling lips moved close, kissing the corner of my mouth. "This is real, and you aren't dreaming."

TWO YEARS LATER

James let us borrow his private jet and crew for our trip to Sofia, Bulgaria. It was a Godsend, with Ming, now a precocious toddler, literally climbing the walls. The flight time was fifteen hours and counting, and it would have been *miserable*, if he hadn't done us this huge favor.

"Nikowash," she said, for maybe the hundredth time. She was practicing.

"That's it. Very good," I told her.

"My brover." She jumped up and down, the yellow ruffles of her dress bouncing. Her hair had gotten quite long, and I'd smoothed it into two pigtails that bounced as much as her dress.

Of course, I was biased, but she was the most beautiful little girl in the world.

"Yes, yes he is," I assured her.

Tristan plucked her from the aisle, settling her in his lap. "Your baby brother. Trust me, you're going to appreciate the distinction as you two get older."

"Baby brover," she repeated dutifully. She was very much her daddy's girl.

His name was Nikolaj. He had the brightest blue eyes I'd ever seen.

He was born in Bulgaria and dropped off at an orphanage by his biological mother at two weeks old. We were extremely lucky to take him home at just ten months old. He wouldn't let go of Tristan's neck for the entire plane ride back to Vegas. Ming kept crawling onto her daddy's lap and giving her new brother kisses on the cheek. She must have done it a hundred times. We couldn't stop her.

He was ours.

Even our little Princess Ming knew it.

I was no more controlled, stroking his back, his little hands, bending to rub my lips on his slumbering, baby soft cheek.

Tristan held him without complaint, often shutting his eyes and pressing his cheek or lips to our baby boy's head. It was official. We'd been through hell, but here we were, in our own little slice of heaven.

TWO YEARS LATER

I had the kids over at Bev's house for some girl time. Nikolaj was climbing all over Bev, and Ming was getting her hair braided by Frankie. It was a pretty typical Thursday afternoon for us all.

Except that it suddenly wasn't. Frankie had just asked me the strangest thing, and then Bev's response had absolutely floored me. I just sat there in stunned silence for a while, trying to figure it all out.

Frankie and Estella wanted a baby, but they were missing one of the important ingredients to make one, so they were in need of a donor.

"Estella wants to breed a linebacker, I think," Frankie joked, but she looked ill at ease. This couldn't be an easy thing to ask somebody.

And..."why are you asking me? Shouldn't you be asking Tristan about this?"

"No, I think this is the proper course of action," Bev butted in. "What could he say, without your permission?"

She had a point.

"But now I just need *his* permission," I said numbly.

"If you told him you were okay with it, he'd do it," Frankie pointed out. And she was right.

"Which one of you wants to carry the baby?" Bev asked her. Frankie's nose wrinkled up. "We're working that out. You're going to think we're demented, but we both want to get pregnant."

Bev nodded. "Yes, you're right. I *do* think you're both demented. Danika, aren't you guys trying to adopt again?"

I nodded. "Yes. Domestically, this time. You know how it goes, though. A lot of waiting. We are very lucky we got our first two babies as fast as we did."

"I might have an idea that will give both you and Estella a chance to go through a pregnancy," Bev said quietly to Frankie, as sweet Nikolaj kissed her all over the face. He was the most affectionate boy.

That stumped me, and I just stared at her.

"Oh yeah?" Frankie asked her, sounding just as stumped.

"One of you can get inseminated, and the other can act as a surrogate for Tristan and Danika. A baby for everyone."

Cue the long pause.

I blinked. Several times. "Bev, you know I had a hysterectomy."

She was unfazed. "I also know they were able to leave your ovaries intact. There's a chance you can still produce eggs, my dear. And eggs, combined with sperm and a surrogate makes baby. And these two lunatics *want* to get pregnant. There are no certainties, but it's certainly worth looking into. The stars seem to be aligning for this."

"I feel a double pregnancy coming on," Frankie said, looking just thrilled about it.

I felt like an idiot. I'd heard the lingo, but I'd never even realized that you could produce eggs after a hysterectomy.

After the idea was presented, I was afraid to even give it too much thought. Though I did tell Tristan, the moment I saw him.

"Frankie and Estella want your sperm for their baby," I began.

He blinked, then bent down and kissed me on the nose. "Will

they buy me dinner first?"

I rolled my eyes and tried to stifle a smile, then waited patiently while our children mobbed him. He had one smiling child on each hip when he looked at me again. "How do you feel about this?"

I chewed on my lip, but this was the easy part. "I'm okay with it. I'm excited for them. I want another baby, too. For us."

Ming chimed in loudly that she would also like another baby. She was baby *crazed.*

"Well yeah. We've already decided we're having at least two more. We just have to be patient."

I didn't bring up the second part until the kids were sound asleep in their rooms, and we were in our kinky bed.

I was naked and straddling him. I'd just given him a hell of a ride, and we were both still panting from our efforts.

He was rubbing the side of my thigh with one hand, my bad knee with the other, and looking at my body in a way that let me know he was quickly going to be ready for a second round.

"There's a chance I can still produce eggs," I told him.

He sat up, then flipped us both until I was on my back, and he was looming over me. "I don't understand." He started playing with my clit, watching the action with enthralled attention, still half buried in me. Clearly, this was not the best time to bring it up.

"Frankie said she'd be a surrogate for us, and there's a chance I can still produce eggs."

He pulled his hand back, looking confused. "I don't understand."

"I guess they were able to leave my ovaries intact with my hysterectomy."

"I didn't know they could do that."

"Yeah, me neither. What do you think? About giving it a try?"

"I'm happy with whatever makes you happy. I want more kids, but I'm not at all picky about how we get them."

God, I adored this man, every single inch of him.

Though a few minutes later, I might have loved several specific inches of him best.

Of course, there were a million ifs and plenty of odds not working in our favor. All three of us were over thirty. After a lot of stressful doctor's visits and nerve-wracking test results, Estella and Frankie wound up being pregnant at the same time. They even wound up with close to the same due date.

Frankie was carrying our baby, Estella theirs. And coincidentally, Bianca and James finally decided to get pregnant around that time. There were a solid twelve months in there where the four of us couldn't be in the same room without talking about all things baby. I loved it.

Jared Jeremiah Vega was born huge and healthy.

Tristan couldn't stop crying when he wrote that name down on the birth certificate.

He was born only five days past his due date, but weighed in at a whopping eleven pounds. Frankie blamed Tristan one hundred percent for that, and cursed him up and down every single time she saw him for nearly a year.

Maria Sosa-Abelli was born just days after Jared. She was only five pounds, but healthy and beautiful.

Ming was in heaven. "We have so *many* babies now!" she said, twirling her pink dress around like a mad woman.

None of the adults in the room could stop laughing about that.

Nikolaj didn't care for the hospital, but agreed that his little brother was, "Pwetty cool."

We'd had to buy a mini-van. I was in heaven. We had so many kids that I was officially a min-van mom. We loaded them all up and took our Jared home.

We didn't sleep the first night. When I say we, I mean all of us. Tristan and I couldn't tear ourselves away from the nursery, and Ming wouldn't stay in her bed. Even Nikolaj couldn't stop coming to check on his new brother.

"Why did we name him Jared, Daddy?" Ming asked between adoring glances at her baby brother.

He got choked up at the question, but eventually, haltingly, he started to tell our Ming the story of his brother, Jared. It was an important story, and though she wasn't old enough to really understand it now, I knew that we would be sure to teach her that, though those we loved may die, our love could keep them close to us forever.

Ming fell asleep halfway through his story, sitting on his lap in the rocking chair. He just held her closer, kissing her on the top of the head. Nikolaj had fallen asleep in his other arm a while back.

I was sitting in a rocking chair facing his, cradling Jared in my arms.

We shared a look. What a journey it had been. I had a whole lot of happy under my belt these days, but never in my life had I been so happy as I was in that *exact* moment.

"I love you," I mouthed at him.

He flashed one ruinous dimple at me. "Love you more."

BOOKS BY R.K. LILLEY
  IN FLIGHT (UP IN THE AIR #1)
  MILE HIGH (UP IN THE AIR #2)
  GROUNDED (UP IN THE AIR #3)
  LANA (AN UP IN THE AIR NOVELLA)
  BREATHING FIRE (HERETIC DAUGHTERS #1)
  BAD THINGS (TRISTAN & DANIKA #1)
  ROCK BOTTOM (TRISTAN & DANIKA #2)
  LOVELY TRIGGER (TRISTAN & DANIKA #3)
  AND COMING SOON...
  THE WILD SIDE (A NOVEL)
  CROSSING FIRE (HERETIC DAUGHTERS #2)
  MR. BEAUTIFUL (UP IN THE AIR #4)

* * *

Thanks so much for reading this series! Keep up to date on all of my current and future projects at www.rklilley.com, and if you liked this book, please, please, please, review and tell all of your friends!

Here's an excerpt from my upcoming standalone erotic romance.
Coming 2014
THE WILD SIDE

ARE YOU READY TO TAKE A WALK?
Alasdair Masters is in a rut. He just hit forty, has been nearly celibate for the past year, and his life has turned into a daily sequence of lonely patterns that revolve around avoiding human contact.

His tidy life is turned on its head when a hot young blonde at the gym that's been pseudo-stalking him decides to rock his world. A *very* young blonde. Way, way too young for him. The problem is, he can't seem to tell her no, and she just keeps coming back for more.

It doesn't help that he's ninety percent sure she's a criminal, and still, he can't seem to turn her down. What is a dull introvert to do when a chaotic cyclone that oozes sexuality comes twisting into his life?

At first, he thinks she'll give him a heart attack, but after his twenty-year marriage ended a year ago, he's been a little lost, and when she comes crashing into his life, he realizes that he's never felt more alive.

Is a walk on the wild side just what he needs to get his life on track or a disaster in the making? Is it possible for someone that much younger to be just what he needs, or is she a fortune hunter, as everyone keeps telling him? Is it his hormones telling him that the mysterious younger woman is the one, or could it be more?

I set my two perfectly folded gym towels down on a chair by the treadmill and got on the machine.

I always brought two. I wasn't even sure why. I was a creature of habit. Once I started a pattern, I tended to stick to it, rain or shine.

Kind of like my marriage. Of course, that hadn't lasted forever, but that hadn't exactly been my choice.

I punched in my settings and began my warm-up. I had already done twenty minutes of stretching at home. My three-hour daily workout was very precise. I had a family history chock-full of heart disease, and so I aggressively fought to stay healthy. I was intelligent enough to know that I'd brought the whole thing to an extreme, but honestly, what else was I supposed to do with my free time? I was busy enough with work, but my work involved a lot of sitting down and tapping away at a computer, and I felt I had to counter all of that physical inactivity, somehow.

I'd just had my dreaded fortieth birthday, and I felt like I was in as good of shape as I'd ever been. My waistline wasn't growing, thanks to my three hours a day in the gym and an impeccable diet, and my muscles were well toned and good sized. I had no idea what age I actually looked, but I figured the liberal salt and pepper at my temples brought it at least close to forty. I didn't really give it much thought, as I stayed largely to myself, and any time I was on camera, I went out of my way to avoid seeing it.

The gym was busy, as it usually was, so my time there was literally the most social I was in an average day, and I usually got away with a nod and a good morning to the receptionist on the way in.

That was it. The only verbal interaction in my day.

Sometimes I had to talk on the phone for work, and once, maybe twice a year, I did a few television or radio interviews.

And that was it.

The scary part was it was effortless for me. It had started with an ugly divorce just over one year ago, and slowly shaped its way into this. A sad, old man that could have easily embraced a life as a complete recluse.

I did still go out of my way to work out at an upscale gym, instead of just building one in my house. I had the room. I certainly had the money. I figured it was only a matter of time before I resorted to that, too.

The strange part of it was, I wasn't worried about it because I was lonely. I was worried because I *wasn't*. I did miss being with a woman in the literal sexual sense, but that was about it. I'd considered the idea of hiring a prostitute briefly, but even that seemed like an ordeal. I detested breaking the law. It was so very chaotic.

A familiar figure moved onto the machine next to me, and I met smiling light green eyes in the mirror, nodded once briefly, then looked back down.

She was a shapely little blonde woman that had started sharing my gym hours nine days ago.

Girl, I corrected myself. She was a girl, way too young for me to even sneak a long glance at, though I was only human, and she was wearing next to nothing, so I'd caught many, many glances.

She probably thought I was dad material, I told myself, as she started to jog on the machine, her full, perky breasts bouncing with every smooth step.

She really needed to go shopping for a more supportive sports bra, I thought to myself, my eyes catching on her, then darting away, then glancing again within a few bounces.

She wore only a hot pink sports bra and the tiniest skintight white lycra shorts I'd ever seen in my life. Her abs were toned, waist tiny, her skin smooth in a way that happened only in the very young.

Way, way too young for you, I reminded myself, my furtive gaze catching on her lithe hips as she jogged her sexy little heart out.

My eyes moved up to her face, and I flushed to find her watching me watching her. I looked down and kept on jogging.

There'd been no censure in her eyes, and so I found mine wandering back to her face.

She was beautiful. Not a scrap of makeup on, her white-blonde hair pulled back in a ponytail, and still she could've stopped traffic. A real bombshell. None of it was artificial either, just plain old good genetics at work.

She was friendly, too. I wasn't sure why, but she usually took the machine next to mine, if it was empty, though there were lots to choose from. She always had a smile for me, too.

Maybe I reminded her of her dad. Or fuck, her grandpa.

It didn't bear thinking about it.

I'd never been with a younger woman, let alone one that much younger. Hell, she'd probably give me a heart attack. I shook off the thought. A flawless little thing like that wouldn't give me a second glance, and I told myself that was a good thing.

For all I knew, she could have been jailbait. Needless to say, for a man that'd never even had a speeding ticket, even the idea of that was too scandalous to linger on.

Still, my eyes were drawn, time and again, to her perfect figure jogging hard on that treadmill. Her legs were incredible, long and slender, bare from the top of her thigh to her ankles, and so toned and tan.

I made myself look away and not look back.

I hit the one-hour mark on the machine when I saw her slow and stop out of the corner of my eye. This had become a pattern, too. I did exactly one hour of cardio, before I hit the free weights. She seemed to be working a similar routine, and every day I saw her, it became even more similar.

I almost jumped in surprise when she approached me directly, standing on the very front of my machine, to get my attention.

My eyes traveled slowly up, trying not to linger on the way her breasts rose out of her sports bra's neckline as she leaned into my machine. She was spilling out of the thing.

She beamed at me.

I swallowed hard, catching the side bar and swinging first one leg, and then the other, onto the footrests on the sides, coming to a stop.

I popped out an ear bud, raising my brows in what I hoped was a look of polite interest.

"Hi," she said.

"Hey," I panted back, shutting the treadmill down. May as well quit, since I'd reached my goal.

She handed me my towel, and I took it, immediately wiping my brow. This was a new development and a strange one, to be sure.

She held up the second towel, my OCD towel, if you will. "I saw that you have two. I forgot mine. You mind if I borrow it?"

I shook my head. "Go for it. Glad I could help."

She smiled again. Her teeth were gorgeous, straight and white against her tan skin. "What's your name?" she asked me.

I was caught off guard, and so it took me a few extra beats to answer awkwardly. "Alasdair."

She raised her brows, looking intrigued. "Nice name. It has a lot of character. Do you shorten it at all, or should I call you that, Alasdair?"

Hearing her say my name made me feel indecent. Just

beastly. I briefly considered cutting my workout short. "Sometimes my friends call me Dair."

"Dair. I like that too. And are you daring, Dair?"

"Not particularly," I said quickly, my heart pounding. I couldn't quite believe that she was hitting on me, but if she was, I needed to put a quick stop to it.

Way too young, I told myself firmly.

I moved to the weights, and she followed like we were old friends. I started doing curls, eyes glued to her as she grabbed some smaller weights and started doing dead lifts with a hammer curl.

The sight of that nearly had me slack-jawed. The move consisted of her bending down at the waist, her legs straight, and touching the ground, then lifting back, her ponytail bouncing, back arched, her incredible ass sticking out, and bringing her arms into a curl.

She faced away from me when she did it, giving me a perfect view. Her shorts were so thin, her skin so supple, that it was more perfectly designed to turn me on than a porno. And I'd watched plenty of porn. The girl was set on giving me a heart attack today.

She kept doing it for the longest time, sending me a look over her shoulder as she straightened on the last rep. She smiled that sweet little smile at me. "Well, aren't you gonna ask me?"

I had no idea what she was talking about, but my mind went very dirty with it.

Could you do that one more time, but pull your shorts down for this one, so I can fuck your brains out? I was pretty positive that wasn't what she meant.

Can I give you a ride home? Or maybe a hard ride on my cock? Nope, those two were out, too.

Or how about, *Want to grab a coffee after this?* That one was better, but I held my tongue.

"Excuse me?" I asked instead. The safest bet of all.

"My name. I know yours now. Don't you want to know mine?"

I smiled politely, sincerely hoping that my raging hard-on wasn't too obvious. I was wearing athletic pants and a long sweatshirt, so I was probably safe. "Yes, of course. Nice to meet you..."

"Iris."

My brows shot up. You didn't see many girls her age named Iris. "Iris?"

Her eyes twinkled at me. She gave very good eye contact. Intense, but good. "Don't you like it?"

"Y-yes," I stammered out. "It's a beautiful name."

"It's always easy to pick out flowers for me. My favorite flower is the same as my name."

"I'll make a note of it." What the fuck did you say that for? I asked myself. Of course, I wouldn't be getting her flowers. Totally inappropriate.

She looked pleased as punch. "You do that."

She bent down, her back arched like a pinup girl, and picked up her borrowed towel. She moved closer, dabbing at her cleavage with it.

I swallowed hard, my cock throbbing in time to my accelerated heart rate.

"Upper body today, huh?" she asked.

I was watching her perky tits as she said it, so I blinked like an idiot. Her nipples were hard. I could see them through that flimsy as hell bra. "Hmm?"

The towel moved down to her stomach. She didn't look to be sweating much, but she patted herself down like she was.

I was in a full on sweat. I designed it that way. It made for a better workout, but just then I wanted to strip down.

Strip down and pin a naked Iris to the floor.

"You're working your upper body today. You alternate, right?"

"Oh yeah."

340

"It's an intense workout you've got going. You training for something in particular?"

I shook my head. "Just trying to stay fit. What about you? You clock in three hours, too, right?"

She shrugged. "That's a new thing, though I do enjoy a good workout. Just trying to keep things nice and tight."

That made my brain short-circuit. "Things are looking very tight." A perfect fit for my cock, my perverted mind added.

She came a little closer, almost into my personal space. "Thank you. That's a big compliment, coming from a gym regular like you."

I couldn't take anymore. I turned, put the weights back on the bar, and went into a round of grueling pushups.

When I rose again, she was a few feet away doing French press reps, her chest thrust forward.

I turned quickly away, and tried not to so much as glance at her.

She kept her distance until I was on the last quarter hour of my routine, making my rounds on the machines.

"I bet you have some super special after workout drink you down after these sessions," she told me as she approached my machine, her tone playful.

She got right up in my personal space, her breasts just inches from my face.

I looked up at her eyes, mine almost pleading. She had to quit teasing me, whether or not she knew that's what she was doing.

I grunted.

"Admit it. You do, don't you?"

My mouth twisted wryly. She even had a good personality. She was a sweet little thing. She didn't need to be. She could have gotten by on sheer good looks alone. "I have a little something I make."

"It's a drink, isn't it? I'd bet good cash you make it with a

Vitamix, and it has kale in it."

I coughed out a laugh. "You aren't wrong. I'm pretty predictable, huh?"

She winked at me. Fucking winked. It was adorable, and I needed to get away from her. "You're a mystery to me. I'm just throwing out guesses, trying to figure you out."

"Now why would you do that? I have to tell you, I'm about as boring as they come."

She shook her head, her eyes soft. "Not at all. You seem fascinating to me, Dair."

I wasn't sure why, but that seemed to be my breaking point.

I politely excused myself and hit the showers. I was the only one in there, and I did give half a thought to rubbing a quick one off, but I refrained. I'd be home soon enough.

I emerged from the showers, clad in a fresh white T-shirt and black athletic shorts, to find Iris still hanging near the weights, still in her workout gear, dabbing at her glistening breasts with *my* towel.

Well, I guess she'll be keeping that, I thought, giving it one last longing look before I turned on my heel and headed out.

I nearly let the door swing shut on her before I realized that she'd followed me, still in her workout gear, duffle bag in tow. I held the door wide for her, a little worried at her beaming smile.

"You shower at home?" I asked, then wanted to take it back. I did not need a visual of her showering.

"Yeah, usually. Here." She draped the used towel over my shoulder.

My mind went really filthy with the things I'd be doing with it later.

"Thanks for that. You just headed home now?"

I nodded, looking over at the parking lot, back at the gym, anywhere but at the too young girl that was too much trouble for my peace of mind.

"Have a good one," I murmured, and walked away.

"Wait," she called out from behind me when I was halfway through the parking lot.

I stopped. She was just a few feet behind. Either she was following me, or she was walking somewhere. My pearl white model S Tesla was the only car parked this far back.

I turned to her, and she was smiling at me, of course.

"Do you mind giving me a ride?"

I took a few deep, steadying breaths, wondering what to do.

Of course, I needed to give her a ride. If the poor girl needed to walk somewhere, she could hardly do it dressed like that. She'd be abducted, for sure.

I wasn't positive that I wouldn't abduct her myself.

"Sure, honey. Where you need to go?"

She pointed at my car, her eyes widening. "Is that your ride? It's brilliant. Wow. A Tesla. Just beautiful."

I smiled, impressed that she knew what it was and waved her on.

I loved my car, and I got a real kick out of her excited reaction to it. She was good at making me smile.

"I've never been in one of these before."

"I just got this one about eight months ago."

"Do you like it?"

"Yes. I'm happy with it."

"Whoa. You got the seven seater? You have any kids?"

I laughed. "No. I have no excuse, other than that the salesman was very good at selling me features."

We were inside and belted before I looked at her again. I could smell her in the small space. She smelled so good that it was playing havoc with my peace of mind. Like vanilla, maybe a touch of lemon, and some hint of what could only be her hot little body after a good workout.

I was shamefully happy that she hadn't showered after the workout. I had a very clear visual of me licking every bit of that salty sweet sweat off her, and since that wouldn't be happening,

I at least had a smell to obsess over in place of that.

She reclined her seat until she was lying down flat. Her mouthwatering breasts pointed straight up in that position. "That is so cool. What is that called? The glass ceiling?"

"An all glass panoramic roof. Like I said, the salesman was very good at selling me features, even ones I didn't need."

I started the car, waiting for her to tell me where to go. When we just sat there for a few minutes, I asked, "So, where can I drop you?"

She brought her seat back up. "Aren't you going to invite me back to your place? I want to see your house. And I'd like to try whatever concoction you make yourself drink after your workout."

I smiled and shook my head. "I don't think that's a good idea, Iris. You are much too young to be inviting yourself to some man's house. Especially an old guy like me."

"How old are you?" she asked, sounding only vaguely curious about that.

"Forty. Old. How old are you?"

"Twenty-four, Alasdair. Old enough for any damn thing."

I gave her a gimlet-eyed look, sure she was messing with me. "I don't believe you. Prove it. Show me your ID."

She giggled like I'd just said the funniest thing, but she did bend forward to fish around in her bag, retrieving a small pink wallet. "What? You think I'm jailbait?"

"Something like that."

She handed me a Nevada driver's license. I studied it, did some quick math, then studied it some more. It was real, as far as I could tell, and it did place her at twenty-four. I could hardly believe it.

"I'm still way too old for you."

"Your cock doesn't agree." Her tone was so innocent that it took me a moment to process what she'd said.

I flushed bright red. "My cock doesn't know what's good for

it."

"But I do." Her voice was whisper soft and breathy.

I put the car in reverse. "You sure about this?"

Mr. Beautiful will be a male POV continuation of the UITA series. The bulk of the novel will take place after the events in Grounded. However, there will also be many, many bonus male POV scenes from the first three books.

A TEASER FROM *MR. BEAUTIFUL*
COMING 2014
WARNING: THIS TEASER CONTAINS SPOILERS FOR THE *UP IN THE AIR* SERIES

JAMES

I couldn't sleep after the shooting.

Bianca slept like a baby, like she never had before, like every worry she'd ever had had disappeared with the death of her father.

But not me. I was more restless than ever. A miracle had saved her, not me, and I felt helpless because of it.

It was not a feeling that fit me well.

In fact, it made my skin crawl in discomfort. In anger.

It had been months since the attack. She and Stephan were healed physically, and it seemed emotionally, but I felt the wounds as though they were fresh. What had *almost* happened haunted me. I was a man that needed control, and I'd been shown, in the starkest way possible, that I had *none*.

I sat scant feet away from our bed, watching Bianca sleep.

346

She was nude, with not so much as a sheet covering her. I'd seen to that. I watched her lithe form shift on the bed, one long leg hitching up to give me a glimpse of the pink between her legs.

I felt like a fucking stalker.

In fact, I was one, watching her for hours on end, night after night.

I tensed when I realized she'd roused. It disturbed her that I couldn't sleep, when she deserved peace more than anyone.

She sat up, and I watched her heavy breasts swaying with the movement. "James." Her voice was the softest utterance.

"Love," I answered, feeling the dark mood that had overtaken me lift in an instant. Just having her eyes on me could do that.

She crawled across the bed toward me. She'd always had an uncanny ability to do exactly the thing that would drive me the most wild, and she'd only gotten better at that over time. She didn't hide her body from me as she moved. In fact, she posed for me, even the exposure of her body an act of submission. As though reading my thoughts, as though even those were a command, she paused on the edge of the bed, parting her legs to let me look my fill before she rose, approaching my chair.

I stood to meet her, my body drawn tight, my cock throbbing as though I hadn't come, buried inside of her, just hours before.

I was a statue as she leaned up to my ear, my brows drawing together in a question. Her lips touched my ear as she spoke.

"Hurt me," she whispered raggedly.

My eyes shut tight, my jaw went slack, and a shudder wracked my entire body.

I'd avoided all of the rough stuff since she'd been injured, but God had I missed it.

"We don't have to, Bianca. It's not necess-"

She gripped my hair, pulling my face down to her injured cheek. She dug her jaw into me so hard that I knew it must have been hurting her badly. It was healed now, but I knew it was still sore.

"I need it," she rasped into my ear. "I'll never stop needing it. Please."

I pulled back, and my hands trembled as I cupped her face in my hands, my eyes searching hers desperately for what I wanted to see. Need. *Yes.* She needed this as much as I did. Perhaps more so.

"Get on the bed," I told her thickly.

Made in the USA
San Bernardino, CA
06 May 2014